TO Kathy

ENJOY

The Chronicles of Mathew

The Chronicles of Mathew

Frozen Soul

Jacob Rensfeldt

iUniverse LLC
Bloomington

The Chronicles of Mathew
Frozen Soul

Copyright © 2013 Jacob Rensfeldt.

All rights reserved. No part of this book may be used or reproduced by any means, graphic, electronic, or mechanical, including photocopying, recording, taping or by any information storage retrieval system without the written permission of the publisher except in the case of brief quotations embodied in critical articles and reviews.

This is a work of fiction. All of the characters, names, incidents, organizations, and dialogue in this novel are either the products of the author's imagination or are used fictitiously.

iUniverse books may be ordered through booksellers or by contacting:

iUniverse LLC
1663 Liberty Drive
Bloomington, IN 47403
www.iuniverse.com
1-800-Authors (1-800-288-4677)

Because of the dynamic nature of the Internet, any web addresses or links contained in this book may have changed since publication and may no longer be valid. The views expressed in this work are solely those of the author and do not necessarily reflect the views of the publisher, and the publisher hereby disclaims any responsibility for them.

Any people depicted in stock imagery provided by Thinkstock are models, and such images are being used for illustrative purposes only.
Certain stock imagery © Thinkstock.

ISBN: 978-1-4502-8947-4 (sc)
ISBN: 978-1-4502-8948-1 (e)

Printed in the United States of America.

iUniverse rev. date: 10/03/2013

CONTENTS

CHAPTER ONE

ANOTHER DAY

With a yawn and the sound of an alarm clock in his ear, Mathew forced himself out of bed and looked out the window. The clouds were thick and dark; a clear sign it was going to rain or possibly snow.

Another horrible day, he thought with a sigh and began to dress himself. At least we have the ski trip soon. That should be fun if we manage to get snow between now and the next two days.

I wonder if a girl lived here before me? He asked himself as he looked at his reflection in the mirror. He examined his once light brown hair that was slowly changing to a darker color—probably black and thankfully, since he was still a teenager, not gray.

"I guess I can never stay the same. So much for some things never changing," Mathew said quietly to his reflection. He felt a bit depressed as he grabbed his sweatshirt. He reached for the large gold cross that hung from a single hook in his room, placed the chain around his neck and walked out the door into the cool November air.

I hope today will be better but with this rain . . . I don't think it will, he thought as he leaned against a tree that was at his bus stop. The rain slowly started to come down.

"No more thinking like that, Mathew," he said to himself. "No matter rain or sleet or snow, we need to think positively even though it's cold and wet. At least I will be able to see my friends at school. That's always something to look forward to . . . I guess. Yes. Yes, it is something to look forward to. Just because I'll probably die alone doesn't mean that I can't seize a few moments of fun with my friends," he said aloud with a sigh and a small smile. "But, then again, you can't count on anyone. They all eventually leave anyway," he said slowly then gripped his cross through his sweatshirt for comfort. The smile faded away from his face just as the bus stopped and the doors flung open.

"Hey, Mathew!" one of Mathew's friends said.

"Hey, Sophie, how are you?" he said as he took a seat across from hers in the back of the bus.

"I'm fine, how was your night?" Sophie asked politely with her usual smile.

"It was alright, I guess. My dad's not back from his business trip yet so I was alone again," Mathew replied guessing that he looked depressed.

"Dude! Call me when that happens. If you ever need me or are just feeling lonely, call me and I'll be over in no time at all. I know your dad is never home and your mom lives somewhere out of state but, then again, they are divorced so I guess that's normal," Sophie said with big, caring eyes.

"Well, thanks. I appreciate you saying that. It gives me something to look forward to," Mathew said with a slight smirk. "Well, you are my best friend and I want you to feel loved," she said with her arms spread out.

"At least someone cares . . ," Mathew said giving her the hug she wanted.

"So Mathew, do you know what we are doing today in school? I can't remember . . . do we have a test today in biology?" Sophie asked.

"No. I think that is tomorrow. Hey! How did that date go with that what's-his-name? Not like I care about him or anything. Just wanting to know how it went," he asked since Sophie always had a story to accompany every event in her life, large and small.

"It was a complete disaster! First, he shows up in the same clothes he was wearing at school last Friday and he did not shower or bother to use any cologne so he stunk the entire time. I texted my friend and asked her to call my cell so I would have an excuse to get the hell out of there," Sophie said rubbing her eyes in disbelief at the memory.

"Sounds like my prediction was right on the money!" Mathew exclaimed when she finished.

"I don't know how you do it. You told me you got a funny feeling whenever I talked about him but I didn't listen. But anyway, I don't need your help with my love life. Speaking of love and life, what type of girls are you into, Mathew? If you have had a date in the years we've been best friends, you've kept it a secret . . . what's up with that?" Sophie asked trying not to sound too suspicious.

"What type of woman am I into? Hmm, let me think," Mathew said receding into his thoughts. This wasn't something he normally thought about and Mathew had a habit of thinking before he responded, even if he knew the answer immediately. His motive was to be as truthful as possible but others often thought he was searching for a plausible lie.

"You think you're like 50 or something? Why do you always call girls 'women'?" Sophie asked knowing Mathew well enough to know his quirky speech patterns.

"Let's see. For one, we are in high school and most girls in high school can reproduce. They are technically women—physically if not mentally. I'm not interested in anyone who is . . . . I'll just say 'under developed' . . . those are girls. I am defining the difference between women and girls." Mathew said plainly.

"I see now, good point. Let me rephrase my question. What type of woman are you interested in?" she asked.

"If I would have to pick the type of personality, I would go with the stalker type," Mathew said after a few moments of thought.

"The stalker type . . . are you insane? That's so wrong!" Sophie exclaimed, slightly startled and obviously thinking of some horror movie.

"I not talking about an ugly stalker, if that's what you're thinking. I want a cute one . . . that would be nice," Mathew said correcting Sophie's image in her head.

"You're a strange boy, or should I say 'man, physically if not mentally'. Seriously Mathew, why you would want a woman peeking at you when you're at home, on the toilet or in the shower?" Sophie asked incredulously.

"Sounds like a real relationship to me! As you know, I'm lonely and it would be nice to have someone with me 24 hours a day. Besides, I'm a real boy, Geppetto. What real boy would turn any woman away?" Mathew said with a calmer voice that expected.

"Well put. You are a boy but a hypocritical one. Why don't you refer to yourself as a man since you are physically, if not mentally, able to reproduce?" Sophie asked pointedly.

"There is no difference between a boy and a man. Both have the same needs and are pathetic in our own way. We crave sex like a baby craves milk from its mother. Until boys can stop craving sex, they will not truly be men," Mathew said with wisdom beyond his years.

"I can't believe you actually think about this stuff! You will be a great philosopher when you get older," Sophie said after hearing his statement.

"I don't need to get older . . . I'm already a great philosopher, in my own mind, that is. Anyway, until you have been secluded for long periods of time, you have no idea how the mind works. It's kind of like prisoners who are put in solitary confinement. The weak ones go completely coo coo. The strong ones find their inner selves and come out stronger. In my own words, your eyes will be opened when you see your own self," Mathew said with his best Methuselah-esque tone.

"What does that even mean?" Sophie asked getting frustrated with the riddle. She was tiring of the intensity of the conversation.

"Well . . . until you are so lonely that your own soul must talk to you . . . Or maybe it's God talking. Not sure yet. It's hard to explain unless you have experienced it. Honestly, it could be just a bunch of crap but it's kind of cool," Mathew said trying to keep the same general tone to his response but knew his last comment ruined it.

"Well we're here, so later on you need to explain it to me . . . okay?" Sophie said heading down the stairs.

"Sure, Soph . . . if we don't forget," Mathew said as he walked down the bus stairs and hopped onto the concrete sidewalk.

"I hate these classes that they have for us. Don't you think that some certain things are completely pointless—like the cell thing in plants—that have nothing to do with anything Human related? How is that going to propel us into our grand destinies? It's so stupid," Sophie said rubbing her eyes.

"Wait . . . what?" Mathew said as if coming out of a dream.

"Forget it, Mathew. I'm not repeating myself . . . again. If you can't pay attention, you don't deserve repeats," she said sounding a little annoyed.

"Sorry, I was getting my mind back together," Mathew said rubbing his head and ruffling his already tousled hair.

"Now what does that mean?" Sophie asked as she pushed open the front doors of the school.

"I needed to gather my thoughts," he replied simply

"Why didn't you just say that? You talk kind of funny now and then," Sophie said still annoyed.

"Thanks . . . Not that I'm not insecure enough as it is," he said with more of a sarcastic tone.

"Why is that now?" Sophie asked calmly.

"I'm joking, Sophie. You can relax a little. I don't need therapy . . . not quite yet anyway," Mathew calmly explained.

"Oh alright. As long as you're okay," Sophie mumbled as she walked next to him. "I've got to run to my locker. I'll see you later," she said before she hurried down the opposite hallway.

Mathew gave a small wave as he walked down the hallway. With a sigh he spun his locker combination till it clicked and he flung the door open. He picked up all the books that he would need before lunch and quickly closed his locker. He moved through the hallways, which were full of rambling teens, just to put his books in his first class. He then decided to head out for a drink of water.

"Hello, Mathew!" a familiar voice said right before he was hugged from behind.

"Hello, Angel, how are you today?" Mathews said recognizing this familiar greeting. He turned around to look into his friend's face. Angel's pixie-like face was framed by spikey, short brown hair, reflecting her hyper personality. She was a little bit shorter than Mathew but not by much as she was still able to peer into his eyes without tilting her head up.

"I'm fine besides a few cramps," she said as she quickly put her small hand over her abdomen just for effect.

"Why do you have . . . oh, never mind," Mathew said remembering a similar, uncomfortable conversation they had a few months ago.

"Ah, ha! You're learning more about us girls," she teased as she put her face close to his and poked him on the nose.

"Perhaps, but isn't that supposed to be a good thing?" Mathew said, confused as usual about this particular topic. He believed that a man shouldn't have to know about menstrual cycles, but most of his friends were female and they all seemed to be very open about even what he considered the most intimate topics of conversation. The bright side of knowing this information was it helped him steer clear of stormy waters.

"Of course it is. Every girl wants a man who can understand her," Angel said with a little spin just to release some of her pent up energy that always seemed to build up quickly.

"Is that all there is to it?" Mathew asked as he thought about this new information.

"Umm, no!" Angel said sarcastically. "There is far more involved but you must learn that on your own," she said simply while waving her finger as if she was teaching.

"Oh, you're so cruel to me," Mathew said crossing his arms and making a fake angry face.

"Well, I've got to get going. First bell is about to ring!" she said before skipping down the hall.

"Okay. I'll see you later, Angel."

"Bye-bye, Mathew!" she yelled back. As Angel left, the bell rang and Mathew walked slowly to his classroom. He sat down in his chair with a sigh and, as soon as he got comfy, he felt a gentle pull on the back of his hair.

"Hey, Mathew, guess who?" Sophie asked playfully with a cheerful tone.

"Sophie, what are you doing in here?" Mathew exclaimed with a quick wave of happiness.

"I'm a victim of a computer conspiracy involving a so-called 'glitch' that has mucked up my schedule. I have been reassigned to new classes so, here I am!" she said trying to braid Mathew's hair even though it was too short and kept coming undone.

"Okay . . . okay, quiet down class. I have a few announcements," the teacher began. "Looks like the ski trip is still going to happen," the teacher said after the class quieted down enough to hear the news. The fate of the annual class ski trip had been in jeopardy as there hadn't been any snow yet that year. The ground was barren with the ugly sight of dirt and dead plant life. "There is the probability of a large snow storm that should bring at least a few inches of snow. That will allow us to go as planned."

Throughout the school, a wave of cheers could be heard as each class received the morning news at about the same time.

"Now that's done, open your textbooks to page 140," the teacher said after the class was under control.

The rest of Mathew's day went extremely well as he had been perked up by the news about the ski trip. He, Angel and Sophie had lunch together and nothing could dampen his good mood, not even Angel and Sophie bickering about something Mathew couldn't understand. Which, of course, ended with them refusing to talk to each other . . . again.

The rest of the school day went quickly and Mathew was surprised to realize that school was a lot more enjoyable when he was happy. He rode the bus home and, as soon as the door flung open at his stop, he could tell there was a serious storm brewing. Huge snowflakes, some the size of fifty-cent pieces, were already coming down. Mathew had a brief fantasy about winning a heavenly lottery with buckets of gold coins snowing down from "Above". The fantasy was short-lived when the logical side of his brain kicked in with how dangerous that would be. He probably wouldn't live to spend a single coin on anything decent. However, within the short time it took him to get from the bus stop to his driveway, it was already snowing harder.

How did it get this cold? Mathew thought as he jogged up the driveway. He wasn't dressed for this extreme cold weather snap and wanted to get inside as quickly as possible.

He went down to his room in the basement and took off his treasured gold cross that a close friend had entrusted to him. He hung it up on its single wall hook and then plopped onto his bed.

I wish something exciting would happen today. The cold is making me sleepy, Mathew thought with a yawn. I believe a short nap is in order he thought and changed into his pajamas. He crawled under the covers and slowly drifted off into a deep sleep.

After what seemed like only moments later, he woke up to the annoying ring of his alarm. Mathew rolled over, looked at the time, grabbed the clock and threw it across the room. It hit the wall with a loud 'bang' and broke into pieces.

Not . . . today . . . no, not today . . . no school, he thought before drifting back to sleep.

When Mathew finally woke up, it was about noon the next day. He couldn't move out of his bed to save his life. He was warm and the air in his room was cold. He had forgotten to turn on the heater when he came home so with each breath he made a white vapor cloud. After a few moments, he forced himself to roll onto the floor. As his body touched the cold carpet, jolts of energy went through him. He ran upstairs and quickly jabbed at the heat button until the thermostat read 90 degrees. He hobbled back downstairs, changed out of his clothes and jumped in the shower so he could warm up while the furnace did its work.

"I feel a little better today," Mathew said to no one in particular after his shower. He didn't eat anything before falling asleep yesterday and was very hungry. He walked upstairs to rummage some food and see if his dad was home yet.

Food. What should I have? Mathew wondered as he scavenged through the refrigerator. I think I will take this leftover steak, he thought to himself before cramming steak into his mouth.

Hmm . . . cold steak. It's like beef jerky. But cold. And a bit crunchy. Not bad, he thought happily chewing on the cold steak. After ripping off a piece of steak large enough to sustain him on his trip downstairs, he went into the basement, chewing noisily, and turned on the TV for some entertainment. Mathew glanced out the window and noticed that the ground was white with new fallen snow and it was still coming down.

"I love the snow. There's something so pure and fresh about it," he commented feeling more cheerful than he had in a long time.

Engrossed in his television program, Mathew lost track of time until he heard the front door slam. Not moving, he just ignored it figuring that it was probably his dad, who he did not feel like talking to at the moment. So he just sat there watching TV until the door to his room flew open and banged against the wall. The shock of the sudden sound and movement spooked him off his bed into a small gap between his bed and the wall.

"Why didn't you come to school today?" Sophie demanded as Mathew tried to wiggle out of the small crevasse. He was surprised that he fit into a space that small. He was even more surprised when he realized that it was very easy to fall into the crevasse but extremely difficult to get out. He had a flashback to when he was 4 years old and got his head stuck in the balcony railing at the mall. His dad had to call the fire department to get him unstuck. Definitely easier going in than out.

"I just didn't feel like going . . ." Mathew's explained in a muffled voice while he was still stuck between his bed and the wall. "Don't just stand there staring at me! Help me out of this hole!" he shouted waving his hand at her.

"Well, you should have called me! I do have a cell phone you know," Sophie said as she yanked Mathew out of the gap.

"Sorry, I woke up at, like noon or something. Way too late to join the living in the Great Halls of Education," he said while rubbing his back where he had scraped it against the wall.

"What exactly happened here?" Sophie asked before sitting down on Mathew's bed. She pointed at the shattered alarm clock and the fresh dent in the wall.

"Just a little scuffle. Which I won, of course," Mathew said trying to remember why he threw it instead of turning it off like a normal person.

"Don't you think that is a bit extreme, Mathew?" Sophie asked looking at the broken alarm clock.

"I don't remember why. I just remember throwing it," Mathew said rubbing his head.

"You are a prime candidate for therapy, in my humble opinion, of course. But that's not my place. I'm your friend first," Sophie said lying down on the bed.

"How deep is the snow out there?" Mathew asked turning on his computer that doubled as a radio.

"Classic topic evasion technique. Believe it or not, it's like 6 inches already," she said looking at her leg.

"It's only been snowing for a few hours!" Mathews said slightly astonished.

"Only a few waking hours for you. It's been snowing for almost 24 hours now. Mathew, the main reason I came over today was to mother you. The ski trip is tomorrow and we are staying for a few days in the hotel so bring extra clothes and clean underwear, too," Sophie said yanking on Mathew's shirt to make sure she had his full attention.

a boundary or two, please! It's tomorrow already? I should et my winter clothes out, then. I heard on the news that the snow ing to keep coming. It was really cold when I came home from school yesterday, is it still?" Mathew asked opening his closet and pulling out an old trench coat.

"Yes, it is. Um, is it okay if I use your phone? I don't have any reception at the moment," Sophie said putting her cell phone away.

"Of course . . . it's down the hall on the right-hand side," Mathew said trying on the trench coat. Luckily he hadn't grown much in the past year.

"Thank you. I won't be long so don't go anywhere," she said with a playful voice.

"Where am I going to go? It's my house, you know!" Mathew said taking off the trench coat. He went to clean up the broken alarm clock and then heard Sophie yelling.

"Everything alright?" Mathew asked offhandedly as he played on the computer so he didn't have to hear her conversation.

"Yes I'm fine! Just yelling at my dad," Sophie replied and went back to her conversation. After a few moments of yelling, Sophie returned to Mathew's room with a funny look on her face.

"Is everything alright?" Mathew asked as he inspected the new dent in the wall and wondered if his dad would notice . . . or even care.

"Mathew . . ." Sophie began with a blush growing across her face.

"Yes . . . is there something you need?" he said turning to face her.

"I . . . um . . . well . . . I'm going . . . to have to . . . to . . . stay here tonight," she finally finished as her face and tone of voice changed dramatically.

"And . . . why is that?" Mathew said as a deep blush spread across his face at the thought of having a young lady in his house overnight.

"There was nothing I could do. My dad said it's not safe for me to be out on the road right now and he'd rather have me stay put. He's mad at me that I didn't have 'enough sense' to go straight home after school. The snow is coming down faster than the road crews can handle. They're shutting down the roads until the storm is over later tonight," Sophie said with her body language changing from just an embarrassed girl to a very nervous one.

"Okay, so you're stuck here till morning . . . there is nothing we can do about it," Mathew said trying to rationalize the situation.

"Mathew . . . this will sound strange . . . but . . . will you be good?" Sophie asked pulling her body into a fetal position while keeping her eyes down.

"What do you mean by 'good'?" Mathew asked still trying to put the pieces together of what was starting to happen.

"I mean you won't try to jump me, will you?" she asked finally.

"Seriously? How long have you known me? Why would you even wonder about that?!" Mathew yelled before thinking.

"Remember our conversation yesterday about what type of girl you liked and you pointed out that you are a man . . ." she said with her voice becoming more shrill than usual.

"Okay, Sophie, don't worry. You're starting to make me really nervous and I won't do or try anything, okay? So, please relax and try to . . . You know, make the best of it . . . here let's . . . let's just watch some TV," Mathew said quickly grabbing the remote and switching it to the movie channel (which, by horrid coincidence, just happened to be a porn film). Sophie let out a quick shrill scream.

"Oh my god! I am so sorry! I had no idea it was porn!" Mathew yelled flipping through the channels as fast as the remote would allow. They sat there for a few moments in awkward silence.

"You know . . . that was kind of funny," Sophie said relaxing a bit more with the beginnings of a smirk on her face.

"You're right," Mathew said with a small chuckle. He looked at Sofie, she looked at him and then the two burst out laughing together. They laughed until they were out of breath and had to stop before passing out.

"That's just what I needed, believe it or not," Sophie said back to her normal self.

"Yeah, I needed that too. That was a good laugh," Mathew said lying back on the bed.

"You wouldn't mind if I took a shower, would you?" she asked standing up and stretching her legs.

"Go ahead but . . . what will you wear after?" Mathew said pointing out the major flaw in the plan.

"I could use some of your clothes while I wash mine, if you don't mind," Sophie asked pushing at Mathew when she was done stretching.

"That's fine, I guess. I'll get clean sheets for the bed while you're in there. You can have my bed for the night. Before you ask, I am going to sleep on the couch," he said looking in his closet for clean clothes for Sophie to use.

"Thanks, Mathew. I appreciate it," Sophie said as she walked out of the room.

CHAPTER TWO

SKI TRIP

Mathew woke up from a restful sleep to the smell of bacon in the air. He rolled off of the couch and looked into the kitchen.

"Good morning, Mathew," Sophie said cheerfully while moving around food that was cooking on the stove.

"Good morning. What is all this, Sophie?" he asked standing up while rubbing the sleep from his eyes.

"What does it look like? I'm making breakfast for us because it's breakfast time. Plus I wanted to thank you for your hospitality. I slept really well. It was a bit too hot, though," she said happily as she flipped a pancake on to a plate. Mathew absently remembered setting the thermostat at 90 degrees some time ago.

"Here you go, my friend. Enjoy a good homemade breakfast for once," she said putting a plate for him on the counter.

"Well, thank you then," Mathews said as he grabbed the plate and started eating. Sophie joined him and they both ate quietly until the front door opened and slammed shut.

"Mathew, my son! What smells so good?" Mathew's father cheerfully asked as he came upstairs.

"Oh dear God, why now?" Mathew exclaimed while quickly standing up.

"Well, well, well! What do we have here? A lovers' tryst while your old man is out of town on business, huh?" Mathew's father said putting Mathew in a headlock.

"NO! . . . Dang it, dad! She had to stay here last night because of the snowstorm. Her dad said it wasn't safe for her to be out on the roads!" Mathew tried to explain as he wrestled his way out of his father's tight grip.

"Well, why don't you introduce me to your lover then?" he said.

"You completely ignored what I just said. But anyway, Dad, this is my friend Sophie. Sophie, this is my dad . . . who is incredibly obtuse with selective hearing," Mathew said now worn down.

"Nice to meet you, Sir. Mathew has told me a lot about you," Sophie said taking off the apron she was wearing.

"Nice to meet you too, young lady. Mathew has also told me quite a bit about you, too. By the smell of your cooking, it seems like you've got some talent. Hey Mathew, you should marry this one, son!" he yelled on his way down the hall to his bedroom. The comment caught Mathew unprepared and made him spit out the milk he was drinking and burst into a chocking fit.

"Time for us to go," Mathew said quickly as he threw on his coat and made a frantic dash out the door with Sophie rushing to catch up with him.

"So . . . that was your dad, huh? He seems fun and he's kind of cute for an old guy. I can see where you get your rugged good looks," Sophie teased, breaking the uncomfortable silence that they had struggled with since his dad's marriage comment.

"He is but he's always so . . . . uncomfortably uncontrollable. He tries to be hip and cool whenever I have friends around. Seriously! Saying those things right in front of us both. I think he knew exactly what he was saying and just wanted to mortify me in front on my friend," Mathew said while rubbing his eyes as the bus crept to a stop.

"Have a nice night, you two?" a sarcastic voice yelled from the back of the bus.

"Timothy . . . Tim, that is you, isn't it?" Sophie asked as she approached the back on the bus.

"Yep, it's me. I got released from the hospital a few days ago. I've been at home resting for the past few days . . . you know, Mathew, you could have given me a call. It would have been nice to hear from you," Tim said giving Mathew a smack on the arm.

"Yeah, sorry. It's not in my usual agenda to call up a guy," Mathew said plainly.

"Well, from the looks of it, you would rather be playing doctor with Sophie here!" Tim said poking fun at both Sophie and Mathew.

"We were not playing doctor! Mathew wasn't at school yesterday so I went to see him and got stuck there because of the snow and the roads were closed until the morning!" Sophie said rather aggressively.

"Sure you were. But anyway, we are going on the ski trip today so where are your clothes for the overnight stay?" Tim asked pointing out the thing that Sophie did not have.

"You know me, always prepared. I packed everything a few days ago. My dad is going to drop my bag off at school for me. And Mathew . . . he said last night he might want to talk to you," Sophie said recalling the conversation with her father the night before.

"The fun never stops," Mathew said to no one in particular.

"Oh, that reminds me, Mathew. I thought you would want this. I put it in my pocket this morning but I forgot to give it to you at breakfast because of your father," Sophie said digging in her pocket and pulling out Mathew's cross.

"Wow! That's one of the most beautiful things I have ever seen," Tim said as he admired Mathew's cross. The cross was indeed beautiful. It was 24 karat gold with small emeralds embedded in each corner and on the bale that connected the cross to the chain. There were delicate patterns that looked like birds with outstretched wings, slightly worn from years of someone rubbing the cross with their fingers in search of comfort, making it difficult to tell the cross' age. The cross looked old because the faded patterns were not a modern design. Mathew had always assumed it was an old gothic design but he wasn't sure. He had searched the Internet hoping to find some history, or similar crosses, without success. He didn't think the cross was one of a kind but it definitely was unusual.

"Why, thank you," Mathew said taking the cross and putting it around his neck.

"I wanted to ask you where you got it. My mom buys a lot of jewelry and I've learned a bit from her. I can tell by the dark color of the gold that it's 24 karat. It looks rather expensive and old, too. Maybe antique, or even Italian in design. No offense, but it looks like more than you or even most people could afford, so I'm wondering if you inherited it or something. Either way, I know it's special to you and would like to hear the story behind how you got it," Sophie asked not trying to sound rude.

"I inherited it from a friend," Mathew said simply.

"Well, lucky you! Is that the reason you're so happy lately?" Tim asked leaning back in his seat.

"Actually this positive mood came yesterday while Sophie was stuck at my house with me," Mathew said examining his recent mood compared to his depression two days before. He was beginning to see a pattern of the depression linked to spending too much time alone.

"One thing's for sure . . . I would be yanked out of a depression too if I was sleeping with someone," Tim said getting a punch from Mathew and a slap on the arm from Sophie for his comment.

When they arrived at school, they went to their classes and were put into groups of 3 to 5. Excitement was in the air and no one was able to sit still for long. Thankfully, they boarded the buses quickly and headed off to the mountain resort that was a few hours away.

"I'm so excited to get there I could just pee my pants. I want to snowboard so badly!" Tim shouted as he jumped and put Mathew in a loose headlock as evidence of his excitement.

"Tim, you doofus! Only girls say that. By the way Mathew, what were you and Angel talking about before we left?" Sophie asked.

"She was just asking about what bus I was assigned to and who was in my group," Mathew replied, his voice distracted as he watched some kids start a fight on the sidewalk.

"Well isn't that just like her . . . nosey whore," Sophie said crossing her arms.

"What?? I had no idea you felt that way about her . . . last I heard you two were good friends," Tim said with a rather confused tone of voice.

"They have been fighting for a few weeks now. They started shortly after you smacked your head trying to do that flip off of the balance beam. I have no idea what they are fighting over, though. I asked both of them and they just told me it's girl problems and walked off. Too much drama for me," Mathew said recalling his knowledge of the fight.

"It's none of your business, Mathew, that's why we won't tell you . . . and I won't tell you either Tim, so don't bother asking me later on," Sophie hissed.

"Okay, okay! Sorry, I didn't know it was such a touchy subject," Tim said trying to calm the now seething Sophie.

"It doesn't matter anyway. The bottom line is we are not friends anymore," Sophie said turning to look out the window and refusing to talk the rest of the ride to the resort.

When they arrived, they were put into two different floors in the hotel. The girls' floor was one floor higher than the boys. After they unpacked, they were directed to go to one of 14 stations to get set up with skis or snowboards that were appropriate for their height and weight. They were then given the rest of the day to ski and do whatever they wanted.

"Come on, you two old men!" Sophie shouted getting in line for the ski lift.

"Hey! It's been five years since I was last on skis," Mathew justified wobbling his way to the line.

"And I'm just hanging back to help Mathew," Tim said now trying to push Mathew to make him go faster.

"Stop that, Tim! I'm not stable yet," Mathew pleaded without relief from the impatient Tim. When Mathew was finally able to get in line and get on the ski lift, they got about half way up the lift when it stopped suddenly. They waited impatiently until the lift speaker blared out an announcement.

"Attention! The ski lift is temporarily disabled. Don't be alarmed. We are just changing a few things on the generator and you should be moving within the next few minutes. Please be patient and thank you for your cooperation," then the speakers went silent.

"Well, what should we do now?" Mathew asked immediately becoming impatient and realizing the irony of being thanked for his patience when he wasn't asked in the first place and had no choice.

"Did you just see that thing?!" Tim blared out pointing at the tree line.

"What thing, Tim? I don't see anything," Sophie said shading her eyes from the midday sun with her hand.

"It was like a bear or something! It was walking around on two legs then it ran into the woods!" Tim said with a frantic voice.

"Tim, there is nothing there! It's just some bushes. Besides, no wild animals walk or run on two legs," Mathew said, rationalizing to calm down from the sudden fright.

"I'm not joking! I saw it moving! It was white and big and . . . and . . . walking in the woods . . . OMG! It was BIGFOOT!" Tim said and then screamed like a girl.

"Seriously, Tim! Calm down. So it was big and white and walking . . . . Oh, my god! It was Frosty the Snowman!" Sophie yelled breaking out laughing after she finished her sentence.

"It wasn't fricking Frosty the Snowman! It had FUR! Frosty wouldn't have FUR! It looked like a big white bear," Tim said getting angry as Sophie continued laughing at him.

"Okay, let's do this . . . when we finally get off the ski lift, let's go over there and check the snow for any tracks," Mathew said trying to end the argument with logic.

The lift started to move again and they finally reached the top. The three friends hopped off and skied to the place where Tim had spotted the two-legged animal. After a few moments of searching, Sophie found some tracks.

"I found something! Right here!" Sophie exclaimed excitedly pointing at the large track she found.

"Well, I don't know of any bear that would make this track," Tim said inspecting the imprint.

"It's a snowshoe track, you idiot. It's way too big for any bear—or any other known animal. What you saw was just a guy going for a hike," Mathew said plainly.

"So, a hiker is out in the woods with snowshoes and a white fur coat??" Tim sarcastically questioned Mathew's logic.

"How do you know it was a hiker, Mathew?" Angel's voice came from a few feet behind them.

"What are you doing here, Angel?" Mathew asked already knowing this would not end well.

"Kim said she thought she saw something and wanted to check the tracks," Angel said pushing Kim in front of her.

"Well . . . I thought I saw something that looked something like a big white bear but I wanted to check the tracks to make sure," Kim said with a nervous tone of voice.

"That's what I said. But Sophie said it was fricking Frosty the Snowman," Tim said defending his original statement.

"You said it was big and white and walking in the woods. Hence, Frosty the Snowman. I hear he was a very jolly old soul," Sophie argued.

"That was hilarious," Mathew added.

"Okay, back to the topic. Mathew, how do you know it's a hiker with snowshoes?" Angel said getting the group back on the original topic.

"Well, just look at it . . . it's too big to be an animal track and it has the pressure marks in the snow where the weight was distributed," Mathew said closing the mystery of the two-legged bear like an iron trap.

"I'm sorry for dragging you out here, Angel. I must have misinterpreted what I saw," Kim said with a nervous voice.

"It's fine, Kim. We are at this hotel all week, you know. So it's fine if we do other things besides ski," Angel said shaking Kim lightly by the shoulders.

"Well . . . it was good to see you, Angel, but we must be going," Sophie said before pushing Mathew down the hill, who quickly crashed into a snowdrift.

The rest of the day was spent skiing with a sullen Sophie who was barely talking to anyone. The group decided to turn in early after Mathew skied into a rather large puddle of water that hadn't quite frozen yet. The three friends spent the rest of the evening hanging out and playing cards in the lobby with multiple apologies coming from Tim, who was the reason Mathew skied into the large puddle. As the sunlight was fading, a strong storm blew in and the students were told to go to their assigned sleeping quarters. Mathew was working on his laptop when he heard a loud banging at his door.

"Mathew . . . Mathew . . . Open the door! Hurry!" an alarmed female voice came from the other side of the door.

Mathew ran to the door, unlocked it and stepped back as it flew open. The small figure of Kim stumbled in and basically fell on him.

"Kim! What's wrong?" Mathew asked putting her on the bed.

"It's Angel . . . She wanted to go for one more run down the hill but I didn't want to go so I told her I was going back to the room. And it's been about 40 minutes and I'm worried, and you're the only other person I could think of who could help," she said before bursting into tears.

"Did you tell someone else about her? You know, like a staff member or a teacher," Mathew said now completely alarmed.

"Yes, I did but that was twenty minutes ago and she isn't back yet," Kim managed to say between sobs.

"Okay, I'm going out to find her. Think, Mathew. Okay, Tim is downstairs getting something. When he gets back, tell him what happened then go tell Sophie. I'm sure she will want to know," Mathew said grabbing his trench coat and other winter necessities like gloves and hats. He even wrapped a few towels around his legs for good measure and dashed out the door.

It was snowing so hard outside that he couldn't see three feet in front of his face but he managed to make out the silhouette of a snowmobile. Mathew rushed over to it hoping it the keys would be there.

"Key . . . key . . . key! Where is the key?" Mathew said looking around the snowmobile for a hiding place for the keys.

"Here it is!" Mathew pulled the key out of its hiding place under the seat, turned the machine on and sped off into the snow. Mathew's eyes were starting to freeze from of the strain of forcing them open. He decided to stop to warm them. He heated his hands by holding them close to the motor then pressing them on his eyes. Once he could see again, he hopped back on and rode off. After about thirty minutes of wandering up and down what he believed to be the ski slopes, he finally saw something in the headlights that he hoped was Angel. He jumped off the snowmobile and ran towards the figure, stumbling through the force of the wind.

"Angel . . . . Angel! Come on, it's freezing out here and we don't have a lot of gas left," Mathew said as he grabbed the figure by the arm and spun it around. To his horror and astonishment, the face he saw was not the face of his friend but the face of an animal.

The animal roared and threw Mathew into the trees. Mathew felt the sharp pain of branches slashing his body. He finally hit the side of a tree and fell into the snow. He tried to stand but collapsed and spit up blood for his effort. He felt his leg, that was now burning and he looked down and saw that a large branch had lodged itself through his skin. His chest started to burn from an even larger branch through it. Mathew could feel his warm blood streaming out of the wounds and he dropped his hands.

So, this is it, Mathew thought to himself. This is how it ends; Death by Frosty the Snowman, he finished with a small smirk as he felt his limbs growing numb. A peaceful sleepiness came over him as the snow slowly covered his entire body.

CHAPTER THREE

REBIRTH

Mathew dreamt about his life and his mistakes he had made throughout his short teenage history. He had a dream about his first dog and his first friend. He saw his departed friend, Meridia, and her passing and felt his heart shatter into tiny pieces all over again. He wandered aimlessly in this dream world for what seemed like a lifetime. Mathew tried multiple times to regain his thoughts but they always came back to nonsense, like words being put through a mixer and sorted back in a scattered, random order.

Throughout the whole experience, there was a voice. A strong, calm voice guiding him through each event, pointing out mistakes that he often regretted like stealing things or avoiding a close friend only to lie about it when that friend cared enough to confront him. And then came the excuses. Excuse after excuse for not doing what he knew to be right and missed opportunities to make things right when he had botched it up. After what he hoped was just a long, virtual journey, he finally came to the last event in his short life; his death. He watched his well-intentioned self dash out of the hotel with an ignorant, not well thought out plan and race around the mountain looking for Angel. Over and over again, he encountered the creature, saw himself fly through the air and felt his body punctured by the branches of the tree. He wondered the purpose of watching repeats of his death until an unfamiliar figure appeared before him. Mathew couldn't see well enough to make out who it was.

"Who are you?" Mathew asked.

"I am The One Humans seek but never find," the figure replied in a strong, sturdy voice that brought peace to Mathew's wandering soul.

"Where am I? Why am I watching my life?" Mathew asked. He was annoyed at the figure's cryptic answer.

"You are in the space between Life and Death," The One answered.

"How do I leave? I feel . . . tired," Mathew said now realizing how exhausted he was.

"You make a choice between Life and Death. If you choose Death, life as you have known will end and a new one will begin. If you choose Life, life as you have known will continue but it never will be the same. Neither choice will restore your previous existence but both choices lead to Life as you have not known. There are rewards and trials ahead of you with each choice," The One said, moving as close as a breath away but still just beyond reach.

"What does that mean? How will my life be different?" Mathew asked struggling to pay attention as he felt a fast approaching deep sleep coming to claim his soul.

"Your life will depend upon which Element you are a part of.

"Wait! How can I choose when I don't know? What are . . . Elements and how do I belong to them?" Mathew asked as his vision blurred and he struggled to maintain mental clarity.

"Enough questions," The One stated firmly and Mathew felt overwhelmed by fear. The One seemed to notice and continued with a new urgency.

"Mathew, you don't have much time. Your soul hangs in the balance for but a few moments more. You need to choose your path or your choice will be taken from you. Your choice is my gift to you. To my left is the path to Life that will never be the same. And to my right is the path to Death where you will begin life anew. You will only have enough strength to travel down one path. Once your choice is made, there is no turning back so choose well," The One finished and Mathew turned to find himself at a crossroads before an unfamiliar, vast forest. As he peered into the forest, he noticed that the bark of the trees looked like brass and the sap seemed to flow like a river of gold. Crystal leaves shimmered in the wind and reflected light from an unseen source. Brilliant silver fruit hung heavily from the branches.

"I choose to continue my life on Earth," Mathew said with such confidence that The One seemed to pause for a moment in surprise. He wasn't sure how he knew that because, even at a close proximity, he still couldn't make out who The One was.

"I am pleased with the confidence in your decision," The One said plucking a heavy, silver fruit from the tree and gently handing it to Mathew.

"Mathew, this is the Fruit of Life. It will give you the strength to travel down the path you have chosen," The One stated as Mathew bit into the silver fruit.

The experience was exhilarating and not like anything he had ever known on earth. When he ate, he not only tasted the flavor but he tasted the smell of it as well. It was bitter and sweet at the same time and seemed to taste like every flavor and smell at once. When Mathew was finished, The One helped him to his feet and walked with him to the path he had chosen.

"Mathew, what I am about to tell you, you must remember. It is another gift for you that will give you strength on your journey," The One said before releasing Mathew's arm.

"What is it, then?" he asked. He still felt very tired but his body was now moving on its own down the Path of Life.

"You are together even though you won't know it until the appointed time," The One said quietly as Mathew staggered on.

"What does that mean . . . ? I can't . . . I don't understand," Mathew asked watching the ground move slowly beneath him.

"Just remember my words. All is well and clarity will come when you are born once again in the world of the living. Until then, you must continue down the Path of Life," The One said, its voice fading with every step until Matthew was overcome by the resounding silence of solitude.

Mathew continued to move slowly down the Path of Life until he saw a bright light in between two large gates. He knew instinctively that the light was good and felt its warmth like a friend welcoming him to a new adventure. The closer he got, the faster he moved until he was running. He ran for what seemed like a long time and finally reached the light. As he moved through it, he felt his entire being change.

A familiar feeling came over him that he couldn't place until he saw lights pass by his head. He looked around as he passed towns, streets, countries and entire continents and then realized he was flying. Mathew quickly focused on a single snow covered mountain that seemed to be his destination. As he approached, he saw his own body lying motionless in an orb of ice then, with a sudden gasp for air, his soul was sucked back into his body. There were several figures around him but he paid no attention to them and fell into a deep, dreamless sleep.

Mathew regained consciousness slowly and found himself inside what looked like a bubble in the ice that was created when water freezes too quickly. He could see his immediate surroundings but couldn't see outside of it. Mathew noticed that the bubble was frozen but still filled with water. He seemed to be breathing without the use of an air tube.

He reached out to touch the side of the bubble and heard a cracking sound. Mathew quickly pulled his hand away. He saw a small crack where water was streaming out of the bubble. As he watched, the crack grew bigger until it split the bubble in two, spilling out all of the water along with Mathew. He hit the ground with an impact so strong that it sent liquid shooting out of his mouth.

With a gasp for breath, Mathew slowly regained his strength and stood up. His first order of business was to check his vitals. He could see, hear, smell and breathe. He had a pulse so he figured there was not much else that was necessary at that point. He reached down and felt his legs where the stick had been lodged during the incident with the killer beast. There was no sign of the stick and both his leg and chest had healed. While checking his fatally wounded sites, he was amazed to see there weren't even scars where the protrusions had been. He wondered for a moment if he was stuck in a dream within a dream.

At that moment, he realized that checking for scars had been way too easy and discovered that he was naked. He frantically looked around the room for clothes or anything that would appease his overwhelming need for modesty. He found something that looked like a white robe with blue stitching around it and various snowflake-like patterns. It was a little too large but he wasn't fussy at that moment. He quickly put it on to make himself as comfortable as possible.

Wondering where he was and what to do next, Mathew decided to see if he could find his way home—or at the very least find out where he was. He left the Bubble Room (as he had dubbed it) and entered a large hallway which looked as smooth as crystal. The floor seemed to be made out of the same material as the walls except it had a common square, tile-like pattern on it. He continued to explore the building but he seemed to be alone. Mathew saw a few signs of life, like other footprints in the light frost that still clung to the ground, so he walked down the hallway to a large window. He decided to look out it, hoping that there would be some type of landmark he would recognize.

It was dark out and there was snow everywhere he looked; he saw sheer ledges where icicles hung like sparkling Christmas lights. It was a picture perfect image right out of "Chronicles of Narnia". After admiring the view for a while, he wondered briefly why he wasn't more freaked out than he was. It's not every day a guy wakes up in a bubble that breaks and ends up walking around by himself in a crystal cathedral. Shaking off the momentary wonder, Mathew continued down the hallway and entered a large room. The room was made out of the same crystal material as the hallways but had a more refined look to it. It was so clear that it was almost invisible. He realized there was more to the elements than what he learned in science class. He wandered out of that room and into another hallway, still trying to find someone to answer his list of questions that seemed to be growing every moment he spent in this unusual place.

Where am I? I might have to be dreaming, that's for sure, Mathew thought to himself after walking up and down endless hallways.

He wandered aimlessly until he heard a female voice singing in the distance. It was hard to tell where the voice was coming from because it seemed that sound traveled through the crystal with amazing clarity. The singing sounded sharper and clearer than any Mathew could remember. He decided to follow the sound to find the source. It led him into a frosted courtyard with Ionic pillars wrapping around a frozen garden. There was a fountain in the center that had crystals forming and disintegrating from it instead of water. Around the fountain circled an abundance of pale white and light blue flowers that delicately chimed in the air in harmony with the sound of the fountain. As he drew closer, he noticed that the singing was another layer of the sounds that came from the garden. He wasn't sure if the garden was carrying the tune or the singer but decided it didn't matter. This was one of the most beautiful singing voices he had ever heard.

Mathew went deeper into the garden with the familiar crunch of frost under his bare feet. He figured he should be cold but wasn't. It was actually quite nice out as far as he could tell. Fresh and clean. When Mathew finally found the girl who was singing, he listened silently as she sang her song. Mathew thought it sounded like some type of ballad that the old medieval bards used to sing.

When she finished, the haunting tune hung in the clear, crisp air and in his head. He couldn't remember the words but the words didn't seem to matter; it was just the tune that caught his ear in the first place. Even the wind seemed calmer as she sang. Mathew desperately wanted to hear her sing again so he decided to speak up.

"Please continue," Mathew said softly. All that did was spook the girl who turned to face him with a startled look on her face. Mathew saw that the girl was young. He estimated she was around his age, or maybe 20 at the most, but her body language suggested that she was older than she looked. Her hair was a light blue and her skin looked as pale as a ghost in the moonlight. She had blue eyes almost the color of her hair that, from where Mathew stood, shone like the sky on a frosty morning. He decided that she was as lovely to look at as her voice was beautiful.

"Oh, I'm sorry . . . did I wake you?" she asked quietly.

"I'm not sure exactly what is going on . . . I woke up and found myself in some type of bubble," Mathew replied. "Can you help me? I don't know where I am or how I got here," he confessed.

"Oh! So you're a new one! Welcome to the World of the Elementals!" the girl said enthusiastically.

"What was that song you were singing just now?" Mathew asked slightly distracted by her welcome but he had a strong yearning to know more about the haunting melody.

"It's called 'The Unknown Melody'. It's my own song that I'm trying to finish but I just can't think of the next few lines," she replied calmly.

"What is it about?" Mathew asked walking up to the girl as she stood near the edge of the balcony. To Mathew's surprise, the balcony appeared to be perilously perched over a deep ravine and was overlooking the entire side of a large mountain.

"It tells the story of a Succubus who fell in love with a Human. When the Human accepted her, she was so happy that she forgot to take care with her, um, 'interactions' with him. She was careless in her joy and her lover died during their wedding night leaving her brokenhearted and bitter," she said simply.

"You have a beautiful singing voice. The only other person I know who can sing half as good as you is my friend, Sophie," Mathew said after he was able to build up enough courage to speak.

"Well, aren't you sweet . . . I'm glad you chose the Path of Life instead of choosing the Path of Death. It's been quite a while since we got a new boy. The last 14 were girls," she said with a caring smirk.

"Wait . . . Wait . . . yes! I remember now! The One and the fruit and everything," Mathew exclaimed as he put his hand to his forehead. He was feeling light headed as the memories flooded his mind.

"What is it . . . are you okay? Do you need me to get the doctor . . . ?" the girl asked trying to figure out what was happening.

"No, I think I'm okay. I just remembered what happened . . . there's no need to worry," Mathew said calmly, his heart now racing from the sudden memory. He reached for his cross like he usually did for support and to his horror discovered that it was gone. He climbed to his feet and raced through the maze of hallways until he found the room where his bubble had been.

When he got there, he frantically searched the room on his hands and knees, looking under everything and anything he could but his cross was nowhere to be found.

"What are you doing?" the girl asked panting from the pace she had to run at to keep up with him.

"Where is it? I have to find it! I had it on . . . before that stupid thing hit me and now it's gone," Mathew said as he continued searching the remains of the bubble. He knocked over everything in the area where his cross could be hidden. He needed to find it. That cross was his only connection left to Meridia and his only solid connection to reality.

"Um . . . darling, you know you're dead, right?" the girl said with a sympathetic voice.

"No. I'm not! I ate the fruit and now I'm alive," Mathew said continuing to search, hoping to see the cross' gold glimmer in the pale light.

"Darling . . . this body is just a copy of your original. And your cross is probably still around the neck of your Human body," she said wrapping her arms around Mathew's shoulders which caused a peaceful wave of calm and understanding to course through his body.

"Do you know where my body is? I have to get that cross! I need it!" Mathew explained practically yelling but still in the tight hug of the girl. His confused mind was at war with the calm in his soul.

"I'm sorry, but I don't know. We have to wait for the Elders to examine you before you can leave the safety of the fortress," the girl said tightening her grip.

"But . . . I . . . . Okay . . . Okay . . . I understood things were going to be different when I took this path . . . so, Okay . . ." Mathew said trying to calm his mind down. He was struggling to remember what The One had told him and understand this new life he was in.

"Come on honey, let's get you a bed. One good thing about being an Elemental is we no longer physically need to eat or sleep, but we sleep anyway just to help our souls relax," she said helping Mathew up off the ground.

"Forgive me. I have been rude . . . my name is Mathew," Mathew said realizing how stupid he was dragging this girl into his problem without even introducing himself.

"Nice to meet you, Mathew. My name is Ilium," the girl said with a charming smile as she helped him down the hallway to a room with a bed.

"Well, where am I, then?" Mathew asked.

"You are in your new home, Mathew. Just sit back and relax now," Ilium replied brushing back his hair.

"You're so kind, Ilium. Especially since I was just yelling at you," Mathew said trying to calm down.

"I've been where you are. I was terrified when I was reborn. It was the kindness of someone that helped me get through it. Just trying to pass it forward," Ilium said simply.

"I don't know if this is too personal but, how did you die?" Mathew asked wanting to know more about this strange girl who was caring for him.

"It's not as personal as you would think. We often laugh at our death stories after we get to know each other. We retain our core, foundational personalities after we are reborn and a lot of our

Elemental personality glitches mirror our Human frailties. My story is actually kind of dreadful. I died because of an avalanche. It was instantaneous so not as traumatic as most. How did you get here, dear?" Ilium asked sitting at the end of the bed.

"Well . . . I don't know what it was. It was like a freaky white bear thing . . . it stood on two legs and its face kind of reminded me of a gorilla . . . wow! I sound like my friend, Tim. He thought it was Bigfoot," Mathew said with a slight chuckle but when he looked at Ilium, her face was extremely serious.

"Mathew, stay here. I'll be right back," Ilium said running out of the room. As soon as she left, Mathew heard small cries and growls that were coming closer to his room. His heart pounded with fear and apprehension until Ilium entered the room with a small animal in her arms.

"Mathew, did it look anything like this?" Ilium asked putting down a small white bear-like animal on Mathew's bed and let it run around.

"Yes! Except it was much bigger. What is this thing?" Mathew said in slight horror as the little animal crawled onto his lap.

"Mathew, that is a Yeti. I am confused as to how you encountered one. Yetis are bound by Ice Elemental law and not allowed to even encounter Humans, let alone kill them. I have to go talk to the Elders about this. Please take care of this little Yeti. It's still a baby so it won't hurt you. Just play with it, okay?" Ilium said quickly and left before Mathew could object to watching the little Yeti.

Mathew slowly got more confident with the Yeti. It reminded him of his puppy when he was a little boy. It wrestled with his arm and chewed on his fingers, which thankfully didn't hurt at all. Then it crawled onto his lap and fell asleep while Mathew scratched its stomach.

"You're like a puppy, aren't you, little Yeti. Little Yeti boo-boo!" Mathew said. A few minutes after the Yeti fell asleep, Mathew heard a 'Thump! Thump!' coming down the hallway. The door flew open and a Yeti larger than the one that killed Mathew stood in front of him. Understandably, Mathew panicked and woke up the little Yeti who jumped into the large Yeti's arm and crawled onto its shoulder.

"*Thank you for watching my cub*", a voice said inside Mathew's head. The large Yeti turned and walked out without another word or motion.

Moments later, a small group of people came into the room and swarmed around Mathew. They were rapidly asking him different questions that were all blurred together in a jumbled mass of confusion.

"QUIET!" a voice boomed from behind the crowd and, through a small opening to the right of Mathew, a man stepped forward. He was pale and had a youthful look. His robe was different than the others; it was blue with gold patterns in the shape of something that looked like a snowflake or a crystal. The man's hair was bright white with a few strands of brown threaded through it. He also had a slight scar under his chin that wasn't big enough to ask about. His eyes were blue but not the blue Mathew was used to seeing; it was if they were frozen.

"Now then, Mathew. My name is Steven. I'm one of the members of the Elder Council. Are you sure it was a Yeti that killed you?" he asked getting directly to the point.

"Yes Sir, it was indeed a Yeti. But it wasn't nearly as large as the other Yeti that came here to take the little one away," Mathew said answering the question while giving as much detail as he could.

"About how big was the Yeti then, Mathew?" Steven asked.

"Where is Ilium? I need a reference," Mathew asked trying to remember the night.

"I'm right here, Mathew. What do you need?" she said wiggling her way to his side. Mathew stood up and held her by the shoulders and spun her around like he did the Yeti before it killed him.

"The Yeti was about one foot taller than Ilium . . . or that's what I remember anyway," Mathew said.

"It must still be an adolescent," someone in the crowd said starting a quick uproar.

"Mathew, where were you killed?" Steven said grasping his shoulders.

"It was a ski resort called Honor's Ledge. We were on a class trip and I was racing around the hills by myself, like an idiot, looking for a friend of mine who was lost in a snowstorm," Mathew explained then a sudden bout of depression hit him. He never did find Angel before he died. Mission unaccomplished.

"Mariah, go search the area for Mathew's body near the Lodge and report to me when you find it. I'll go there personally to handle this matter," Steven said barking orders then turning to leave.

"Steven, wait!" Ilium said grabbing his shoulder before he got too far.

"What is it Ilium? We have a rogue Yeti on the loose threatening Human lives! I don't exactly have time for small talk," Steven said seemingly annoyed by being halted from his work.

"Since you're going to Mathew's body, would you do him a favor?" Ilium asked trying to use a flirty voice but even Mathew could see right through it.

"I guess so. What does he need?" Steven said trying to speed the conversation up.

"There is a cross that Mathew would like returned to him. It's of great sentimental value to him so if you would be so kind as to have it sent back," she said stating the favor.

"What does it look like, Mathew?" Steven asked

"It's larger than most crosses. It's gold with green gems on each corner of the cross. There are golden patterns of a weird symbol on and around it on it," Mathew said recalling the cross he had worn so many times.

"Okay. I'll keep an eye out for it," Steven said and turned to head out the door.

"Ilium?" Mathew asked still thinking about Angel being dead because of him.

"What is it, Mathew?" she replied detecting Mathew's depression.

"How often does someone survive a snowstorm?" he asked trying to think of how to word it.

"Depends on the storm, Mathew. Why do you ask?" Ilium answered simply as she kept her gaze on Mathew.

"When I died, I was trying to save a friend from the storm and I didn't get to do that before I died," Mathew confessed as he felt tears of loss and failure creep up on him.

"Oh, don't you worry, sweetheart," Ilium began. "I'm sure whoever it was survived if you were at a ski lodge," she said as she rubbed Mathew's back gently.

"How can you be sure?" Mathew said after a while.

"You were at a ski lodge and all the hills lead directly to the lodge, yes?" Ilium answered after she thought about it.

"You know, you're right," Mathew said after thinking about it. It had been snowing but all the hills lead back to the lodge or the ski lifts that were nearby. "Angel is smart I'm sure she made it back ok," he finished feeling a little bit better. He did realize, though, with conflicting emotions that if he had thought of this before his mad dash, he would probably still be alive.

"There you go. Now tell me a little about yourself," Ilium said with a small smile.

"Excuse me for interrupting," a new person said as he quietly entered the room. It was obvious to Mathew that knocking was not really a courtesy Ice Elementals practiced. "The Elder Council is ready to process Mathew," he explained quickly, giving Mathew the impression that he had other things to do besides talk to them.

"Okay, I'm coming. Ilium, are you going to come with me?" Mathew asked simply.

"I think I will. I don't think you would be able to find your way back," she replied with a smile then a laugh before they all left the room.

Mathew was led down a few crystal hallways to a large room where he was going to be examined. Mathew was expecting a simple check-up at the doctor's office but, when he entered the room, it was anything but a doctor visit experience. Two people he didn't know were in charge of grilling him with questions, some very personal, such as "have you had any problems adjusting to your new body?" and "have you experienced any depression-like systems?" Mathew, trying to make the best of his discomfort, answered all the questions as accurately as he could.

After the examination, Mathew was given a blue crystal the size of a baby aspirin. He looked at the crystal and was skeptical about his body's ability to process it properly but swallowed it anyway, also in the spirit of cooperation. After he swallowed the pill in blind faith, the interviewers told him it would dissolve in a few hours and be absorbed into his system. Its main purpose was to allow him to leave the frozen mountaintop without melting. The interviewers also decided that Mathew was healthy enough to attempt the 'Art', as they called it, but weren't too specific on what it was or what it was about.

"So Ilium . . . what exactly does that little crystal pill do anyway and what the heck is the Art?" Mathew asked after his examination was complete. He was still confused and mentally off balance even after it had been explained to him in the big room.

"Let's see. Mathew, believe it or not, that little blue crystal keeps us from being affected by other elements outside of our home," Ilium started explaining to the best of her ability. "Like . . . because we are Ice Elementals, we are already are immune to the cold but . . . we end up being extremely prone to heat, so the crystal prevents our bodies from melting in warm to incredibly hot temperatures," she said with a few pauses in between to gather her thoughts.

"What?! I can melt?" Mathew asked not believing what she just said.

"Yes . . . I don't know why but apparently it's true. And the 'Art', as they called it, is our ability to control our element. It's like magic and we can do wonderful things with it," she finished her explanation.

"So I can control ice and snow? Let's start that now! Come on, Ilium, teach me!" Mathew said now incredibly motivated and excited.

"Hang on, Mathew. I'll teach you but first you need to learn how to get around in the snow using the Art. I know a girl named Sara who is probably better at that specific ability than I am; we will go find her after we get you new clothes," Ilium said leading Mathew through a door to an area that was considered a market. There were approximately 10 shops (most of which were clothing stores) and a small store that resembled a gas station. Its only purpose was to supply free food and other items from the Human population to help newcomers (like Mathew) adapt to their new life. There was also an Elemental bookstore that gave away everything free.

"Why is everything free?" Mathew asked after he browsed the shelves of the food store.

"We are supposed to live forever, Mathew. We don't need sleep and we don't need food so none of this stuff has any value to us. It's all about supply and demand, even in the Elemental world," Ilium explained taking a bag of potato chips from the shelves, opening them on the spot and started nibbling on them. "Num. These are so good . . . like an explosion of tiny flavors in the mouth. Ok, grab what you want. I want to get this done so we can get started on your Art. It will take a while . . . just to let you know," she said before she popped another chip into her mouth.

"Okay, give me a second," Mathew said grabbing a small soda and following Ilium into another store to get new clothes.

CHAPTER FOUR

NEW FRIENDS

"Are you happy with your new clothes, Mathew?" Ilium asked also wearing a new outfit she had picked out.

"Yeah, they're nice but what was with that lady who kept touching me?" Mathew asked, complaining about his experience even though it was, all in all, quite interesting. The clothes were also free because they were made from the Art that Ice Elementals could use to create cloth by weaving it together almost instantly.

"I should have mentioned this to your earlier but, don't think of me in any different way, okay?" Ilium said trying to sound serious.

"Okay . . . it's not like I have anyone else to talk to right now so go ahead and tell me," Mathew said trying to figure out ahead of time what it was going to be. He often got nervous whenever someone started a conversation by telling him not to "take it the wrong way" or "don't think of me differently". Or, better yet, the "I probably shouldn't say anything" conversations. In most instances, those were the conversations that should never have started in the first place.

"Mathew, for some reason it's extremely rare for men to appear as Ice Elementals so . . . how do I put this . . . . you're in high demand, I guess," Ilium said not trying to sound weird.

"So . . . there aren't any rules that apply to men around here?" Mathew asked also trying not to sound weird.

"You are required to take a spouse after a certain amount of time, usually like 10 years. It's more common, though, for you to be given away like a gift to the female who has the best connection to the council. I need to warn you, Mathew. You seem like a nice boy . . . some females are honorable but others will just try to seduce you," Ilium said now feeling a little awkward. "Mathew, I don't know if you know this but . . . well . . . we don't age here. So looks can be deceiving when it comes to women . . . or even men if that's your taste," Ilium said with a funny look on her face.

"Yeah, um . . . men aren't my type," Mathew quickly said to clear any ideas in Ilium's head. "So . . . how old are you then, Ilium?" he asked deciding to use this newfound knowledge.

"Don't you know that it's rude to ask a lady her age, Mathew? I don't have any hang-ups about age so I'll just say I'm over 10 and younger than 100," she replied giving him a gentle slap on the back.

"Wow. You're lookin' good for your age, that's for sure. So where is this Sara person, then?" Mathew asked excited about this new adventure.

"Don't worry, Mathew. We will find her eventually, or she will find us," Ilium said giving Mathew a little push.

"Do you ever miss your friends you had when you were alive?" Mathew asked.

"Everyone does at first but you make new friends and move on. I know that sounds callous but you have to make the best out of every situation here or your life will be just . . . miserable. Who wants to be miserable for all eternity? Definitely not me!" Ilium said changing her tone.

"That's what I thought. I'm sure it would be strange if I were to show up after I'm dead," Mathew said flatly but he was already getting a little homesick and it was even worse knowing that he could never go back.

As soon as Mathew realized that he was outside, he felt something hovering behind his back. He spun around to see what it was and found a young girl with short light blond hair. Her bangs were pushed to the right side of her face and partially covered her bright green eyes. The word "impertinent" popped into his mind.

"This is the new boy I heard about, isn't it, Ilium?" the girl asked before introducing herself.

"Yes, Sara. This is Mathew. Please don't scare him. He is fresh out of the bubble as of yesterday," Ilium said as if this happened regularly.

"I know. I can smell the bubble juices on him . . ." she said sniffing Mathew which was just weird to him.

"What?! I have juices on me?" Mathew asked, smelling himself as he tried to see if he smelled funny but he couldn't tell.

"Oh yes . . . it's like a sweet yet bitter smell. The bubbles are gender specific and, because you're a boy, the water has a little different scent to it. That's okay, though. It's like a pheromone to me," Sara said still sniffing Mathew while gripping his arm tightly so he couldn't back up.

"Okay, Sara. Enough with sniffing the boy," Ilium said pulling the resistant Sara away from him.

"Fine, then. I heard you were looking for me. Did you need me for something?" Sara asked.

"You need to teach Mathew how to use Travel Art," Ilium explained and Mathew wondered what this Travel Art was.

"Fresh out of the bubble and you want to use Art. Well, well, well. Aren't you a resilient one? I like that," Sara said with a quirky smile on her face.

"When can we start, then? I want to get a move on and do this Art stuff," Mathew said just trying to speed up the conversation.

"First off, how much do you even know about us and the other Elementals?" Sara asked.

"As there's not much to go by in Human existence, I don't have any history about the Ice Elementals. Other Elementals? I didn't know that there are other Elementals . . . why aren't they around?" Mathew asked as he admired the mystical, frozen mountain landscape as the sun shone on the frost that sparkled like diamonds.

"Sara, before you say anything, remember that he is new here," Ilium said in defense of Mathew.

"Right . . . well, anyway. Long story short, there are five main Elements. They are Earth, Air, Water, Fire and Ice. We're Ice. Our relationship with each Elemental race is based on how we can be of use to each other . . . and sure, the occasional war pops up every few years or so because even dead people aren't perfect," Sara explained while Mathew took a seat on a nearby bench.

"How are we 'of use' to each other, then?" Mathew asked.

"Let's look at Ice and Water. You would think they are the same thing because they are both made up of water but no. Ice is a solid so it somehow became its own element. Don't think too much into it. It's kind of like the Human concept of the Trinity. You will never find an exact answer so why bother getting your brain all twisted up about it? If the Water Elementals needed us to, like, freeze a certain area for some reason, we would and they would owe us something. None of us have any use for money or physical possessions so think of it as a favor," Sara started explaining to the best of her ability. "Like that 'issue' awhile back where part of the Antarctic ice shelf supposedly collapsed. That's one of the favors the Waters wanted . . . that area gone so we went in and got rid of it," she continued to explain giving Mathew a good example of the only currency that seemed to matter to an Elemental; favors.

"Okay. I get the favor thing but what do I need to know about Art?" Mathew asked still excited but trying to hide it. He didn't want to give off the impression that he was in a hurry but he really was and wanted to play it cool . . . as ice.

"I'll take this one, Sara," Ilium began.

"You see, Mathew, Art is still a bit of a mystery. Each Elemental is unique in the abilities we have to perform Art. None of us are good at everything. I think that's how the balance of power takes place here. For instance, I'm better at using ice to shape objects such as chains and other things that I could use. Sara here is better than I am at shifting the snow around her," Ilium started explaining as best she could. "It depends on the person. Not everyone needs to make functional items like I can but using the snow to travel is a must for everyone reborn into Ice. Think of them as . . . what are those people movers called? Um . . . cars!" she finished giving her fingers a snap.

"Okay, I understand that each person is better at some things that others aren't. It's like having different talents . . . so, can I do it now?" Mathew asked again trying to speed up the conversation.

"You're like a child, Mathew! Impatient, curious and always seeming to want to rush through things. But yes, we can start now," Ilium said with a sigh.

"Okay, my turn," Sara said pushing Ilium out of the way.

"First you must close your eyes and feel the snow; it helps if you get in the moment like holding out your hand while you concentrate. But, after a while, you won't have to move a single muscle to shape ice," Sara said holding out her hand signaling Mathew to do the same.

"You may want to close your eyes to understand what I mean by 'feeling the snow' . . . try that now," she instructed so Mathew obeyed.

"Mathew, you want to concentrate on the essence of the snow below your hand . . . I know it sounds weird but just try it," she finished.

Mathew began to concentrate on the snow itself. He felt a slight vibration throughout his hand.

"Good! You're doing well, Mathew! Now think of a shape. Try something simple like a square or a circle," Ilium said.

Mathew thought of a circle and the circle reminded him of a picture he saw on the Internet a few years ago. The picture was of a ball with a delicate snowflake inside. He focused on the picture for a while until he felt his body being shaken by someone. Mathew snapped back to present, opened his eyes and saw it was Ilium shaking him. What caught his attention, though, was the beautiful object in Sara's hand. It was a sphere made of ice so clear and as smooth as glass that it was transparent. In the center of the sphere was the snowflake in the picture he had been thinking about. The snowflake was a shade darker than the sphere itself and the contrast made the snowflake stand out like a holograph or 3D image.

"Wow! Did I make that thing?" Mathew asked taking the sphere out of Sara's hand to look it over.

"Yes you did, Mathew! I'm actually impressed. You went above and beyond the exercise. Most beginners get half a sphere or a corner of a box, never anything so detailed and complete. So, how did you do that?" Ilium asked taking the sphere away from Mathew so she could look at it.

"I'm not sure . . . just thought of a circle then the circle changed into a sphere then I thought of a picture of a clear ball with a snowflake in it," Mathew explained simply.

"Okay. Well . . . you're probably ready for actual ice forming. I wasn't expecting to start it this soon in the training but, whatever. Now Mathew, do the same thing but picture a snowboard made out of ice . . . or skis if you prefer," Sara ordered so Mathew, who was more than willing to perform more Art, obeyed happily.

Mathew closed his eyes and repeated the creative process except, this time, he thought of a simple snowboard. He pictured its sleek shape and size with small patterns on the bottom like his cross (which he was still feeling empty and naked without it on), but his imagination took off in all directions of possibilities. When he was satisfied with the image in his mind, he slowly stopped thinking about it and opened his eyes.

Mathew was amazed at his result. Before him was a snowboard but one that was unlike any he had ever seen. It was even different than the snowboard he had pictured in his mind. His snowboard had no place to strap on his feet and was curved a little less. And, what really made him happy was the pattern of his cross embossed all over his board, and not just on the bottom as he intended.

"Well, Mr. Bigstuff . . . think you can ride it?" Sara asked with a smirk.

"Probably not . . . I can barely ski. Remember that I had to steal a snowmobile at a ski resort to try to save my friend," Mathew admitted feeling a little embarrassed.

"Point taken but you're on the fast track and about to learn. Let's begin with the basics. Controlling the board itself is very tricky and will probably take you a long time so, the sooner we get started, the better," Ilium said giving Mathew a friendly slap on the back as the three walked back inside.

Mathew worked harder than he had ever worked on most things that required practice; he began to become very skilled with his new abilities. The greatest challenge he had was dealing with a board made of ice without the standard curve of a Human board. What did help a bit, though, was the engraved pattern of his cross. Without the pattern, the board would be unstoppable down the hill. With it, the board would slip down the hill faster than any skis Mathew had been on but the pattern added enough drag to ensure Mathew was almost able to stay on the board. All in all, it took about a week to get used to his new mode of transportation. That week of learning also included Mathew learning the essence of snow. As time went on, he learned how to use the snow under his board to move even faster. Once he mastered the essence of snow, he was no longer limited by standard downhill velocity and was able to go up hills without slowing down. He even mastered several tricks that took Humans years to accomplish. Though it took all of his concentration, which was very tiring, snowboarding gave him a sense of limitless freedom. The more skilled he got, the more he enjoyed his time boarding.

"Okay, Mathew. That's all you need to know about traveling with ice. Don't worry about going up the hills. You will be able to do that much faster in about a week," Sara said pleased with Mathew after he was able to 'board up an incredibly steep slope, which was the final test Sara and Ilium had given him.

"Why do we say what Art we use so strangely?" Mathew said offhandedly.

"Well we . . . rephrase the question?" Ilium asked getting confused as she tried to answer his question.

"What I meant was why do we say like 'traveling with ice'?" Mathew clarified.

"No other words describe it in our culture besides magic," Ilium said patting Mathew on the back.

"This will sound stupid but, wouldn't you call it something like 'Ice Magic' then instead of 'Art''? It's really confusing how it is now," Mathew said feeling kind of childish and stupid.

"If it will help you, there is no problem with that," Sara said

"Actually the title of Art has been under negotiation for years now because it makes more sense to use "magic" for people who lived as a Human first," Ilium said recalling a previous conversation she had a while ago.

"Really? There people who are born as an Ice Elemental?" Mathew asked switching the topic after a few moments of thought.

"Yes, Mathew. I'm one of them," Sara answered with a big proud smile.

"But how? You are a teen. I thought Elementals didn't age," Mathew said surprised.

"We don't . . . I'm a teen because they used Art; I mean 'magic', to change my body to what it is now. They call it the 'Right of Frost'," Sara said and the look on her face made Mathew assume that she was remembering a fond memory.

"So . . . how does it work? Do they like, stretch you out or something?" Mathew asked.

"They don't tell us how they do it because it's a well-kept secret. The only people who know are the ones who perform the ritual. But, then again, they ask us what we want with our body. Now that I think of it, it was seriously uncomfortable talking to them. They're kind of freaky Ice weirdoes or something," Sara said recalling her Right of Frost.

"It must be like plastic surgery," Mathew said making the connection between Elementals and Humans.

"What's 'plastic surgery'?" Sara asked.

"You lived with Elementals all your life so I can't blame you for not knowing. Well, it sounds similar to the Right of Frost in choosing your body . . . but most people, especially girls, have it done to make them look better," Mathew explained using the simplest example he could think of.

"What do they have done, Mathew?" Sara asked interested.

". . . Ilium, you want to take this one?" Mathew asked Ilium, watching her trying not to burst out laughing.

"Sure, Mathew. Now Sara . . . in Human society, beauty is often measured by the size of three things: thin body, size of nose but, what seems to be the most popular is a larger chest size," Ilium said letting out a few quick giggles now and then.

"So weird. I thought the Right of Frost was strange. Why is breast size more important in the Human world than nose size? How does that work? Why should breasts be large and noses be small? I would think a larger nose would be more beneficial because you could actually use a heightened sense of smell. Large breasts would just . . . get in the way. I wouldn't like my breasts to get in the way when I wanted to do something," Sara reasoned and Mathew fell on the ground just for effect.

"Let's ask the man of our group . . . oh, Mathew? What's a better size?" Ilium said shifting her gaze to him.

"Most men like the big Boing Boings," Mathew replied feeling stupid the moment he said it.

"Most men? What about you, Mathew? This is the first I heard about this and it seems like nonsense to me," Sara stated leaving Mathew speechless.

"Are you crazy? I'm not talking about that! That's private!" Mathew yelled as a blush quickly covered his face.

"Oh come on, Mathew! Tell us what you like . . . smaller ones like Sara's or bigger Boing Boings like mine?" Ilium asked trying to expose more of her cleavage just for comedic effect.

"I'm not going to tell you two anything!" Mathew said with the two comparing sizes right in front of him, even though he knew they were doing it as a joke.

"What the hell are you three up to?" a voice came from across the hallway.

Mathew spun around and saw Steven looking at the group with the strangest look on his face.

"Oh hey, Steven. What's going on?" Sara said. She was the first to recover and drop out of the competition.

"You first! Why were you showing off your cleavage in front of Mathew?" Steven asked with as much seriousness as he could muster after viewing and understanding the strange situation.

"We're trying to find out what size Mathew prefers," Ilium said pretending to drop something out of her pocket only to perform a perfect bend-and-snap to give Mathew a clear view of her generous cleavage.

"Oh, my god! Mathew, come with me!" Steven said grabbing Mathew and dragging him away from the two girls.

"Thanks, Steven. I owe you one," Mathew said grateful not having to reveal his preference.

"That's two you owe me now. And I keep track," Steven said pulling Mathew's gold cross out of his pocket. It was a little dirty with moss growing on one side but it was still as good as new to him. The dirt looked like it had been on there a while but Mathew thought it should come off with a good cleaning.

"What the heck! How did this get so dirty? I've only been dead for a few days," Mathew said taking the cross and, with a wave of his hand, created a small ice cloth to wipe off the dirt. "That rabid Yeti must have chewed on it and spit it out for it to get this dirty so quickly. If I weren't already dead, I'd kick its butt, that's for sure. Don't mess with my cross!"

"Oh dear . . . no one told you yet, did they?" Steven asked.

"Told me what?" Mathew asked as he rubbed the dirt off the cross and quickly created a small pointy icicle to get the dirt out between the patterns and small areas. Mathew was getting good at making small items and he was thankful for the increased handiness of his skills.

"This might come as a shock to you but . . . you have been dead for about a year," Steven said. The shock of that statement was a little too much for Mathew and he stumbled backward in disbelief.

"A year . . . How could I have been dead for a year?" Mathew asked.

"Let me rephrase that . . . You were dead for a day. Your body reconstruction took a week. You were in a coma for about 11 months so, yeah, about a year," Steven said recalling how long Mathew was out of commission.

"So judging by the snow fall, my school should be about ready for the annual ski trip to the lodge. I think I will go and visit them," Mathew said quickly doing the math in his head.

"Mathew, you are free to see them but, before you do, you must know the rules to interacting with Humans," Steven said with all seriousness.

"Why are there so many rules around here? A guy should have some death benefits! I'm not human anymore and shouldn't have to deal with rules and regulations. I mean, I woke up about two weeks ago and have made great progress with Ice Magic. I think it's about time I should get some more respect and not have to be told rules!" Mathew demanded like a rebellious adolescent.

For a response, Steven thumped his staff (which Mathew figured was a status symbol of the Elder council members) on the ground and sent a wave of frost around him, causing Mathew to fall to the ground in a weakened state.

"Mathew, I respect you for your accomplishments so far but you're more comparable to a toddler at this stage in your life. I, on the other hand, have been around for years," Steven said pulling Mathew back up off the ground.

"I'm well aware, Mathew. That's why I took you down with a weaker attack," Steven said with a slight chuckle.

"How old are you, Steven? I know we don't age so I'm curious," Mathew asked.

"Officially, I lived 28 years but I have been around here for about 232 years . . . My Rebirth day is going to be in about a month . . . what about you Mathew?" Steven said leaning up against the nearby wall.

"Well, I was 17 when I died and my birthday is in October so I guess I'm 18 now . . . . But can I ask how you died?" Mathew asked remembering the question he asked Ilium

"I fell through the ice while I was messing around with a few friends," he said simply. "That reminds me, Mathew . . . your body is still where it was. You had the nastiest death I have seen in a while,"

Steven said remembering seeing Mathew's body, which was impaled by multiple braches.

"Must have been pretty rotten by now . . . sorry, I guess," Mathew said trying to figure out what to say.

"Our bodies don't rot, Mathew," Steven replied

"Why . . . I mean . . . It's not like I'm using it, or anything," Mathew said.

"We don't know either. It's the same for the other Elementals, too. We think it has something to do with the soul not being departed from this world yet so the body stays intact," Steven said reviewing this as if he had talked about it before.

"So, what are these rules you were talking about?" Mathew asked wanting to change the topic because he was getting a kind of funny feeling.

"What . . . Oh yeah, sorry. The first rule is that they can see you but they can't know it's you . . . get it?" Steven asked

"No, I don't" Mathew said simply

"Just hide your face so they don't know it's you . . . but, then again, you could probably just walk in front of one of your friends without them knowing it's you . . . you and your body look completely different now. Here, take a look," Steven said making an ice mirror for Mathew to look in to.

Mathew couldn't believe the change that has happened. His skin was very pale but still had a touch of color on his lips and cheekbones. His face was leaner than it had been before his death and the small scars he had on his face from a tree climbing accident when he was seven were now gone. His hair was now a light white instead of dark brown. His skin was clear and void of all the dry patches, which he had problems with since he was a baby. Mathew's conclusion was he actually looked a lot better as an Elemental.

Not bad at all, he thought to himself. He looked a bit longer in the mirror to admire his new eyes that were like a mixture of ice blue and white, like a frosty blue sky on a cold, sunny morning. He really liked that.

"Wow! You weren't kidding I look completely different," Mathew said checking out the rest of his other visible body parts and wondered briefly about those that weren't so visible. This was the first time he realized he had changed.

"Okay, rule two. No using your Art in front of Humans. It freaks them out. Other than that, have a great trip if you're going. Oh, by the way, you can interact freely with the Humans that don't know you . . . so just obey rule number one at all times," Steven said finishing up the short list of rules that Mathew found reasonable and easy to remember.

"Okay, but where is the lodge? What ever happened to the Yeti that killed me?" Mathew said remembering his death, which caused a slight bit of horror to twinge through his mind

"The lodge is at the bottom of this mountain. We were quite surprised when we found out and we put the Yeti down . . . turns out it was rabid and was thrown out of its pack. Yetis are very particular about pack health," Steven said remembering his recent task.

"Hey, speaking of Yetis, do they ever talk out loud rather or do they just use telepathy?" Mathew asked remember the mother Yeti's use of telepathy.

"They do speak audibly but not frequently. They are a quiet race. We call on their aid during wars now and then . . . but anyway, Mathew, I have to get back to the council and report the situation with the Yeti . . . and you have my permission to see your friends but know your limitations," Steven stated before walking off down a different hallway.

Mathew went to find the girls. They were still standing nearby and he invited them to go along on the small trip to see Mathew's friends. They quickly agreed right before Sara caught sight of Mathew's cross hanging around his neck and demanded to see it. The ordeal ended up with Mathew on the ground being sat on by the two girls who were looking at the cross. When they were satisfied, they placed it back around his neck.

Mathew and Ilium decided that they should each go pack everything they could think of for the quick trip. When they were ready to head out, they gathered at the frozen garden and stepped over the small safety rail. They stood together on the other side of the rail overlooking a steep drop. They decided that was the best location down the mountain because it was steep and rough for short ways but seemed to smooth out quickly.

CHAPTER FIVE

OLD FRIENDS

"Same here, Mathew," Ilium said from her room as she walked out wearing an Ice Elemental robe.

"So . . . what else do Humans do here?" Sara asked.

"Well, the last time I was here my friends and I would go down to the store and get hot chocolate . . . what happens if we eat? I know that Elementals don't need to eat, right?" Mathew asked.

"Well nothing . . . it's kind of like an extra boost for our magic," Ilium stated.

"Well, let's go get some hot chocolate then," Mathew suggested.

"I'll go but I have to change first. I'm in the nude under this robe," Ilium said with a chuckle. Then she waltzed into the other room.

"The sad thing is I know she's lying," Mathew said with a stupid look on his face.

"That's Ilium for you," Sara said sitting up getting excited.

The three went down the elevator and into the café. They were the only customers because it was late at the moment and half of the shop was dark because half of the lights were off to save energy. Mathew had to teach Sara how to use the cocoa vending machine and, during the ordering process, he had to scold Sara to stop her from saying "Yay! Human food!" every time she thought about eating.

"How do you like it, Sara?" Mathew asked once they were sitting down in a nearby booth in the darker part of the café.

"I've never had it before and it's delicious," she said taking another sip.

"It's been years since I had something like this," Ilium agreed but her tone seemed more calm and relaxed.

"Oh, crap! It's them," Mathew said nervously as he spotted his old group of friends who all came to have a drink. The group consisted of Angel, Sophie, Kim, Tim and a new boy that Mathew didn't recognize. They took a seat at the booth in the lighted area of the café. To Mathew's surprise, Angel and Sophie appeared to be friends again. Then he remembered it had been a year and things changed.

"Remember girls, my name is 'James' now," Mathew whispered refreshing their memory.

"James, can I get another cup?" Sara asked out loud.

"Of course you can, I have plenty of money for our trip," Mathew said trying not to act suspicious but then realized he was pushing his budget by saying that.

"I can't believe it's been a whole year," Sophie said sadly to her group as Mathew and Ilium eased into their booth and Sara guzzled down hot cocoa.

"Try not to think about it," Tim said trying to console her.

"I'm sorry every one," Kim said then burst into tears. "I didn't know Angel was back in the lodge when Mathew went out. It's my fault! I killed him!" she sobbed.

"Kim, don't blame yourself. It's my fault. I stayed out longer than I should have and it's my fault," Angel said her face buried in her hands also starting to cry.

Mathew felt badly for being unable to say anything at that moment. He really wanted to pop up and say, "Don't cry! I'm right here!" But he knew he couldn't so he just clenched his hand tightly and held himself back. And, anyway he looked at it, he was still dead to them.

"I'm sorry. I know this is a touchy subject but who is this Mathew person? I've heard you guys talk about him before and it's obviously a very personal subject," the new boy asked.

"Well, Jacob, Mathew was a part of our group before you came to our school. One year ago we went on the annual school trip to this hotel. The first night we were here, Mathew rushed out of the hotel to find Angel and never came back. After about two months of searching the police pronounced him dead and called off the search," Tim explained because he was the only person besides Jacob who wasn't about ready to burst into tears.

"Oh, I'm so sorry . . . I had no idea," Jacob said with more sympathy than Mathew expected.

Not being able to take it anymore, Mathew stood up and walked to the sullen group. They gave him looks that seemed strange but Mathew just put one of his fifty-dollar bills he had on the table and said, "I'm sorry for your loss, the drinks are on me," then he turned to walk away.

"Hey, James! Wait for us!" Sara said chugging her hot cocoa and ran to catch up with him.

When the group got back to their room, Mathew went straight to bed while listening to Ilium learning new songs off of the radio and Sara asking silly questions like, "Why is the demon box singing?"

The next day, the group was lazy getting up. It was noon before everyone was up and when their door received a few knocks on it. Sara rushed to find out who it was. When she opened the door, she found Kim standing outside.

"Hey, you are one of the Humans from the café," Sara said still on her hot cocoa high.

"Um . . . okay. I just wanted to give you fair warning that our little group from yesterday is coming here to thank that boy," Kim said before dashing off towards the elevator.

"Yay, Humans!" Sara shouted jumping at the thought of talking to actual Humans. "Hey, Ilium! We are going to have visitors!"

"Okay. Hopefully Mathew . . . I mean James, will be out of the shower by then," Ilium said right as a knock came on the door. This time Ilium went to answer the door and was greeted by the entire group. Ilium invited them in.

"So, what brings you all here?" Ilium asked trying to make idle conversation.

"Well, we wanted to thank that boy . . . where is he?" Sophie asked.

"Oh, I'm sorry. He is still in the shower. He should be coming out any moment now," Ilium said and like clockwork Mathew opened the bathroom door with nothing but a small towel wrapped around his waist.

"Which one of your girls took all my towels?" Mathew asked not noticing the visitors until he was standing out in the open.

"Ooo-la-la! It's like living in the house of a model," Angel said checking out the pale boy who was just standing there with nothing but a skimpy towel for protection.

"What the heck! Why did no one tell me we were going to have guests?" Mathew yelled dashing into his room to change, with his heart rate up. He was now very nervous with his friends here and was concerned that they would recognize him.

"Well, James . . . I wanted to surprise you . . . and I took your towel. I thought you could use mine," Ilium said taking the blame.

"Yuck! Why would I want to use your towel?" Mathew yelled from his room.

"I didn't think that far ahead," Ilium replied.

"So, why did you take the towels, Sara?" Ilium said looking directly at her.

"I wanted to see him without his clothes . . . you even heard the one girl say he looks like a model," Sara said in her own defense.

"You are right on that account, Angel. That boy has a good body. Excuse me but . . . why do you all have the same pale complexion? Are you related . . . you aren't sick, are you? "Sophie asked now realizing how pale the two girls are compared to the others.

"We just live in the same area . . . We don't get a lot of sun," Ilium said thinking fast. "Oh forgive us! We have been rude. My name is Ilium and the one to my left is Sara," Ilium said introducing the girls.

"Well, who is the cutie boy you're staying with?" Kim asked this being the first time she spoke up.

"Oh, that's just our friend James. He is paying for this trip," Sara replied, this being her first answer.

"So his name is James? He has a nice body. Sent a shiver up my spine when I saw him . . . . Hey, you two aren't sleeping with him to pay off your end of the trip, are you?" Angel asked lowering her voice.

"Oh no . . . he isn't that perverted . . . but your friend has been staring at my chest since he got here," Ilium said and Tim quickly turned his head away.

"Excuse us for intruding on your girly fantasy but we haven't been introduced," Jacob said irritated by the comments about Mathew/ James.

"Oh, that's right. Sorry about that. The girls left to right are Sophie, Angel and Kim. The boy, however, is Jacob. Don't mind him.

His stomach has been upset lately . . . and my name is Timothy and if any of you young ladies need company up here in this big room well, don't be afraid to ring me up," Tim said trying to put his arm around Ilium and received a kick in the pants from Angel for his effort.

"Hello, everyone. I'm sorry for that spectacle . . . that's not how I usually make friends," Mathew said casually, coming out of his room trying to be completely calm and discrete. He watched every word he said hoping to not fall into any speech patterns that his friends might recognize.

"Well, maybe that's how you should from now on; you never know what will happen, James," Angel said looking straight at his body and not even trying to be discrete about it while checking him out.

"Thanks, Angel . . . but can't you be a little more inconspicuous when checking me out?" Mathew said feeling kind of funny with his friend checking him out.

"How do you know her name? You were in the other room when we introduced ourselves," Jacob pointed out being the only one who was actually paying attention.

"Well . . . . I heard you through the wall. Believe it or not, these walls are incredibly thin . . . Ilium, you moan in your sleep and it gives me weird dreams," Mathew blurted out as he thought of the first believable thing. And as a matter of fact, the walls were poorly made and Ilium did talk in her sleep.

"Dreams and moaning . . . you are a pervert," Angel said as a joke and got a good laugh from the girls.

"That reminds me . . . we were wondering if you three would like to go skiing with us today," Kim spoke up remembering the main reason they came up to the room.

"That would be great!" Sara said before the group could talk about it.

"Great! Meet us by the café when you're ready. Come on, people!" Sophie said taking charge of the little mob and they walked out of the room.

"Thanks Sara. Now I have to be on my toes the entire trip and try to act like someone else," Mathew said a little irritated by her sudden decision.

"Don't mind it, Mathew. It's not like they know it's you. They think you're a model," Ilium said with a chuckle.

"Well, then feel honored girls that you know a model," Mathew said flexing a little bit just as a joke.

"Yummy," Sara said playing along and they all got a few good laughs with other sarcastic comments.

They got ready which, for Ice Elementals, was quick and easy. Sara wore just a simple shirt and jeans and Ilium wore more standard clothes. Mathew wore whatever he put on. He was now immune to the cold and was going to exploit this ability every chance he got. Then the three friends went down to the café to wait for the other group to arrive. During that spare moment, Sara was introduced to soda pop for the first time and downed ten of them in less than five minutes. Mathew still couldn't believe that Sara didn't know much about Human culture or even the simplest of beverages like hot cocoa. The other group showed up without Jacob. He had stayed in his room because of his upset stomach.

"So, where is your skiing stuff . . . ? And is that all you guys are wearing," Angel asked looking at the lightly dressed group compared to the heavily dressed group who looked like a tribe of Eskimos.

"We have a high tolerance to cold," Mathew said proudly not really lying this time.

"Well, if you insist. Let's go," Sophie said.

When they got outside, Mathew, Sara and Ilium ran around the corner of the hotel to create their snowboards and slid around. The group of Humans gathered around them to check out their snowboards and proceeded to ask a lot of questions of why it was made out of ice and why there was nothing to keep your feet in place.

"Well, what should we do first?" Kim asked. Mathew noticed that she always had a nervous tone to her.

"We could enter the race that's going on in a few hours," Sophie suggested.

"That sounds like fun! Where do we register?" Tim asked.

"I assume it would be those two gentlemen over there," Ilium pointed to two miserable individuals sitting at a booth out in the cold.

"Well, then. Let's go register!" Angel said without any more discussion from anyone.

So the group went over and everyone registered in the race. There were two different races, one for boys and another for girls. The girl's race was before the boy's. The group spent the time in between practicing on a hill that was similar to the one used for the race as the one for the race was taped off to prevent interference.

When it was time for the girl's race, the boys sat on the sidelines and cheered. Jacob joined them when he was able. The girls took their positions at the top of the hill. Mathew, Sara and Ilium decided not to use their skills with snow to help them win the race. Each of them had varying degrees of competitiveness and all liked to win but they decided fair and square was best.

The girls lined up at the top of the hill and waited patiently. The shot rang out and the downhill race took a surprising turn. It was shy little Kim who was in the lead. Mathew saw the happy glow on her face that she was doing something and winning. Then a rather snobby looking girl slid next to her and drove her elbow into Kim's gut and she fell from the blow. A wave of gasps and boos came from the crowd. But the girl sealed her fate as soon as she attacked Kim. After helping Kim up and getting her back up to speed, Ilium, Sara, Sophie and Angel swarmed Kim's attacker like hornets and forced her off the track into the trees. Surprisingly enough, this group effort caused a round of cheers from the crowd. Sophie won the race but pulled little Kim up to the judges' box to ask that she be put in first place because of the interference. The judges gladly agreed and Kim was put in first for the female competition.

Now it was the boy's competition. Mathew stood next to Tim and, even from the top of the hill, they could hear the constant cheers of the girls.

"Good luck, James!" Tim said giving him a light punch.

"Good luck to you, too, Tim!" Mathew said as the shot rang out.

Mathew pushed himself off and accelerated using his Snow Magic. Before he knew it, he was in second place. He looked straight into the eyes of the person in front of him and saw the same look the girl had before hurting Kim. Before Mathew knew it, the boy in the lead tried the same trick but he was more skilled than the girl. He waited until Mathew was a little bit in front of him and acted like he was going to pass. That was when he went for a jab to the Mathew's gut. Mathew, who was expecting this, simply slid to the side and popped a smile that obviously struck a nerve. The rogue skier didn't bother to hide the strike the second time but Mathew dodged it with ease by going faster than the boy. Mathew ended the race in first place.

"James, you did it!" Ilium yelled sarcastically because she knew Mathew cheated.

"Good job, James! You showed that cheater why he doesn't win!" Sara cheered even though she also knew Mathew had cheated.

"Okay, you two. We need your picture," a man with a camera said. He pulled Mathew and Kim to the side and took their victory picture. He then took one with the group.

"Okay, just a few questions then, you two," the man said pulling out a pad of paper and a pen.

"Oh . . . Okay," Kim said with her normal skittish voice.

"Now . . . first of all, I noticed that you two are friends. So . . . is there love in the air or not?" the man asked.

"Oh, no. We just met yesterday," Mathew said with a generic answer.

"Ok. So you're just getting to know each other, right? Next question . . . This should have been my first question but, what the heck . . . What are your names?" the man said taking down some notes.

"M . . . my name is Kim Tamber," Kim replied this being the first time Mathew heard her last name.

"Is Kim short for Kimberly or some other name?" the man asked as he continued to write.

"No, it's just Kim," she replied

"And yours, young man?" the man asked looking straight at Mathew.

"My name is James," Mathew suddenly panicked a little he realized that he never thought of a last name.

"James what? You forget your name, son?" the man asked with a slight chuckle.

"Sorry about that brain fart . . . My name is James Arclight," Mathew blurting out the first thing he thought sounded believable.

"Arclight! Ho . . . I like it! It's snazzy . . . Oh, next question; what motivation did you two have to join the race?" the reporter asked taking down everything that the two said to each other.

"Well . . . we just joined because we were bored and we thought it would be fun," Kim said

"Okay, okay . . . just one more question, alright? You said you two just met. So, when did you meet?" the man said adjusting his glasses.

"Well . . . the first time I saw him, my other friends and I were reminiscing about a friend," Kim stated but not telling him that Mathew (or in this case, James) gave them a fifty-dollar bill.

"Well, if it's alright . . . what was that friend's name?"

"It's, okay . . . but I might start crying . . ." Kim warned before she took a deep breath. "His name was Mathew . . . and yesterday was the one year anniversary of his disappearance," she finished.

"I'm sorry to mention it . . . wait! Wasn't that the name of the kid who disappeared here last year?" the man asked and Kim couldn't take it. She started crying at the question so Mathew had to answer for her.

"Yes, that was him . . . and I didn't know him so don't bother asking me." Mathew said consoling Kim who had latched onto him and sobbing with her tears soaking into his clothes.

"Well, thank you for the interview. I'm sorry for upsetting you, little lady. I'll leave two copies of the article at the front desk for you two. You can pick them up about noon," the man said before walking off into the parking lot.

"What happened to Kim?" Angel asked as the group approached.

"Oh, the man asked how we met so the topic of Mathew came up," Mathew said feeling a little funny that he was talking about himself as if he weren't there.

"Oh, poor dear. Please stop crying," Sara said trying to calm her by offering part of her candy bar, which Kim took in a quick snap and nibbled on it slowly.

When Kim finally stopped crying, the group went inside to get away from the cold. Sara kept pestering Mathew for hot cocoa again until he finally caved and gave her the money to buy herself a few more cups.

"Well, everyone, what should we do now?" Angel asked.

"I'm not sure. It's rather late don't, you think?" Sophie said.

"Well, we could . . . . Oh, never mind," Kim said taking back her idea.

"What is it, Kim? Come on. Share with us . . . we don't bite," Ilium said getting her to speak up

"Well . . . why don't you and Sara visit with us in our room? . . . I mean if you want to . . ." she finished.

"That is a splendid idea," Angel said giving her a friendly hug.

"I wouldn't mind a little chit-chat," Ilium said happily. Mathew suddenly remembered that Ilium was older than she looked, but she blended into the 'teenage girl' role rather well.

"I'll go as long as they have this cocoa stuff there," Sara said sipping her drink.

"Well, then, I suppose that just leaves the boys to do what they please," Sophie said looking at the raggedy group of boys.

"I don't know about you two, but I'm going to bed," Mathew said with a monotone voice. He really didn't feel like hanging out with Tim or Jacob.

"Hey, dude . . . you're no fun. I guess that just leaves me and Jacob," Tim said wrapping his arm around Jacob's neck who was, obviously, used to this kind of treatment.

"I suppose the best we can do then is escort you to the elevator since we're not allowed on your floor," Jacob said breaking out of the headlock.

The group went up the elevator. First Tim and Jacob got off then it was the girls. Mathew gladly went to his room and proceeded to hop into his bed and fall asleep after watching a little bit of television.

When Mathew woke up, he noticed voices already talking in the other room. He checked the time and it was 7:38 AM. He got up to go inspect why people were talking so early. He walked into the other room and was greeted by Steven who was chatting with Ilium and Sara.

"Hey, sleepy head. It's about time you woke up," Steven said cheerfully to Mathew.

"Hey, Steven. What's going on?" Mathew asked in a sleepy voice.

"Nothing much. Just decided to drop in on your vacation . . . don't worry about the sleep, when you adjust you will no longer need it," Steven said scooting over on the couch allowing Mathew room to sit.

"Well, Mathew, we were just discussing what happened the last few days, like us getting to know your friends," Ilium said.

"Great. Just what I need, a strange guy knowing about my friends," Mathew stated. As soon as he finished, a knock came at the door followed by shouts from Mathew's friends.

"Well, speak of the devils," Steven said chuckling a bit.

"Hey, honey! Come out here quickly!" he shouted into the other room. A young woman entered the room and smiled kindly.

She had a beautiful smile that made Mathew feel happy even though nothing had happened. She had light brown hair and eyes that were a nice light green, which added to her smile wattage.

"Oh hello, you must be Mathew . . . you caused quite a commotion at home," she said sweetly as another knock came followed by shouting outside the door.

"Yeah! Hang on a second," Mathew shouted at the people standing on the other side of the door.

"Um . . . ok. I don't know if you two have been told but while my friends are within ear shot, my name is James Arclight," Mathew said explaining the situation.

"Hello, loud people. What do you want?" Mathew said as he opened the door.

"Why didn't you get the door the first time?" Sophie said as the entire mob moved in.

"I was talking with my other guests," Mathew said pointing out Steven, who was whispering to the new woman, and Ilium.

"Oh, great . . . more pale people," Kim said noticing the other Elementals in the room.

"Well, have a seat . . . If you can find one," Mathew said noticing Ilium was whispering to Sara.

I have a bad feeling about this, Mathew thought feeling awkward with all the whispering going around. He was starting to catch onto how much Elementals liked practical jokes.

"Now James, Julian and I have something we need to discuss with you," Steven said giving Mathew a little bit of insight into the secretive scenario. Mathew decided Julian was the name of the new woman to whom Mathew hadn't been introduced to yet.

"And what is that now, Steven?" Mathew asked politely, taking a seat across from Steven between Sara and Ilium.

"You know what this is about . . ." Julian intimated, drawing everyone's attention to her.

"No, I don't. What are you two getting at?" Mathew said getting another funky vibe with the situation.

"It's okay, James . . . . I already told them . . ." Ilium said trying to act embarrassed but Mathew saw right through it.

"James . . . we know that you and Ilium . . . ," Sara said with a more believable embarrassment act but still not good enough for Mathew's eyes.

"How could you do that to my daughter?" Steven suddenly roared.

"What the hell are you talking about, Steven? That is so not funny!" Mathew shouted back figuring out their prank.

"You're going to make this right, James Arclight!" Steven said putting on the "angry dad" personality (and making it seem quite believable)

"I didn't do anything so I won't be making anything right!" Mathew yelled getting suckered into the imaginary fight.

"What the heck is going on?" Sophie asked confused by the sudden argument.

"By the sound and look of it . . . James slept with Ilium and that person, who I believe is named Steven, is supposedly her father," Tim said breaking down the data, which was rare for him to express that level of insight or intellect.

"James! How could you do something like that?" Kim shouted and slapped him across the face making his neck crack.

"Okay, okay! That's enough of that joke. It's getting too serious," Julian said standing up to inspect the red handprint on Mathew's right cheek.

"Why, I mean he slept with Ilium . . . how are we supposed to take it?" Kim yelled a little angry.

"You shouldn't have reacted at all . . . it was a joke," Sara said enjoying how the situation turned out.

"What . . . why would you joke about something like that? That's just . . . so WRONG!" Angel asked with a shocked look on her face.

"It was getting a bit stale in here and we had nothing else to do. Also, it was a way for me to get to know Ma . . . I mean James, a little bit better but it didn't work out as expected," Julian said babying Mathew's face despite his objections.

"Is this your first meeting, then?" Tim asked inspecting the new girl which seemed to have developed into a bad habit while Mathew was away.

"Yes, it is. Steven said that he was an alright person but I wanted to make sure that this new boy I was hearing about wasn't a bad influence on my little sisters," Julian said finally releasing Mathew who was rubbing his cheeks.

"Wait! Are you, Sara and Ilium related?" Sophie asked looking at the three girls.

"Not genetically, but our bond is like sisters. We've known each other for a very, very long time. We also live right by each other, which helps with the female bonding. You know . . . . proximity makes a good bedfellow and all. Or, something like that," Julian said with such a convincing performance that it actually made Mathew wonder about the real relationship between the three girls.

"That's how Angel and I are. We used to live by each other before I moved and then I started riding the bus with Mathew . . . he was such a nice boy," Sophie said drawing back into her memories.

"Who is Mathew?" Julian asked playing dumb. But the question was now like a trigger for poor Kim. She let out of few sniffles that were a warning sign for her approaching tears.

"Oh, I'm sorry. I didn't mean to upset you," Julian apologized.

"It's okay. Excuse me, I'll be right back," Kim said running out of the room with tears in her eyes.

"Is she going to be okay?" Julian asked the others.

"Don't worry about it. Even though Kim starts to cry whenever Mathew's name comes up, she always tries to put on a smile for everyone else . . . for some reason she has been crying more often here than usual. It must be the memories and location association," Angel said simply thinking about her nervous friend.

"Well, anyway. Mathew was our friend. He disappeared here exactly one year ago . . . and Kim was the last one to talk to him before he went out into the blizzard, that's why it's a bit of a tender subject," Tim said speaking up.

"Do you guys want to do anything later? Now that I'm thinking of it," Angel asked just as Kim walked back in to the room.

"Well, usually we would but I would like to talk to James a bit more," Julian said.

"I suppose we should get out of your hair then. Nice talking to all of you. Come on, guys," Tim instructed heading out the door followed by the others.

"I'll catch up to you guys in a second. I need to talk to James first," Kim said as she returned and continued to close the door behind the group.

CHAPTER SIX

A DEPRESSING DEPARTURE

"So what do you need then, Kim?" Mathew asked as she walked over to him.

"You . . . I can't believe I didn't see it before," Kim began hiding her eyes behind her long hair.

"What didn't you see?" Julian asked curious to what the girl was getting at.

"Mathew," she said simply.

"What about Mathew?" Ilium asked getting nervous.

Without any warning Kim threw her hand down Mathew's shirt and pulling out the one thing she knew would be there and exposed it. It was Mathew's gold cross, which was a clear give-away to his true identity.

"Oh man . . . this isn't good," Steven said pulling Kim back from Mathew's neck.

"I knew it . . . but Mathew . . . Why? Why not tell us that you were alive?" Kim shouted. It was obvious that she was holding back tears.

"Um . . . . Steven, I need help. What do I do?" Mathew asked. Trying to figure out what would happen now that someone knows who he actually is.

"Well, there is no point in hiding it. Kim, in our society, you knowing Mathew's true identity is a serious offense for him. I'll pull a few strings with the Elders so he won't be thrown in jail for 40 years but you need to promise not to tell anyone of this conversation,"

Steven said simply putting a lot of emphasis on '40 years' to make it stand out above anything else in his comment.

"What?! Jail? Why? Okay, I promise. I won't say a word to any one! But now I kind of understand why you didn't tell us. Are you in the witness protection program? I had no idea you were facing 40 years in prison if you told us," Kim said picking up as Steven intended the punishment Mathew would get if she told anyone.

"How did you find out it was Mathew, though?" Julian asked Kim who was latching herself onto Mathew and crying her eyes out.

"Look at the newspaper. They have Mathew's previous school picture with a story about his disappearance and the one from the race," Kim said slowly as she started to calm down.

"Mathew, did you see this yet?" Ilium asked handing him the paper.

"This is not good," Mathew said seeing how Kim was able to put the pieces together. Last year's school picture had Mathew's cross lying on top of his shirt and the picture from the night before had the cross there too, but not as visible.

"How did that happen?" Sara asked looking at the picture.

"It must have slipped out after that punk tried to knock me out of the race," Mathew said looking at the most probable event.

"Mathew!" Kim began still crying into Mathew's body.

"What is it, Kim?" Mathew said with a consoling voice.

"I'm so sorry! I didn't know she was back and I was just hysterical. But now you're alive so it's okay . . . right . . . please tell me it's okay," she said looking right into Mathew's eyes for any sign of forgiveness.

"Kim, I don't blame you for anything. You did what you thought was right at the time and I did what I thought was the right thing to do at the time. There's nothing to forgive," Mathew said. He gently patted her head and gave her a tender hug as he struggled with his emotions.

"So you'll come back to school, then?" Kim asked excited with her voice full of hope and cheer.

"I'm sorry, Kim, but it isn't that easy," Sara said plainly

"Why? . . . Why can't you come back to school?" Kim pleaded not understanding the situation.

"Kim, look at me," Mathew began making Kim focus her gaze on him. "I know you probably won't believe me but you're going to have to . . . . Kim, the Mathew you knew is dead," he said trying to figure out the right way to explain the situation he was in.

"What?! How can you be dead if you're right here? That sounds messed up," Kim asked now completely confused.

"Mathew, I'll take over. I know how to explain this probably a little bit better than you can. Kim, Mathew was killed that night he left but his soul was sent back into this new body. He just came out of a coma less than a month ago. Do you understand?" Steven asked after he explained to the best of his abilities.

"I understand but I don't understand . . . you died but you are here because you were sent back. Like reincarnation or something like that?" Kim said struggling to figure this out with logic.

"It's not really like reincarnation but it's too complicated to explain. Listen, I know it's hard to understand but . . . just believe what we're saying," Ilium said trying to get the issue over with.

"Okay. I'll believe you but . . . who are you people then?" Kim asked looking at the others with disbelief in her eyes. It was obvious that she was earnestly attempting to believe the story no matter how far-fetched it sounded.

"Just think of us as ghosts. Each of us has died, with the exception of Sara who was born into this little world of ours," Julian said taking this question.

"Okay . . . I somewhat understand now. But really I don't. It's too much for me right now. Thanks anyway for telling me . . . but I should be going before the others start wondering what I'm doing in here with you," Kim said standing up and headed for the door. "Oh, and Mathew, one more thing. Thank you for forgiving me. It's been tormenting me for the entire year. I've been obsessively eating and not sleeping well at all. Maybe I'll start sleeping better and lose a few pounds now. Maybe not be so tormented anymore now that I know you are alive . . . or not dead . . . or whatever," she said before she walked out of the room.

"So what now, Steven? Are you going to turn Mathew in to the Elders?" Julian asked.

"Turn him in for what?? I just woke up from a nap and I didn't hear anything," Steven said faking a yawn and a stretch.

"I know. It's weird how we all suddenly just fell asleep," Ilium said with a small laugh and a fake yawn.

"Thanks, guys. I appreciate it . . . that was nice. It felt great to tell her. I have been feeling badly about her crying all of the time. I can't even imagine how I would feel carrying all that guilt around every day," Mathew said thankful for a friend in the Elder council who was willing to bend the rules a little bit.

"This could get complicated but we can hope for the best. Mathew, you really should ditch the cross for a while," Steven said after some thought.

"Maybe, but I'm not going to. This cross only comes off when I'm going to take a bath or when I'm dead. Well, skip that. I'm already dead . . . kind-a," Mathew argued but unwilling to budge on the issue. This cross was his only connection to his Human life and he wasn't ashamed of showing it off.

"Okay, but don't say I didn't warn you. Oh! That's right. Mathew, I have taken the liberty of signing you up for a few 'Ice Elemental 101' classes," Steven said remembering his original reason for being at the resort.

"School?! Why would I need classes on being an Ice Elemental? It's not like I need training to breath or anything," Mathew commented wryly. He did not want to take classes he didn't need to. He had just gotten out of high school a little while ago and he had no interest to go back. If he had to be dead, he wanted some perks and eternal school was not his idea of fun.

"Mathew, the classes aren't like that. They are an overview on Ice Elemental history, culture and the other creatures that live hidden in the world," Julian replied trying to pique Mathew's interest.

"Hidden? Interesting. What do you mean by 'creatures'?" Mathew asked, his interest piqued as his brain went on a wild run around the unusual topic.

"We know you've seen the Yeti. It's not the only creature out there like that," Ilium said leaning back on the sofa while cracking open a soda and taking a quick sip.

"What are some others, then? I want to know," Mathew said with his interest growing.

"That's what the classes are for," Julian pointed out but Steven quickly interrupted.

"Let's see. There are four separate classes: Mutants, Demons, Monsters and The Unknown. The Mutants are basically Humans with extra features. Demons are just as they sound. There are the Succubi and other Demons . . . that list is one of the longest," Steven started. "But Monsters are the most basic on the list. Prime examples of a Monster are the Yeti, Minotaur, and so on and so forth. But, The Unknown are the things that we still fail to understand such as Phantoms and Night Terrors," he finished pulling his own memories of the class out to give Mathew a good visual example.

"What? All those things exist? I thought they were . . . you know, just fairytales or folklore! Why don't Humans know about them?" Mathew said his head spinning with this new information.

"Obviously Humans know about them because you have the written and oral legends. But, most of the people who have had a run-in with them often don't make it back home alive. Unless, of course, that creature is under the command of Elementals or they are turned into Demons themselves," Julian said as she left the conversation and went into the other room.

"What did she mean by under the command of Elementals?" Mathew asked.

"Well, certain Monsters, like the Yetis for example, are under the watch of the Ice Elementals and don't usually wander far from snow. If it's that type of Yeti anyway . . . but the one that killed you was rabid and, under any other circumstance, wouldn't have hurt you. Wouldn't have even made itself known to you," Steven stated recalling Mathew's horrid death.

"When do the classes start, then?" Mathew asked willing to at least hear them out on this issue.

"Tomorrow. Classes start tomorrow so we need to head out tonight. That's actually why I came here. Unfortunately to cut your fun time short," Steven replied being honest.

"Well, we'd better get packed then," Mathew said, not in the least bit saddened by the news. At that same moment, there was a loud thump on the entry door.

Sara opened the door and, this time, the whole group of friends came waltzing back into the room with Tim rubbing his nose.

"What happened to you?" Ilium asked.

"I turned the door . . . thought it was open . . . I was wrong . . ." he muttered

"That was hilarious! Saved us a knock or two," Sophie said sending a slight chuckle through the room.

"So, what are you guys up to?" Kim asked noticing the group moving back and forth between rooms.

"We have to leave today," Sara stated trying to stuff her clothes into her small traveling bag. She was having a difficult time because the bag was already packed to the brim with soda and chips and she was refusing to leave without it even though all the extras in her bag were stocked at the Elemental stores. She appeared to place more value on things that Mathew's money had purchased over free soda and snacks at the Fortress.

"Oh . . . that's sad news. We have three more days here before we head back home," Angel said helping Sara by applying force on the bag.

"Yes well, something came up that I must attend to," Mathew said politely as he neatly folded his clothes and put them into his bag.

"Hmmm . . . it is a shame that you three are leaving . . . but, on a brighter note, do you ladies need any help packing your more delicate items??" Tim asked but all he got for an answer was Ilium's foot in his face, which made Mathew wonder how she managed to do that without falling down. Tim was much bigger than she was.

"That's what you get," Kim said as if she had seen this before.

"You know that never works, Tim. If it doesn't work on us, it won't work on them," Angel said who was out of breath from wrestling with Sara's bag.

"But then, how did Mathew pull it off? I remember a few years ago he helped you two pack up your clothes!" Tim said trying to prove his point.

"See, what you don't understand is Mathew just saw those as clothes and nothing else . . . at least he did at that point in time anyway," Angel replied simply.

"And I think that was before I met you two, wasn't it?" Kim pointed out.

"Yeah, but Mathew was still the same person when you met him," Sophie commented.

"You mean he was always quiet like that?" Kim asked.

"No. He was far worse when I first met him," Sophie began.

"He always had this look . . . I can't explain it. Sad but more than sad. His eyes constantly looked glazed over. When I talked to him for the first time, he used the most depressed tone of voice I had ever heard. Think of Eeyore from Winnie the Pooh on depression steroids. It was as if he had lost everything that mattered to him. Lost the will to live or something," Sophie finished recalling her first encounter with Mathew.

"Do you know why he was like that, Sophie?" Ilium asked exploiting the fact that Mathew couldn't say anything without giving away his secret if they started talking about something personal.

"I asked him on several occasions but he would always say 'that's something you really shouldn't ask about.' So I never got an official answer out of him," Sophie answered sadly.

"This is total hear-say but, I heard through one my friends who went to school with Mathew before he joined ours that, before he moved, his closest friends died from some disease. That seriously crushed Mathew's heart and turned him into a completely different person," Angel said going off of a completely unreliable source. Actual source or not, a tidal wave of emotion hit Mathew harder than expected and he frantically bit the side of his lip to hold back the emotions.

"Do you have a name of the friend? Or even the reason Mathew was so crushed at the time?" Sophie asked.

"Unfortunately, rumors spread like wildfire after her death. The only thing I know for certain is it was a girl and that she died holding Mathew's hand . . . or something like that," Angel said not noticing that each word pierced Mathew like an arrow through his heart.

"When did you find out about this? I had no idea and I was Mathew's best friend," Sophie asked shocked at the new news about Mathew, her closest friend.

"I found out over the summer from my friend. But I didn't do any actual research about it until last night," Angel replied.

"I don't mean to be rude . . . but I don't think Mathew would like us talking about his life like this," Kim said realizing Mathew's distress.

"Sorry, Kim. You are right, though," Angel replied agreeing to drop the topic.

"Well, now that that's over, would you girls mind helping me pack my 'delicate clothing'?" Ilium asked clearly just to watch the expression on Tim's face turn from sad to dejected.

"Of course, Ilium. I would love to see what you prefer to wear!" Angel said just jumping into the girly-talk.

"Oh come on girls! I can help, too . . . . I can give you opinions on what to wear," Tim pleaded.

"We don't want the advice of a pervert," Kim said sharply.

"Mind if I join you girls? It's been a while since I did this sort of thing," Julian asked with an angelic smile.

"I don't mind, Julian. I would enjoy hearing your opinion," Ilium said giving her a friendly smile back.

When the girls left the room, the three boys just sat and listened to the giggles and muffled voices coming from the other room. Then the door opened and the girls came out still talking but Mathew interrupted them mid-sentence. He wanted to preempt any understanding he might gain on what they were talking about.

"Well, ladies. How did it go?" Mathew asked politely.

"It went alright. But the garment preferences are unique from girl to girl," Julian replied calmly as she took her previous seat next to Steven.

"I'm surprised that doesn't irritate your skin, Ilium," she continued.

"You would think so but it's actually extremely comfortable. I do, though, seem to need to constantly adjust the straps," Ilium replied simply.

"Okay that's it! Since I didn't get to help, I'm going to hang out with Jacob. The poor guy has been sick all week," Tim said marching out of the room frustrated because of the girl-talk going on.

"Phew. Now that he is gone we can actually talk," Sophie said.

"James, would you be a dear and go grab the thing on the stove?" Julian asked.

"Yeah, sure. I'll be right back," Mathew said as he stood up and headed for the kitchen. He took the "thing" that was cooking on the stove and poured whatever it was into a cup. Mathew figured whatever it was it wasn't worth drinking because of the smell. But he brought it to Julian nonetheless.

"Thank you, James," Julian said taking the cup.

"What is that stuff, Julian? It smells like hot tar!" Mathew asked moving away from the vile substance. He nearly threw up as she took a sip of the dark liquid.

"It's my medicine. I need to take this at least once a week," Julian said between sips.

"What is it for?" Kim asked inspecting the liquid.

"It helps me focus during Art," Julian said using the word for magic so only the Elementals in the group would know.

"It smells nasty but looks can be deceiving . . . want a taste?" Julian asked holding out the cup.

"Don't fall for it . . . she did that to me the first time I saw her make that stuff. It will make you throw up a lung. Seriously," Steven warned as a putrid expression came across his face.

"You're no fun, Steven," Julian said annoyed that her prank was ruined.

"I'm an extremely liberal guy and throwing up for an hour is not funny," Steven said recalling the horrible event.

The eight friends sat around until it became dark outside. Steven suggested that they head out before it got too late. Sara, Sophie and Kim walked the Elementals down to the lobby to say goodbye. Mathew assured them that they would be back next year for the annual ski trip. Before they left, Mathew pulled Kim aside to ask for her address. He wanted to write to her for updates on his friends.

It was time to go. The group of Elementals left the lobby and Mathew was so sad to say goodbye to his former classmates that he was close to tears. He was able to hold them back as best as he could. Mathew glanced back several times at the lodge where, for the past couple of years, had been a place of fun with his friends. He realized now that he may never get to see them again. Nonetheless, "life" as he now knew it must go on. He turned from his past and walked towards his future.

When the group entered the tree line, they each created a snowboard for themselves and shot up the mountain. During their journey back, Mathew was introduced to the game Slow Snow. The rules were similar to tag except the objective of the game was to knock the other person off of their snowboard. That person then became the tagger. Since Mathew was new, he was given a handicap and was allowed to tag rather than dis-board. When he became more stable on his board, he would enter the game full on.

Mathew felt joy swell up inside his soul as they played the game. They dashed from the tagger, weaving in between trees and bushes and eventually big rocks as they climbed higher up the mountain. Mathew was having so much fun that he didn't even notice the sun slowly creeping over the mountain's ridge. Sunset made the game even more fun. The light from the fading day caused the snow to sparkle in the air. All in all, it was a magical end to a trying day for Mathew.

CHAPTER SEVEN

QUICK CLASSES

Mathew got up the next day surprisingly energized and remembered that he didn't need to sleep anymore. He looked at the clock and quickly got ready for his classes. They were scheduled to start at 9:00 am and he didn't want to be late. Ilium went with him to wish him good luck and to show him where the class was going to be at. Mathew still didn't know the area well enough to find it on his own. When Ilium left, Mathew felt like he was back at pre-school. All the faces were new (and mostly female) and Mathew noticed that there weren't as many people attending as he expected. He thought there would be a full class of 20 or 30 people, but the total looked closer to 15.

When everyone started taking their seats, Mathew moved to the back of the room. This was a force of habit from years of schooling and wanting to go unnoticed. The class calmed down until everything was quiet. The teacher appeared and Mathew had no choice but to do a face palm.

The teacher was Julian. She was dressed in what Mathew assumed was the standard Ice Elemental teaching attire that, from what he could tell, was a simple top and a skirt. He noticed quickly that the simple uniform managed to look different on her from the others he had seen. He also noticed that the current female Ice Elemental fashion statement was a top and some type of skirt.

Mathew was handed a few books that he was going to need for the class. The class books were constantly being updated so he was free to keep them. His list of schoolbooks contained interesting titles such as "Demonology", "Bites and Markings", "The Elemental History", "The Big Book of Creatures", and "Mutations and Adaptations". In addition, there was a really skinny book simply called, "The Unknown", whose title alone spoke volumes.

Mathew flipped through each book trying to get an understanding of the topics on the upcoming syllabus. "Demonology" was a book with a record of all known demons and how to deal with them.

"Bites and Markings" was self-explanatory; it defined each bite mark and other markings of the individual demons and monsters. Mathew looked up Vampire just for fun and saw that the bite mark wasn't as he expected. There were two generic puncture marks on the neck of the person in the example picture, but Mathew saw that some had more than 2 holes, or sometimes none at all. It seemed that the skin would heal instantly under the right circumstances leaving no indication of the encounter. He made a mental note of it and dismissed the other example pictures.

"The Big Book of Creatures" was exactly as it sounded; it was a big book based on all the other creatures that lived in secrecy. Mathew didn't bother to open "Mutations and Adaptations" or "The Elemental History"; he was already focused on learning all he could about Demons.

Mathew couldn't help but read throughout the entire class even when Julian was talking. It wasn't that he disliked the class; he just couldn't put the Demonology book down. He quickly read chapter after chapter and even jumped around to different Demons from the Index. As class ended, Julian asked Mathew to stay behind.

"So . . . how is my little bookworm?" Julian said poking fun at Mathew.

"This 'bookworm' is alright. I was just skimming over the Demonology book," Mathew said flipping open to the page he was on and continued reading.

"What did you look up, then?" Julian asked

"I looked up the Succubi . . . they sound interesting," Mathew said as he flipped open to that page and skimmed over the section again.

"How cliché . . . that's what most boys look up," Julian replied with a disappointed tone.

"I actually find them rather romantic," Mathew said feeling kind of funny talking 'romance' with a woman he barely knew.

"I'm sure you find it romantic. Most boys think that an entire race that survives off of the energy from sexual intercourse is romantic," Julian said with even more disappointment in her voice.

"No. It's not that. Have you actually read the full section on the Succubi?" Mathew asked as he continued to skim through the book.

"In all honesty I haven't . . . we spend a very small amount of time on Demons and their races in this class," Julian replied, a little ashamed.

"Hmm. I don't blame you but . . . give me a second," Mathew said flipping back a couple of pages.

"Okay, here it is . . . Succubi may feed off of the energy from sexual intercourse but will only breed with one member of the opposite gender of another race, and then continue a strictly monogamous relationship with that individual until he or she dies of natural causes. The Succubus picks this individual from millions of experiences with various people. Unlike popular belief, the Succubi do not take the entire life energy of their victims. They restrain themselves to about one year of life per person . . ." Mathew said closing the book. "The point I was trying to make was that Succubi go through millions of people in order to find that one person to breed with, then they stay with that person until he or she dies. Only then do they move on," Mathew said feeling like a scholar.

"I have to admit that I was unaware of their dedication to their mate . . . Mathew, what page was that on?" Julian asked grabbing pen and paper.

"That paragraph was on page . . . . 410. The Succubi sections start on page 400," Mathew replied.

"Well, thank you, Mathew. And thanks for the information. I'll give you a couple extra points on the tests," Julian said flipping open to the page about Succubi.

"Wait! Isn't this class just informative?" Mathew asked confused.

"I guess we forgot to tell you . . . If you pass the class you can apply for a license that allows you to . . . how do I put this . . . umm . . . I guess be eligible to be an ambassador to the separate races," Julian said flipping the page.

"I don't quite get it," Mathew said still confused. He had been okay with taking the class to just learn for fun but adding tests was not what he had signed up for.

"Let me explain; if you obtain a Demonology license, it allows you to go negotiate with certain Demon races like the Succubi you were reading about. And if you get the Elemental license, it lets you into other Elemental Fortresses," Julian replied recalling all the information.

"So . . . if I had a Demon license I could go hang out with a Succubus?" Mathew asked just to set the record straight.

"Yes and since Elementals are immortal, you could probably have a hay-day with the girls down there," Julian said letting out a chuckle.

"Wow! My teacher just told me to go play with a Succubus," Mathew said jokingly.

"Remember Mathew, just because I'm your teacher doesn't make our friendship any less important. So expect to see me around more often," she said simply.

"Thanks. I'll remember that. I'll catch you later then, Julian," Mathew said as he walked out of the room.

With no particular destination in mind, Mathew slowly backtracked his way to Ilium's room. He had nowhere else to go and decided to catch up with her before his next class. When he walked in, Mathew took a good look at her room for the first time. It was a respectable space, perhaps a little bigger than a Human's living room but more sparsely furnished. It was mainly a functional room with a bed and a couch (which Mathew had been sleeping on) and Mathew decided that Ilium did not spend much time there.

The walls of Ilium's room were covered with intricate designs that looked similar to vines climbing up the walls. The ceiling looked like a canopy of trees with intermittent carvings of birds that gave the room a fresh, outdoor look. It reminded him of the garden he had first found her in. All in all, it was definitely very feminine; there were even a few stuffed animals on her dresser that resembled a bear and a fox. What impressed Mathew the most about the room was the intriguing feeling of stability that made him feel safe, secure and comfortable. The room's best asset was the view; there was a large window overlooking a small gorge that was as pretty as it was deep.

"Hey, Mathew! How was your first class?" Ilium asked enthusiastically as she walked into the room.

"Not bad at all, Ilium. What were you doing, anyway?" Mathew replied.

"Oh, I had to talk Sara out of doing something stupid . . . and I had to get this thing," Ilium said opening something that looked like a cage.

"What's in there?" Mathew asked but found out quickly. It was the little Yeti that he had watched when he first became an Elemental. It greeted him with a hug-like motion then proceeded to jump up and down on the bed.

"The mother asked us to watch him for the day. She was sent out on an assignment," Ilium said picking up the little Yeti.

"I don't mind . . . but why us?" Mathew asked as he watched Ilium play with the Yeti.

"Apparently the mother personally requested us to watch him. I have no idea why," Ilium replied passing the Yeti to Mathew

"What's up, you two?" Steven asked as he barged into the room.

"Knock much? Why didn't you tell me Julian was the teacher?" Mathew asked as he lunged to catch the Yeti that suddenly started to run around the room.

"It just slipped my mind . . . but anyway, I see you have a little Yeti," Steven said picking up the ball of fur. "Oh you're a chunky one aren't you!" he said jokingly to the Yeti.

"Yeah, the mother's off doing something," Mathew replied simply.

"Mathew, where have you been staying?" Steven asked, seemingly randomly, as he put the Yeti down. It ran toward Mathew, climbed up his leg, onto his back and hung there.

"At the moment, I'm staying here with Ilium," Mathew said spinning around looking for the Yeti, not realizing that it was on him.

"I'm surprised you allow that, Ilium . . . in my experience, you're not one to trust easily," Steven replied.

"Well, Steven, it's not like he has anywhere else to go. I'm just being a good neighbor by letting him stay here until his permit comes in," Ilium replied unhooking the Yeti from Mathew.

"If that's truly the case, I could place a rush order for that permit. I do have considerable pull with the Registration Team," Steven said flexing his muscles to emphasize his power as an Elder.

"Yes, Steven. We know you're all powerful but what the heck is this permit thing you guys are talking about?" Mathew asked. Since he was still relatively new to the ways of the Elementals, he didn't fully understand the entire procedure with all the laws and regulations.

"Nothing to be too concerned about, Mathew. The permit is a permission slip that allows you to live here . . . think of it like a birth certificate, passport or, in your case, a Green Card," Steven explained, putting it in terms Mathew would understand.

"Really? What needs to happen for me to get a permit? Don't take this the wrong way Ilium, but I don't know where my clothes are and I'm afraid to open anything," Mathew said.

"Why are you so skittish about those things, Mathew?" Ilium asked

"Well, I was an only child and my mom left when I was young so I . . . don't know how girls react when you see their underwear," Mathew replied feeling rather embarrassed.

"What about that story I heard about you packing with Sara and Angel?" Ilium asked remembering the similar conversation.

"I was invited to do that so it's like getting their permission to look," Mathew said in his defense. "Also, I was kind of out of it back then and didn't care at all," he said as he recalled his emotional year when he moved from place to place like a zombie.

"Well! I'm letting you sleep here! How is that not giving you permission?" Ilium asked more than a little irritated with him.

"I suppose . . . that would be a new perspective on this situation that I hadn't thought of," Mathew replied admitting defeat.

"When you two are done bickering like an old married couple, would you like me to get that permit or not?" Steven asked when there seemed to be a small pause in the argument.

"If you could Steven, that would be great," Mathew said feeling rather excited that he would be getting his own place soon. He also felt a little badly for getting into an unnecessary argument with Ilium.

"Okay. It should be to you within the week," Steven began. "Well, if you will both excuse me, I have to see to my wife now," he said standing up rather quickly.

"You're married, Steven?" Mathew asked in a slightly shocked tone.

"Of course I am and you know her . . . her name is Julian," Steven said with a chuckle.

"Oh, come on! Why didn't I put that together?" Matthew asked himself feeling rather stupid now.

"It's only obvious to those who look, Mathew. I'll see you two later," Steven said before he walked out of Ilium's room. He left whistling an unfamiliar tune.

"In the meantime, Mathew, there is no reason why you should be afraid to look in the drawers . . . but just to make you feel better, my clothes are the bottom three. I put yours in the top drawers," Ilium said respecting Mathew's privacy issue and, at the same time, inadvertently apologizing for the argument.

"Thank you, Ilium. I appreciate that," Mathew replied calmly.

"Mathew . . . do you gamble?" Ilium asked off of the topic.

"Not so much. I couldn't gamble my way out of a topless box," Mathew said while pulling the Yeti down from curtains it decided to climb on.

"Hmmm . . . if you don't mind, would you allow me to teach you? I don't have a gambling partner at the moment," Ilium said taking out a bag from one of the bottom drawers.

"I don't mind. I would love to learn," Mathew said sitting on the couch next to her.

Ilium then opened the sack and pulled out ten dice. He was baffled for a few moments until Ilium told him the rules of the game. Whoever had the most pairs or die on the same number would win unless the other person had more pairs of a higher number (three 5s trumped two 6s). They spent the rest of the day having fun gambling on silly things like the winner gets a quick backrub.

The next day came and Mathew was off to his class again. He walked into the room and took his seat, opened "Demonology" and continued where he left off yesterday. A few snippets from his classmate's conversations caught his attention; "hey, did you start that 'Art' stuff yet?" and "I can't believe there aren't enough guys to go around in this place!" Not much was piquing Mathew's interest until he saw, out of the corner of his eye, a skirt sit on his table right next to him infringing on his personal space. After about five seconds of annoyance, the skirt's wearer spoke.

"Hey, you're kind of cute! You got a girl friend? What's your name? Where are you from?" the girl asked making Mathew look up. She looked really young—a little too young for Mathew's taste.

"How old are you?" Mathew asked saying the first question that came into his head.

"I'm 14, sweetie. How old are you?" she asked right back, not even bothering to hide the flirty tone in her voice.

"I'm 18. When did you die?" Mathew decided to ask knowing that she may be older than she looked.

"I died a few months ago. You sure are asking some strange questions," the girl said as Julian walked into the room and ordered everybody to their seats; unfortunately, the girl sat right next to Mathew and kept glancing at him, which made him uncomfortable and agitated.

By the end of class, the girl seemed to have decided Mathew was her life-long bosom buddy and decided to stick to Matthew's side like glue as he gathered his books.

Before Mathew was able to leave, Julian asked him to stay after class. Thankfully, the strange girl was forced to leave with a few of her friends.

"Seems like you have a little admirer," Julian said noticing the girl outside the door gabbing to her friends about Mathew.

"Could you do me a favor and like, move her away from me or something? She keeps looking at me and it makes me feel weird in a bad way," Mathew asked anxiously while closing the door to prevent the flirtatious girl from peaking in the room and eavesdropping.

"I would never have guessed a guy would 'feel weird' when a girl looked at him," Julian said with a slightly humorous tone in her voice.

"That's not the main reason. She's only 14, died a few months ago and she still has hormones rushing through her body . . . I guess I don't know if that translates," Mathew said picking out all possibilities.

"I'll move her tomorrow if you would like but I can't guarantee that you will enjoy the next person that will sit by you. I have noticed a few girls giving you the eye," Julian said making a note on a pad of paper.

"What kind of eye and why?" Mathew asked.

"I have a few ideas but will leave it to you to figure that out. It does, though, probably have something to do with 69% of the Ice Elemental population being girls . . . I remember when I was taking these classes I did exactly the same things," Julian replied a little embarrassed.

"Why aren't there enough guys, anyway?" Mathew asked recalling the same question he heard in the class earlier.

"I think it's because girls are more susceptible to temperature and may die quicker in this cold weather than guys do . . . but that's just a theory," Julian said remembering her time in classes.

"May I ask how you died?" Mathew asked realizing this was a standard question around here.

"Me? I just got lost on a family trip and froze to death . . . now that I think about it, it wasn't that bad. But . . . I heard about how you died from Steven. That was gruesome," Julian replied with a sympathetic voice. "Oh, I almost forgot. Steven asked me to tell you that your permit will be ready shortly," Julian said remembering the initial reason she called Mathew aside.

"Well then, tell him 'thank you' for me. I'll see you tomorrow then, Julian."

Mathew's night consisted of gambling with Ilium and Sara, who was also new to the game. Sara suggested playing 'Strip Dice' but Mathew was strongly against it because he didn't want to take advantage of a complete newbie, or that's the reason he said out loud anyway. Eventually, Steven and Julian decided to wander into the room wanting to play, too. Unfortunately, Julian was considered a pro and, if they had been playing for cash, everyone would be in debt to her about two grand.

Before the friends knew it, the sun was coming back around. Julian and Mathew decided to walk to class together which, of course, started a lot of gossip going around the classroom. Mathew took his usual seat and opened "Bites and Markings" to check if the Succubus had a specific mark, which it did. The Succubus mark seemed similar to a black tattoo and the shape and pattern of the mark were "user" specific that varied from succubus to succubus. As he continued to read about this unique mark, the book was pulled from Mathew's hands. He looked up, expecting to see the annoying girl from yesterday, but it was Julian wanting to see what he was reading.

"What's this now, Mathew? Still looking up things about the Succubi?" she asked as she skimmed through the chapter Mathew had been reading.

"Just curious . . . you know how it is," Mathew said as he took the book back.

"Teacher, what's a Succubus?" someone yelled from across the room. By the tone of voice, Mathew assumed it was a boy.

"We'll go over that today," Julian replied to the person.

"All right, everybody. Turn your "Demonology" books to page 400," Julian ordered.

During the lesson, students were asked to read a portion of the chapter out loud, with the exclusion of Mathew who had read the chapter already. Mathew followed along and would often glance around the room at the other students who were shifting in their seats. He assumed they were uncomfortable with the subject matter or bored. Just as they got to the place in the current chapter that was detailing the mating rituals, Steven entered the classroom and walked right up to Mathew.

"Here you are Mathew, the permit to your new home. You lucky dog! Ask Ilium to show you were it is," Steven said sounding louder than a dying pig and completely interrupting the class.

"So my dear wife, what are you learning about?" Steven asked Julian.

"We are learning about Succubi, their rituals and habits," Julian replied showing him the book.

"Oooh, Succubi. How yummy," Steven said sending a ripple of laughter through the room.

"Hmmm . . . Did you know that Mathew has already been through this chapter on his own and gained enough knowledge to give even me a small lesson on them?" Julian commented which was one of the worst things to say to someone like Steven.

"Aha! Mathew is into those types of girls . . . you perverted bastard!" Steven said obviously trying to make a friendly joke but that didn't keep the rest of the class from whispering.

"Let's settle this over a game of dice tonight, Steven! Just you wait!" Mathew yelled.

"Okay, fine. Winner gets a Succubus!" Steven yelled as he walked out of the room, not giving Mathew a chance to defend himself.

"He had better not bring a Succubus tonight or I might just have to 'Sock-his-butt' to him," Julian said to herself as a small joke.

After class, Mathew received a few friendly jokes about his supposed choice in girls, but he had more important things to think about. He had his permit in hand and was anxious to get settled in his own room. Mathew made his way quickly to Ilium's room to find both Ilium and Sara waiting for him. Julian had decided to join them and arrived shortly after he did.

Ilium marched ahead of the group because she was the only one who actually knew where it was. They walked for about 15 minutes when they reached a dead end.

"Okay. Here it is!" Ilium said pointing at the hard wall of ice.

"Ilium, are you okay?" Mathew decided to ask since their quest ended where a solid ice wall started.

"Oh, Mathew dear. You have to use Art to get in . . . put your hand on the wall and think of a door," Julian said ascertaining the problem before anyone else.

So Mathew did as he was told. He placed his hand on the wall, fingers straight and spread wide, and pictured a door. He felt a quick tingle on the palm of his hand. He opened his eyes and in his hand was a freshly created doorknob.

"Mathew. Before you go in, put your hand on the door and think of what the inside should look like," Sara ordered him just as Julian did.

Mathew's imagination took flight. He thought about his room back home and had always wished it bigger. His mind jumped to Ilium's room and thought about different things, like a desk and the dice gambling he was taught. As he continued creating the foundation for his Art to work with, other objects randomly came into his head. He wanted a statue, a big cozy bed and patterns on his wall. His room would be like a forest with big pine trees covered in snow—just like Christmas.

"Okay Mathew. That's enough. You can stop now," Ilium said calmly. Mathew opened his eyes and decided to go in.

As Mathew was still learning the power of his Art, his room was a pleasant surprise to him. It was larger than he had thought of. It had a large, comfy looking bed, two couches and, in the corner, five chairs around a smaller gaming table mainly created for Dice. In the midst of planning the more obvious pieces of the room, Mathew somehow managed to think of smaller necessities such as a bookshelf and a sculpture of a Yeti. He was amazed at the detail and completeness of his room and had a hard time believing his eyes at first. He had no idea he could do this with just thoughts and a block of ice. Julian assured him that ice had the ability to take on any form and any texture, which was true. When it came to the wall designs of a forest on his walls, each wall looked like Mathew could just wander off into them and get lost. The only slight disappointment was the colors in the room. As everything was made out of ice, the only colors in the room were shades of white or blue.

"Nice place, Mathew! I especially like the texture of the bed," Sara said lying under the blankets.

"Hey, Mathew! Great idea on the dice table!" Julian said rather pleased with the little table.

"Knock, knock! Anybody home?" Steven's voice came from the doorway.

"Hey, Steven. Come check this out! Mathew's quite an interior designer!" Ilium exclaimed making Mathew feel proud of his little room.

"Everybody, gather 'round quickly," Steven said.

"What do you need, Steven?" Julian asked.

"I thought it wouldn't be proper without a house-warming gift . . . so I brought him a little something," Steven said.

"Show it to us, already!" Sara demanded her interest piqued.

"Okay then . . . Here it is! TA-DA!" Steven yelled pulling in a small girl with a big ribbon wrapped around her head; she looked like she was maybe 10 or 11. She had big, blue eyes, black hair and her skin was as pale as an Ice Elemental's. However, Mathew got the feeling that she wasn't an Elemental. She looked around the room at the different people standing in the room with a weird, intense focus.

"Steven, what's this?" Ilium asked inspecting the girl. Then Mathew noticed she had a Demon looking tail that was moving around and doing apparently random little flicks and twists.

"Steven . . . you didn't . . ." Mathew said now realizing what this present was about.

"What . . . what is it?" Sara asked still inspecting the girl.

"He brought me a fricken' Succubus," Mathew said rubbing his eyes but couldn't help but noticed that when he said "Succubus" the girl looked up at him.

"Steven, I thought you were just joking about betting on the Succubus!" Julian yelled nearly strangling Steven.

"I was but, when I found out that this girl was going to be attending your class for the rest of the week, I couldn't resist," Steven said trying to escape his wife's death grip.

"We'd better see if she's anything to worry about," Mathew said walking over to the girl.

"Excuse me, may I look at your tail?" Mathew asked the girl who simply shook her head and handed him her tail. Mathew inspected the color and length.

"Okay, would you open up your mouth for me?" Mathew asked as he moved onto her canine teeth and looked at their length.

"Mathew, what are you doing?" Ilium asked as she watched Mathew move about the girl.

"He's checking what stage she's in," Julian replied.

"What is a 'stage'?" Sara asked.

"A stage is technically the age. A Succubus doesn't become sexually active until it's at the Patriarch stage. That would equate, in Human age, to around twenty. For a Succubus, though, age isn't a good marker for the stage they are in. They can have sudden growth spurts when they aren't feeding so she could change stages with very little forewarning," Julian said using her newfound knowledge. "So, what's the verdict, Mathew?" she continued to ask as she looked at the girl who didn't seem to mind being inspected by Mathew.

"Well . . . I would say she is still in her Latriarch stage. I would assume we have about three months before she hits Patriarch," Mathew said as he gently patted the girl on the head.

"What the hell is the Latriarch stage?" Sara asked frustrated because she didn't know anything about this topic.

"Sara, according to what we know about the species, Succubi have three Stages: Latriarch, which is their childhood and teen years which lasts from seven months to one year; Patriarch, which is like their late teens and adulthood which can last indefinitely; and Matriarch, when they live with their mate until he or she dies. The Succubi mate for life. If the mate dies too early, they may go back into the

Patriarch stage and regain any lost youth. It's actually an interesting process," Mathew said going to sit down for a little bit. "So, where is she staying?" he decided to ask just to keep the conversation going.

"Well, I was assuming . . . . here," Steven said who obviously didn't put any thought into this joke of his.

"I think she should stay with one of you girls," Mathew calmly suggested.

"Is she any real threat at the moment?" Ilium asked kind of keeping her distance from the girl.

"No, not at the moment," Mathew replied taking another quick look at the girl.

"Well, why don't we ask her?" Sara suggested.

"I don't think that will work out the way you think it will, Sara," Mathew said in a matter-of-fact voice.

"How do you figure, Mathew?" Sara said feeling kind of insulted.

"She is a Succubus. She is going to be more inclined to naturally pick a male over a female; so it either going to be me or Steven," Mathew stated just thinking of the most logical outcome.

"If it's all the same to everybody, I would like to spend a night with each of you," a sweet voice rang out from the girl.

"That sounds reasonable," Julian answered.

"Why didn't talk until now?" Steven asked the girl.

"I was still deciding whether or not to accept you . . . I was just abducted and had a ribbon put on my head," she said with a glare directed at Steven.

"You have an incredible vocabulary for someone so small. What is your name?" Mathew asked surprised.

"My given name is Catharine but the others just call me Dee. Even though I look young, I have the intellect of a Human college student. It is one of the perks associated with the fast growth . . . and if you're wondering, I already know how babies are made so don't bother to dance around the topic if it comes up," Dee explained with complete seriousness.

"It sounds like you have been given this talk before," Ilium commented. Mathew noticed that Ilium paid attention to subtle nuances in people's communication so she was quite good at picking out little pieces of unsaid information and putting them together to create a better understanding of what was really going on.

"This isn't the first place I have stayed. My mother wanted me to get knowledge of the different Elemental groups before I went into the Patriarch stage, and 'Mathew', was it . . . you were close, I have about two and a half month left. I'm surprised though; your scent tells me that you haven't been an Elemental for very long. You still have some Human left in you," Dee said picking Mathew out of the group to make a comment to.

"Well, if you knew how long you have till your Patriarch stage, why didn't you just tell us?" Mathew asked.

"To be honest, I have never been examined before and my mother always said to try everything at least once," Dee replied with a cute little smile.

"Your mother sounds nice," Sara said just to be part of the conversation.

"Yes, she is. I know this will sound rather rude but I'm getting tired. I have had a long day . . . you know with the kidnapping and everything," Dee said letting out a yawn and the group went to giving Steven evil looks.

"Oh, well . . . sorry. Who do you want to stay with tonight?" Julian asked sweetly with one of her powerful smiles.

"I honestly don't feel like going anywhere else so I'll stay here tonight," Dee said crawling up onto the couch.

"Fine with us, then. Come on everyone, let's get out of here," Ilium said pushing every one out of the room like a herd of cattle.

"Where do you want to sleep, Catherine?" Mathew asked once everybody was gone.

"Please call me 'Dee' and I don't mind sleeping here on the couch," she replied gathering a few pillows from Mathew's bed.

"Here, take one of these blankets . . . don't you have any extra clothes?" Mathew asked.

"Thank you for the blanket and I put my bag over there in the corner. I'll change tomorrow," Dee said throwing the blanket over her and snuggling in.

"You aren't cold, are you? I can't feel the cold myself," Mathew decided to ask because for all he knew she could be freezing

"I'm fine, thank you. It's warmer in here than you think," she replied.

"Ok. Well, goodnight then, Dee. I'll see you in the morning," Mathew said before turning off the lights, which were more like glowing ice chunks than light bulbs.

The night passed quickly. Mathew slept better than he had in weeks but awoke to someone shaking him so he had to get up.

"Mathew . . . Mathew! Get up!" a voice shouted. He opened his eyes and saw Dee leaning over his bed, which startled him a little.

"Oh . . . good morning, Dee" Mathew said sitting up and realizing something was different about Dee. "What changed?" he decided to ask.

"Oh, I grew a few inches in my sleep. No reason for alarm," Dee said grabbing her bag and left the room to change quickly.

"Hey, Dee! You're going to class with me this morning, right?" Mathew asked as Dee returned.

"Yes, that's right so don't leave without me. I don't know where I am or where class is from here so you will have to show me," she replied.

After Dee changed, the two headed out to the classroom where they had to get Dee set up with class material. Mathew sat down with Dee next to him and they both looked up different things in "Mutations and Adaptations". They would tell each other a page number whenever they found something interesting.

"Okay, class. Butts in seats!" Julian ordered as she walked to the front of the class. "We have several things on the agenda today. First is an introduction to a new classmate and then we have my husband, Steven, coming in to talk about the Elder council," she announced.

"Oh great, more problems," Mathew decided to say loud enough that Julian could hear him.

"Thank you, Mathew. First on this list is the introduction. Dee, please come up here and introduce yourself," she continued and Dee obeyed.

"Hello, my name is Catharine. But most people just call me Dee," she said in the most basic introduction Mathew had ever heard.

"Welcome, Dee. Would you like to tell us more about yourself?" Julian suggested.

"No, thank you," Dee said as she was going back to sit down.

"I hate it when strange people know what I am. It always freaks them out," she vented quietly to Mathew.

"Alright, then. Please come in, Steven," Julian ordered and Mathew decided that she wasn't in the best of moods today.

"Hello, people!" Steven yelled as he entered then he spotted Mathew and Dee sitting together. "Hey, Mathew did you enjoy the Succubus?" he yelled sending the word 'Succubus' through multiple whispers throughout the room.

"Shut up, Steven! Whenever you show up I end up having trouble," Mathew yelled back knowing exactly that Steven was doing this just to get a rise out of him.

"That's not true, Mathew. And how are you, Dee? Did you have a nice sleep at Mathew's place?" Steven said purposely setting things up so Mathew would have problems.

"Mathew! How could you!" the one 14-year-old girl yelled for no apparent reason.

"Excuse me . . . wait no . . . shut up and sit back down," Mathew replied coldly, he was not in the mood to deal with her today.

"How dare you! I thought we had something special!" she continued.

"I don't even know your name and we just met yesterday! How can you say that crap?" Mathew yelled.

"Crap! All that was just crap to you!" she screamed back.

"Oh, shut up you pathetic bitch! You're giving me a headache!" Dee ordered as she rubbed the side of her head.

"What do you care? You took Mathew away from me with your Succubi magic that we read about yesterday!" the girl continued to yell.

"I did no such thing! I can't even use Charm yet!" Dee yelled and the alarming thing was, Mathew noticed that she grew a few inches when she shouted.

"Why don't we just ask Mathew? Mathew, who do you want? Do you to be with me, who can give you all the love in the world, or Dee, the Succubus, who would enslave your soul with the flick of her demon tail?" the girl asked silencing her cries for a few moments.

"I choose Dee," Mathew said in frustration and without a thought in between the question and the answer. His answer caused the girl to go over the edge and she ran out of the room, followed by a few of her friends.

"Mathew, we need to go home. I grew so I need to change my clothes," Dee said pulling Mathew up by the arm.

The walk back to the room was quiet and unpleasant as Dee went from pulling Mathew's arm to holding his hand. Mathew didn't mind either because to him Dee was still a child.

After the two got back to Mathew's room, Dee changed into clothes a size larger than she needed just that very morning. She and Mathew decided that they would not go back to class that day. They decided they had both had their fill of drama and there was probably too much commotion still going on at class that neither wanted to deal with. So they kicked back and played Dice, which was turning out to be one of Mathew's favorite pastimes.

"Hey Mathew, would you please do me a favor?" Dee asked after a while.

"Sure. What do you need?" Mathew replied intent on his dice throw.

"I need you to measure my wings," she said standing up.

"You have wings? Duh, of course you do. I forgot about that . . . um, sorry," Mathew said sitting up.

"I need to warn you in advance that I have to take off my shirt. Don't worry, though. I have something on underneath," she said before she did anything.

"Okay, I understand. Thanks for the advanced notice," Mathew replied.

Dee took of her shirt and she was wearing a small, white cotton cloth that was tied around her neck and waist so it covered her entire chest. Mathew saw the wings come out quickly, which startled him because they made a loud "whoosh" sound. He almost started laughing because they looked like the Vampire wings that were in some of the old cartoons he used to watch when he was a kid. Not wanting to offend her, Mathew managed to contain himself and, after his initial amazement wore off, he walked behind her to measure them like she requested.

As he looked at Dee's wings, he tried to understand where he should measure them. Mathew gently placed his hand on one of the main bones extending outward from Dee's back and couldn't help but run his fingers up and down it to feel the texture.

"Mathew! Please be careful . . . they are very sore," Dee stuttered as she jumped a little bit from the discomfort.

"I'm sorry, Dee. Why don't you tell me a little about yourself? It's not like we met under normal circumstances," Mathew said as he gently touched the fine skin that was stretched across the wing.

"I supposed you deserve some honesty. Well . . . where to start? My first my name isn't actually Catharine. It's just Dee. My mother's name is Catharine. I have a bad habit of using her name when I'm nervous," Dee said revealing this truth to Mathew, which didn't seem like the truth.

"That's interesting, Dee. By the way, your wings are close to identical and have about 54 inches to them . . . so, where were you born?" Mathew asked, deciding that questions where far more comfortable than uncomfortable silence.

"I was born in the Demon world," she said simply.

"Wait! There is a Demon world?" Mathew asked.

"Yes. It is very similar to the fortresses you Elementals live in, but are only found in ancient areas of the world where Humans don't like to go . . . even if they live only a few miles away. So, in short, if you're not a guest or a Demon, you're not getting in . . . or in some cases getting out," Dee said wincing again as Mathew touched the soft skin on her wings.

"Sorry about that," Mathew said making his way back to the couch.

"It's okay. I know you're not used to this . . . but thank you anyway. You're the first person I let do that," Dee admitted as her wings folded neatly inside her back. Mathew was amazed that the wings, so significant in length, could fold so compactly that they were virtually undetectable.

After a few more hours, Mathew and Dee decided to call it a night and went to bed without anyone coming to visit them. This surprised Mathew because his new room had become an entertainment center for his friends. Dee didn't seem to mind that she was staying another night in Mathew's room and they both quickly fell asleep.

"Mathew . . . Mathew! Wake up!" a voice came to Matthew's body as he was being violently shaken

Mathew opened his eyes to see two glowing pink eyes close to his face. He was about to scream but a soft, feminine hand covered his mouth. The hand seemed to break apart and move around inside its skin, which scared the hell out of him, so he shot up to confront the eyes.

"Mathew! It's me, Dee . . . . I did the math wrong. I'm . . . I'm going into the Patriarch stage right now!" Dee explained best she could. It was obvious that she was in incredible pain and her body seemed to be moving inside of her. "My body is reconstructing itself; I need to get back to the Demon World for it to be done properly. We need to find Steven!" she urgently said.

Mathew jumped to his feet and had to pick up Dee because her entire bone structure was rearranging. Mathew could feel it as he carried her to Ilium's room. He didn't know where Steven's room was so Ilium's was his only choice. Dee's hands were clenched tightly around the shirt Mathew was wearing as he ran through the halls. When they reached Ilium's room, Dee leaned in and whispered into Mathew's ear, "If I don't see you again, I want you to know I won't forget this."

When they were able to finally get Ilium out of her room, she quickly led the way to Steven's room. It took Steven even longer to get out of bed. But, once he was awake and up to speed, there was no stopping him. He barked orders to a few random people in the hallway and a few moments later a group of people rushed in and started setting something up. Mathew was ordered to put her in the middle of whatever it was they built, so he did.

Once Dee was settled inside the object, Mathew stepped back and noticed that it looked like a big arch extending over Dee's helpless body. Dee stood up, shook and cried at the pain that must have been surging through her.

"Dee, listen to me!" Steven ordered getting the little Succubus's attention. "We're sending you home. I've sent word ahead to your mother and she promised that someone will be there to help you get through this so just hang in there, okay?" Steven encouraged as he went to work. He stood near the arch and placed his hands firmly on the outside. Mathew watched as Steven's face settled into a fierce resolve. A red light began to swirl around Dee and in a bright flash she was gone. Steven then collapsed in a nearby chair.

"It's been a while since I did that," Steven said after getting some of his energy back.

"What exactly did you do?" Mathew asked confused about what happened. The structure that Dee had been lying in had dissolved into a pile of blue and white snow.

"I sent her home. To send a Demon in an emergency like that is extremely difficult for anyone to accomplish. Dee could not take the regular portal because bone rearrangement makes the translation dangerous," Steven said leaning back in the chair and slowly closing his eyes.

"Will she be okay now?" Mathew asked still concerned.

"Yes. I sent her to her mother. Wow! What a way to wake up, huh?" Steven commented, trying to calm his nerves with a breathing exercise.

"Here, Mathew. Drink this," Julian said bringing out a drink for him.

"Thank you, Julian," Mathew said taking a sip of the warm liquid.

"That must have been horrible for you, Mathew! Having to carry that girl when her entire skeletal system was being rearranged," Julian said as her head did a small twitch at the thought.

"It was just strange. The poor girl was holding in her screams. I could tell how bad the pain was by how tight she was hanging onto my shirt," Mathew confessed taking another sip.

"How was it living with a Succubus for two days?" Julian decided to ask.

"It was a lot like living with Ilium, but I think it would have been quite different if she had been in a different stage," Mathew said as his vision started to spin and he quickly fell asleep.

CHAPTER EIGHT

DISPATCHED

After the incident with Dee, life settled into a less dramatic pace and Mathew continued his classes. The "Magic" classes, as Mathew called them, were officially 'Art Classes' but it was difficult for him to take them seriously calling them by that name.

After classes finished each day, Mathew was always found doing something extracurricular. Steven forced him into the Basic Swordplay class with the suggestion that Mathew may need that skill later (he did not, though, give any details as to why). After Mathew completed all the required classes, he continued his studies with classes that would fine-tune and expound on his specific areas of interest. He was amazed that, as a Human, school had never been "his thing" but as an Elemental, he could not seem to get enough knowledge to satisfy his soul. Learning made him come alive inside in a way he had never felt before. He especially wanted to review and correct some of his own assumptions about certain Demons, or mutants. The entire process of going through classes took about four months. By the time Mathew was done, he was exceptional at using Magic and was able to spontaneously create an Ice Blade to fend off any attackers that might come his way. Steven had stepped up and appointed himself as Mathew's mentor and taught him many things that were not a part of any class syllabus.

But Mathew had only one goal in mind; he wanted a Demonology license. He worked hard in all his classes and did exceptionally well on every test. Even though it had been a few weeks since he had completed all of the required classes, he hadn't been awarded his license yet. Mathew knew he was going to get one sooner or later because Steven kept making really stupid comments that made it obvious to everyone.

"Well, if it isn't our own resident Demonologist," Steven said mockingly as Mathew entered his room. While Mathew was preoccupied with studying, his room had become the central hangout for his friends.

"You know, I haven't gotten my license yet so don't go calling me that," Mathew said sitting down on an ice chair he had recently created due to the increasing popularity of his room.

"Well, not anymore, Professor," Steven said throwing him an envelope.

"Open it, Mathew. That's the reason why we invited you here," Ilium said with her regular tone of voice.

"You do realize this is my room, right?" Mathew said as he opened the envelope, pulled out the letter and began to read aloud so the whole group could hear.

> Dear Mathew:
>
> We are pleased to inform you that the Elder Council has granted you the "License of Demonologist".
>
> By accepting this License, you fully agree, should the need arise, to make yourself available to carry out emissary missions with various Demon races on behalf of the Ice Elemental Community.
>
> By achieving this License, you are also granted a title by which you may own and/or publish new information on any new race of Demons that you may to discover. That information must first be sent to the Demonologist Committee to be examined and revised if need be. If approved, the Committee retains the right to use the information in any future books for academic or personal use.

In closing, as a token of our gratitude for strengthening the relationship between Ice Elementals and the Succubi community, the Elder Council will be sending a package containing a special gift.

Congratulations on your accomplishment.

Respectfully yours,

The Elder Council

"How did I 'strengthen' the relationship between Ice and Succubi?" Mathew asked.

"Steven, didn't you tell him?" Julian asked giving him "the eye".

"It must have slipped my mind," Steven calmly replied in his usual offhand manner.

"Mathew, it turns out that Dee's mother is actually a Succubi Matron. Apparently Dee was sent to interact with each Elemental race and analyze which race would be the best fit to help to the Succubi community," Julian said.

"Cool!" said Sara. "What did we do that was so special?"

"I was given a copy of Dee's mother's report on the Ice Elementals to review. It stated that there was a young man who went 'above and beyond the call of duty' to care for her daughter. This young man took the responsibility of personally inspecting the daughter in her current Latriarch stage. Along with caring for her and giving her a place to stay, the young man personally helped the Matron's daughter get back home when she began an unexpected transformation into the Patriarch stage. There was, though, an unfortunate mention of a 'crazy' member of the Elder Council who presented the Matron's daughter, wrapped in a ribbon, to that special young man out of a bet," Julian finished looking at Steven who was quietly trying to sneak out of the room.

"Well, at least he did something good for once," Ilium said as she watched Julian drag her husband back into the room.

"Speaking of, I wonder how Dee is?" Mathew wondered aloud remembering the small girl he only knew for two days.

"I heard she went through the morphing process just fine. Other than that, I haven't heard a thing," Julian said sipping her "medicine" that still smelled like hot tar from the Jurassic period.

"Well, I don't mean be rude, girls," Mathew started and Steven made a fake loud coughing noise requesting acknowledgement. "And Steven . . . but I think you all should head home. I want to recreate my room tonight," Mathew said as he stood up and opened the door for everyone.

"You should have more statues in your room," Ilium suggested as she and Sara skipped out of the room with their arms linked.

"What's wrong with those two?" Mathew asked jokingly but forgot he had two even stranger people still in his room.

"Is that a challenge?" Julian said with the funny grin. Mathew had come to learn that expression as her "tell" that she had started to think of a joke or prank to play upon some unsuspecting person. Even though Mathew had only seen that grin a few times, he was well aware of the potential threat associated with it. As threatening as it was, that funny grin was nothing compared to Julian's "Mighty Saint" smile that made whoever it was directed at happy with a warm feeling as an after effect.

"Um . . . no," but Mathew was too late. Steven and Julian had already joined forces and used Art to make a sled out of Mathew's couch. With a loud "Mush!" from Julian, Steven pranced like a sled dog and pulled the couch out of Mathew's front door into the hallway and continued as they slid around a corner.

"Hey, wait! That's my couch! Oh, forget it . . . just keep it. I have BIG PLANS in here anyway!" Mathew yelled as he ran after them. He then remembered that his couch was made out of ice and would be easy to replace by using Art. Or, he could do without and create something really unique to replace it. He walked back into his room, placed his hand on the wall and closed his eyes.

Mathew decided that the Yeti statue was nice but he would rather have a few statues of armor like the ones he had seen in books about old castles when he was Human. In just a few moments, he created those along with one set of Japanese Samurai armor, just for looks, and placed in the corner of each room. He also decided to create a coffee table and another couch since Klondike Julian and her mush dog, Steven, ran off with his.

When Mathew was finished, he rearranged everything and decided to amuse himself by bad talking to the different suits of armor. He especially got in the face of the Japanese one by acting like he was a big, puffed up Japanese General. Mathew laughed at himself and decided to practice using his Art to design a sword. He thought hard about what he wanted the sword to look like and decided to add a few designs on his blade for creativity's sake. He didn't want any plain looking blade in his newly designed room when he had unlimited creativity at his fingertips. Mathew reached around his neck and tried to take off his treasured cross. For some reason this was difficult but after a few attempts, the cross came right off into the palm of his hand. As he studied the shape, size and texture, Mathew decided to shape his blade to look like the cross. He even managed to get a few blue ice gems in the handle. The gothic look of the cross, however, was very difficult for him to copy but he eventually managed to craft the blade to at least look decent before he called it quits for the night.

Once settled into his new bed, Mathew realized he wasn't all that ready to close his eyes. He decided to practice his Art in little ways because he had nothing to do and didn't want to stare at the ceiling for hours to come. So he made a few darts to throw at the wall. He eventually drifted off into his thoughts but thought he saw something move in his line of sight. Startled, he sat up ready to inspect whatever it was. He didn't see anything move again so he just announced it was his mind playing tricks on him and put his head on the pillow again. The next thing he knew, his mind settled down and he fell into a sound sleep.

A loud knock on his door woke Mathew and, when he opened it, there was nothing there except a package placed at the base of the door. Mathew took the package into his room and proceeded to open it. Inside there was the formal uniform of a Demonologist and, at the bottom, was a beautiful, leather bound book thick with blank pages. Mathew assumed it was for recording any information that he would gather on Demons. He had a brief thought of how much more convenient a computer tablet would be but let it go in his excitement over the package. He then noticed a small vial with something in it that looked like liquid. Mathew leaned over, picked it up with a curious glance and decided to tuck it away on the shelf when another knock came at the door

"Hey, Mathew! You've got to come to Steven's place! He has your letter and is refusing to give it up. He is just like a child, I swear!" Sara said before even saying hello. But her description of Steven refusing to give up Mathew's letter made Mathew think of an old western where Steven was holding up a bank and using the letter as a hostage for his escape plan. The image made Mathew laugh a little.

Once Mathew finished laughing, he forced himself to go to Steven's room to retrieve his letter.

"Okay, Steven. Hand it over," Mathew demanded but, when he got a good look at the letter, it was more like a small package and Steven reluctantly handed it over to him.

Inside there was a Demonology badge of authority along with a chain for the badge that was supposed to hook to Mathew's vest or pocket, along with a letter that Mathew also read out loud. Mathew couldn't decide if he would look like Jesse James or Sherlock Holmes.

Dear Mathew:

By the Order of the Elder Council of the Ice Fortress, 'Illumination', and in correlation with the Demonologist Selection Process, you are hereby given the Title of "Half Light"

Enclosed please find the badge that gives you all-encompassing authority over all Demon-related matters not limited to Issues, Negotiations, Investigations, Etc.

Respectfully yours,

The Elder Council

"Congratulations, Half Light!" Ilium cheered using Mathew's new title.

"Well, thanks but you don't have to call me Half Light," Mathew said feeling rather embarrassed, yet proud and fulfilled. He felt this would have been like his graduation back home if he hadn't died.

"I believe it's time to celebrate! I'll get muffins," Julian said hurrying into the other room.

"I'm not eating those muffins! They look funny!" Steven yelled after Julian.

"You're having a muffin, Steven, even if I need to shove it down your throat!" Julian yelled with a much angrier voice.

"What's wrong with her?" Sara asked picking up the tone.

"I'll tell you when she lets me know . . . I'm on a rather short leash at the moment. I seem to be a victim of Ice Elemental hormone hell or something," Steven said sulking down into his chair.

"Okay, here we are!" Julian said with a much happier voice placing a basket of purple muffins on the coffee table and ordered that everyone should take one.

The group reluctantly took a single muffin, while silently acknowledging that Steven was right; the purple color made you think twice about taking a bite. Eventually everyone took a nibble and found out it wasn't as bad as it looks. Julian returned to the room, cut a muffin in half, put it on a plate and firmly placed it in front of Steven.

"I am NOT eating that!" Steven said as he stared at the strange food with a look of horror on his face.

"Eat the damn muffin," Julian ordered threatening Steven with the butter knife she had in her hand.

"Julian! What is wrong with you? I have never heard you use profanity before," Mathew asked with slight shock. Julian's mood was nothing like the caring woman Mathew had gotten to know over the months.

"Oh, it's nothing, Mathew dear. You know I'm just having one of those days," she said giving him a friendly kiss on the forehead, which confused Mathew for a few moments.

"Uh huh . . . I see now," Ilium exclaimed somehow putting something together.

"What do you see? Please indulge us," Mathew said confused enough as it was.

"I might as well tell you," Julian said taking a seat on the couch. "A few weeks ago I found out something . . . . I found out that I'm pregnant," she finally said with a blush and a girlish giggle.

"Steven, you dog, you!" Mathew yelled happily as, unfortunately, he had picked up some of Steven's way with words over the past months.

Mathew then discovered that just the mention of the word "pregnant" was enough to get the girls to gather around, squealing, and chatting up a storm. Mathew and Steven were forced to retreat out of the room entirely because they couldn't hear each other over the excited chatter of the three girls.

To celebrate the good news, Mathew and Steven went downhill racing against a couple of younger Yetis who could run as fast as Mathew and Steven could snowboard. The Yeti group included the first Yeti Mathew had been introduced upon his arrival. It was a small cub when they first met but now that same cub was about as tall as Mathew. During those few meetings, Mathew had learned quite a bit about Yeti culture, tendencies and how their minds worked. They were able to telepathically communicate to Ice Elementals. Mathew wasn't sure how they communicated with each other. He did notice a lot of grunting and gestures akin to sign language but Mathew decided that it didn't make sense for them to be so advanced as to communicate telepathically with one race and be confined to gestures and grunting with each other. By the time Mathew and Steven got back to the room, Sara and Ilium were gone and Julian was in bed, so Mathew went home to get some rest.

Mathew was up all night. His body was still adjusting to the Elemental lifestyle and that rarely included sleep. This lack of sleep was not that they were always busy but because they didn't need it. Mathew passed time having fun throwing things at his wall—especially since he was able to quickly fill the holes in the wall when it got to unpleasant to look at. He was living a childhood fantasy and having a good time doing it.

Around 9:00 am the next morning, a letter was delivered from the Elder Council. The letter contained orders for Mathew to report to the Council chambers immediately upon receipt. He felt it was appropriate to wear his Demonologist robes so he got dressed went out the door. He had to wait for about an hour before he was allowed inside the chambers but, as he was a little nervous, he didn't mind the wait. This was his first summons and his first time seeing the chambers. Once inside, Mathew took a moment to settle his nerves and look around. He was intrigued by the setup; the room was nothing more than a large, circular space with multiple balconies overlooking the main floor. It appeared to him that the "guest" would speak or receive orders in the center of the room where all could see him or her. It reminded him of the ancient Roman amphitheater set-up. Following his instinct, Mathew walked to the center of the room and was not surprised when the first voice he heard was Steven's. As what now seemed to be the norm, Steven's comments and stupid statements were drawing Mathew into another pointless argument.

"Quiet, Steven! We didn't request this meeting just to listen to you verbally joust with him," one of the Elders yelled, or it sounded like he yelled but could have been more like an echo.

"We're just having a bit of fun . . . so shut up," Steven said coldly to the Elder who interrupted him. "Now, down to business. Take it away, Samantha," he said to an Elder who was seated behind Mathew.

"Now Mathew, we don't usually do this but your services and newly acquired expertise are needed. We are requesting that you investigate a string of homicides that are possibly Demon related," the girl said calmly.

"Excuse me, 'Samantha', is it? I have had my license less than a day and you are sending me out to investigate murders? Shouldn't I be starting out with something of less importance? Or, at the very least, send someone who is a little more . . . qualified?" Mathew asked politely.

"We are aware of this fact, Mathew, and yes, we would usually start you out on something simpler but you are the only Demonologist we have on hand at the moment," Samantha said admitting that this was indeed unusual request.

"I am not in favor of sending him out alone," another Elder said from across the room.

"I agree," Steven said and followed with a more serious tone than usual, "I think we should send two others with him."

"We must remember that this is a murder case. If Mathew, who is relatively new to our ways and being sent on his first assignment, discovers who it is and the perpetrator eludes capture, he himself could become a casualty of his own investigation," another female Elder stated.

"Well, perhaps we should send a Vanguard with him. That should be enough protection," another Elder chimed in.

"Yes, but what about the other person we are going to send?" Samantha asked.

"We shall ask the person who it affects the most. Mathew, you have a preference on who you believe should accompany you on this mission?" Mathew was asked.

"Well, by the sound of it . . . I think I should take someone trained in Medical Science, in case the murders aren't Demon related. Either way, if this is or isn't Demon related it would be good to know what the victim died of. For example, if the victims died of blood loss, I would be able to cut out entire species of the Demon race," Mathew said after thinking about the possibilities.

"I accept the terms of use of a medic and vanguard," an Elder said.

"Then it's settled," Steven began.

"Mathew, please remain here until the other two members of the team have been selected and assembled," Steven finished.

"Excuse me, I know I'm probably out of place for asking this but I'd like to request another member," Mathew said as he thought of a key detail.

"Why would we grant you the assistance of a third Elemental?" another Elder asked who sounded rather insulted by Mathew's request.

"Let him speak, Andrew," Samantha ordered. "Mathew, what is your reasoning behind this request?" she continued to ask.

"Just for argument's sake, let's say that the murderer is a Werewolf. We know Werewolves can move incredibly fast for extended periods of time," Mathew began. "I can identify Demons at the drop of a hat but I have no way to track them if they escape. I also won't have the stamina and speed to chase something with as much speed as a Werewolf," Mathew finished laying out reasonable arguments.

"What do you other Elders think? I have no objection to add a tracker to the squad," Steven said convinced by the argument.

"I also agree! What's the point of knowing what or who the killer is if we aren't able to apprehend it?" Andrew said enthusiastically which sent nods and universal agreement throughout the room.

"Very well, Mathew, you are granted the use of a tracker," Samantha announced walking out of the room for a moment then returning quickly. "Mathew, the rest of your squad is being assembled. Please remain here," she said simply.

Mathew stood alone in a rather awkward silence, in the middle of the ice amphitheater, until Steven started making his coarse comments again sparking yet another meaningless argument. This caused chuckles from a few Elders of the Council.

Just then the door opened and two boys and a girl walked in. The girl was dressed in what Mathew thought was the dress blues of the Ice Elemental military uniform. Mathew assumed by her appearance that she was a high-ranking officer. She was far more proper looking than the others but her hair was a striking contrast to her professional attire. It was a soft looking light blue and much longer on her left side than her right. Even though she was in full military attire, Mathew thought she still looked quite lovely. Her face stood out more than her uniform did. The only movement Mathew noticed on her expressionless face was an occasional blink now and then.

Mathew turned his attention to one of the boys who had entered the room with the girl. He was almost the perfect description of a medic; his studious glasses hung precariously from the tip of his nose, his hair was brown and clean cut. As he stood there, his facial expression was focused but lacked the formidable glare of the girl. The boy still seemed like a force to be reckoned with.

The other boy, however, was not even dressed properly. Mathew was momentarily offended by the boy's lack of propriety until he realized that the boy was probably hired to crawl around in the mud to find even the smallest trace of the most obscure element. If he had been properly cleaned up, this boy would have been very handsome. Mathew noticed that the boy's skin was an unclean "Ice" pale, his hair was the blackest of black and contrasted starkly with the long scar on his left from cheek to ear.

"State your name, rank and profession . . . all of you," Samantha ordered.

"I'm Mathew and I'm a licensed Demonologist," Mathew said nervously because Samantha ordered it so suddenly.

"Bell, 2nd Vanguard of the Ice Elemental military," the girl said in a monotone voice as she snapped to attention.

"I'm Doctor Victor. The 'doctor' part should speak for itself," the medic stated with an intelligent sounding voice, nodding his head as acknowledgement to himself.

"Marsh. Ice Tracker," the last boy said simply with not another word.

"Please pay attention. The following is the detail of your mission," Samantha began once introductions were over. "You are being dispatched to investigate a string of homicides with possible

Demon cause. I say "possible" because the evidence, at this time, in inconclusive," she finished with a calm and composed voice.

"Pardon my interruption, but why am I being sent out to deal with such an insignificant matter as this?" Bell said in a clipped, loud military voice.

"We are currently unaware of what or who the killer is. With that in mind, please note that this string of slayings could possibly have been committed by something or someone as deadly as a Vampire Lord," Samantha replied.

"Understood," Bell said with the same monotone.

"The place you four are heading to is near a Demon Sanctuary and, even though all the victims to this point have been Human, the population there is getter nervous about these homicides. They believe it's only a matter of time before people start hunting for the murderer. You four have been given clearance to enter the Sanctuary. Because of the circumstances surrounding this situation, I would suggest beginning your investigation there. Once you arrive in Demon territory, you will be met by a Demon police officer," Samantha explained.

"How will we be getting there?" Victor asked.

"There is a portal nearby that will take you to the closest sanctuary and you will return the same way unless something happens," Samantha replied.

"You will be leaving tomorrow. Please report here before you leave. Naturally you will be in Demon territory so Mathew will be in charge during your time in the Sanctuary. Is that understood?" Steven asked calmly.

"Yes, Sir!" Bell shouted.

"Of course," Victor replied.

"Whatever," Marsh said reluctantly.

After the meeting, Mathew went straight home to get a good rest. When he woke up, he threw on fresh clothes and packed a small bag with the blank book from the package he received the day before and a few tools for Demonology study, and then headed out the door. When Mathew arrived at the council room, Bell was the only other person there. She had also packed a few things that were neatly folded into a small bundle.

"Hello, Bell," Mathew said trying to be friendly.

"Good morning, Commander Mathew," she replied simply.

"What's with the "Commander" part?" Mathew asked surprised by Bell's formality.

"My experience with Demons has been limited to the occasional few that have come to our fortress on business or personal issues. You, Sir, are a licensed Demonologist and outrank me when we are within Demon borders. So you are my commander during this mission," Bell replied with the same monotone voice she used the day before.

"No need to call me that. Just call me Mathew, okay Bell?" Mathew asked realizing at that moment that Bell was a bit nervous and that probably accounted for her formality.

"Mathew . . . that will take time to get used to," she replied simply.

"Why is that?" Mathew asked

"I served in the Werewolf Revolt 539 years ago and have been on active duty in the Ice Elemental military ever since. It's been a long time since I have been in an informal setting and I am not accustomed to being on a first name basis with many people," Bell said with all seriousness.

"Okay. Just keep in mind that it's fine with me when you decide to be a little more relaxed," Mathew said trying to lighten the mood a little; it was difficult for him to talk to someone this serious.

"Thank you. I'll keep that in mind . . . Mathew," Bell replied just as the others started arriving.

"So, are we ready to go get this thing or what?" Marsh asked seeming to be in a better mood than yesterday.

"We might as well head in. No point in sitting around here waiting for another murder to happen," Victor said coldly before heading into the council room first as the others followed him in.

"Well, are you all ready?" Steven asked with a yawn.

"I believe we are," Mathew said speaking for the group.

"Okay. You have permission the head out. The teleportal is down the hall and I believe Bell knows the way," Samantha said simply.

Bell led the way down the hall to the room that contained the teleportal. With Bell leading, one at a time the team walked into the teleportal that looked like an inconspicuous mass of floating water. Mathew soon discovered that inconspicuous mass was not so inconspicuous at all. It attached itself to his skin before he even realized it.

Mathew found himself standing at the beginning of a street that led into a town. The group slowly walked down the road and Mathew noticed that Bell was constantly checking all of her blind spots. Just then, someone ran up to the group. Mathew was nervous that Bell would go military on newcomer.

"Hey! Are you the Ice Elementals here for the investigation?" the man asked out of breath from running.

"Yes, I suppose we are," Mathew answered after he let the man catch his breath.

"Oh good! I thought I missed you already. I'm just here to bring you to our inspector, the one in charge of our side of the investigation. Please follow me this way to the police station," the man said leading them deeper into town. They arrived at a building with an emblem of a large star, carved in stone, above the entry door with the word "Police" engraved into the star.

"Hey, John! They're here!" their escort yelled excitedly as a very tall man walked in. He was wearing a button-up vest with brown pants.

"Welcome. I'm Jonathon, Chief Inspector for this Demon community. Come this way and I'll fill you in on the details that we've gathered so far," he said motioning the group to follow.

The Inspector led Mathew and his team down the hallway to a large room filled with people and a lot of commotion. Mathew assumed this was the heart of the police office where clues were gathered and cases solved. The occupants of the room were enthusiastically discussing details of various cases they were involved in until the team's presence became known. As soon as the group caught sight of them, a deafening silence came over the room. All activity stopped so that the only sound that was heard was their footsteps as they walked through the room to the Inspector's office. John showed them into his office and closed the door quietly.

"Please excuse the others in the office. When Elementals show up, it usually means something bad is about to happen," John said sitting down behind his desk.

"Why do they assume that?" Mathew asked.

"It is our experience that Elementals usually believe that they outrank the Demon population. Demon attacks are reported from time to time but most are instigated by Elementals," John explained as he leaned back a little farther in his chair. "Oh! Pardon me but I forgot to ask for your names," he said simply, sitting back up.

"My name is Victor. The one with the white hair is Mathew and the other one is Marsh. The girl is Bell," Victor answered before anyone else could answer.

"Well, it's nice to meet you all. Anyway . . . down to the unfortunate business at hand," John began. "The victims have all been Human so far. Cause of death appears to have been blood loss through 2 puncture wounds on the front side of the neck. The puncture wounds alone would have closed the case but, in addition to these wounds, each body has had multiple bruises. Bruising is very rare in a Vampire attack so we are not able to draw any solid conclusions yet," John said stating a few important details.

"Have you confronted any Vampires about this?" Mathew decided to ask.

"We have interviewed the known Vampires that live within the city but we can't talk to the major population because they are outside of the Sanctuary. Other than those two, the only Vampires in here are just students at the local school for Demons. They are part of the local community so it's pointless to search there," John replied after thinking it over.

"Do you have a body that I can inspect?" Mathew asked feeling kind of sick thinking about what he was about to do.

"Of course. Follow me to the freezer," John said and exiting the room.

The group went down a flight of stairs to the morgue. John pulled out a corpse and flipped up the thin sheet that was over it. The body was of a young woman who wasn't exactly pretty but Mathew thought she was at least easy on the eye.

"Have they all been female?" Mathew asked trying not to breathe in too deeply and swallowing hard to calm his stomach.

"No, there were a few males, too. This one was found approximately two weeks ago so . . . it's fresher," John replied calmly.

"Hey Victor, what she die of?" Mathew asked.

"That will require me to do an autopsy so you better inspect the bite mark fist," Victor replied.

"That's what I was thinking; give me a little room please," Mathew said pulling out one of his demonology tools to inspect the depth of bite marks. The tool, called an ortho-yard, was basically a long, skinny cylindrical measuring stick. It was similar to the tool jewelers used to measure ring size. Mathew slowly inserted it into both of the punctures wounds and took readings.

"Glad I checked. If the cause of death was the puncture wounds, our murderer is not a Vampire. The wounds go past the carotid artery and are at different depths. This alone is highly unusual—a Vampire would have to have one tooth longer than the other one, perhaps from breakage. Also, there is no trace of the saliva acid that usually seals the wound once the teeth are removed. Were there any other marks that I should look at?" Mathew asked feeling surprisingly okay now with touching a dead body. He was amazed that he got use to it this quickly.

"Nope, just the marks on the neck and the bruises on the lower parts of the body, but I don't think you will be able to tell anything from them," John replied as he worked with a few papers.

"Alright Victor. You're up," Mathew said announcing he was done with the body.

"Right. I assume you have a room I can do this in?" Victor asked.

"Of course, right this way," John said showing Victor into a separate room as a few other officers brought in the corpse.

A few hours passed while the autopsy was being done. At the fourth hour mark, Victor emerged in a white medical apron and mask. Both had traces of blood splattered on them. The blood splatters seemed strange to Mathew. The body was cold and should have had no pressure build up within the veins. Strange, indeed.

"So, Victor. What's the verdict?" Marsh asked standing up to stretch.

"She died of suffocation. The marks on her neck were made just so a telltale bruise wouldn't form. Quite clever, actually," Victor said giving his answer.

"So! They all are strangulations!" John exclaimed after hearing the diagnosis.

"As I've only examined one body, I can't affirm that all deaths were due to suffocation. This one was," Victor stated.

"Can you show us where the bodies have been found?" Marsh asked.

"Of course, but are we able to do that tomorrow? I'm all most done with my shift," John asked hesitantly.

"You don't want to solve this?" Marsh asked.

"Of course but, as the killings have no pattern to them and occur within the span of a few months, I highly doubt that another body will appear within the next few days," John said in his defense.

"I would also like that we take this up tomorrow; I want time to study the Demon races who suffocate their victims. None are coming to mind at this moment so I need to do some research," Mathew said thinking out the strategy.

"Sounds like a plan, then," John agreed.

"Is there any place that we could stay?" Mathew asked.

"Now that you mention it, an Ice Elder named Steven already booked your place," John said before the group could discuss it.

"Oh god . . ." Mathew said already expecting something bad.

"Excuse me, Commander . . . I mean Mathew. What is so bad about having an Elder book our rooms?" Bell asked with her regular military tone.

"You don't know Steven . . . alright tell us quickly . . . where did he place us?" Mathew said holding his breath.

"He asked me to check you four into the Succubus palace," John replied a little confused by Mathew's reactions.

"Of course he would book us into something like that," Mathew complained.

"Hey, you shouldn't complain. I heard that place is pretty pricey and rumored that anyone could request . . . um . . . companionship for the night," John argued.

"What's the price?" Victor decided to ask.

"Three years of your life. But as you are all Elementals and have unlimited years, that's pretty cheap to you. So, my new friends, party hard," John said giving Victor a friendly punch.

"Would you mind showing us where it is then?" Mathew asked as he rubbed his eyes.

"Yeah, sure. It's not far from here. I'll take you there now," John said as he quickly grabbed his coat and led the group out of the room.

Mathew had a brief opportunity to get a good look at the city. He noticed that most of the buildings were made from stone and the gothic-style architecture reminded him of his cross. As this was a Demon sanctuary, there were multiple Demons of all shapes and forms everywhere he looked. At first glance, it seemed like a normal town but then Mathew noticed that very few of the inhabitants followed traditional methods of travel. There were roads and sidewalks but few Demons used them. Most climbed up the buildings or flew around to get where they were going.

When the group arrived at the Succubi palace, they were all impressed by the size and beauty of the building. It was, literally, a palace or a mini castle. When they entered the building, a very large breasted Succubi wearing minimal clothing greeted them. For some reason, Mathew thought of the French when he saw them.

John was kind enough to get the room numbers for them and a message that arrived earlier for Mathew, then he quickly said goodbye and left.

The group was escorted to their individual rooms by Succubi. This was a form of courtesy but, more specifically, a way to advertise to potential customers. The only person who didn't have an escort was Bell. She had refused her escort for unknown reasons.

When they reached their rooms, the Succubi escorts left them with promising smiles and a flick of their tails. Mathew thought this was very clever of them.

The room Mathew was staying in was beautiful and, to his surprise, completely set up as a visual aphrodisiac. Mathew noticed a musky scent in the air and the bed was covered in sumptuous red silk. There were several erotic sculptures placed in strategic areas throughout the room and the pictures hanging on the walls were all nude to partially nude paintings. Mathew redirected his attention and decided to open the message he had received earlier:

Hey, Mathew.

Just to let you know, I ordered a 'special' service for you. It should arrive about midnight, and knowing you (which I do), I know you will NOT reject it no matter what shape or form it comes in.

So have fun!

-Steven.

That bastard! Hiring me a Succubus without consulting me first! Mathew thought as he hopped on the bed that was wonderfully soft and relaxing. Mathew had just settled in when he heard a knock at the door. Reluctantly he got up, opened it and found Bell standing at attention.

"Excuse me, Sir, pardon the interruption but do you have a minute?" Bell sounded calm but Mathew noticed that something in her voice was off.

"Of course, Bell. Please come in," Mathew said happily and made way for her to enter. He was happy and relieved that it was just Bell and not the "special service" Steven mentioned in his letter. But Bell just stood there at attention like she did at the police department.

"So, something up, Bell?" Mathew asked after a moment of awkward silence between them.

"First of all, I apologize for interrupting your rest, but I was feeling a bit uncomfortable for a reason I have yet to understand," she stated still standing.

"Well, before we can go any further, we have to get you to relax. No formal apologies, please. I'm your friend not your commander . . . actually I'm more like your acquaintance but that's beside the point," Mathew said trying to get Bell to relax.

"Okay, Sir. I will work on being less formal in the future," Bell replied relaxing her shoulders a bit.

"Now, where were we? Oh, yes. You were feeling uncomfortable," Mathew said getting back to Bell's problem.

"Yes, Sir. Something isn't right here. It's hard to explain but, well, I'm a seasoned Ice Vanguard yet I find myself feeling insecure and vulnerable in this place," Bell explained and she looked over her shoulders as if she was expecting someone to be there.

Mathew thought for a moment and then responded enthusiastically, "Oh, I know what's going on!"

"Please tell me. What is it, then? I would rather resolve this quickly," Bell asked still in her military monotone.

"It's this place we're in. It's made more for men than women, and even though you're a Vanguard who could probably kill me in a heartbeat, you're still a woman. It's just your instincts telling you to protect your body," Mathew explained calling on his knowledge of the Succubi culture, even though there was no such thing as lesbians in their culture or history, the enchantments in the room are unable to read gender so it affected both in different ways.

"How do you know that for certain?" Bell asked.

"All the items in these rooms are saturated with various levels of enchantment to encourage the urge for sex. Take the bed, for example. Lie down for a second and think about your emotions," Mathew suggested, so Bell did just that. She put her head down on the pillow and closed her eyes.

"I feel it; they are switching rapidly from things like embarrassment and nervousness to feelings of love and interest," Bell replied with more honesty than Mathew had expected.

"Now, you need to be aware of the enchantments to resist them. My method is simple. I just remember who I am and my regular position on certain topics," Mathew explained sitting at the end of the bed.

"What should I do then?" Bell asked sitting up and taking a seat next to Mathew.

"I'm sorry but I can't help you. I can only speak for myself," Mathew explained looking straight into Bell's eyes and, as soon as he did, Mathew felt a thump in his chest. They stared at each other until Mathew gathered enough willpower to speak.

"Bell, I need you to do something for me . . ." he began.

"We can't do that . . . it would look bad on me . . ." Bell said in a sweet nervous voice that sounded unusual for her but made it clear that she too was caught in the trance.

"No Bell . . . I need you the slap me," Mathew said trying to correct her.

"I didn't expect you to be into that sort of thing, Mathew," she said still taking it the wrong way.

"No . . . It's so I can get my senses back. Bell, just do it," Mathew said as he felt his self-control failing.

"If you insist," Bell said simply as she gave Mathew a slap across the face so forceful that it made him fall off the bed and onto the floor. Luckily that was enough to break their intoxication with each other. Mathew slowly got to his feet and stood silently.

"I'm sorry, Bell. I had no idea how powerful that specific enchantment would be," Mathew explained.

"That's okay . . . I'm sorry about what I said . . . you know," Bell replied trying to regain her military composure but the blush on her face wasn't helping. This was the first time Mathew had seen another elemental blush and he noticed that the color wasn't red but instead light blue that slowly spread over her cheeks.

"It's okay. Our minds were clouded," Mathew said trying to make the situation better.

"Well, I had better let you rest . . . have a good night sleep, Mathew," Bell said as she quickly walked out the door.

I'm glad that ended the way it did, Mathew thought lying back on the cursed bed, which caused him to fall asleep faster than usual.

In his sleep, Mathew felt the bed shift, which caused him to wake up. He opened his eyes sleepily and looked around. He was startled to see a pale pink eye looking into his. He jerked fully awake as a soft, feminine hand covered his mouth before he could yell.

"Just like last time," a familiar voice said before Mathew's eyes could adjust to the dim light of the fireplace. Mathew saw a face that jogged his memory but was more mature that the last time he saw it.

"Dee, is that you?" Mathew asked sitting up.

"Yes it is, Mathew! It's good to see you again," she replied with a smile.

"Come over to the fire so I can see you better," Mathew said pulling Dee with him.

Dee was now a lovely young woman instead of the small, girlish figure he had known. Her hair had turned jet black and seemed to shift in the darkness with a life of its own. Her once blue eyes were now a pinkish color and seemed to have a glow to them. Her skin was still as pale as it was last time but what had changed dramatically was the size of her breasts—Mathew couldn't help but notice that they were a lot larger than they had been when he saw her last time. He decided that Dee was now a very beautiful woman.

"So what do you think, Mathew?" Dee asked standing up and doing a little spin for him.

"You're beautiful, Dee! I'm glad I was able to help in getting you home," Mathew said as he felt warmth come over him from his good deed.

"I'm grateful to you for doing that. Speaking of that, I've been curious since that night—what did I feel like when my bones were rearranging?" Dee asked inviting Mathew to sit on the couch next to her.

"Let's see . . . digging into the dark recesses of my mind, it was creepy. I remember that it felt like holding a leather bag with things moving inside of it," Mathew said recalling the weird feeling.

"Ew. That sounds disturbing. I want to apologize again. I didn't expect to go into the next stage so soon," Dee explained scooting a little closer to Mathew.

"I figured that's what happened," Mathew replied calmly. He was still happy with himself and his body had a warm and fuzzy feeling flowing through it.

"I know this will seem strange but would you mind checking my wings again," Dee asked.

"Sure, but . . . why do you need me to do that again?" Mathew asked as he was getting up moving behind her like he had done before.

"I'm not allowed to fly until my wings have grown to about 82 inches and I don't have anyone else I trust to check them," Dee explained.

"Alright then, I'll take a look. I don't suppose you have a ruler or anything on you?" Mathew decided to ask before he started.

"Yep, I brought it along," Dee said handing him a measuring tape. She quickly removed her shirt to expose her wings, which were obviously larger than before. "And remember, Mathew, they are still sore," she said simply, feeling Mathew's hands run across her wings like before.

"You're about 71 inches now," Mathew said closing up the measuring tape.

"Thank you, Mathew. That's good news," Dee said as she stretched her wings. The sight was interesting for Mathew to watch because he hadn't seen anything like it before.

"Why are they so smooth?" Mathew asked

"They just are. Would you rather they were wrinkled and rough?" Dee replied as Mathew sat down.

"No, I guess no. Tell me . . . what have you been doing in the last three months?" he said as he took his previous spot on the chair.

"Hmm . . . to answer your question, at the moment I'm taking classes on proper etiquette," Dee said.

"What is the etiquette class for?" Mathew asked.

"Do you want it bluntly or do you want me to actually explain it to you?" Dee asked.

"I'll just take it bluntly," Mathew said wanting to know the overview but not so interested in the details.

"It teaches us how to be a Succubus," Dee replied which wasn't as blunt as Mathew expected.

"So . . . is that all it teaches?" Mathew asked as his curiosity got the better of him.

"We are taught many other things. The focus of the class right now is how to restrain ourselves to not steal the entire life force of our prey," Dee said understanding how Mathew's mind was working.

"So by "prey" you mean anyone, right?" Mathew asked giving her a little glare.

"Of course, technically even you are prey," Dee said casting a playful yet dangerous look back at him.

"I just remembered something . . . why didn't you tell me you were 'examining' each Elemental race to help your mom with work or something like that?" Mathew asked remembering the reason they first met.

"Because looks and rumors can be deceiving," Dee said quietly. It wasn't quite the answer Mathew wanted but it was true.

"What about you, Mathew? What have you been doing these past months?" Dee asked.

"Lots of stuff. I've actually been very busy. I'm now a full-fledged, licensed Demonologist and I have taken a few classes in using Magic. You may know it as Art. That along with a swordplay class," Mathew answered proudly.

"So you took an Art class? How . . . artsy of you," Dee teased with a giggle.

"I know, I couldn't take it seriously either," Mathew said agreeing with a chuckle.

"Oh, I get it now. You're not here specifically to renew our friendship. As a Demonologist, you are probably here to handle that unsolved murder cases, correct?" Dee asked leaning in a little bit.

"Actually, yes. It's my first job," Mathew stated still feeling rather stupid about that.

"So, who's the girl?" Dee asked from out of nowhere.

"Girl . . . you don't mean Bell, do you?" Mathew asked confused.

"When I came into the room, I picked up a female scent that's quite fresh," Dee explained.

"Yeah, that would be Bell, one of my team members on this case. She was feeling uncomfortable because of the enchantments on a lot of the things around here. Because of the stinking sheets on the bed we almost, um, had 'relations'," Mathew replied.

"Well that explains that, then . . . but back to the murders. Listen, Mathew, I believe my mother knows something and I'm sure she will tell you if you come with me to see her," Dee said giving him an offer he couldn't refuse.

"Sure, when can I see her?" Mathew asked as he began to stand up.

"Right now. Come on, let's go!" Dee yelled, pulling Mathew up the rest of the way before he had time to answer.

Dee dragged Mathew up multiple flights of stairs with only a few stops along the way to catch their breath. When they reached the top of the stairs there was a large plain, contemporary door that looked out of place with the rest of the more ornate decorations in the palace.

"This is the room where we all live," Dee said quickly before opening the door.

The door opened and Mathew was surprised at the large number of Succubi in the room. He made several mental notes and found it fascinating to see firsthand how the Succubi lived. The room was large and, unlike any other in the palace, had several smaller rooms stacked together that all opened up to the great room, which was obviously their community area.

As Mathew walked down the hallway, he self-consciously noticed a variety of looks directed at him. Some were friendly, others nervous and multiple others seemed to be interested or just plain curious. He also noticed desire but, before he had any other chance to sort through any of the other "looks", Dee dragged him into the room in the middle of the hallway.

"Mom! Are you in here?" Dee yelled as they both entered the room.

"Yes, I am. Come in, dear," a kind voice replied.

"Mom, this is Mathew. The Elemental boy who helped me," Dee said as she caught sight of her mother sitting at a desk full of papers.

"So this is the brave Mathew," the woman said standing up. She was almost an exact copy of Dee except her hair was nutmeg brown and her eyes were a more vibrant pink than Dee's. Her chest was also bigger than Dee's. Her face had a kind look to it and she had a nice smile. Mathew noticed that something was different about her—a certain type of innate elegance that can't be learned in etiquette classes.

"Well, well, well. You're a busy bee, aren't you? We just met and you already are checking out my body," the woman said with a small laugh.

"Can you read my mind?" Mathew asked suspiciously because she figured it out really fast.

"No. I am an expert at reading sexual levels," she said with a charming smile. "Oh! Excuse me, dear. My name is Catharine and I am the Matron of this beautiful home. I am also a key member of the local Succubi community. I won't get into details because you wouldn't understand anyway," Catharine said with another smile and moved in to give Mathew a hug that he couldn't resist or not enjoy.

"It's nice to meet you, Catharine," Mathew replied as he pulled out of the hug.

"What can I do for you, sweetie?" Catharine asked putting her arm around his neck like they were old friends.

"At the moment, ma'am, I'm here on business," Mathew answered not sure how he could word it.

"'Ma'am!' Okay, then. What business is that?" Catharine replied leaning in closer to Mathew's face.

"Dee mentioned that you might have information about the recent murders that have happened in this community," Mathew said getting straight to the point.

"Hmm. One of my girls says that the responsible party is a Human Vampire cult in the nearby town. Apparently the cult worships some book series that's been coming out over the last few years, but I know the Elder council is going to need more evidence than the testimony of a single Succubus," Catharine said after giving Mathew the information he needed.

"Thanks for the information. I'm heading to the murder sight tomorrow to hopefully find evidence there that might close the case," Mathew replied simply.

"Well, now that that's settled, is there anything I could personally do for you?" Catharine said with a seductive tone in her voice that caused Mathew's mind to get all slow and foggy.

"I don't have anything I need at the moment but I'll keep that in mind," Mathew said valiantly trying to break out of the fog that seemed to overtake his thoughts and replace them with more suggestive ones.

"Just ask for it and you will get it, dear boy. I owe you my little girl's life," Catharine said as she started giving Dee's shoulders a good squeeze. "As long as you are here, how about a game?" Catharine asked as she slowly pulled out a blindfold.

"Mom! We are not having him play that game!" Dee exclaimed in a horrified voice. Mathew figured this was some inside joke that was between them both.

"Okay, okay! It was just a joke," Catharine said putting the blindfold away.

"I don't think I want to know," Mathew mumbled under his breath.

"Just out of curiosity, Mathew, what's your title?" Catharine asked as she sat back down at her desk.

"My title . . . oh yeah . . . My title is 'Half Light'," Mathew said with his words full of pride.

"Mathew, the Half Light Demonologist . . . has a nice ring to it," Catharine said as a knock came at the door, making her look up from her desk. "Come in!" she answered.

"Excuse me, but this Elemental was about to break down the door," a Succubus said before pushing Bell into the room.

"So! Here you are, Mathew. Good to see you're not hurt and my concern was for nothing!" Bell said as she threw a glare at the Succubus who pushed her in here.

"Bell! What were you doing here?" Mathew asked.

"It's my job to protect you while were on this investigation so, when I saw you being dragged away by a Succubus, I feared the worse and trailed you," Bell said simply.

"That is understandable," Catharine said forgiving the incident without another word.

"Well, okay now, introductions. Bell this is Catharine and her daughter, Dee. Catharine and Dee, this is Bell," Mathew said simply. He never had enjoyed making introductions.

"It's a pleasure to meet you," Bell said with her usual military monotone.

"Same here," Dee said inspecting Bell by circling her like a shark.

"Well, Mathew, I'm going to have to take you back to your room now. We have a big day tomorrow and I can't have our only available Demonologist tired from messing around with Succubi all night long," Bell said as she led Mathew out of the room by the wrist.

Mathew was then ordered into his room and forbidden to leave until she came for him in the morning; she ensured this by completely freezing the doorway with advanced magic so even Mathew couldn't melt it away. He did try, though.

The next morning, the group met up and was later joined by Inspector John, who took them to the murder site. The site was located in the dense woods. When they arrived, Mathew dispatched Marsh to find any traces of tracks that would indicate Human involvement while Mathew looked around for any other evidence. Bell was being particularly cautious with Mathew's wellbeing and stuck to him like a shadow.

Just then, they heard a crack from a twig in the woods, followed by a large burst of flame from the same area the sound seemed to originate from. Bell pushed Mathew to the ground for protection as she sent a wall of ice toward the fire. Immediately the fire was extinguished in a very impressive display.

"Come out slowly and show me your hands, Fire Elementals!" Bell ordered into the area with an ice blade in her hand, the area that was now full of smoldering trees, bushes, and twigs.

"Sorry about that, Ice. We didn't expect you to be around here as well," a voice came as two figures stepped out from their hiding spots in the thick woods.

"Who are you?" Bell demanded authoritatively, sending chills down Mathew's back.

"I'm Charles, the Impulsive Blaze Demonologist and this is my apprentice, Keira," he explained as he came closer.

"Why are you here?" Bell asked, continuing the interrogation.

"We were sent by the Council of the Eternal Flame to investigate the recent murders here. Why are YOU here?" Charles demanded.

"The same reason you are. I'm Mathew, the Half Light Demonologist," Mathew said standing up from the hole he had been pushed into and quickly flashed his badge.

"Happy to make this easy for you, then. As a courtesy, I'd like to inform you the murders have been a series of Vampire attacks. The puncture wounds on the neck should be enough proof for you," Charles said completely convinced in his theory and happy that he was able to flaunt his intellectual superiority.

"Sorry Charlie, it seems you were misinformed. The death of each victim has been by suffocation. The puncture wounds were made to mask the true cause. Apparently, the perpetrator wanted us all to believe that it was a Vampire. In actuality, the blood of the victim was drained from the puncture wounds in the neck to prevent a telltale bruise from forming. Word on the street is the culprits are a cult of Human Vampire worshipers who are interested in a book series that is particularly trendy right now," Mathew said laying out all the facts he could list.

"Well! It appears you have done your homework! How long have you been on this case?" Charles asked with an ambiguous tone in his voice. Mathew figured he was just offended by a newcomer challenging his theory—especially since that theory was directly opposite of his own.

"I've been here two days," Mathew said being honest.

"Wow! You're quite impressive! We have been wandering around for days." Keira said

"Thanks but it's because of the team I had put together," Mathew said as Marsh ran up.

"Mathew! I found old tire tracks, probably about two weeks old, that have been dried in the mud along with dried blood and this," Marsh said as he handed Mathew a high school or college insignia ring. Mathew quickly looked it over and assessed it was a college ring because of the approximate age of the dead girl he had inspected.

"Good work Marsh, case closed! We can go home now," Mathew said happy that the information he got from Catharine was legit.

"AND . . . there's another body but I didn't inspect it. I figured you or Victor would want to look at it first," Marsh continued.

"Damn it! Well, we had better go check it out then," Mathew said disappointed that another body showed up overnight.

When Mathew saw the body, a sense of horror came over him as he realized that the body wasn't Human at all.

This isn't good, Mathew thought while running up to the body.

The body was propped up against a tree and was a young female. Her hair would probably have been a vibrant grey or silver but it was covered in mud so it was anyone's guess to the true color. Mathew decided to go through his basic checklist before doing anything to hopefully prevent any mistakes or false assumptions.

Teeth . . . canine and larger than usual. Jaw muscles have more mass. Skin is pale but not too pale. Fingers . . . standard with no alterations to indicate constant use. Conclusion . . . species Vampire, Mathew thought to himself as others watched him work. Okay what to do? What to do? He continued mulling things over until an idea dawned on him.

"Bell, animate a sword and cut my hand!" Mathew ordered. Bell obeyed without hesitation and, with a quick jab, blood started dribbling from a small cut. Mathew had a surreal moment when he realized this was the first time he seen his own blood as an Elemental. His blood had gone from the red of Human blood to a shiny silvery color.

As the blood continued to flow out of the cut, Mathew held the Vampire's mouth open and dribbled the silvery substance in. After about sixty seconds the girl began to move and open her eyes. She frantically grabbed at Mathew's hand and started sucking on the cut for all she was worth.

"It's okay. Take it from my neck," Mathew said, understanding how dire the situation truly was. He quickly exposed an area on his neck of his choice for the starving Vampire. She didn't argue and quickly sank her teeth into Mathew's flesh. As she drew blood, Mathew felt a heavy stream of blood go into her mouth and, after about a minute of letting her feed, he became dizzy and passed out.

Dee

CHAPTER NINE

VAMPIRES

Mathew woke up in a large dark room. He hazily looked around and noticed heavy curtains were blocking out most of the sunlight. As his last memory came back to his mind, he reached up and felt his neck for any wound. With a sigh of relief, he found none. From his vantage point, Mathew saw that he was in a strange room with no idea of what happened or how he got there.

"Well, look who's awake," Bell's voice came from the corner of the room, which made Mathew jump a little.

"What happened?" Mathew asked sitting up.

"Let's see. Where to begin . . . you passed out after you let the starving Vampire suck out half of your blood. It took all three of us just to get her off your neck," Bell said summing up the incident.

"How did I get here then?" he replied.

"The Vampire picked you up and ran here. It took poor Marsh three days to track her . . . although he could have just followed the trail from the city but we didn't know about it until we got here," Bell explained sitting down on the bed. She started peeling an orange for Mathew. "Eat this. You still need more blood. By the way, it took a week for you to wake up," Bell said handing him the orange.

"So where are Marsh and Victor then?" Mathew mumbled with his mouth full of orange.

"I sent them back home to deliver the report about the murder and explain that you are now incapacitated in this Vampire Manor,"

Bell said giving Mathew a small idea of where he was, even though he didn't know where the "Vampire Manor" was.

"Why did you stay?" Mathew again asked still trying to understand what's going on.

"You're my friend, remember. Also, leaving you here would have been against our military code . . . you know, 'No Man Left Behind', and all that," she explained. Mathew realized that Bell was more relaxed that she had been originally been.

"I appreciate it, Bell," Mathew said with a kind smile.

"There was also something I wanted to talk to you about," she said before handing him another orange.

"What is that, then?" Mathew replied

"What would you think if I left the military after this is over?" Bell asked which did surprise him. He had only known her for a few days and he didn't expect her to confide in him about something this big.

"Why are you asking me?" he asked.

"Remember when we were caught in that enchantment? This will sound weird . . . but it's not as it sounds, okay?" Bell said giving Mathew a warning. "Well . . . anyway. As we were staring at each other, the emotions that were present at that time made me envision the life we would have had. You know . . . us married with children. But the thing is . . . I liked that thought a lot and I have been thinking about it since that incident," she explained as best she could. "Well, not my life with you exactly . . . no offense Mathew," she said correcting her statement.

"I understand; you just liked the thought of being married," Mathew summed up, pulling the strings of her choppy explanation together.

"Yes, that's it. But the thing is, I have been in the Elemental military over 900 years. It's all I know, all I can remember really. So I need your unbiased opinion on this matter," Bell confessed to him.

"900 years? Wow. I really don't know what to say to that. If you feel strongly about having a family then I think you should leave. I mean, you certainly put in your time with the military, so it's more like they owe you," Mathew said stating his opinion.

"But how will I adapt from my regular habits?" Bell asked.

"Just start at the basics. You start slowly, get to know people and make an effort to change, I guess. When we get back, I'll introduce you to a couple of my friends."

"Thank you for helping me then," Bell said as the door opened.

"Oh, so you're awake," a young voice said from the doorway.

"Excuse me but . . . who are you?" Mathew asked when the person was in sight.

"Oh yes, I'm Victoria. It's nice to finally talk to you, Mathew. I'm here to thank you and apologize for nearly sucking you dry. You saved my life," she said with a smile that didn't make her seem dangerous at all.

Mathew calmly looked her over now that she didn't need saving from imminent death. He liked what he saw. Victoria's hair was a silvery blonde color and, from his vantage point, looked like it was down to the middle of her back. There was nothing special about her demon red eyes, but her smile was charming and alluring at the same time. The only evidence of her recent ordeal was a bandage on the right side of her head.

"That's alright, Victoria. It was an impulsive move but I understood how dire the situation was," Mathew said.

"How bad was this supposed 'situation'?" Bell asked not clearly understanding the scope of the incident.

"I was very close to a Vampiric coma. Which means I was close to going insane, or dead, and would have drank any amount of blood I could get my hands on," Victoria explained as she approached the two Elementals. Mathew noticed that her body had a gentle sway when she walked but he couldn't tell if that was conjured up for his benefit, a natural grace or the head wound taking its toll.

"So, what happened exactly?" Mathew asked curious how a Vampire would end up in dire straits.

"I can't remember what happened. I think I hit my head," Victoria replied vaguely and, with another smile, she pointed at the bandage on her head. "By the way, Mathew, my father would like to talk to you when you're able to walk," she said remembering one of the main reasons she was there.

"Okay, Bell. Please help me up," Mathew said as he stretched out his hand. He felt that he was strong enough to accomplish at least this one little task. Bell reached out, grabbed his hand and pulled Mathew to his feet in one swift move. He was a little wobbly but he was able to walk. "Alright, let's go. I think I may need some help," Mathew said shifting a good portion of his weight on Bell.

Though it was a short distance away, it took nearly ten minutes for the small group to reach their destination. Mathew needed several breaks along the way to combat the dizzy spells from low blood pressure. When they finally arrived at the main hall, Mathew was impressed at the size and beauty of the room. There were red drapes drawn together to display a black, embroidered insignia and allowed little to no light to filter in. Long balconies graced both sides of the long room and had supporting pillars with beautiful, horizontal carvings of bat-like creatures. After a thorough once over, Mathew noticed someone sitting in a big, throne-like chair at the end of the hallway.

"Hi, Daddy. Here is the boy I told you about but please, be gentle with him as he isn't fully recovered yet," she said to the imposing, undistinguishable figure in the chair.

"Seriously?? You've got to be kidding me," Mathew said a little annoyed.

"And what would I be kidding about, young man?" the man asked calmly in a distinguished voice.

"No, not you . . . this whole situation is way too contrived and all too convenient for me. More than that, it's suspicious. First, the girl I let stay in my place turns out to have a Succubi matron as a mother and now I rescue a Vampire princess . . . What the hell is going on?" Mathew yelled quickly spiraling into a rant.

"Calm down, young man," the man quietly commanded. "I am not aware of other situations in your recent experience but what you have described would give anyone cause for suspicion. This all may seem 'contrived' to you but you have my word that this is completely a coincidence," the man said as he drew a little closer. Mathew was still not able to see him clearly yet as the room was only dimly lit and he was becoming dizzy again.

"Okay fine . . . your name, please?" Mathew said with more rudeness than usual.

"I am known far and wide as Count Dracula but, as you have recently saved my daughter from near death, you may address me as ‘Count’,” the man said causing an astonished Mathew to silently stand for a few seconds as he processed his thoughts.

“. . . What the hell!” Mathew yelled after he registered the name and significance of the entire situation. “Now you’re telling me you’re the infamous ‘Count Dracula’ from all the movies . . . and the shows? The sideshow, ‘I vant to suck your blood’ freak??” he continued as he quickly lost his usual composure.

“I suppose the ‘sideshow freak’ is loosely based off of me,” the man relied with a calm yet serious voice.

“Oh, don’t give me that crap . . . you . . . you . . . blood sucking bastard!” Mathew said as the dizziness overwhelmed him and he passed out from over exertion. The last thought through his mind was how inconvenient it was to lose consciousness in the same room as Count Dracula. His body was caught before he hit the floor and Mathew’s last sight was the grim smile of Dracula.

Mathew woke twice in the same day in the same room. Just as before, Bell was faithfully watching over him again. He felt like he was in a video game and this was just a checkpoint.

“Matthew! You swore at Dracula! And you were SERIOUSLY rude to him! You’re lucky to still be alive and living as a free man. Mathew, you’re not leaving that bed again until I know you’re healthy,” Bell said sitting down next to him.

“What? What did I do?” Mathew asked not entirely knowing what happened.

“You don’t remember? You didn’t have enough blood in your system yet for ‘conversation’ then you swore at the KING OF ALL VAMPIRES! And then you blacked out . . . oh, by the way, he took your cross . . . don’t worry, though. He is going to give it back,” Bell said explaining what happened.

“I heard screaming so I assumed Mathew was up,” Victoria said with a smile as she walked gracefully in the room. She certainly did know how to make an entrance.

“Did I actually swear at Dracula, Victoria? Your father?” Mathew asked praying for a different story.

“Yes, you did Mathew. It was, though, actually quite hilarious; dad got a good laugh out of it,” Victoria replied with a small laugh.

“So, he isn’t mad?” Mathew asked a little worried and confused by the turn of events.

"Certainly not 'mad' and most definitely not angry. He's been around for several centuries and understands that you were reacting brutishly because of the lack of blood flow to your brain . . . I think he actually found it refreshing in a way. No one still living has EVER dared to speak to him that way. Especially the 'sideshow freak' comment," Victoria said with a small chuckle as she reached out her hand to feel Mathew's forehead. "You're chilly," she stated simply but Mathew just rolled his eyes at the comment.

"I'm an 'Ice' Elemental . . . chilly is not an issue for me. Well, that's good . . . Sideshow freak? What was I going on about?" Mathew asked recalling some shouting but couldn't exactly remember.

"Oh, you know. Something along the lines about how great stuff has been happening to you lately. First you aid the daughter of a Succubus dignitary and then save the life of the daughter of Dracula himself. Yada-yada," Bell said summing up the incident.

"Now that I think about it, what's with that? It's like this life is perfect . . . charmed. Everything seems to work out. It's just not right . . ." Mathew said examining his short history as an Elemental.

"Chalk it up to cosmic coincidence and don't go jinxing it," Bell said giving Mathew decent and wise advice.

Mathew stayed in bed for another day until Bell allowed him to actually get up and walk around for a little bit of exercise. Another day passed before she decided he was able to hold a proper conversation. Then, taking her duties very seriously, she waited an extra day before bringing Mathew before Dracula again . . . just to be on the safe side.

As Bell slowly escorted Mathew down the hall, he felt his heart start to race as they got closer to the main hall. His mind kept drifting back to the old horror movies where Dracula was this unstoppable force that hated all Humans and anything that resembled a Human. Mathew could feel his heart pounding hard from nervousness. He leaned up against the wall for a few seconds to calm himself with a quick deep breathing exercise. He tried his best to focus on the small, motivational pep talk Bell was giving him. As they got closer to the main hall, his apprehension was at an all-time high. Rounding the corner, he was finally able to see the lightly illuminated figure sitting in the throne. Fire was burning in each of the four fireplaces surrounding the throne, even though Mathew could see electrical chandeliers high above him. He wondered if the heat was necessary to keep the cold-blooded Vampire comfortable. He then realized that the phrase, "cold blooded killer", probably originated from Dracula.

"Welcome back, Mathew. It seems that you have made a full recovery," Dracula said as he stood up from his throne and slowly started moving toward Mathew. It seemed to Mathew as if Dracula was floating across the floor rather than walking, casting dark shadows all around him. Really dark shadows.

"Yes, Sir. I have to thank you for your generosity and it appears that I must humbly apologize for my rude behavior during our first meeting," Mathew said rather embarrassed as, the closer Dracula got to him, the more nervous he became. His worst nightmare was about to morph into existence and it was taking all of what was left of his depleted resolve to not run screaming like a mad man from the room. Mathew watched as Dracula approached him with shadows dancing across his pale face and hands.

"Relax, Mathew. Your heartbeat sounds like a drum," Dracula said giving Mathew a good slap on the back and started shaking him to loosen him up. "There we go! Much better, eh? Don't worry about our first meeting. Honestly, I had the best laugh in centuries over it," he said with a chuckle that allowed Mathew to calm down a bit. "But, on another note, where did you get this cross?" Dracula asked pulling Mathew's gold cross from his pocket.

"I inherited it from a friend when she died," Mathew explained quickly.

"Do you happen to know anything about the history of this cross?" Dracula asked with a tone that made Mathew expect a story.

"Unfortunately no, I don't. My friend died before she had a chance to explain its history and her parents didn't know anything about it because it was a gift from her grandmother," Mathew explained as he recalled the events that led to his receipt of the cross. The memories made him a little depressed because they were all connected to Meridia. "Why . . . is it important or something?" Mathew asked when he was sure he had full control of his voice.

"Indeed it is, dear boy! This cross is named 'Vampire's Crucifixion' and I'm its original owner; unfortunately I lost it in a fight against a Demon Hunter named Van Helsing," Dracula explained with a strange tone in his voice as he examined the cross.

"Van Helsing? A real dude? Wow. How did you manage to lose it?" Mathew asked out of curiosity. He had always watched movies and read stories about Van Helsing and Dracula but he didn't believe any of it until he came face to face with the living (or dead) Dracula.

"That sneaky bastard threw a stick of dynamite at me and my entire left side was caught in the blast. The chain was destroyed and it fell off as I made my escape," Dracula said recalling the event.

"Does the cross 'do' anything special?" Mathew asked on a hunch.

"Not any longer. The source enchantments inherent in its creation were broken when the gems were put on to disguise its identity. That, coupled with age, was enough to redirect its energy. You see these little marks?" Dracula asked indicating the small, bird-like engravings. "Those were once bats. Time has not been friendly, that's for sure," he said as he brushed his fingers over the old patterns with a strange but happy look on his face. "When I originally received this cross it had a strong enchantment on it to ward off damage. That alone is probably the reason I'm still alive today. It helped me make it through the years of growing wisdom," Dracula commented as his Vampiric eyes looked at the cross' pale gold like a long lost friend.

"Could the enchantment be restored?" Mathew asked politely. He didn't like the look Dracula was giving his cross and was fighting the urge to yank it out of his hand. The cross was his only remaining connection to his memories of Meridia and, even though Mathew knew from reading about vampires that Dracula was no doubt much strong than he was, Mathew was still willing and ready to fight to the death over the little cross.

"Hmmm . . . just because I like you, I'll ask around and see if anyone knows how to cast it," Dracula said handing Mathew the cross and ended Mathew's preparations for a sudden fight.

"So Mathew, there is something that has been bothering me about the circumstances around your encounter with my daughter. How did you happen across my Victoria?" Dracula asked, leading Mathew into another room with a table and chairs and invited him to sit.

"It's a long story, Sir. It goes back a ways to when I first received my Demonologist license. Barely a day had passed when I was assigned my first mission of solving the recent string of homicides around here," Mathew explained.

"One moment . . . Your first job was to discover the perpetrator of a murder case?" Dracula said observing the same fact everybody else had.

"I know. Weird, huh? The Ice Elemental Council told me that I was the only Demonologist available. When I arrived at the nearby Demon sanctuary and inspected the body of one of the victims, I got a lead that the suspect was Human and not Vampire as previously assumed," Mathew explained thinking hard of how to explain it.

"Good man. At least someone is still teaching Demonologists not to jump to conclusions," Dracula commented with a smile that exposed his large, yellowing fangs. Mathew was taken aback a bit and thought pearly white would have made a better impact.

"When we arrived at the site where the bodies were found, we discovered that it was indeed Humans that were responsible and, for some reason, had disguised the killings to make it look like Vampire attacks. My tracker found your daughter, assumed dead, against a tree. He immediately directed my attention to the scene of the supposed crime. When I arrived at the scene, I had a suspicion that the victim really wasn't dead so I attempted to revive her by providing her my own blood. After that, I blacked out for reasons I'm sure you know and now I find myself before you, Dracula, retelling the circumstances surrounding this situation," Mathew said finishing the short story. He paused a moment to take a few breaths.

"Was there anything at the murder site that could lead us to the killers?" Dracula asked.

"Yes, there was . . . Hang on . . . oh no . . ." Mathew said searching frantically in his pockets for the signet ring. When he came up empty, he realized he wasn't wearing the same clothes he had been wearing when he was knocked out.

"Here, Mathew," Bell said quietly as she put the ring into Mathew's hand and then adjusted her white gloves that she seemed to fidget with when she was uncertain about a situation. "I decided to have your clothes changed as you wouldn't have wanted to be wearing the same clothes now as during your bed rest," she said with her characteristic monotone voice.

"Oh well . . . thank you, Bell," Mathew replied because he was unsure how to react. He thought it best to let it pass until a more appropriate time. "Ok, here you go, Sir; Marsh found this ring stuck in the mud near where your daughter was found," he said handing the ring to Dracula.

"I see . . . Yes. I know exactly where this is . . . but it's farther than I expected. Thank you, Mathew. The problem will be dealt with . . . under the table of course," Dracula said with a nod and a poker face.

"Thank you, Sir. It was a pleasure doing business with you . . . I guess," Mathew said putting the ring back in his pocket.

"Young man, regardless of everything, I don't know how to thank you for helping my daughter," Dracula said calmly. "Victoria is my youngest daughter . . . so far, and she is very precious to me," he explained with the utmost sincerity in his voice.

"There is no need to thank me, Sir. I just did what I believed was right," Mathew said with characteristic modesty.

"I believe you'd make a fine Vampire, young man. I could arrange a transformation for you, with your permission, of course . . ." Dracula suggested.

"Thanks for the generous offer but . . . No. I would probably only allow that if I knew I was going to die as an Elemental," Mathew replied with a polite grin.

"I'll keep that in mind . . . by the way, why do you smell like Catharine? No, scratch that . . . how do you still smell like Catharine?" Dracula finally asked, unable to help himself, as the puzzle had been bothering him for quite some time.

"I know her daughter, Dee. As for why I still smell like her, I'm at a loss on that," Mathew said simply and, after he put the connection together, he then realized that he probably hadn't had a bath since Dee's mother had hugged him. Since becoming an Elemental, many things had changed—he didn't sweat anymore so he didn't have to think about bathing much. He would have loved that as a Human.

"A moment, please. Now I remember where I heard your name before! You are the young man who helped Catharine's daughter, aren't you?" Dracula asked.

"Yep, that was I. Dee was spending the night at my home when her bones started to shift," Mathew replied as a shiver ran up his spine at the memory of Dee's bones rearranging themselves as he held her in his arms.

"Good man!" Dracula exclaimed as he reached out to give Mathew a slap on the back. The slap sent Mathew flying out of his chair and across the room, straight into the opposite wall over twenty feet away.

"My apologies, Mathew. There are times when I still forget my own strength," Dracula said as he rushed over and helped Mathew back up to his feet.

After a few more hours of talking over a variety of things, Bell suggested that they head back home. Mathew was fully healed so Dracula ordered an escort for them back through the dangers of the thick forest path to the Sanctuary's main rode. From there Mathew and Bell followed the road that led to the teleportal, but neither was in a hurry to return. They took some time to browse through a few stores along the way. Most of the shops were different than Elemental shops and Demon fashion was very different than Elemental shops. Most stores offered suits that were vintage to retro in style but seemed to Mathew like musty, outdated old suits. They did, though, happen to find more common attire like jeans and Mathew's favorite; different types of T-shirts.

After a leisurely afternoon spent in the town, Mathew and Bell made their way to the teleportal. Even though he liked the speed at which travel took place, Mathew had taken an extreme dislike to the sensations caused in his body by teleportal travel. When they finally arrived back in Elemental territory, Mathew was thankful.

Their arrival was highly anticipated and Mathew and Bell were escorted directly to the council room. When they entered the room, Mathew had his head held high and he was proud of himself for having solved his first murder case (with a lot of help, of course). Above his success, he had the opportunity to meet the infamous Vampire, Count Dracula, and his totally cute daughter.

"Hey, Mathew, you bastard! You're back," Stevens shouted from an upper balcony in the room.

"Hey, Steven. I'm not a bastard. Never have been; never will be. But, it's good to see you, too," Mathew replied dryly.

"Hello, Mathew. Welcome back. The Council is anxious for your report as the other members of your team were rather vague on the details," Samantha commented as she looked through a few papers.

"Sure. After two days there, I discovered that it was actually members of a Human cult who were committing the murders. The motive is still unknown. The bodies were prepped so all obvious evidence pointed to Vampire involvement. As Humans are outside of my official jurisdiction, there was nothing else I could do to bring the cult members to justice," Mathew said summing up the report as best as he could.

"Is there any indication of where the murderers are from?" an Elder asked with a scratchy voice.

"Marsh found what appears to be a college insignia ring. We believe it was left behind by one of the murderers or one the victims, so it should lead you straight to the general area of where the crimes were committed," Mathew said as he tossed the ring to the Elder who asked.

"But why the extra delay in both your and Bell's return? Did you run into some sort of trouble?" another Elder chimed in.

"I can answer that," Bell began as she confidently stepped forward; Mathew wasn't aware until that moment that she had come into the room with him.

"While Marsh was recovering information about the surrounding area, he reported to Mathew about a fresh body he found. As we approached the body, Mathew ascertained that, rather than dead, it was a female Vampire who was approaching something called a 'Vampiric Coma'. Mathew alone realized the danger and, as she was starving to death, fed the Vampire his Elemental blood," Bell explained with a loud voice that filled the room. "The girl took more blood than she should have and caused Mathew to black out, near death. He was then taken to the recovered victim's home, for reasons we still are not aware of. After an additional two days of tracking with Marsh, we found Mathew and discovered that the Vampire he had saved was the daughter of Count Dracula himself," after Bell said the name, gasps and whispers surrounded them.

"Are you positive it was THE Count Dracula?" one Elder questioned.

"We're positive. He even identified the cross Mathew has around his neck as the one and only 'Vampire's Crucifixion' which Dracula himself wore during his battle with the legendary Van Helsing," Bell said as more whispers went around the room.

"You two are dismissed," Samantha said before going back to the loud commotion of arguing with the other Elders.

"You sure can cause a lot of noise, Mathew," Bell said after they left the room full of bickering politicians.

"Well, I guess I have accomplished a lot in the four months I have been an Elemental," Mathew said realizing how short his new life has been.

"Only four months . . . it sounds more like forty years," Bell said with a small smile.

"Oh, yeah. I just remembered . . . I promised to introduce you to my friends, Ilium and Sara. Let's go now," Mathew said off topic and proceeded in pulling Bell down the hallway.

"What . . . where are we going?" Bell asked.

"I'm taking you to meet some of my friends, Bell. Remember our talk about that?" Mathew said letting her wrist go when she was walking next to him.

"I remember and I do appreciate it, Mathew," Bell said with a slightly nervous tone.

"Buck up, military girl! You're a Vanguard, and as your Commander, I'm ordering you to make some friends," Mathew yelled trying to use a tone Bell would have been use to but he couldn't help but feel silly as he tried to push the sound of a commander; it reminded him of when he was talking to the suits of armor in his room.

"Sir, yes Sir!" Bell said reacting to the tone as naturally as she usually would, she stood at attention and held her hand to her forehead for a salute.

"Alright, then. Let's go!" Mathew yelled giving her further encouragement.

They proceeded down the hallway, marching like they were in the military. Mathew made several attempts at marching in sync with Bell until he finally managed to get the rhythm. It seemed like the one thing that had not improved with his new existence was his rhythm.

When they got to Ilium's room, Mathew pounded on the door because Ice Elementals did not use doorbells. The doors were created out of ice in such a way that the occupant of the home had total privacy but external sounds in the immediate vicinity transferred well. He noticed that Bell was still nervous so Mathew got her to relax by giving her a slap on the back and a good shoulder shaking like Dracula did to him. He sensed her immediate response to the maneuver.

Wow! He really knew what he was doing, Mathew thought to himself. As the door opened, Mathew was greeted with an excited hug from Ilium.

"Mathew! How are you? It's been rather lonely around here during the time you've been gone," Ilium said quickly.

"Well, I'm all better now so no need to worry. By the way, this is Bell and she wants some help learning how to do some . . . I guess, um, 'girl stuff'," Mathew said trying to explain the situation.

"Say no more Mathew, any friend of yours is a friend of mine," Ilium said smiling at Bell who was trying to keep a straight face but Mathew knew that she was nervous again.

"Bell! What were my orders not ten minutes ago?" Matthew yelled using his commander tone to rouse Bells fiery spirit.

"Commander, your orders were to make friends!" Bell replied compulsively as ingrained habits die hard.

"Commander?" Ilium said with a confused voice. "Mathew, trivial question but, what kind of role-play are you into?" she asked taking it the wrong way.

"No Ilium, it's not any role-play. She is a Vanguard so when I need her to snap-to-it, I raise my voice in an authoritative tone to get her spirit up," Mathew replied defensively.

"So you ordered her to make friends? That seems kind of mean," Ilium replied as she started inspecting Bell.

"Hey, Mathew's back! Hello, dear! How did your first job go? I still think that was nonsensical for your first job," Julian said as she gave Mathew another friendly kiss on the head then a warm hug.

"Hello, Julian. I'm doing just fine. I'd like you to meet my friend, Bell, who's here to widen her circle of friends," Mathew said trying to get introductions done with quickly.

"Careful, Julian. Apparently these two have some sort of military role-play going on," Ilium said trying to make things worse. Mathew had decided that drama and gambling were Ilium's private hobbies.

"Oooooh . . . that's sounds kinky. How long have you two been an item then?" Julian asked not realizing the truth of the matter.

"Excuse me, but Mathew and I are <u>not</u> in that sort of a relationship," Bell explained calmly.

"Hmm. Such a shame. You two look good together," Julian replied vaguely causing Mathew to blush a little. "I have my medicine cooling. Nice to meet you, Bell. Talk to you later, Mathew," she said cheerfully as she disappeared behind the door.

"I suppose we should get to girl-talking then. Bye-bye, Mathew," Ilium said as she dragged Bell into the room and slammed the door shut before Mathew could say anything else.

"Poor Bell . . . you were an excellent soldier in a rank of your own but I think you've met your match," Mathew joked out loud to no one in particular.

Mathew quickly made his way back to his room. He had been gone a long time and was looking forward to getting back to the comforts of home. Mathew opened the door and the smell of frost, which was always a comfort to him even when he was a Human, rushed out of the room. As he walked in, he spotted something dark in the corner of the room. Mathew took a brief glance and then quickly looked back in astonishment. The dark object in the corner was a bat the size of a Great Horned Owl. Mathew screamed in shock and fell over his coffee table.

"My apologies, young man. I neglected to remember that you haven't seen me in this form yet," the bat said while still hanging from the wall.

"What . . . the bat can talk? Seriously?? I'm going insane now . . . I know I am!" Mathew said not taking his eyes off the large bat.

"Mathew, it is I, Dracula. This is the form I take to travel quickly from place to place," the bat said as it dropped from the ceiling while transforming into Dracula. Apparently cats were not the only creatures that always landed on their feet.

"You scared the crap out of me! What are you doing creeping around in my room? How did you know this was my room?" Mathew yelled as he tried to calm himself down a little.

"I apologize, Mathew. For clarification, I was hanging; not creeping. I am as comfortable in that form as I am in this. It's just something I'm used to and you're not," Dracula said patting Mathew on the back.

For the first time, Mathew actually saw Dracula in decent light instead of a dimly lit throne room. He was quite surprised—at hundreds of years old, Dracula looked quite young and naturally handsome. His clean-cut hair was black and went halfway down his neck. Dracula's body was lean, his clothing style fit him perfectly and his eyes were no longer the reddish Vampire color that Mathew had noticed at the Manor. The one thing that Mathew wasn't expecting was Dracula's skin color; yes, he was pale but wasn't the paper white Mathew was expecting from years of hiding from the sun.

"Hey, Daddy! Mathew, did you know there is a whole other room behind those doors?" Victoria said walking into the room blocking the sun from her eyes with her hand.

"I have another room back there?" Mathew asked not knowing about the additional room where he had called home for a little over three months now.

"Yeah, it's rather large, too," Victoria replied.

"Mathew, are you okay?" Bell's voice came through the door.

"You can come in, Bell, and yes, I'm fine," Mathew replied as she opened the door.

"Oh hello, Count, Victoria. How did you get here so fast?" Bell asked.

"We used the teleportal like everyone else. We just didn't have to stop and bicker with Elders like you two did, so naturally we got here way before you did," Victoria replied with a big smile. "Here, Mathew. I brought you a present because I never properly thanked you for saving me," Victoria said shyly as she handed Mathew a small paper wrapped package,

"Thank you. Victoria, but you didn't need to give me anything," Mathew said as he ripped open the package and found out it was simple yet stylish Vampire clothing.

"Well, I also got an outfit for Bell, too, because I felt sorry for leaving her to watch over you alone," Victoria said handing her a similar package.

"Thank you very much, Victoria. I don't often get gifts. I'll try them on right now. Mathew, where can I change?" Bell asked as she looked around his room.

"Apparently I have a whole other area for you to change in, so be my guest," Mathew said opening the door to the completely empty room.

As was characteristic of her, Bell changed quickly and efficiently. The results, though, were unexpected. Bell was stunning and, despite her not being a Vampire, she looked great in the outfit. Mathew wasn't able to tell if the outfit was supposed to be a suit or just casual clothes so he just stopped thinking about it.

After seeing Bell, Victoria began pleading with Mathew to change into his new clothes. There were also a few prods coming from Dracula. Mathew eventually caved and went to change in the other room. He gently closed the door then turned his attention to the small bundle of clothing, Mathew couldn't help but notice that Bell's clothes were neatly folded and placed out of the way. He realized she was probably organized and efficient in every area of her life but, then again, it had to be easier to be when family or friends weren't around to complicate things.

As Mathew put on his new clothes, he was happy to see that they fit like a glove. He couldn't have chosen better for himself. Mathew did a quick check to make sure he had everything on right. The outfit looked like it belonged in a thrift store but he liked it. The cloth felt good on his skin; no scratchy or irritating feeling he usually got when trying on clothes. Mathew decided he should follow Bell's example so he folded his clothes neatly and placed them aside instead of just strewing them about.

"Well, how do they look?" Mathew asked quietly as he stepped out of the room where he had been changing.

"It looks good on you. I'm not surprised, though. My daughter has always had an excellent eye for fit and style," Dracula commented as he pulled Mathew's cross out so it was visible around his neck. "That's better. Gives you a more elegant, aristocratic look . . . a bit 'edgy' as the kids say these days."

"I'm so happy it fits! I had to guess on your size," Victoria said with obvious excitement.

"Mathew! Where are you? We have so much to discuss!" Steven said as he barged in through the door without knocking like everybody did. As soon as he saw Mathew and Bell in their new outfits, Steven froze for a moment as if he was trying to figure out what to say. "Is there a reason for the Vampire getup?" he asked after several moments.

"Just a simple gift from my daughter, Victoria," Dracula replied as he started standing up to be polite.

"I don't believe we have met, Sir. My name is Steven. I'm an Elder for the Council here," Steven said introducing himself with a curious look on his face as he shook Dracula's hand.

"Dracula . . . Count Dracula. A pleasure to meet you," Dracula said with a smile that exposed his fangs, and, as soon as Steven processed the name in his mind, he ran out of the room yelling for Samantha.

"Well. This should be fun," Mathew said sitting down knowing that it was about to get very loud in his room.

"No worries. I'm used to it. Every time I visit an Elemental's home, favors are usually requested . . . and not by me," Dracula stated as he sat back down again.

"That sounds troublesome," Bell replied also sitting down.

"Of your many admirable qualities, young man, the one thing I admire most about you is that you don't treat me like some Royal King or legend. You treat me with a casual respect just as you would to any of your other friends . . . as far as I know, anyway," Dracula stated leaning back on the couch with a small chuckle.

"So, is there any other reason you two are here besides the gifts?" Mathew asked because to him it seemed like too much trouble for them to go through.

"Yes and no. We are here mostly because my little flower, Victoria, wanted to see you again . . . even though you left not 5 hours ago," Dracula replied as he looked around the room.

"Daddy! You're not supposed to say stuff like that!" Victoria exclaimed as her cheeks tinged pink.

"Victoria, my dear girl. There is not much that I do not understand, modestly speaking. Your first Elemental blood is always going to be your favorite flavor so there is no point in hiding it," he replied simply.

"Blood has different flavors?" Bell asked as she peeled back her sleeve to look at her pale wrist.

"Yes, it does. Like fingerprints, each person's blood has a special flavor that is uniquely their own. Victoria, dear, what did Mathew's blood taste like?" Dracula asked out of curiosity.

"Hmmm, let me think . . . . It was like drinking out of a river of fresh glacial water. It was divinely delicious," Victoria said licking her lips at the memory.

"Hey! You know I'm not a juice box, right?" Mathew asked which got a good laugh from the two Vampires.

"Don't worry, Mathew. I'm sure she will ask your permission before she decides to bite you again," Dracula said giving his daughter a little nudge.

"Hey, Mathew! Did Bell come in here? She just ran off when she heard you scream," Ilium said walking into holding a tiny skirt in her hand. She stopped quickly as she spotted Mathew's unexpected guests.

"Yes, she's right here. Took you long enough to show up. Who knows what could have happened in the amount of time it took you. Did the tiny skirt slow you down?" Mathew asked as he pointed to Bell sitting in one of the chairs.

"What's going on here, a role-play party?" Ilium asked with a laugh, taking another jab at Mathew.

"No, Ilium. It's not a role-play party and I'm still not wearing that skirt! It's way too tiny," Bell said with an annoyed tone to her voice. Mathew just assumed Ilium was trying to play "dress-up" with Bell.

"So. Who are your friends, Mathew?" Ilium asked simply.

"This is Count Dracula and his daughter, Victoria," Mathew replied.

"You lie! I don't believe you, Mathew! I get the joke and it's easy enough to ask someone to dress up as a Vampire then invite your friends here to meet Dracula," Ilium said poking him in the arm a bunch of times just as Samantha and Steven sprinted in to the room.

"See, I told you!" Steven yelled pointing at Dracula then leaned against the wall to catch his breath.

"Easy, Steven. Take a few deep breaths. You need to watch yourself now that you're going to be a dad," Samantha said as she patted Steven on the shoulder.

"Excuse me, but I assume you're Dracula," Samantha asked the only person she didn't know that was male.

"Count Dracula. You assume correctly. Now, how may I help you?" Dracula asked in a less than pleasant tone.

"I'm not going to beat around the bush here so I'll just come out and say it. We would like to offer you a contract and would like to discuss the details privately," Samantha stated calmly.

"I'll hear you out, madam, but only because I am indebted to the Ice Council for sending Mathew out on the murder case," Dracula said as he gave Mathew a pat on the back, which felt more like a blow because of his strength.

"Please follow me to the Council's room," Samantha said as she turned to leave.

"Mathew, while I'm in this meeting I expect you to take care of my little girl," Dracula said before he left the room. Steven followed him and Ilium just seemed to run out of the room for no apparent reason.

"So, I guess I'm staying here for the night," Victoria said after a few moments of silence.

"Why does this always happen to me?" Mathew asked, now suspicious again over all the strange coincidences that seemed to happen at random since waking up from his transformation coma months ago. What if he had never really woken up from that coma and all of the special circumstances were just figments of his grand imagination?

"I think it has something to do with that cross, but I'm not positive," Bell said bringing up a new theory.

"Why do you think that, Bell?" Victoria decided to ask.

"I noticed that the atmosphere around Mathew changes at certain points in time," Bell said pointing out something she had noticed since spending time with Mathew. "And when did that big gem in the middle of the cross get there?" Bell said pointing to Mathew's cross that was hanging in plain sight for all to see.

"What? Well, what the hell is that thing?" Mathew asked he inspected his cross, which now had a large blue gem in the middle of the cross. The gem resembled an eye.

"I don't know but it certainly does give the cross added character," Bell decided to say after a while of inspecting the cross.

"Okay, enough about my cross. How about a game of Dice?" Mathew asked since there didn't seem like anything else to do to pass the time.

"I don't know how to play but will you teach me?" Victoria asked as she smiled sweetly in Mathew's direction.

"Sure I can. Bell, do you know how to play?" Mathew asked.

"Yes, but it's been a few years. I usually spend my free time practicing Art and Swordplay," Bell replied calmly.

"Well then, let's begin," Mathew said as he created a few sets of dice.

As the night passed, Mathew discovered that Bell was as good as Julian but not as consistent in her wins, because of her irregularity of playing. He guessed that she played like she fought but the irregularity worked better in combat than Dice.

After a few more hours of gaming and a weird snowball fight between Mathew and the only other person who could make snow, Bell decided she should go report to her actual commander. She was planning on requesting her discharge or retirement as originally discussed with Mathew while in Vampire territory. After Bell left, Mathew was alone with Victoria so he decided to use his newly found room to create a temporary living space for her.

They both went to bed after Mathew finished furnishing Victoria's room. Even though Mathew did not need sleep any longer, he still liked the routine of sleep in his schedule and enjoyed dreaming now that his entire reality had been turned upside down.

The time passed slowly as Mathew just lay there. He couldn't sleep and his mind was still thinking about how everything was working itself out. He was plagued a bit by his earlier thought of still being in a coma.

Mathew continued to be deep in thought until he heard the door to the other room open up and close with a little slam. He sat up to ask what Victoria wanted but he ended up gazing into blood red eyes instead. Mathew felt a chill run up his spine for a moment, even though she was across the room he felt like she was right up next to him.

"You can relax Mathew; when the sun goes down our true eyes come out," Victoria said taking a seat on the couch.

"Scheisse, Victoria! You scared me. So, I take it you can't sleep then," Mathew said as he got up out of bed.

"Unfortunately, yes. Vampires don't usually sleep at night . . . but if we do sleep, at the most it's three hour cat naps," she replied as she scooted over to let Mathew sit down.

"So, what is it like being a Vampire? I know that may sound weird but . . . being an Elemental is just like being a Human. It's just that I can control ice now. And, I'm better at just about everything," Mathew explained because he was thinking about being a Human.

"I guess it's similar to being Human but getting thirsty is something you experience often even if you feed regularly," she replied simply.

"How do you feed regularly? And I mean like getting prey," Mathew asked noticing Victoria's beautiful ruby red eyes looking at him

"Let me show you," she began pulling Mathew up out of his seat.

"Well the simplest way is to find someone by a street or something abandoned. Now, try to walk by me," Victoria ordered so Mathew did trying to figure out she was up to. Victoria bumped into him, fell back and looked like she hurt herself. Mathew instinctively bent down to help her up.

"Just like that and I would have you," she said looking into Mathew's eyes putting him into a slight trance.

"See, all I need to do is make eye contact then feed until I'm satisfied," Victoria continued as she ran her finger up Mathew's neck.

"Clever girl," Mathew said simply, breaking out of the trance with ease.

"Mathew, if you don't mind?" Victoria said obviously implying that she was thirsty.

"It's your nature so I don't mind," Mathew said sitting down.

"This may sting a bit," she said before sinking her teeth into Mathew's neck.

Mathew sat motionless as Victoria fed. He couldn't help but sympathize with the Vampires on their thirst. When Mathew was Human, he couldn't go a day without a soda because of the small addiction he had. But still this was different than drinking a soda. Mathew noticed she was being more careful than their first encounter with each other where she was taking entire mouthfuls of blood, now it seemed more like small steady sips. It took about five minutes for her to feed until she was satisfied; Victoria slowly removed her lips from his neck, which had a light silver color on them from the blood. It went well with her silver hair.

"Thank you, Mathew," Victoria said happily as she started wiping the blood off of her mouth.

"No problem. I'm glad you didn't suck out huge mouthfuls this time," Mathew said as he let Victoria wipe his neck with a small cloth.

"I still feel badly about that, but I was starving so please understand why that happened," she replied simply.

"About that . . . why exactly did you take me to your home, then?" Mathew asked.

"Partly because I felt badly for my lack of self-control and you would have died if I hadn't done something," Victoria said with kind tone.

"What was the 'something' that you did?" Mathew said still not satisfied with the quality of information of had been given.

"We gave you a few blood tablets to stimulate your cell reproduction and secluded you until Bell showed up," she said and something about her expression and tone made Mathew uneasy.

"'Secluded'? By your tone of voice and expression, it seems like seclusion was more for my safety. What happened that I would need protection from your own family?" Mathew asked noticing her sudden mood change.

"Well . . . yes, everyone who lives at the house isn't exactly related but you have to understand that me bringing you, an unconscious Elemental, into the house was a first. I am the youngest Royal Vampire there so having such a unique situation happen to beings that are centuries old, and believe they have seen it all, would naturally cause quite a stir. Don't misunderstand me . . . we've often had visitors over, usually other Demons, but I never knew how savage they could get over an unconscious Elemental. Because of the unexpected manifestation of the baser nature, my sister, Allyson, and I watched over you to keep you safe. Still, it became apparent after your first day there that more drastic measures needed to be taken so my father banished all of them out of the house and told them not to return until he summoned them back," she said shuddering at the memory. "If my dad hadn't stepped in, there would have been nothing left of you to protect. I haven't seen him angry in a long, long time. I had forgotten how terrifying it is."

"I didn't know you had any siblings. Next time you see Allyson, please tell her I said thank you," Mathew said now extremely grateful to the members of the ruling Vampire family.

"I will and I'm glad you were calm the entire time . . . excluding the first time you met Dad," Victoria said with a smile and small chuckle as she remembered that particular encounter.

"I still think our first meeting was rather humorous," a voice said from above them; Mathew looked up and felt his heat skip a beat when he saw Dracula hanging over him in giant bat form.

"Damn it, Dracula! Don't do that!" Mathew yelled as he took a few deep breaths to calm his nerves and his pounding heart.

"Daddy! How long have you been there?" Victoria gasped as a vivid blush slowly crept over her face.

"Let me see . . . I came back, decided to take a quick nap and I woke up when you came into the room. So, the entire time," he replied transforming back into person form and landing on the couch next to Victoria.

"So you were watching us the entire time?" Victoria yelled getting either extremely angry or embarrassed but Mathew wasn't able to tell at first.

"What's the big deal?" Mathew decided to ask since he didn't understand.

"What's the big deal?? Feeding is a very private, intimate time for a Vampire," she cried covering her face with her hands.

"Do not be embarrassed, my little flower. I am proud of you. It is not every day I witness how mature you have become over the years," Dracula said as he made a move to hug Victoria but, as he approached her, Victoria ran back to the room Mathew had recently created for her.

"Is it true that the other Vampires were trying to eat me?" Mathew asked just to confirm the story.

"Unfortunately yes, Mathew. I was disgusted and extremely dismayed at their behavior. I thought we, as a race, had evolved far beyond our savage beginnings but it appears that the progress I have prided myself on was only skin deep and did not hold up under unexpected circumstances," Dracula replied with a sigh.

"What makes you and your family so special. Or different?" Mathew asked trying not to sound rude.

"We are Royal Vampires with an ancient royal heritage. We have an innate self-control and only feed when we choose . . . the feeding urge does not control us. Aside from myself, I have five brothers and our royal family tree is indeed large with many branches. Yes, there have been instances when our bite may accidentally have turned a Human to Vampire but Humans become hybrids and only transform into base, lower class Vampires. To become a Royal Vampire, a specific amount of our royal blood must be injected which, of course, we do not part with casually, if ever," Dracula confessed. This information was new to Mathew because the book he read hadn't said anything about a Royal Vampire creation process.

"So where are the other royal lines now?" Mathew decided to ask.

"We are stationed in various places around the world and only meet in our familial citadel if there is anything we need to discuss or vote on. For posterity's sake, I am not at liberty to confide the exact location where we meet," he explained. "So, what about you, young man? Where were you living before your death?" Dracula decided to ask but his tone made the question sound important.

"I lived in a town called the Golden Hovel. I doubt you or anyone else but me knows where it is," Mathew said.

"Actually, I do know where Golden Hovel is. It is only a few miles away from the Manor. I have been there more than once looking for leads on an old Vampire Slayer's guidebook that has been floating around. Needless to say, I have been unsuccessful in my quest as of yet," Dracula explained and his tone not as happy as Mathew had thought it should be.

"I wish I had moved from there when I could . . . but now I am an Elemental!" Mathew said actually happy with his death for the first time but he ignored Dracula's comment about the Vampire Slayer's book.

"Yeah, I know how you feel. When I found out why my mother was feeding us the so-called red milk, I was pleased as punch because I could live forever. So much to do and plenty of time to do it," Dracula said with a big smile.

"This may be a personal question but who were your first Human and Elemental feedings?" Mathew asked simply.

"The first Human feeding I had was the village beauty. I caught her in a trance and sank my teeth in; she tasted like sun-ripened strawberries. The first Elemental . . . I seem to recall that she was a Fire Elemental with a rather large character flaw of assuming she was the most powerful being walking in that particular forest," the Count said savoring the memory.

"So, Mathew . . . what about you? Who was your first? And I don't mean for feeding" Dracula replied with a crooked smile.

". . . I haven't had one," Mathew admitted reluctantly feeling very ashamed of himself.

"Ah, cheer up, son. Don't feel badly. You could always give Catharine's daughter a go. She is rather charming and easy on the eye," Dracula said giving Mathew jab with his elbow.

"Hey! Dee and I are just friends," Mathew explained.

"Oh please, do you, too, think I was born yesterday? I can still smell her hormones on you," Dracula said giving Mathew something to think of.

"But why? It's not like I was setting her up while she was here," Mathew said trying to figure this situation out.

"Mathew, Mathew, Mathew . . . you helped her get home during her transformation. Nothing is more personal or intimate to a Succubus than trusting another person with the vulnerability of that stage," Dracula pointed out.

"I didn't think about that and she really didn't have a choice. Well, what can I do about it?" Mathew asked.

"In all honestly and from my experience with Catharine . . . just let it happen. It's a constantly under-estimated fact that Succubi have a much stronger trance than Vampires do," Dracula said explained. "Yes, I excel with trances, but I'm not even close to the level Catharine is," he commented.

"You dated Catharine?" Mathew asked.

"Not precisely. It was more of a seduction than relationship. Remember, Catherine is a powerful woman and, not to mention the obvious, still very attractive," Dracula confessed and Mathew saw a hint of embarrassment in his face.

"Dee isn't your daughter, is she?" Mathew asked cautiously as the thought came to mind.

"Not that I'm aware of," Dracula said thinking about the topic.

"Okay, that's enough of that," Mathew said deciding to end it before it got weirder that it was.

"What are you two talking about?" Victoria asked finally emerging from her room with her head held high with as much pride as she could muster.

"Oh, just this and that," Dracula replied.

"So, Victoria, how are you feeling?" Mathew asked politely.

"Seriously?? I'm embarrassed that my father watched me . . . but I understand that he had nowhere else to stay. I should have checked every nook and cranny of the room before I started. He could have, though, said something," Victoria said refusing to look directly at her father.

"Darling, you're a big girl now so I'm not going to stop it. Your sisters were doing the same thing at your age," Dracula said tying to comfort his daughter.

Mathew sat for a few more hours talking to the Vampire family, and, as the sun slowly came up over the side of the mountain, Victoria lost her demonic energy that was fueled by the mood light and returned to her regular self again. Mathew didn't get to see this, though, as Dracula wanted to talk to his daughter alone. Mathew left the room to give them some privacy and decided to walk to the local market area. After browsing through a few stores, he decided that the "gas station" was his favorite. The Elemental culture had no use for currency so Mathew picked up a can of soda and cracked it open. The fizzing sound, bubbly smell were a link to his humanity and he wanted to savor the flavor like he used to do before his death.

After he was done exploring the market area, Mathew decided to walk out to the balcony where he had first met Ilium when he was just born (or "Reborn" as Elementals prefer to call it) into the Elemental dimension. After watching the horizon for the sun to come up, Mathew decided to see if he could find out what Sara had been up to while he was away.

Victoria

CHAPTER TEN

A UNION OF BLOOD AND ICE

With a little help from Ilium, Mathew finally found Sara's room. This was rather refreshing because the situation in his own room had prevented him from actually relaxing there. As a Human, Mathew hadn't been comfortable around a lot of people and he had started to notice that some of his Human characteristics still seemed to dictate a lot of his actions in the Elemental dimension.

"Mathew! How did the case go?" Sara asked after they entered her room.

"It went well and quickly. I was fortunate enough to come across 'inside information'. That tip led me to solve the case without much effort, not to mention the extra help I had recruited," Mathew replied calmly.

"I heard that you solved the case in just two days—very impressive! What I don't understand, though, is . . . why you were gone for a whole week?" Sara asked.

"I was unavoidably detained because a starving Vampire sucked out more than half of my blood . . . Ah, crap! I forgot my stuff!" Mathew exclaimed as he remembered he didn't pick up his belongings from the Succubi Palace before he returned home.

"I'm sure you could get your stuff back," Ilium said simply.

"Hey, Mathew, did you hear that the Count Dracula is actually staying here? In Ice Elemental territory? How exciting!" Sara said not knowing that Mathew was the reason that he is here.

"Yes, I know Sara . . . I'm the reason he is here," Mathew said not wanting to explain the entire story.

"Cool! How did you manage that?" Sara asked now eager to hear the details.

"Ilium, do you know the story?" Mathew asked.

"To confess, I, um . . . inadvertently came upon this summary of your debriefing from Steven while he was still running around last night," Ilium said as she pulled the paper out of her pocket for Sara to read.

"Wow, you are lucky, my friend," Sara said after reading the paper. "I met Bell last night. She is a good person. It's a good thing she ended up going with you," she commented.

"Ah, so here you are, Mathew. May I speak with you for a minute?" Steven asked as he poked his head into the room.

"I guess. What's the problem, Steven?" Mathew asked after he exited the room and started walking down the hallway with Steven.

"Mathew, first of all I did not agree with what I'm about to tell you," Steven commented. "I don't know how to put this . . . The council has agreed to sign a particular contract with Dracula; by the way, this is something that the Vampires have never done outside of their own race," Steven explained but Mathew knew there was more to come.

"So what does the 'particular contract' have to do with me?" Mathew asked getting impatient and a little bit jumpy.

"Mathew . . . the condition of the contract is that you marry the Count's daughter, Victoria. Dracula is more 'old school' than we are," Steven said spitting out the news as gently as he was able to.

"What! So . . . I have to marry Victoria? What if I don't want to?" Mathew asked, still trying to register the statement. "I assume by your tone of voice and how you told me that I don't really have a choice," he continued.

"Sadly no, Mathew, this is an order from the Council and the Council has 100% final authority over all Elementals. Marriage contracts are a way of showing trust and forming allegiances between two races," Steven explained and his voice told Mathew he wasn't exactly happy with the decision.

"Excuse me, Steven . . . I've got to get out of here before I really freak out. I want to be alone to think on this for a while," Mathew said before walking off down the hallway.

Mathew couldn't find a place to be alone with his thoughts and his head was spinning; he never thought he would be ordered to marry someone, especially as an Elemental. Mathew decided a spontaneous visit to his Human grave was in order. It was a short distance down the mountain and he just needed to think things through. The trip took about an hour but once there, it seemed like ten minutes because his mind was still stuck on every detail he could think of regarding the news.

He ran the remaining distance to his grave and skidded to a stop near the ice cross Ilium and Sara put there. The cross was still standing and the area, in general, seemed to resonate with a peaceful calm. The ground around his grave was still frozen and a mini ice oasis was starting to form despite the soon arrival of spring. The mountain's summit where the fortress was stayed frozen all year but the area farther down was starting to thaw.

"Hey . . ." Victoria's voice came from behind him, which startled Mathew.

"Hey. I'm surprised you found me down here," Mathew said as he checked out the Vampire.

"I take it you got the news, too," she said quietly.

"Yes . . . I don't really know what to say or think about any of this. Especially since I know very little detail about the whole situation. I can understand why you but why me? I have more questions than answers. Would you be happy with me? Would I be happy with you? Why doesn't that matter to anyone here? I mean, we have known each other for only a few days at the most. I'm sorry, I lost track of days while I was in that room," Mathew asked, trying to figure everything out.

"You're nice enough. I know you wouldn't give me any real problems," Victoria replied.

"Were you offered a choice?" Mathew asked.

"No. My father said I needed to do this . . . I don't know why . . . he didn't want to sign any contract to begin with," Victoria stated.

"Me neither. I'm locked into this because of the Council. I guess any personal freedom of choice I had died with my old body. The Council must need this arrangement for something," Mathew said.

"So . . . we're getting married," Victoria said it was obvious she was also still getting used to the idea.

"I suppose so . . ." Mathew replied unsure of what else to say.

"Is this your body?" Victoria asked with a slightly depressed tone.

"Yep, this is where I bit The Big One," Mathew replied, reaching for humor while looking at the frozen coffin that was still visible.

"I don't want things to get awkward between us," Victoria blurted out suddenly.

"I don't want that either but . . . we just need to work through it," Mathew said in complete agreement.

"Come on, Mathew. Let's go back," Victoria said as she gently took Mathew's hand in her own and started walking up the mountain. Both of them knew they could have used their individual abilities to get back to the village faster but chose to walk together in a comfortable silence.

It was all happening so quickly and didn't seem to be possible or practical yet, whenever Mathew would glace at Victoria during their climb, he eventually came to simple conclusion; he had no actual arguments against the marriage. Victoria was attractive, confident, seemed to be a good conversationalist and, in the back of Mathew's mind, he couldn't help but note that she was Vampire royalty. However, that line of thought somewhat made him feel shallow.

When they returned to the room, there was still a hint of awkwardness between them but most of it had been worked out on the trek back. Mathew opened the door and they were greeted by all of his friends, including Bell, who was actually out of her usual military uniform and dressed in civilian clothes like everyone else there.

"Congratulations, Mathew and Victoria!" Sara yelled who was obviously the one who put this surprise party together.

"Mathew, I told her not to do it but she didn't listen," Steven said with his voice still a little depressed.

"It's okay . . . not like I can do anything about it now so might as well enjoy what I can," Mathew replied before sitting down.

"Lucky you, Mathew . . . you getting married before me," Bell said with her monotone voice but her happy smile made up for that.

"And how is your search going Bell, any luck?" Mathew asked.

"Nothing so far. I figured there isn't enough guys in this place for everybody to have," Bell answered with a disappointed tone.

"Just don't give up, Bell. We get a few new people here several times a week. A few are bound to be new boys," Ilium said happily.

"Here Mathew, have a drink of this. It will make you feel better," Julian said as she handed him a cup of something.

"No, Mathew, don't!" Steven yelled as quickly as he could but it was too late. The thick liquid coated Mathew's throat and his stomach lunged. He made a mad dash for the window and expelled everything that had been hanging out inside him.

"Sorry, Mathew. I just had to see your reaction," Julian said bringing him something actually good to drink instead of her 'medicine'.

"Come on, Julian. You pulled this on him when he just had the news broken to him. You should have a few boundaries by now," Steven said as he gave Mathew a few pats on the back.

"Hey, Mathew, you want some cake?" Sara asked with a full mouth.

"Please! I need to get this taste out of my mouth," Mathew pleaded still trying to calm his stomach.

"Don't worry about it, honey. The feeling should pass within a few hours at the most," Julian said giving him the worst-case situation.

For the rest of the party, Mathew kept his mouth shut because he feared if he opened it he would throw up again. Despite everything his mind was going through, the small party was rather enjoyable. When things started to wind down, another Council meeting was called and both Dracula and Steven had to attend. The others left as a group to go shopping and left behind Mathew and Victoria, the supposedly "happy" couple. They sat for a few moments on the couch together in silence.

"I don't suppose you know when this thing is going to happen," Victoria asked after a while.

"Sorry, I don't. Should we plan something or do you think the Council is going to do that for us?" Mathew replied looking into her eyes

"If you don't mind, I would like to plan something. I need to feel as if I have at least some control over my own marriage," Victoria said reasoning with her own emotions.

"Alright, that sounds like a good idea. So what are you thinking, then?" Mathew asked, hoping that she had at least thought about this topic before. He considered himself way too young to have ideas on his wedding and was valiantly struggling to make the best out of this unexpected situation.

"Well, I have always wanted to have a spring wedding," Victoria confessed.

"That sounds nice. I just don't want to have it in the summer, for simple reasons," Mathew replied. He felt as if he were discussing someone else's life. Maybe it was easier that way for now.

"So you're okay with April, then?" Victoria asked turning her head to look at him.

"That's fine. But I would be more concerned about what you're going to wear," Mathew said as he remembered how long it takes for girls to prepare for a wedding.

"You're right . . . what is going to happen?" Victoria asked obviòusly distraught over the entire ordeal.

"Don't worry about it. I know it will be strange between us for a while but we will get used to our situation," Mathew said trying to comfort her. Then she started to cry.

"What? What is it? Come on, tell me?" Mathew said pulling her closer to him.

"It's just . . . I don't know. I never thought of getting married before and now I'm being pushed into it. I know I should have been at least thinking about it but I was content with my life," she cried as she laid her head on Mathew's shoulder. "Before I was a Vampire I was just an abandoned Human baby that was found during a storm," Victoria confessed to Mathew even though it was off topic

"Tell me your story . . ." Mathew said feeling that this topic may calm her down.

"Right after I was born, I was abandoned by my family for reasons I still don't know. Mathew . . . I know I have never told you this but I was born when the Black Death was ravaging Europe," Victoria said giving Mathew a hint of her age. "I was found by my father, the Count, who took me into his home and family and cared for me during my childhood. At first, I never thought it weird that Dad and my siblings drank blood while I ate simple foods that someone had prepared for me, like bread and soup. I also didn't think much about their eyes being red at night. Vampires raised me so you could guess my childhood was 'different' than other children's. I didn't have anything else to compare my upbringing to until I went into the village for the first time to get my dad a present for his birthday. He came with me, of course," she said with a smile at the memories.

"When is his birthday?" Mathew decided to ask.

"He says February 21, but I don't know for certain . . . he keeps changing the date," Victoria replied with a silly chuckle.

"That's a shame, so anyway . . . you were saying," Mathew said wanting to hear more about her story.

"Ah well, when I was in the village, I noticed that things were different from the environment at the house. People were moving around slower than usual, no one was drinking blood, those types of things. I asked dad and he just told me that they were strange people," Victoria explained with a smile on her face. "But I discovered truly what my family was when a burglar came into my room. Naturally, I screamed and my father, along with a few of my brothers and sisters, rushed into the room. The man held a knife up to my neck and told them to stay back.

Unfortunately for him, even the slowest member of my family can move at least three times faster than any Human. Dad got hold of his hand and crushed it . . . and I don't mean he squeezed it until the man let go of the knife. He crushed it along with the wooden handle until the hand and knife were completely fused together," she said, shuddering. That must have been both horrifying and disgusting at the same time especially for someone that age.

"After Dad did that, the man let me go and my sisters rushed me out of the room. The only thing I remember clearly was the man screaming and that I was told to stay out of my room for a few days. During that time I slept with my sister Carmen, which was okay because I was afraid to be alone for a little while. When I was allowed back in my room, everything was rearranged and there was the addition of decorative "safety bars" on my windows. Everything except my furniture was new," she said quietly. Mathew could only guess at what happened to the poor man who was unfortunate enough to break into Dracula's home and threaten his daughter.

"After that, things settled down to the normal I was used to and, when I turned nineteen, dad asked me if I was ready to be a Vampire.

Of course, out of love and respect for my family, I said "yes". Quite a few years later, here I stand before you, a Royal Vampire, engaged to an Ice Elemental. I have to admit, I have never been one to think that far ahead," Victoria finished her story with a smile then she gave Mathew an alluring glance. "What about you, Mathew? I told you my story so you tell me yours," she said sitting up to give him her full attention.

"Me? I was born in this state, I attended school like a good little boy and I made a good friend while I was in preschool. We stuck together like glue and I still remember the fun times we had together as we went up through the grades. Sadly though, during our sixth grade year, she started getting sick a lot more and began missing school every now and then, she had a disease that baffled every doctor her parents took her to. And believe me, there were a lot of doctors involved," Mathew began and immediately, as usual whenever he talked about that time of his life, he felt a heavy weight over his heart. "At first, it was just a couple days a month . . . but then it got worse and she was out of school for weeks at a time. Her house was only a block away from mine so I checked on her every day," he continued as he felt a knot of choked emotion start to form in his throat.

"One day while I was at home, there was a phone call and my mother told me to go to her house. As soon as I entered, her mother greeted me normally but I knew something was wrong. Very wrong. I went up to her room and she greeted me with her usual smile and then continued to tell me that she was going to die soon and she didn't want to be alone. I sat with her the entire night," he continued but held his hand over his eyes and acted like he was scratching an itch when he was really trying to regain control of his emotions.

"At about 11 at night, she sat up and, even though she was very weak, gave me this cross that I have worn almost every day of my life since that night. She valued this cross because it was her grandmother's and she was very close to her. About an hour later, my friend said she was feeling cold so I crawled into bed with her and held her with a blanket around us. I felt this horrible feeling of helplessness as her breathing slowed then finally stopped altogether. I checked her pulse even though I knew in my heart there wouldn't be one. I laid her down as gently as possible, tucked her in and gave her cheek a small kiss as our final goodbye. I went to tell her mother and father. Her mother hugged me, thanked me and told me to go home. But I didn't go straight home. I went to our secret place in the park where we would always go when we wanted to be alone with each other. Our favorite place by the park was an old drainage pipe that was no longer in use. A fence with a locked gate blocked the entrance but we soon found the key under a nearby rock and turned it into our own little club. We brought in a table, lights and whatever else we could get our hands on. I went straight there, lit the oil lamp we had found one day while rummaging about in an alley and sat there until I heard police sirens," Mathew paused reflecting on his memories.

"Can I ask her name?" Victoria asked.

"Her name was Meridia and, no offence, but after tonight I would appreciate it if we never talked about this again," Mathew explained.

"I understand . . . What was she like?" Victoria replied making Mathew search through hundreds of precious memories that he had locked tightly away.

"She was . . . wild, crazy and very kind. When we were at our closest, she declared herself my girlfriend and literally fought off any other girl who got too attached to me," Mathew said as he laughed at the memory.

"How long did that keep up?" Victoria asked trying to hold in her giggles.

"Until she died . . . the thing that scarred me the most were her last words, 'Mathew . . . my love, goodbye'. The sad thing is . . . I haven't been that close to anyone besides her . . . ever," Mathew said as tears started to fill his eyes. "I'm sorry Victoria . . . here I am talking about my childhood friend and crying like a baby," he said forcing a smile as he wiped the tears from his face.

"You loved her very much, didn't you?" Victoria said as she wrapped her arm around him.

"I did . . . I miss her everyday . . . and I have never been able to let go. I'm a man trapped in the past of a boy . . . I need help to move on," Mathew cried as the tears began to flow like all the memories that were flashing through his mind. He could still hear her voice in some of those memories. "I'm sorry . . . I know I'm pathetic," Mathew said when he managed to stop the tears but not the heavy breathing.

"You're not pathetic! You've been carrying this heavy burden of pain for a long time and it seems like the memories are still fresh in your mind. Mathew, I've lived many, many more years than you and Vampires are very emotional beings. We see death and life of our partners and family. So, what I'm trying to say is that I understand," Victoria said softly as she held him.

"I can still see her and hear her voice like today was the last day I saw her. Worse of all, the feelings of guilt are unbearable . . . like I was the one who let her die," Mathew said and then fell silent.

"Mathew . . . those feelings are very common but they are very wrong. You didn't kill her and you couldn't have saved her so, at the moment, you just need to focus on the fun memories you had with her," Victoria said in a very caring tone.

"Victoria, thank you for listening to my story. I appreciate you taking care of me like you did but . . . I'm tired. It's been a long time since . . . I even said her name," Mathew said and after a few moments he regained most of his composure. He started to feel foolish about crying in front of her and wished his moment of weakness had been private.

"Of course, Mathew. You need to rest for a while . . . you went over things that had hurt you in the past so I'll leave you be," Victoria said giving him a kiss on the cheek then quietly went to her room.

Mathew walked over to his bed and lay awake for hours. Something seemed wrong since he released the memories and the emotions that went with them. He couldn't understand why his emotions were acting the way they were. Especially why he reacted the way he did in front of Victoria, the woman he was going to marry. Now he felt like he had lost any pride he had gained by crying in front of her. Finally, Mathew couldn't stay awake anymore. He was emotionally and mentally exhausted. This was the first time in his Elemental life he truly needed sleep.

"Get up!" a voice yelled and Mathew was pushed off of his bed.

"What was that for?" Mathew said sitting up his mind clear and sharp from his impact with the floor.

"What's that?!" Julian screamed pointing at Dracula hanging from the ceiling as a bat.

"It's OK, Julian. It's just Dracula. Hey! I told you to stop doing that!" Mathew yelled as Dracula was waking up from the loud noise.

"Would you rather I sleep in the bed with you?" Dracula asked with a sleepy glare.

"You got a point . . . Fine. Keep hanging from the ceiling then," Mathew said rubbing the sleep from his eyes. "I'm going to get a soda," he mumbled not used to this much excitement in the morning.

"When did that get there?" Julian asked calmly when Mathew reentered the room with his soda

"When did what get where?" Mathew asked, confused. He started looking around him room for something different or out of place.

"On your cross," she pointed to the new, shiny blue gem on it.

"It just showed up. Bell was actually the first one to notice the other day," Mathew explained.

"That is unusual! It wasn't there when I looked at it a few days ago . . . Mathew; may I see your Cross?" Dracula asked a little confused.

"Yeah, sure . . . I thought you put it there before you gave it back to me. Funny, it doesn't seem to want to come off," Mathew said as he tried to pull the cross over his head but the chain seemed to be somehow attached to his body. It still moved loosely but he couldn't get it off.

"Here let me try," Dracula said pulling the cross off with one swift motion but, when he removed it, Mathew was unable to stand. His vision blurred, his head spun and it felt like his body was going to split in half. The pain caused him to black out as he hit the floor.

Mathew had dreams of his friends from his old high school. Next year was going to be their junior year and, even though he was 18, he was still a junior because of a slight family mistake about enrolling him a couple years later than usual. His mom seemed to have had separation anxiety or something along those lines. Mathew dreaded the dream. He didn't want to graduate because that was the end of his "supposed" life. The only thing he really knew at this point in his life was school so school was his entire life.

Mathew's dreams kept swirling around until he came to a dream about the party the night before. Everyone was having a worry-free good time and reveling in the thrill of just being alive and having fun with friends. Though the drink Julian gave Mathew made him puke, it was still in the name of fun. At that point, Mathew realized that he had been given the gift of new life and needed to accept that his old life was over. In spite of the tragedy that took his Human life, he had been given a fresh start with good friends. He was even going to end up getting married to a Countess and, after a while, he would probably start a family of his own. In this dream, all of his Human hopes and dreams were coming to pass much more quickly than they probably would have in his old life.

He finally woke up with water all around him. Mathew had seen this before. He was in one of those birthing, embryonic bubbles that Ice Elementals are born in. Confused, he quickly looked around and saw the room was empty so he decided to stay in the bubble and reflect on the things that he had dreamed about.

His mind was now a lot clearer than it had been the last few days. As the epiphany evolved, he could see all the little things that led him to his current situation, especially his meeting with Victoria.

Victoria had supposedly been suffering from a head injury and wasn't able to hunt normally. Without regular 'meals' she started to starve and, when her baser Vampire instincts took over, she went to a nearby place that had the scent of fresh blood. That place just happened to be the place where the bodies with holes in their neck had been dumped. Even though the bodies had been removed, they had been there a few days and the ground was saturated in the blood of the victims. Unfortunately for her, the scent of blood was all that remained, leaving nothing for her to feed off of.

After a few hours of deep thought in the bubble, Mathew heard muffled sounds. He turned around to see what was causing the sounds and saw his friends gathering around the bubble. They were excitedly waving at him, writing something down on a pad of paper and holding it up for him to read.

"How are you feeling?" the notepad said.

The only thing Mathew could do was give them the "thumbs up" for a reply.

"You will be able to get out of the bubble tomorrow. We will explain everything then," Victoria wrote after she wrestled the notepad away from Ilium (who didn't seem to appreciate that at all).

Mathew nodded and saw someone he assumed was the doctor moving around his birthing bubble. He couldn't clearly see through the bubble because the ice was distorting the image like a fun house mirror. The "doctor" checked what he assumed to be his vitals and then injected some type of liquid into the bubble that was a blackish color. The liquid seemed to take on a life of its own and attach itself to Mathew's body. Slowly it worked its way into Mathew's skin. He could feel it coursing through his blood stream. Mathew felt a sleepy lethargy come over him and shut his eyes to rest.

Mathew woke up in his room, out of the bubble, to find Victoria and Dracula intently watching over him. He thought this was nice but unnecessary since he was just sleeping.

"Kind of creepy to wake up being stared at. What happened?" Mathew asked with a crackly voice as trying to sit up but a sharp pain came over him forcing him to lie back down.

"Easy Mathew, you're not quite ready for activity yet," Dracula said simply.

"What happened?" Mathew asked again in a clearer voice. The crackle was still there, just not as prominent.

"A lot has happened. Do you remember that last thing that happened before you blacked out?" Dracula asked.

"Party. Necklace that wouldn't come off. You pulling off necklace . . . lots of pain," Matthew replied.

"Close enough. The new gem that appeared on your cross was what we call a 'soul gem'. To be precise, it was your soul gem. Unfortunately, I didn't realize that your cross had enough magic left in it to accomplish anything as significant as soul gem creation. Because I didn't think through the situation, when I pulled off the cross it caused a rending between your body and the cross. This is my fault . . . I deeply regret my carelessness and I apologize," Dracula said with a funny tone in his voice. Mathew guessed that the Count was not well acquainted with apologies.

"Well . . . ok. That's not too bad," Mathew said still happy he was alive and out of the birthing bubble.

"Mathew . . . honey . . ." Victoria said obviously trying to be more wifely. "When Dad removed your cross the gem wasn't completely formed so . . . he inadvertently ripped your soul in two. Don't ask me how but when the cross was separated so quickly from your body, you slowly began to die. We quickly put you in that ice bubble thing to preserve you until we could figure out what to do. It was Dad who remembered something that you said," she continued.

"What was that?" Mathew asked again beginning to get very frustrated at how long it was taking them to tell him what happened. He eventually understood that the situation was probably hard to explain.

"Our conversation, in a nutshell was 'I could always turn you into a Vampire.' 'Thanks' you said 'but I would probably only allow that if I knew I was going to die as an Elemental.' I concluded that I already had your permission for what needed to be done so I proceeded with the Transformation," Dracula explained slowly in a calm voice.

"What?! 'Transformation'? What does that mean? I'm a Vampire now?" Mathew replied shocked and realized that he was quickly recovering.

"Not exactly. You are more accurately a "half breed". When your soul was torn, I found a way to replicate and repair that section by giving you a dose of my royal blood," Dracula tried to explain as best he could.

"So I'm half Vampire/half Elemental is what you're trying to tell me? I'm a nothing now?" Mathew asked, trying to put the pieces together.

"On the contrary, you are not 'nothing', you are something entirely new. It's a very elementary explanation but it's appropriate for the situation we are currently working through," Dracula replied.

"So do we officially know anything about me? Meaning, am I the same old Elemental me or am I different?" Mathew asked as he now had a better understanding what had happened.

"That is where the opportunity starts—there has never been an actual Transformation combining an Elemental and Royal Vampire. That's why I was extremely cautious while I worked on you. The answer for the time being is no. Honestly, I am very thankful you are merely a half-breed. I was concerned that if I were to actually try a complete Transformation, it might have been too much for your body to handle and you would have . . . expired. None-the-less, even though only part Vampire, we have embraced you fully as a member of the proud Royal Vampire family," the Count said with an encouraging smile that seemed to make the situation feel better.

"Let me get this straight. You got your 'permission' to turn me into a Vampire from my response to your offer the other day and yet, it's never been done before. Why the hell did you offer?" Mathew asked a little angry at this realization.

"I don't know . . . I actually still surprise myself even after all these centuries. I fall back on common courtesy. Honestly, what greater gift could I offer than renewed life to the man who saved my beloved daughter before she went on a murdering rampage? Victoria's soul would have been irreparably damaged by such a heinous act," Dracula replied. Mathew could not believe that this was the very same legendary Vampire and laughed at the Count's response.

"A bit dramatic, maybe. I can't see her going on a murderous rampage," Mathew admitted after he examined the silver haired Vampire that tilted her head sideways as she was mentioned.

"By the way, where does her silver hair come from? Unless you've hit the bottle, your hair is still jet black . . . and I know Humans don't get white or grey hair until they are older," Mathew asked just to change the topic.

"The silver hair comes more from my brother's side of the family blood, but never this deep a sliver, usually a light gold. However, I have no idea how she got that gene though me," Dracula explained

"Another mystery? I shouldn't be surprised. Why does my chest hurt so badly?" Mathew asked, pulling the blankets back and exposing a large black spot that nearly covered his chest. "What the hell is that thing?" Mathew asked as he poked at it he realized that it was causing the sharp pain.

"Oh, that . . . that's where your soul was supposedly ripped apart; I'm surprised, though, that it's still there," Victoria said as she peered curiously at the black spot.

"Will it go away?" Mathew replied not wanting to go through life or, more technically, his third life with a large black spot covering his chest.

"No worries, my son. It was the size of your entire chest before we put you into a recovery bubble," Dracula stated. Mathew did catch the "son" part of his comment that made him feel as if he had betrayed his Human father in some way.

"How long ago was that now?" Mathew asked.

"About two weeks of intensive care. In all honesty, Mathew, I take the entire blame of the situation on myself. In my carelessness, I neglected to follow standard procedures for dealing with the cross. I should have inspected the cross before I had you take it off," Dracula apologized again with a strong hint of guilt in his voice.

"Two weeks! I didn't think I would have been out that long!" Mathew complained rather loudly.

"Mathew, Dad wanted to make sure that you wouldn't die during you're small but steady blood injections so he spanned it over a larger amount of time than usual. The whole situation is extremely unusual," Victoria said defending her father, which was understandable.

"Okay, I get it. Back to my half breed thing . . . do we have a name for me yet?" Mathew asked randomly.

Victoria tilted her head again and asked, "What do you mean, Mathew?"

"Well, I'm not entirely an Elemental but I'm not entirely a Vampire. So what am I?" Mathew clarified his question.

Dracula paused a moment to give the question thought and replied, "I believe you would be a Blood Elemental."

CHAPTER ELEVEN

BLOOD ELEMENTAL

Mathew was confined to his bed for a number of days as his body recovered and adjusted. His friends were his constant companions and, while still in recovery, he heard through the grapevine that the Elder Council had given permission to an Earth Elemental Ambassador to inspect this "new race" of Elemental. Mathew considered this strange because he himself had noticed little to no difference and how could one person be considered an entire race? But as long as he could still control ice, he didn't mind his transformation.

"So Mathew, have you noticed any other changes with your body that you can tell so far?" Steven asked after a few moments of idle conversation.

"Not much. I have noticed some of my senses are keener than I remember," Mathew answered after thinking it over.

"Care to explain? I know I'm shoving this down your throat but put up with it please . . . the council keeps riding me about you," Steven explained with a calm, clear voice.

"I understand. Well, my night vision has greatly improved . . . and I mean seriously improved. It's like I have night vision goggles on or something. Also my sense of smell has increased . . . don't take this the wrong way but Julian wears a little too much perfume for my taste," Mathew admitted.

"You can smell that? Anyway, is there anything else you can tell me before you're able to walk again?" Steven asked with more tension in his voice.

"Yeah, my hearing is rather sharp. If I concentrate I can hear your heart beat," Mathew said thinking about it again.

"That settles it! You have the traits of a Vampire," Dracula butted in like a proud papa.

"It's positive that he successfully inherited the Vampire gene?" Steven asked Dracula.

"We won't be able to ascertain the success of the transformation until he matures a bit more, but neither Victoria nor I mentioned any details about our special abilities and Mathew was able to detail each one of them. Then again, he could have knowledge of that information from his Demonology classes . . . but knowing Mathew I don't think he would lie about something this significant," Dracula replied as if he had known Mathew for a lot longer than he actually had.

"Okay, ya'll. I need to make a report to the Council. Thanks for the update, Mathew. I promise I'll try putting an end to these stupid interviews soon," Steven said as he hurried out the door.

"Mathew, after you are strong enough to walk again, we would appreciate the honor of your company at the Manor for an extended period of time. In layman's terms, Mathew, would you mind coming to live with us for a while?" Dracula asked with a strained tone in his voice.

"Is there a specific reason or you just want to hang out . . . get it? 'Hang' out?" Mathew chuckled at his own joke. He didn't mind the idea of going to the Manor but he still wanted to know what the motivation behind the invitation was.

"Yes, I 'get it'. No specific reason. I'm just having a dark feeling about something . . . I would call it a premonition," Dracula stated, his face more serious than Mathew had seen.

"I know what you mean. Something doesn't seem right," Mathew agreed. He had been burdened by a similar sense of inexplicable worry for the last couple of hours.

"So, is that a yes?" Victoria asked her eyes all hopeful.

"It's a yes; I want to get away from this place until I'm able to do things for myself again," Mathew said sitting up and moving to the edge of the bed.

"You are going to try walking now?" Dracula asked.

"It's been a few days since I tried last, so I might be able to walk. I'm feeling optimistic and a sense of urgency to get a move on,"

Mathew said as he forced himself to his feet. After a few moments of pain and regaining his balance, he was able to slowly hobble around.

"You're able to walk! Should we leave now?" Victoria asked politely but Mathew detected a hint of joy in her question.

"Yes, but can you do me a favor, Victoria?" Mathew replied as his body was in a momentary pain.

"Yeah, sure. What is it?" she asked happily.

"Can you go tell my friends that we're leaving shortly? I don't want them think I just walked out on them after all they've done for me," Mathew said with a kind smile

"Of course, Mathew, no problem. I will be right back," Victoria said as she turned into a little silver bat and flew out of the room.

"I will assist you in your packing. What specific items do you want to bring along? Where is your satchel?" Dracula asked as he got up from the couch.

"Satchel? I keep forgetting that you've been around for centuries and then, out of the blue you come up with a really old word like 'satchel'. Just help me find my Demonologist badge and, if you could throw some clothes in that bag there, I would really appreciate it," Mathew said as he waved his hand at a random bag in the corner of the room. "Where's my cross?" Mathew asked since he hadn't seen it since he regained consciousness.

"Nothing to be concerned about; I'm having the magic drained from it so it will not cause any more unfortunate incidences," Dracula answered as three men in tan uniforms came into the room. Two of the men looked like ordinary soldiers and the other had a more professional appearance. The weapons each were carrying, though, Mathew hadn't seen since he left his Human form. They were guns.

"Which one of you is Mathew, the 'so called' Blood Elemental?" the professional looking soldier asked.

"Who wants to know?" Mathew said using the line he heard on so many TV shows. He felt so cool for using it.

"I'm Rune, the All Seeing Demonologist and Sergeant in the Elemental Military Police. I'm here to ask you a few questions," the man said flashing a badge that had the symbols of every Elemental race on it.

"It would seem to me that if you were truly 'all seeing', you would have fewer questions to ask. Anyway, what's with the guards?

If you're only here just to ask some questions, why have an armed escort?" Mathew replied using the insight he had developed when he was studying to become a demonologist.

"Hold your questions! They will be answered at the Earth Elemental capital," Rune said lowering his voice.

"I don't think that's going to happen," Mathew said getting ready for a fight even though he already knew that he wouldn't last long in his weakened state.

"You don't have a choice," Rune said motioning to the guards.

"Step away from the Blood Elemental," a firm voice came from behind before the guards had a chance to do anything.

"On whose orders?" Rune demanded, turning around only to face the tip of an Ice blade not more than a few centimeters away from his nose.

"By order of the Ice Elemental Military," Bell said with two other people dressed in all white, blades at the ready.

"What is the meaning of this? You are in direct violation of the Universal Law of the Elements Section 59!" Rune yelled.

"No, you are in direct violation of Demonic Negotiations protocol, Section 1, under the proper procedure for Royal Vampire inquisitions," Bell shouted even louder.

"This is an Elemental, not a Vampire!" Rune argued.

"Fortunately for us, you are quite wrong," Dracula said coming out of the same shadows he had faded quietly into. Even Mathew had forgotten he was still there.

"Who the hell are you?" Rune yelled.

"Royal Vampire Count Dracula and this Elemental is carrying my blood within his veins," Dracula said in a calm but threatening tone of voice.

"Why hasn't this anomaly been registered? We demanded an update two weeks ago!" Rune yelled.

"Because you were ordered to wait until our next update," Samantha said calmly as she stepped into the room with Steven and a few other Elders. None looked happy with the current situation.

"You people were given a very specific time limit and details of proper procedure, including the course of action we would take with or without your cooperation. You knew full well when we would arrive!" Rune shouted and showed no sign of compromise. Mathew thought Rune was overreacting just a little bit and wondered about the real motives behind this visit. He also wondered why an "all seeing" Demonologist seemed so in the dark about things.

"Look at your options here, 'Rune', was it? You are trespassing on Ice Elemental territory and you have threatened to arrest one of the highest-ranking demons without a Universal Warrant from the Council of Elemental Kings and Queens. That alone is punishable by death. So, I have one question for you and your men; are you willing to die for your mission?" Samantha asked and the two soldiers looked at each other a moment.

"No, we're not," one of the soldiers said as he disintegrated his weapon.

"Hey, I'm just a volunteer," the other said also disintegrating his weapon.

"What are you two doing? You are under my command and I have not given you orders to stand down!" Rune shouted, still refusing to admit defeat.

"Bell, arrest this man," Samantha ordered.

"Yes, ma'am. Rune, you are hereby under arrest for entering an Ice Elemental citadel without a permit and for harassment of a Royal Vampire," Bell said as her fist landed across Rune's head when he tried to resist. It took only moments for Bell to wrestle Rune to the ground and freeze his arms to prevent further struggle. Once subdued, Rune was quickly escorted out of the room. Mathew was thankful all over again that he and Bell were on the same side. She was really a force to be reckoned with. Rune was twice her size with an ego to match.

"Excuse me, but are we free to go?" one of the soldiers asked nervously.

"Yes, because you cooperated no punishment will come to you," Steven replied.

"Okay, let's get out of here then," the soldier replied.

"Hang on, Jack," the other soldier said. "No hard feelings, Mathew. We were just doing our jobs," the soldier continued as he held out his hand.

"Don't worry about it," Mathew said shaking his hand.

"Same here, Mathew. Lance and I have been friends for a while and we weren't about to die for some cocky bastard like him," the other soldier said whose name was supposedly Jack, also shaking Mathew's hand.

"Like I said, don't worry about it. I understand following orders," Mathew replied as the two Earth Elemental soldiers quickly walked out of the room.

"I hate Earth Elementals. They are so . . . earthy," Samantha said simply with a slight shudder of disgust.

"What was that about?" Dracula asked after the room was clear of outsiders.

"The Ice Council was accused of creating artificial demons. The Earth Elementals sent a Demonologist to deal with the issue," Samantha explained though her voice didn't have its usual calm tone.

"Opportune for the 'gentlemen' that Bell came in when she did as I was about to permanently settle the matter," Dracula replied with a cold, serious voice.

"Mathew, I suggest you go stay with the Vampires for a while until you're able to handle yourself," Steven suggested even though that was Mathew's original plan.

"Actually, we were just about to do that before they interrupted us," Mathew explained.

"No argument then. Is there anything you want us to do?" Samantha asked out of courtesy.

After a moment of thought Mathew answered, "Yes, Samantha. Are you able to keep an eye on Ilium and Sara while I'm away? The Earth Elementals might go after them since they are my friends and are very important to me."

"Don't worry, Mathew. I'll take care of that immediately," Samantha said heading out of the room.

After that, Mathew was able to pack at his own pace with the help of Dracula and Steven (who seemed to just linger about whenever the Count was around). When Victoria finally returned from her task, and after everything was gathered, Steven showed them to a portal. Despite his aversion to the liquid looking mass that just hovered in midair like some ominous creature, Mathew drew a deep breath and stepped into the portal. It always seemed to latch onto his skin and pull him in like it was some horror movie monster.

"Ugh. I have always hated teleporting. Flying is much more enjoyable," Dracula said when they arrived at the small demon town.

The group's first stop was the police department. Mathew had been there before on his first visit but this time it was the Count that needed to talk to someone.

"Well, well, well. What do we have here, fellas? Two Vampires and an Ice Elemental! Not the usual combination!" John exclaimed as he saw the group enter the station.

"Correction, John, three Vampires. Mathew is an official half-breed now," Dracula said giving John a friendly punch which John seemed more than able to sustain the force of.

"No kidding? Well! That'd be good news then, I guess," John replied as he slapped Mathew on the back so hard Mathew lost his balance. Luckily for Mathew, Victoria was able to catch him before he hit the ground. That was the first time Mathew realized how strong she actually was and wondered if a female Vampire was that strong, how strong would he be as a fully recovered half-breed?

"Oh, I'm sorry about that, Mathew! Didn't realize I hit you that hard," John apologized.

"You didn't, John. I'm just weak at the moment," Mathew said as he regained his balance.

"That's a shame . . . anything I can do for you? I owe you one for getting those Fire Elemental political bastards off my back," John said offhandedly complementing Mathew on his investigation.

"Thanks, but I don't have anything at the moment . . . Oh, wait! There is something," Mathew said as an idea dawned on him.

"Tell me and I'll see what I can do for you," John said motioning them into his office.

As Mathew walked through the station a second time, he recognized some of the same faces but they were more inquisitive and looked a little friendlier than his first time there.

"Is there something about me that the others don't like?" Mathew asked when the door was closed.

"What . . . oh, you mean the other officers. You smell a tad different and most of us here heard the rumors of you having another Demonologist guest arrested," John said, his chair creaking as he leaned back on it. It was clear news can travel fast even without technology. Mathew wondered if there was a communication portal lying about somewhere. That would take care of the lack of technology.

"Actually, the demonologist part is true," Mathew began, catching the inspector's attention. "Anyway, John, I need to keep my presence here on the down low. If any Elementals besides Ice come looking for me, don't tell them anything. After they leave, please contact the Ice Elemental Elder Council and inform them of the situation then come and give us a heads up at the Mansion," Mathew finished and took a few deep breaths because his chest suddenly started hurting.

"Deal. Now don't take this the wrong way but apparently Dale just brought in a regular of ours and I have to cut our little get together short," John said walking out of the room to deal with one of the criminals.

"That's our cue. Let's make our way quietly and quickly to the Mansion," Dracula said and the group headed out of the police station

On the walk back to the Manor, Mathew began noticing all the curious looks and whispers that followed them. When the local demons spotted them, he even noticed some nose twitching. Mathew guessed they were catching his scent to try to establish who and what he was.

The walk through the woods was relaxing and, as Mathew had been too busy with the investigation last time he was here to notice, it was as if he was seeing everything for the first time. When they approached the Manor, he noticed that it was also created with the classic Gothic architecture; it made the building look more like a castle than a manor.

"Home sweet home!" Dracula said stretching his arms when they entered the dimly lit atmosphere.

"A little too grand to be called sweet, that's for sure. I do have to admit, though, that there is something special about this place and it has a certain air about it," Mathew said inspecting the sweeping entryway that had large curving staircases on both sides of the room leading to areas that he wasn't familiar with yet.

"Let me show you to your room. You will be staying in the same room you had the first time you were here," Victoria said motioning for Mathew to follow her.

Victoria led Mathew up the staircase, to the right, down the hallway to his room and left him alone to unpack and settle in. As he started reflecting on his first encounter with the Vampires, Mathew couldn't shake the feeling that came with the room. He kept feeling a sense of extreme comfort and safety. This didn't bother him but it did put him on the alert to be cautious about things that were happening around him.

"Excuse me, Mathew, may I come in?" Victoria said as she came into the room and quietly closed the door behind her.

"Sure, what's up?" Mathew asked with a welcoming smile.

"Can I have a little sip? Dad told me I couldn't drink your blood until you were better. Now that you appear to be better . . . may I?" Victoria asked keeping her distance for the meantime, as if she was stalking her prey.

"Um, yeah, sure I guess . . ." Mathew said his stomach did a flip-flop and started to give him the butterflies.

"I have been wondering if your change would affect the taste . . . you may feel a slight twinge of pain," Victoria said before she sank her fangs in and went about her little ritual that again lasted about five minutes.

"So, ah, how was it?" Mathew asked when she removed her lips from his neck.

"Well the taste isn't affected too much, but there is a slight change in it . . . I'm trying to put my finger on it. Maybe a little peppery. I can't place the taste at the moment but it isn't bad," Victoria began as she started cleaning Mathew's neck with a cloth. "But I am relieved that I'm able to still do this," she said with a smile.

"Why are you relieved?" Mathew asked a tad curious about her choice of words.

"Well . . . usually we Vampires don't feed off of each other unless it's for relationship purposes. There's something about Vampire blood that has an unpalatable taste to another Vampire. That's why we usually seek out others not of our kind. But it seems that you, on the other hand, still have enough of your sweet, silver Elemental blood to keep the pleasant taste to it," Victoria explained and that explanation somehow made complete sense to Mathew.

"May I ask you a question, then?" Mathew said wondering about the butterflies.

"I suck on you, you suck on me . . . that sounded like a bad excuse to me," Victoria said trying to make her own version of the phrase, 'you scratch my back and I'll scratch yours.'

"It's okay. Anyway . . . What level of intimacy is there when Vampires feed on each other? I mean, compared to Humans so I have a better understanding," Mathew asked feeling a little embarrassed.

"The level of intimacy . . . I would say it would be comparable to making out or a marriage proposal but don't quote me on that as I have absolutely no idea. Why do you ask, Mathew?" she replied with complete honesty.

"Well, before you fed I had serious butterflies and I was just wondering if it's like, my new hormones or something," Mathew explained as some other emotions rolled through him.

"Butterflies . . . I haven't had those in a while but it could be your body still adjusting. If that's the deal, you should start trying to hone your body to use both Ice and Vampiric abilities," Victoria suggested before leaving the room to allow Mathew to settle in.

Mathew rested until nightfall so he could practice. He went through his mind and concentrated on certain perks like the night vision and a heightened sense of smell, but what he was really after was the ability to transform into a bat like Dracula and Victoria. Everything was new again and the entire process in learning all of these things on his own reminded him of when he first became an Elemental.

So intent on learning his new abilities, Mathew didn't realize how much time had passed until the sun came up. He decided that he should take a break for a while and, after an hour of rest, he worked up enough courage to take a look around his temporary home. The great hall was as magnificent as Mathew remembered from when he first met Dracula and then proceeded to insult him—the second introduction, though, was much less dramatic and they were actually able to speak like civilized people.

While he was looking around at the pillars, Mathew spotted the throne that was made out of a type of wood that was naturally a deep charcoal color and had a few red crystals imbedded into the back of the chair. After he finished examining it, Mathew couldn't resist himself and sat down on the chair just to get a feel for it.

Wow . . . this is actually rather comfy, Mathew thought as he looked out at the large hall that was empty. It seemed lifeless and still. The only sign of activity was a few red embers burning in the fireplace. Even then, they only emitted a small glow.

"Now my servants! Bring out the dancing girls! Chop, chop!" Mathew said aloud just for a little bit of fun. He immediately became embarrassed when he heard laughing coming from behind him.

"Mathew, if anyone else but you took the liberty to sit in my chair and command dancing girls, they probably would not fare well. However, I never expected you to say something like that," Dracula said stepping out from behind Mathew while he was still laughing.

"Oh, excuse me, Sir. I couldn't resist," Mathew said as he quickly got out of the chair still feeling embarrassed.

"Relax, Mathew. Don't believe all those movies that are out about me; I'm actually a rather nice guy. As long as you don't get on my nerves, mind you," Dracula said not the least bit upset.

"I managed to figure that out myself. So is there anyone else here or is it just us?" Mathew asked looking at the empty hall.

"Just us at the moment . . . but my brother may be joining us later," Dracula said thinking the question over.

"Your brother . . . one of the original Vampires?" Mathew asked. His stomach did another flip-flop as he thought about the probability of meeting someone with that type of prestige who wasn't Dracula.

"You are not feeling well?" Dracula said as if he knew.

"Yeah, lately my stomach has been acting strange . . . and I have been getting a little dizzy now and then," Mathew answered and quickly created a glass of iced water. He drank the water quickly, disintegrated the glass and then watched as the water seemed to sink back into his skin.

"Show off," Dracula said with a soft laugh. "I think there is something I can do for you but I need to wait until my brother arrives," Dracula replied after thinking it over a little more

"What's on your mind?" Mathew asked.

"My brother is a master at creating items that are able to carry enchantments. He created Vampire's Crucifixion, although he might be a little upset that I'm having the remaining magic drained from it," Dracula said with another loud laugh as he reflected on his memories of his brother.

"Hey, Dracula . . . something just hit me," Mathew said rather quickly.

"Well, what is it then?" Dracula replied.

"Do you have a first name?" Mathew asked out of a slight realization.

"I do but I haven't told anyone and it is only used by those who already know it," Dracula replied. He seemed to insist on being secretive.

"I know this is hardly related to our previous topic, but can you tell me about yourself? We have known each other for a while but I would like to know more about you from personal experience, not just hearsay," Mathew explained with a simple, yet honest tone because he wanted a better understanding of this ancient Vampire.

"We went over a similar topic a while ago. Do you have something specific so I don't have to repeat myself?" Dracula replied recalling the previous conversation.

"Well, nothing comes to mind right now. I'll ponder that question. However, which one of your brothers am I going to be meeting, anyway?" Mathew asked after a little thought.

"Aiden. He is currently living in a castle somewhere in Europe. Life isn't as safe for Vampires in Europe as it is here. I don't think the latest Vampire craze has hit the Old World yet and there are still people around whose family lines were significantly impacted during our more, um, active days. It's amazing how the Royal lines can actually manage to locate each other when we want to visit," Dracula replied giving a very small and meaningless description of his brother.

"A castle? That must be quite a crowded tourist place if it's out in the open," Mathew exclaimed.

"It's not like that. The castle itself is within a Demon sanctuary so it's completely safe from Humans," Dracula corrected. "Now Mathew, my apologies for cutting our conversation short but I have to prepare for my brother's arrival," he said before leaving Mathew alone.

With an unknown amount of free time on his hands, Mathew decided to explore the mansion again and came to the conclusion that it was as 'Human' as it could get. The mansion had everything that a Human house would like bathrooms, kitchen, bedrooms and even a TV room (which didn't seem to get much use).

"I wonder how they got the money to pay for all this?" Mathew asked himself before sitting down in the TV room just to relax.

"When you have lived as long as my dad has, you know how to make money quickly and easily," Victoria said catching Mathew's comment.

"Hey, Victoria! What's going on?" Mathew said happily.

"Oh, I heard you walking around so I decided to join you," she replied sitting down next to him.

"Yep, this place is huge so I decided to explore when I finished practicing my skills," Mathew said as a small dizzy spell hit him.

"Oh? May I help you with your practicing?" Victoria asked with a soft, sweet voice.

"Are you able to teach me how to turn into a bat?" Mathew quickly asked, he tried his best to hold back his enthusiasm; but now that he was part Vampire, he desired to be able to do and experience all the perks that came with that territory as soon as possible.

"I could probably do that . . . I need to ask dad for the elixir though," Victoria replied.

"Wait . . . it's a potion?" Mathew asked not hearing of an elixir before now.

"Not really, you can still do it without it . . . but it's a lot easier with the elixir, just think of it as a steroid," she clarified. "Stay here I will be right back," Victoria said before running off.

Mathew flipped on the TV to catch up on the news. An announcement that surprised him was that of the murder that he solved; apparently the cult was ironically caught at a costume party, thanks to an anonymous tip off. Mathew knew the things the cult did were terrible but that just made him laugh. How could a brain mastermind a series of complex homicides and then get caught at a costume party?

As the program switched to a different news story, Victoria ran into the room carrying a bottle of something that looked very questionable to Mathew. Dracula came in immediately after her and watched while Victoria wrestled with the lid of the bottle.

"Okay Mathew, drink this," Victoria ordered handing him the bottle of questionable liquid. It was an acid blue color to it and looked like it had the ability to cause serious gastrointestinal issues.

"Why are you here, Dracula?" Mathew asked as Victoria handed him the bottle of strange liquid and, unsurprisingly, it was just as foul smelling as its appearance was bad.

"Just overseeing the process . . ." Dracula stated but he seemed to cut his statement short.

"Alright then. Okay . . . down the hatch," Mathew said before downing the liquid that burned as it went down. It continued to burn as it settled in his stomach.

The reaction was painful and lengthy. Mathew couldn't see what was happening to him but he could definitely feel it. He put his hand against his chest and instantly knew what was going on. His body was beginning to rearrange just like Dee's did but not as severe. Instead of his entire body transforming like Dee's, the only visible transformations were his chest and legs. By the amount of pain though, Mathew was fairly certain that some internal organs were shifting around and changing positions—perhaps even size—but he couldn't tell. The most painful of the adjustments was when something attached to his spine shifted. After what seemed like hours, the pain finally stopped and Mathew sat up feeling extremely tired but remarkably well.

"Wonders never cease," Dracula said after everything had finished moving.

"So, I guess that isn't supposed to happen," Mathew said finding it hard to talk.

"The process is unique to each individual but there are some standards we've come to expect. What happened to you was something entirely new that I haven't witnessed myself before," Dracula corrected himself.

"So . . . What now?" Mathew said struggling to stand up.

"Now you go to bed to recover and we will talk tomorrow," Victoria said as she helped Mathew up.

When Mathew was finally able to get to sleep after all the excitement, he had a nice, dreamless sleep. This was perfect for him because he wanted to learn how to transform and it was just like when he was learning how to use his Ice magic for the first time. After a good, long rest, Mathew hopped out of bed and bit down on his lip by accident. His canine teeth seemed to have gotten a tad bit longer.

"Feeling better now, Mathew?" Victoria asked with a smile. It was clear that she was just as excited as he was.

"I feel great! I don't know exactly what happened to me but I like it!" Mathew exclaimed with more enthusiasm than usual. "So how do I transform?" he continued to ask.

"Okay, now everything is mental. Your body will react to your mind. So, basically, if you think about turning into a bat you will," Victoria explained.

"Okay, I'm going to try," Mathew stated closing his eyes and picturing his body transforming. Mathew felt his skin crawl, so naturally he tried to itch himself but something was holding his hand back. So Mathew opened his eyes finding Victoria was extremely larger than he.

"Awesome! You managed to do it on your first try!" Victoria exclaimed with apparent glee as she picked him up and took him to the mirror.

Mathew was indeed a bat. He was white and rather furry and he realized with disappointment that he wasn't the size of Dracula. He was, though, still a large bat. Mathew struggled to get upright but his wings were getting in the way and he wasn't used to them yet. Finally Mathew was able to get situated by lying across Victoria's arm. Mathew then decided to try to fly . . . and fell to the cold, hard ground for his efforts.

"It seems like you can't do everything on the first try," Victoria teased. "Just flap your wings around like wild fire and try to use the air currents . . . if there are any in here," she continued trying to give him simple flying lessons.

Finally Mathew was able to get off the ground a couple of inches and attempted to fly higher. After a few tries, he began to realize when he was going to crash and aimed for something soft like the couch or Victoria, if she was close enough. He eventually mastered the basics of flying and landing after lots of bruises and lots of time. The next thing Mathew tried to do was learn how to hang from random objects. This was an entirely different challenge and he kept slipping and falling off.

"Well, Mathew. You will get the hang of it eventually," Victoria said with a silly chuckle at her own joke. "Come on, Mathew! Let's go show Dad," Victoria said obviously having fun as she skipped down the hallway. Mathew flew after her, trying not to run into a wall or a lamp or some strangely placed paintings.

"Hey, Dad! Mathew did it!" Victoria yelled when she saw her father.

"I'm a bat!" Mathew said pleased as punch with himself as he flew around the room. Then Dracula transformed into his big scary black bat and dwarfed poor little Mathew.

"And I'm a much larger bat! Now I will teach you about the food chain," Dracula said menacingly as he started to swoop at poor Mathew who was still getting use to flying.

"No fair! You have more mass than I do," Mathew pleaded as he tried to out fly Dracula. The atmosphere was full of fun and joy and Mathew relished it while it lasted.

"I haven't had that much fun in a long time . . ." Dracula laughed as both he and Mathew transformed back to their regular self. "But now I need you two to get ready for the little get together tonight. Apparently my brother decided he wanted to see the Blood Elemental as soon as possible," Dracula explained with his voice still full of joy.

"Do we need to dress up then?" Mathew asked still smiling.

"Just a little more formal than usual. It's not every day two ancient Vampires get together with their families," Dracula explained.

"Who is coming over, Daddy? Victoria asked.

"Do you remember your Uncle Aiden who lives in Europe?" Dracula asked.

"Oh, him! He has that beautiful castle. I haven't seen him in about 15 years," Victoria said after a moment of thought.

"Yes, darling. It's just going to be him . . . I was hoping that he would bring his daughters or maybe his son but they all have plans," Dracula said with a slight, depressed sigh.

"What time did he say he was going to be here?" Mathew asked trying to get a few more details as a chime rang through the house.

"Apparently right now. Go put on more formal attire while I go greet him," Dracula said quickly walking out of the room.

Mathew dashed to his room to find some nicer clothes. He just threw on the fanciest looking thing he could find and then quickly moved to meet their esteemed guest. Mathew found Aiden in the entryway chatting with Dracula. He was a very majestic looking man. Aiden's hair was different than Dracula's. It looked like a honey brown color with blonde and red highlights, but Mathew was still uncertain. Aiden wore an emerald green cloak over his clothes that were a purplish color with a dash of red and black.

"Brother! Is that him?" Dracula's brother asked noticing Mathew who was inspecting them from the balcony.

"Ah yes. Mathew, please come down and introduce yourself," Dracula ordered so Mathew obeyed trying to make a good impression.

"So. You are Mathew. Even in Europe we have heard about your small achievements. So far, so good," he said a little more coldly than expected. Mathew analyzed him carefully. Aiden obviously wasn't as easy going as Dracula was. His voice was extremely formal, cold and semi-monotone but he seemed nice in his own way.

"Thank you very much, Sir. May I ask your name?" Mathew said pulling out his best manners.

"Polite for an Elemental. Yes, you may. I am Dracula, Count Aiden Dracula," he said in his cold voice.

"A pleasure to meet you, Count . . . Dracula," Mathew admitted a little confused as how to address the 2nd Count.

"Count Aiden, please. Nice to meet you as well, Mathew," Aiden said as he shook Mathew's hand. "Now, let me see you," he said and, before Mathew had a chance to react, Aiden was examining him.

He held Mathew's head up by his chin and Mathew didn't understand what he was looking for. Aiden moved Mathew's head to the left then the right, pressed down on Mathew's cheeks for a few moments and then spun him around a couple of times.

"You're a fine young Vampire, Mathew," he said after he finished examining him.

"That reminds me, brother. I need to talk to you about a cross for Mathew," Dracula stated.

"I remember. We will discuss that later," Aiden replied.

"I'm sorry I took so long," Victoria said running down the stairs in a beautiful blue dress.

"My darling Victoria! How are you?" Aiden asked with a small smile.

"I am well, Uncle," Victoria replied using more proper grammar than usual. "And how are your daughters? I was disappointed when I was informed that they would not be accompanying you on your visit," Victoria asked again using the proper grammar that sounded to Mathew that she was trying too hard.

"Victoria, you don't need to be so refined. I am no different than when you came to see me when you were younger," Aiden explained patting his niece on the head.

"Oh thank god . . . no offence, Victoria, but that was really strange," Mathew said happy that he was able to break the formality and be himself.

"It's not often that I get to see my uncle and I would like him to remember me as the proper girl I was," Victoria said.

"What do you mean by was?" Aiden asked calmly and Mathew suddenly caught a glimmer of evil intent in Dracula's eyes.

"Oh, I haven't told you the big news, have I?" Dracula said trying to keep a straight face but Mathew caught a glimpse of a mischievous smile.

"And what news would that be, brother?" Aiden asked as his curiosity piqued.

"Our little Victoria is now engaged," Dracula said and Mathew instantly saw what the Count's plan was but couldn't say anything.

"My, my, my . . . that is rather big news! A little younger than I expected but you are of that age and I'll be expecting plenty of nieces and nephews. It will be nice to hear young laughter again," Aiden said simply but the comments were enough to thoroughly embarrass Mathew. Mathew's face turned light blue as he began to blush and he was unable to look anyone in the eye.

"Guess who the lucky man is," Dracula said slightly nodding towards Mathew.

"You're joking . . . Mathew's her mate?" Aiden asked the surprised tone in his voice irritated Mathew. But he was still too embarrassed to actually do anything about the comment.

"Yes, he is," Dracula said with a grin that seemed to grow wider as he saw Mathew's embarrassment. Victoria just stood there with a smile and a light blush doing a small swishing movement with her body.

"A little young, isn't he? He isn't even an adolescent Vampire yet," Aiden asked.

"Well, thank you so very much for your vote of confidence," Mathew said thoroughly discouraged.

"My apologies, young Mathew, but usually Vampires don't mate until they have at least reached the adolescence stage. Most wait until the adult stage. You're still considered a toddler . . . no offence or anything; your body just needs time to mature and adjust . . . before you can perform a husband's duty," Aiden said making Mathew lose some of his self-esteem.

"Don't feel badly, Mathew. I haven't even gone into my adult stage yet," Victoria said trying to make Mathew feel better.

"Yes, but at least you're an adolescent . . . I'm just a baby," Mathew replied still discouraged and depressed.

"Now brother, let's discuss that cross," Aiden said as he and Dracula left Victoria and Mathew for another room.

"So . . . how many do you want?" Mathew finally asked when the embarrassment eased up and he could talk again.

"I don't know . . . we will probably end up having like . . . six," Victoria answered quietly.

"Six? Don't you think that a tad overdo?" Mathew asked because he had never pictured himself having six screaming children. He consoled himself with the thought that a Vampire Countess would probably have plenty of help.

"It's not like we would originally plan for six. It's just that we are immortal and, as we never grow old or go sterile . . . accidents happen," she explained calmly with a smile.

"I guess that makes sense. There are no old Vampires then?" Mathew asked after he thought about it for a few seconds.

"No, there aren't. Take Dad for example. He is seriously old but he still looks like he is in his twenties or thirties. I personally think it's so we can continue to hunt and attract the opposite sex," she said with a small yawn that gave Mathew the impression that she had gone over this a few times before.

"Are you tired?" Mathew decided to ask after noticing the slight bags under her eyes.

"Just a little bit . . . I think I'm going to go to bed," she said as she gave him a little kiss on the lips. Victoria walked off while Mathew was standing there stunned from the sudden kiss. It made him feel like his first kiss all over again.

After Mathew got over his sudden happy feeling because of the kiss, he wandered back to his own room. Adapting to his new body was starting to become a problem for him and the only way for him to regain his proper mental state was to practice swordplay.

Luckily his room was large enough to do that activity and regain some equilibrium.

The methodic exercise of swordplay calmed Mathew's mind and he figured it had something to do with the fluid movements. Now that he was half Vampire, they felt more like shadow movements but, as soon as he thought that, he felt like a stupid nerd.

As Mathew was finishing a swing, his door flew open and hit the wall with a loud bang, which startled him, and he released his blade that somehow managed to spin around and cut his arm wide-open. He stared in startled silence as silvery blood quickly splashed onto the floor.

"I'm so sorry! Hang on, let me see the cut," Aiden said grabbing Mathew's arm. Mathew already knew it was bad seeing how quickly his blood was running onto the floor.

The cut was deep and Mathew noticed the smell of his own blood, it smelled like water from a special lagoon or something along the same lines as Victoria's interpretation of the taste.

"I'll be right back. I'm going to get the med kit . . . if they have one," Aiden yelled as he flew out of the room.

Mathew knew he didn't have time to wait for help as his blood was draining fast. He quickly looked at the blood and noticed that it was shifting colors from silver to a dark shade of red then it completely separated in half, one side was silver and the other side the dark red.

Mathew stood frozen with his hand clenched around his arm. He was scared and closed his eyes to calm his thoughts and just to think. As he heard a single splash from his blood as it hit the floor, he had a brilliant idea.

He quickly collected his thoughts, grabbed the base of his arm and, in an instant froze it solid to stop the blood flow. He was still in a lot of pain because of the large cut, but put his only working hand into the large puddle of blood and closed his eyes. When he sensed the essence in his blood, he took control. His blood began to slither like a long snake toward the open wound and into the small vein which was cut open just a little bit, but it was still enough to be life threatening. The pain was the worst part of the process. He ripped his shirt, rolled up the cloth and put it in his mouth so he wouldn't break his teeth when he clenched them together because of the pain. As bad as that was, it was far more painful when Mathew forced the two parts of the cut vein together and froze around it thoroughly so he was positive that his blood wouldn't be leaking inside of his body.

"Okay . . . you're doing well, Mathew, just a little bit more," Mathew coached himself as he drew a deep breath and took a quick five-second break.

He turned his attention to the open cut itself, forced the torn skin together then froze the entire skin layer until it was smooth and in a thick layer of ice. He then removed the ice at the base of his arm, which was acting like a tourniquet, to allow the blood to flow freely again. The feeling of the blood rushing back through his veins was kind of soothing yet painful as hell. Mathew was exhausted after he finished. It was very difficult to stay calm enough to save his own life. Using his Ice Magic with his life's blood gushing to the floor was an opportunity for panic for most people. Mathew was finding it very difficult to think as barely enough blood was left to circulate to his head but he somehow managed to close the wound. Now all he could think about was sleep and he leaned back against the bed with his frozen arm and quickly drifted off to sleep.

CHAPTER TWELVE

COMPLICATIONS

Mathew woke up and instinctively felt his wounded arm that was now stitched and neatly sealed. Instead of having the thick layer of ice he had originally put on it, it was wrapped in a crisp, white bandage. He slowly got up and felt something smack against his chest. He looked down and inspected what it was; the shape puzzled him for a moment until he realized it was his new cross. This cross was silver in color and the arms had details engraved into the smooth metal, not vines this time, but unusual symmetrical patterns that didn't appear to have any rhyme or reason.

The details puzzled him for a few moments. Then it struck him where he had seen them before; along with the unusual patterns they were the same bat imprints that were once on Vampire's Crucifixion and, in addition to the bats, there were snowflakes carved into each end of the cross. It was the gem in the middle that really captured his attention, though. It wasn't like anything he had ever seen before. It was ice blue on one side and ruby red on the other with a pure white slit down the middle that made it look like a cat's eye. All in all, it wasn't as beautiful as he previous cross but it did make a huge visual impact. Mathew took his good arm and tried to take it off it wouldn't budge. He followed the chain and found that it was imbedded into his skin. There was no possible way of removing it.

"Well, looks who is finally up!" Victoria's cheerful voice said as she opened the door. She was carrying a bowl of something that smelled very good.

"How come I'm always knocked out when something big happens!?" Mathew yelled getting annoyed at this increasingly common scenario.

"Even though you did a great job in getting your blood back inside your body, you still lost enough to put you out for a while," Victoria said as she set the soup down on a tray for Mathew. "I didn't know you could control blood," she continued.

"If it's a liquid, I can control it. What's in this soup?" Mathew asked as he gave it a few more sniffs.

"Just stuff that will help you heal . . . by the way, Dad went to a meeting with the Ice Council so only Uncle Aiden is here. Oh, and myself of course," Victoria said with a small laugh.

"Do you smell something?" Mathew asked catching the scent of something that wasn't the soup.

"Now that you mention it, I do," Victoria agreed standing up trying to track the scent.

"It smells familiar but I can't figure out why," Mathew said as he began on his soup.

"Hey, do you two smell something?" Aiden asked walking into the room.

"Yes, but we can't find out where it's coming from," Victoria replied.

"What's up, Aiden? I like the new cross . . . so thanks," Mathew said giving a proper thank you.

"You are welcome. I thought it would be better for me to put it on so you would adjust to it in your sleep. And, by the way, it's actually a good thing I put it on you when I did," Aiden said looking around the room for the smell.

"Why is that?" Victoria asked a little curious.

"One moment . . . here it is," Aiden replied as he started to search for something in his pocket.

"Your blood wasn't mixing at all since your soul is half Vampire and half Ice Elemental. It appears you were producing two different types of blood . . . and they were rejecting each other . . . think of it like oil and water," Aiden explained throwing Mathew a small vial of Mathew's own blood. The blood looked like two different substances that stayed as far away from each other as possible.

"Well that makes sense, I guess. Does the cross have a fancy name like 'Vampire's Crucifixion'?" Mathew decided to ask on a hunch.

"Yes, it does. I named it Blood Ties because of the chain that allows both Vampire and Elemental blood to mix properly. You can never take that off so I hope it's comfortable," Aiden said sarcastically as he started looking around the room.

"I understand and thanks again," Mathew said before Aiden left the room still searching for the smell.

Mathew again spent more of his time incapacitated in bed. It was starting to become an irritating habit and somehow accidents were the source of all his wounds. He had experienced more life threatening accidents in his short Elemental/Vampire life than any accident he had in his entire Human existence.

At the same time Mathew was again able to use his body to the fullest; Dracula returned from his short trip and wanted to talk to Victoria and Mathew alone. He explained the main reason for the trip; apparently the Council wanted to reevaluate the pending marriage contract and decided that, because Mathew was now a cross breed never seen before in the Elemental or Demon world, the fact of his mere existence was already enough to void the contract.

As quickly as they came, Mathew and Victoria's marriage plans were now gone. Dracula left the two alone to discuss this turn of events.

"What do we do now?" Victoria asked breaking the heavy silence between them.

"I don't know . . . should we actually do this right?" Mathew suggested.

"I would like that . . . . but not right now. We need to give it some time," Victoria said with an unhappy tone.

"That's agreeable," Mathew said not in the mood to argue.

"So . . . . Are things going to be weird between us?" Victoria asked obviously feeling that way already.

"No . . . absolutely not. I hate it when relationships end because of stupid things. I was just getting used to the idea and now . . . nothing," Mathew said thinking quickly.

From past experiences he knew he only had moments to work before their friendship (and possible future together) was in jeopardy. As he quickly thought, an idea popped into his mind and it seemed like the only option to prove he didn't feel any different about her.

"Are you thirsty?" Mathew asked using his idea that had potential to work.

"Now that you mention it, I am a little parched," Victoria said happily accepting the tribute.

The awkwardness that had started to settle in between them was gone after Victoria's feeding, and everything seemed to be okay by the time she left.

Mathew started contemplating his life again. The weird feeling of everything always going right was fading fast and with it, his positive outlook. He now realized that when he was Human, he was a pessimist and anything that went right was always a bad omen of a disaster just waiting to happen. Now that he was an Elemental, everything was better and the everyday things such as eating and sleeping were something Mathew disliked and no longer needed in his new life. His body was fine tuned to control ice at will (which he was getting good at). He decided he was now more of an optimist than he had been in his Human life so he wasn't paying much attention to the unfortunate events that had happened along the way (like his multiple brushes with death). His thoughts engulfed him so much that he didn't notice the figure moving towards him.

"What are you thinking about?" a voice came that made Mathew jump to his feet. "Oh, calm down, big boy. It's only me," Dee said when she stepped into the moonlight that was shining through the windows.

"Dee! What are you doing here?" Mathew said then invited her to sit down on the bed with him.

"I heard you were here so I came to give you a personal visit. Also, I did hear about the transformation. Why didn't you let me know you wanted to be a half-breed? I would have gladly given you some of my Succubus essence," Dee complained for no apparent reason.

"Well, it's not like I had a choice, and I don't think it works like that," Mathew said in his own defense.

"Yeah, sure. Oh, that reminds me. I still have your stuff at the house and mom wants to see you again . . . I don't know why," Dee said with a strange tone.

"She is a nice lady . . . don't take this the wrong way, but I kind of get nervous around a group of Succubi I don't know," Mathew admitted.

"You mean the girls at home? Most of them ask about you and would like to meet you. You are becoming quite popular among the

Demons here. Come on, let's go right now I'll introduce you to them," she said encouraging Mathew to come by pulling on his arm.

"Okay, okay . . . I just need to tell Dracula where I'll be at so we don't cause a crisis," Mathew said leaving the room quickly then returning just as quickly after he delivered the news.

"Alright, let's go," he said heading to the front door.

"Here we go," Dee said as her wings flew out with a "swoosh" and she took to the air.

Mathew turned into a bat and enjoyed flying around outside. There was a nice breeze and seeing everything from above was exhilarating. Eventually he needed to be flown in Dee's hands because he couldn't keep up with her larger wing span. Mathew liked the feeling of flying. It was so freeing and invigorating and, from above, the small demon town (which he didn't actually know the name of yet) looked beautiful. When they reached their destination, they came to a slow descent and landed gently on the sidewalk.

When Mathew entered the Succubus Palace, everyone stared at him making him feel very uncomfortable. Dee noticed this and quickly led him to her own room on the top floor with the rest of the Succubi rooms. Her room was similar to the room Mathew stayed in the first time he was here except it had more personal effects. There were pictures and a few books that they both used during their short class time with each other. Dee's room was not at all what he was expecting. Mathew thought it would be more seductive like the room he stayed in where everything seemed to have an aphrodisiac, but Dee's room was nothing close to that. There were splashes of pink and purple on the walls with little statues of gargoyles and, after looking around, Mathew couldn't help but notice Dee's closet contained quite a large selection of lingerie. Dee quickly closed the closet door after she noticed it was open.

"Don't you know it's rude to look into a girl's closet?" she said making a quick joke out of the situation.

"Well, it's not like it was closed. An open closet is an invitation to look," Mathew pointed out with a small grin.

"Fair enough. So what do you think? It's not every day I get a visitor . . . especially of the male variety," Dee said for no apparent reason.

"It's a nice room but, don't take this the wrong way, I'm not comfortable talking about your . . . I'll just say 'business'," Mathew said putting it bluntly so it wouldn't get awkward.

"Don't worry about it. I still have three years before I need to start doing that stuff and I'm planning on making those three years last," Dee explained even though she didn't say where she got the three years.

"Good enough. Honestly, Dee, I don't want to think of you that way," Mathew said trying to keep the conversation going.

"Funny, because if there is any Elemental who could understand us, it would be you, Mathew," she said as her tone of voice changed to a more sweet and comfortable.

"Why do you say that?" Mathew decided to ask when he picked up her tone.

"Most Elementals don't have the training to understand us or the desire to know us. They are rude. But when I first met you, you knew that I was a Succubus without me telling you and you treated me the same. You weren't afraid of me like the others," Dee confessed recalling her experience with other Elementals.

"What's going on, Dee?" Mathew asked curious about all of these personal revelations about him.

"I heard about your engagement with Victoria. And I wasn't sure if you would ever want to see me again . . . because of you being a Royal Vampire now," she admitted as she took a seat on the bed next to him.

"Dee, the only thing that is different about me is the color of my blood. I'm not any different than I was last time you saw me, and besides, I'm not one to forget who my friends are," he explained.

"Excuse me, but I hear that a special boy is somewhere in here," Catharine's voice came into the room as the door opened.

"Yes, I'm here, Catharine," Mathew said with a smile when she entered the room.

"Hello, Mathew dear! How are you?" she asked before surprising him with a friendly hug.

"I'm feeling better than ever due to my new upgrade," Mathew replied with a little smile and did a flexing motion just for effect.

"So sorry about your engagement, dear boy," Catharine continued. Mathew was surprised that she heard about it so quickly.

"Don't worry about it. This will sound mean but it was political so it's not affecting me as much as I think it is Victoria. How well do you know her?" Mathew asked as a thought entered his mind.

"I knew her before I had my Dee so I know her rather well," Catharine replied. "I thought of her as my own daughter. I would dress her up in cute little dresses and brush her long hair," Catharine said with a giggle as she thought of the fond memories.

"It's not my place to ask, but would you mind going to talk to her? You know just to make sure she gets everything she needs to say out in the open?" Mathew asked.

"Yes, I can do that," Catharine stated.

"So what will you do now, Mathew?" Dee asked.

"At the moment I'm just waiting for the Council to handle things on my behalf," Mathew replied.

"I certainly hope things get settled quickly but, if you ever need a place to stay, I can always have the Temptation room reserved for you," Catharine offered with a big friendly smile.

"Um . . . I don't think I would want to stay in the Temptation room," Mathew admitted, not trusting a room with that type of name or reputation title.

"What's in a name? Don't worry about it, silly. Come look for yourself," Dee said leading Mathew to the room.

The doors opened into a huge room. It was well furnished with black silk everywhere. The room had a hot tub on the balcony with a great view of the city.

"Well . . . what do you think?" Catharine asked although she already knew the answer.

"I'll take it!" Mathew exclaimed simply, eyeballing the super-sized bed which was twice as big as a king size. He felt like a little kid wanting to jump on his mom and dad's bed.

"Oh, that's so wonderful, Mathew! Why don't you spend the night here?" Catharine asked politely.

"I would love to but I'm not too safe outside the protection of the Royal Vampires right now . . . no offence or anything," Mathew said walking up to the bed.

"Mathew, look at me," Catharine ordered.

When Mathew turned she was right up next to him. She had moved as quickly and as silently as a wolf. She opened her eyes and caught Mathew's gaze.

"Mathew . . . you need to rest, so sleep," she said stroking his face like a cat would do when it played with a helpless mouse. With a single tap to his head, Mathew was out like a light.

He woke up the next day feeling refreshed. He sat up and noticed that he was in pajamas that weren't his and there was a funny smell in the air that smelled like candles or perfume . . . he couldn't tell which. Mathew got up and sniffed around the room trying to track the source of the smell. To his surprise, he found a few extinguished purple candles and, even though he was feeling great, he felt a bit violated that a person who was supposedly his friend put him into a trance without his permission. After a moment of thinking things over, Mathew changed into his regular clothes and tried not to think about who changed him out of them in the first place. He was certain that no one would confess to it.

"Mathew, are you okay?" Dee asked as she crept through the door.

"Yes, I'm fine but I'm not very happy about what has happened here. What was that trance about?" Mathew asked a little agitated about being hypnotized.

"Mom was showing me how to use charm. I did ask her to show me a different way but she said it would be better if it were going to be with someone who would agree to it. I'm sorry, Mathew. I hope you're not angry with us," she replied with big eyes trying to soften him up.

"I'm did not agree to it and I do feel betrayed," Mathew admitted.

"Pardon me for caring about my daughter!" Catharine said who just seemed to show up.

"Well if it isn't the wicked witch herself," Mathew said partly joking.

"Do you know what I like about you, Mathew?" Catharine asked as she drew closer.

"No I don't and it doesn't really matter to me after what happened last night," Mathew said after a moment of trying to think ahead.

"You're got a good sense of humor . . . and you're cuddly," Catharine said suddenly giving Mathew a hug that he wasn't ready for due to it being so early in the morning.

"Mother! Stop it! I know what you're doing," Dee said giving her one of the worst looks Mathew has seen in a while.

"Oh, my apologies, Mathew. I just enjoy playing with my food . . . forgive the analogy," Catharine said letting out a slight chuckle.

"So now I'm food?" Mathew was offended and feeling a tad violated.

"You are aware of how we work, darling boy. By the way, some of the girls would like to talk to you. I'm just mentioning that because they are interested in the new hybrid that is staying here for the moment," Catharine explained.

"I am not staying here by choice but I guess I could see a few of them. A *few* of them . . . not a whole room full," Mathew said trying to be pleasant about the issue in spite of what had happened.

"If you say so; I'll be right back with the girls," Catharine said leaving the room.

"Mathew, what are you thinking?" Dee asked out of the blue.

"Nothing really, why do you ask?" Mathew replied.

"I'm just reading your sexual level," Dee said.

"Why are you doing that?" Mathew asked a little curious.

"Practice," Dee said quickly but Mathew figured there was more to it than that.

"Okay, girls, here he is," Catharine said swinging the door open to allow a swarm of women (who were wearing a variety of costumes) to mob him. They were all asking questions that were completely unrelated to each other such as "can you last longer than regular Elementals?" or others like "what does blood taste like?". The chaos was too much for him and he thought he would rather die than answer half of the questions, so he did the only thing he could think of.

Mathew transformed into a bat and flew out the window as fast as he could. Lucky for him, the Succubi weren't expecting it so they screamed and got out of the way.

Mathew decided that it was best if he went back to the mansion despite his urge to sleep in the "Emperor sized bed", as he called it, again. The mansion was in sight when Dee and Catharine flew up next to him.

"I'm sorry about that, Mathew. I told them not to mob you," Catharine apologized but Mathew knew she wasn't sincere and he didn't care.

"Well . . . It's okay . . . . I forgive . . . you," Mathew panted between breaths. He wasn't used to flying such long distances yet so it was quite a work out.

"Oh, you poor dear, come here," Catharine said as she grabbed Mathew out of the air and held him close to her chest. "Your fur tickles," she said with a giggle.

"Catharine . . . you don't . . . need to hold me . . . . directly on your chest," Mathew said trying to catch his breath.

"Mom, let me hold him," Dee said trying to take Mathew away from her.

"Sorry, dear. Mathew stays with me. He is tired and is recovering the best way he can," Catharine replied, tightening her grip on poor Mathew who felt like he was being body strangled.

"Okay, thanks. I want to fly on my own now," Mathew said while he wiggled his way out of Catharine's grip and flew the rest of the way to the mansion.

"That was a bunch of fun!" Catharine said as she landed.

"You're not supposed to do those things, Mom," Dee argued.

"As long as I'm here, I will have that chat with Victoria. You two kids have fun," Catharine replied before she disappeared inside of the Manor.

"I'm truly sorry about her, Mathew. She has been like that for as long as I can remember," Dee said trying to explain her mother's odd behavior.

"Ah, there you are, Mathew. Good to have you back . . . and with Succubi of all things," Dracula said poking his head out from the door before they had a chance to enter.

"Hello, Dracula, Sir," Dee said politely.

"Hello, Dee. Good to see you but I need to have a private chat with Mathew," Dracula said quickly pulling Mathew aside. When they were inside a private room with the door locked, both Dracula and Aiden confronted him.

"Mathew, how did you get the blood back in your body?" Dracula began.

"What? Oh, it's a liquid so I froze it and forced it back in," Mathew said after recalling the event.

"Mathew, no one, even Ice Elementals, can freeze and control blood," Aiden corrected.

"Well I did it . . . Maybe they've never tried. All I remember is blood has quite a bit of water in it, if I'm correct that is." Mathew tried to explain, his memory of that situation was fuzzy because of the panic and blood shortage to the brain.

"Mathew, blood isn't just a liquid. It's one of the very basic essences of life itself. It is life. And there are no 'Life' Elementals that we know of," Dracula pointed out.

"So how did you manage to do it?" Aiden asked.

"I told you how I did it. Do you think it's part of my Vampire side . . . you know, instead of drinking blood I control it?" Mathew said trying to piece things together.

"That seems possible . . . do you know what this means?" Aiden said giving Dracula a look.

"I'm three steps ahead of you, brother," Dracula said pulling out a bowl of liquid that Mathew identified instantly as blood but it looked odd; even for blood. It looked like a pool of black goo that didn't seem to be very healthy.

"Now freeze it," Dracula ordered with an incredibly serious voice.

"To anything in particular?" Mathew asked.

"Just freeze it," Dracula repeated except he wasn't his usual pleasant self. Mathew had a strange feeling that the gloves had come off for a reason not apparent to him.

"Okay, sure," Mathew said as he held out his hand over the bowl.

He closed his eyes like he when he was working with his own blood. He searched for the same sign as he had before and, when he found it, took control. A vivid picture popped in his head. It was the memory of him flying over the mansion and seeing everything from a unique vantage point. He then felt a thump of power ripple out from his cross. Mathew opened his eyes and was amazed to see his creation; it was a perfect miniature replica of the mansion out of red ice.

"Incredible! He can even freeze a mixture," Aiden said with his eyes wide while standing in his usual serious pose.

"Excuse me but a 'mixture'?" Mathew asked confused by the statement.

"We mixed every Elemental blood type into that bowl and you froze it as easily as if it were water," Dracula said.

"My apologies, brother, but I'm going to be returning home now. I must tell the others about this extraordinary ability," Aiden said leaving the room.

"Mathew . . . do not tell anyone about this. I must have your word," Dracula said with his usual composure but still a hint of seriousness in his voice.

"Yeah, sure. I give you my word," Mathew agreed still not understanding the significance of this new ability he had. It had been so easy for him to transform the blood that he didn't think it was such a big deal but, as it even made Dracula serious, it must be something unusual.

After Dracula dismissed him, Mathew went to his room and was alone for a while until none other than Steven showed up to deliver some news.

"How have you been, Mathew? Seriously! I had a hell of a time finding this place," Steven complained in character. Mathew felt refreshed to have someone act normally around him again. He was getting tired of everyone seeming to walk on eggshells around him.

"Oh, I'm alright. Accidentally cut my arm open with my blade but otherwise it's been fun," Mathew said with a smile.

"Wow that sucks. But anyway, I'll cut right to the chase; your new transformation has every Elemental nation on edge. We're actually trying to figure out how they found out about you so quickly but the main problem is the Fire Elementals have accused us of trying to create a super soldier. The Water Elementals, flakes that they are, think that we have evolved into the next generation. Who knows what the Earth Elementals think! You know how it goes. Anyway, the bottom line is that there is meeting at God's Step. Purpose is to discuss what's going to happen next," Steven explained quickly.

"Interesting . . . What do you mean 'what's going to happen next'? And I assume the only reason you're telling me this is because I'm going with you," Mathew replied simply.

"Smart lad. That is exactly the reason; we need to prove that you're not just a weapon," Steven said.

"Just a weapon? Interesting . . . I hope I don't sound too girly when I say this but . . . will I be safe enough?" Mathew asked trying to strategize and figure out in advance what could possibly go wrong.

"Don't worry yourself, girly dude. King Stanly of the Earth Elementals has restricted the number of troops to one hundred for every race except Ice. Since we are your 'native tribe', we are allowed to have a maximum of three hundred troops," Steven replied.

"That seems excessive. That huge amount of people just to protect me?" Mathew said a little ashamed that so many people were going through a lot of trouble because of him.

"Mathew, the only reason we have that amount is because you're more of an asset as an Ice ambassador and Demonologist than you are as a Blood Elemental," Steven explained.

"Ice Ambassador? When did I get that job?" Mathew asked, he never recalled taking any classes on that.

"It's just one of our leverage points for the conference, and hard to argue when I'm visiting you in Dracula's own house." Steven pointed out.

"Point taken. But why does the King of the Earth Elementals make the rules for every race? Why's he the boss of everybody?" Mathew asked trying to sort through the details to get the big picture. He was a little confused as he dug through his memory banks. He had studied the other races extensively but was quickly discovering that not everything had been covered.

"Good question. My understanding is, to put it simply, we all live on dirt and Earth Elementals control all the dirt so they make the rules," Steven explained in a simple but effective way.

"So when is this thing going down?" Mathew asked and figured he had better start packing now.

"It's in two weeks and, before you ask, there is special teleportal that takes us there. So, it's not like we will be swimming through rock, lava or anything like them," Steven explained sarcastically.

"What's it like?" Mathew asked trying to figure out what he is dealing with.

"It's just like it is up here. It was created when every Elemental race joined together to make a sanctuary for all the 'special people'. It's where we have our wars, meetings, celebrations, so on and so forth," Steven said giving Mathew a visual of Earth as if it were just inside of a big cave.

"Will anyone else I know be there . . . other than you?" Mathew asked, he believed he would be more comfortable with people he knew around to calm him if he got nervous.

"I'm bringing Julian, obviously, and last I heard Vanguard is all up and arms about something involving you. That may be it but you know others will come if they want to," Steven answered and Mathew couldn't help but wonder what kind of mayhem Bell could be calling forth.

"Okay. I had better go back with you so I can pack some fresh clothes," Mathew decided.

"Come on then, girly dude. We need to technically hurry because I, personally, still have a lot of work to do with the council," Steven said as he stood up.

Mathew quickly packed up a few things he felt he would need and explained to everyone what was going on. As a goodbye present, the Count gave Mathew a bag with a gland (or something equally as gross) from a punished Vampire that, even though removed from its original body, still produced an unlimited supply of blood. The Count explained that Mathew would need to have it on hand in case of an emergency.

Catharine gave Mathew a hug and a wet kiss on the cheek, which sent Dee into a slight fit. Victoria said her farewell different than the others. She said a simple goodbye, gave him a hug and a stealthy nip on the neck that no one else seemed to notice. With a smile, she let him be on his way.

"So Mathew . . . have you been playing around with that girl?" Steven asked giving him a funny look.

"What girl?" Mathew asked while he started preparing his mind for another one of Steven's stupid argument.

"The one that just gave you the nip on the neck. She was clever about it but I saw it," Steven said giving him a funny look.

"That girl is my former fiancée, if you recall. We haven't been 'playing' but we have grown close since we were engaged to be married until about 24 hours ago," Mathew said a little depressed.

"You can always ask her to marry you on your own. I'm sure she wouldn't mind," Steven replied.

"We have brushed over that topic. We decided that we were going to do it right . . . if we decided to even try after this. No more questions, please," Mathew said as he started to feel a heavy weight of depression coming over him.

The trip back to the Ice Fortress was quick. Mathew was now used to the walk into town since he had done it several times before. Mathew had become oddly attached to the little Demon town even though he rarely went into the town itself because of the circumstances he currently was in. This time, though, as he walked right through town and spotted a store with the town's name on it. The town's name was Dark Cove.

Dark Cove was comforting to Mathew. He enjoyed walking in the street and looking at the beautiful buildings as he passed by them. He was still glad to return to the cool mountaintop fortress he had called "home" since his Human death. The first thing Mathew did when he got back to his room was create a super-sized bed like the one in the Temptation Room at the Succubi palace. He then happily went to sleep because he couldn't resist the bed's allure.

Mathew woke up in a great mood . . . so great, in fact, that he decided to turn into a bat and fly around the room just to burn off some of the extra energy he accumulated during his rest. As he happily flew around his room, Bell entered. Unfortunately for Mathew, Bell was not aware yet that Mathew could transform into a bat. When she saw him swooping around, Bell created her sword and began to swing at him with great fervor. She only stopped when Mathew screamed at her, "Don't hit the bat!"

"Oh! I'm sorry, Mathew! I heard you came back but I had no idea you could do that," Bell quickly apologized.

"Good news is that at least you didn't sever a wing or decapitate me. Your retirement must have decreased your skill," Mathew joked when he was back in his original form.

"Mathew, I know you're going to the conference of the Elementals," she stated.

"Yes, I am . . . is it classified?" Mathew said trying to figure out what she wanted.

"No. Maybe . . . Only a little bit. Okay. Anyway, since you're going, I'm going with you . . . and I'm not debating about this," Bell said which sounded more like she was ordering him to take her along.

"That's fine with me. I'll enjoy the company," Mathew replied simply just happy to have her go with him.

"Oh . . . I expected you to be opposed to me going with you," Bell said caught off guard and became slightly confused.

"Is there a specific reason you want to go along?" Mathew asked curiously.

"I just want to make sure you come home safe," Bell said as her tone changed from assertive to worried.

"What's on your mind, Bell?" Mathew said now positive this was more than her just wanting to go on a trip.

"I'm just concerned about a few things. I'm fairly certain that something is going to happen . . . so that's why I'm going. Just to watch over you," she answered.

"Bell, if you're that determined . . . how about I just make you my bodyguard?" Mathew said trying to compromise even though he actually wanted her to come with.

"I don't think I would be allowed to do that because of the protection already assigned to you. I mean, you basically have the entire Ice army to protect you," Bell said trying to work out all the facts.

"I don't think it would hurt to add a shadow guard," Mathew said trying to come to terms with her decision.

"I don't think it would hurt either but I won't go against regulations," Bell stated as Steven and Julia walked in.

"What's this about?" Julian asked.

"Julian! Nice to see you again. I'm just trying to convince Bell to be my bodyguard during the conference," Mathew said even though it was originally Bell's idea.

"I don't see a problem with that," Steven said simply.

"What about the troop limit?" Bell asked.

"I don't think one extra Vanguard is going to cause that much of a problem . . . not to mention a retired Vanguard," Steven said ending the problem.

"Okay then, it's settled. I'm going," Bell affirmed for no apparent reason.

"Get packed then. I can't have any bodyguard in my employ without anything decent to wear. I'm a stylish guy, after all," Mathew said which inadvertently kicked Bell back into her military personality. She saluted and was off to fulfill the task given to her.

"Weird girl. Very weird," Steven said after watching her march out of the room.

"She's not weird, Steven. She's sweet," Julian said argued. "Welcome home, Mathew. Are you nervous about the conference?" she continued.

"A little bit. I'm just not sure what will happen. I haven't been to a shindig as official as this before," Mathew replied.

"Not many of us have. Don't worry about it, though. You weren't some type of secret project. You are a product of necessity and the circumstances surrounding your transformation are very easy to prove," Steven said trying his best to calm Mathew.

The day continued like it usually did with Steven poking fun at Mathew then Mathew getting mad and storming out of the room. When he had had enough of Steven's raw sense of humor, Mathew went to visit Sara and Ilium. Sara, though, was out on a task for the Elder Council and Ilium was in a relationship so Mathew didn't stay long. After an awkward introduction to Ilium's boyfriend, Mathew left but couldn't shake the feeling that the man Ilium was dating was actually afraid of him.

Mathew then caught up with Bell who was practicing her swordplay routine. Impressed by her skill, Mathew made the mistake of asking her to teach him a few moves. Bell agreed but the lesson ended in a horribly humiliating defeat for Mathew. Bell, though, refused to let Mathew quit and insisted he continue until he knew how to hold his own. It took Mathew three hours to learn how to block only a few of Bell's swings. After a little while longer, Bell ordered him to return the next day after he had rested.

The next morning, he returned and was given the hardest lesson in swordplay he had ever had. He had to hold different poses, memorize different strikes, and develop a talent called Quick Draw, which was just the ability to summon a functional blade in a matter of milliseconds instead of Mathew's usual thought filled fifteen seconds.

These lessons continued for several days. He endured hours of straight swordplay with a highly skilled Vanguard. Once Steven found out, he insisted Mathew expand his skills to other things than just straight swordplay. Steven forced Mathew to fight using just Magic. Mathew didn't mind as much because Magic didn't cause his feet and hands to blister or exhaust his body. When Bell was satisfied with Mathew's progress, she decided to call it a day. Mathew was traumatized by the physical strain he had endured with the constant blows to his head, arms and a few to the groin which made him eager to learn how to parry that attack faster than the others.

"Mathew! Blink a couple of times, will ya? You're freaking me out!" Bell exclaimed as she sat him down on a nearby bench.

"What was that all about?" Mathew asked while trying to stop the motion sickness that came on him due to the unusual movements of the last exercise.

"The motion sickness will go away after a while," Bell said knowing what was going on. "And we did this because I wanted to make sure you could handle yourself in a fight," she explained.

"Dear God! I'm totally traumatized. Why, though? I still can't stop the images of your swings. Every time I blink I expect to be hit by something . . ." Mathew managed to say before he started muttering to himself.

"Mathew . . . Mathew! Snap out of it!" Bell ordered before she gave him a light smack across the face.

"See? Thank you, though. I still don't know why but I'm never doing that with you again," Mathew continued to complain.

"You would never want to be a Vanguard; the final is a 72 hour battle with your commanding officers. That will really traumatize you . . . try warding off both a blade and Art attacks at the same time," Bell said remembering the horrible memory.

"72 hours! No, thank you! I'm so sorry, though . . . why would you do that?" Mathew asked seeing Bell in a different light.

"I wanted to be a Vanguard and would have done more than that if I had to. I am proud of you, though. I didn't expect you to keep coming back every day," Bell said with a laugh but her tone made it sound like she was implying that Mathew was a moron.

"What else do I have to do? Anyway, did you have time to pack?" Mathew asked out of curiosity.

"Of course . . . we're leaving tomorrow. I am always ready on time. Did you pack?" Bell asked back.

"Well . . . Since I was so burnt out after our exercises everyday all I really did was sleep," Mathew admitted.

"Come on. Let's go," Bell said yanking him up by the arm and leading him to his room like he was a little boy.

"I can pack my clothes on my own, thank you," Mathew argued.

"Our present circumstance does not support your claim. You had two weeks to pack and yet . . . it isn't done," Bell pointed out which silenced Mathew's arguments.

After Bell forcibly helped Mathew pack his clothes, they parted ways and Mathew was left to himself. He didn't know what to do now. He was used to constantly having someone to talk with but now he was alone with his thoughts. Which were not a very good companion at the moment. Mathew ended up practicing his Ice magic so he didn't need to concentrate as much when he actually needed to use it.

Mathew didn't sleep that night. He was too entertained with making shapes and figures and lost track of the time. When Bell came to get him, Mathew grabbed his bag and the blood bag (as Mathew named it) and then followed Bell to the meeting spot. Steven was there already and greeted him with a snowball to the gut then proceeded to goad him about being such an easy target, even after all the training.

The teleportal that they were going to use was on the other side of the frozen fortress. To get there, they needed to go into an area that Mathew hadn't had the chance to visit on his own yet. When they arrived, Mathew saw the portal in clear view. It was almost impossible to miss. The portal was in the middle of a well-kept circular garden that had a small, bubbling brook running through it. There was an archway that seemed to support what looked like a dormant portal that hovered slightly above the ground.

The group stood in silence in front of the arch until Julian hit Steven, who seemed to have been daydreaming, on the back of his head. Steven jumped slightly and took action. The simple action of Steven tapping his staff on the ground caused the portal-like orb to go from its calm, dormant state to a wild and sporadic whirlpool that was glowing with a soft light.

"Alright! In we go. Me first!" Steven said as he walked into the unwelcoming, weird mass of liquid, which still looked to Mathew like a monster had just swallowed Steven whole.

Mathew stood back to contemplate the necessity of this trip. He was a little nervous and intimidated by the thought of walking into the liquid again and had no intention of going next but, then again, he didn't expect Julian to push him in either.

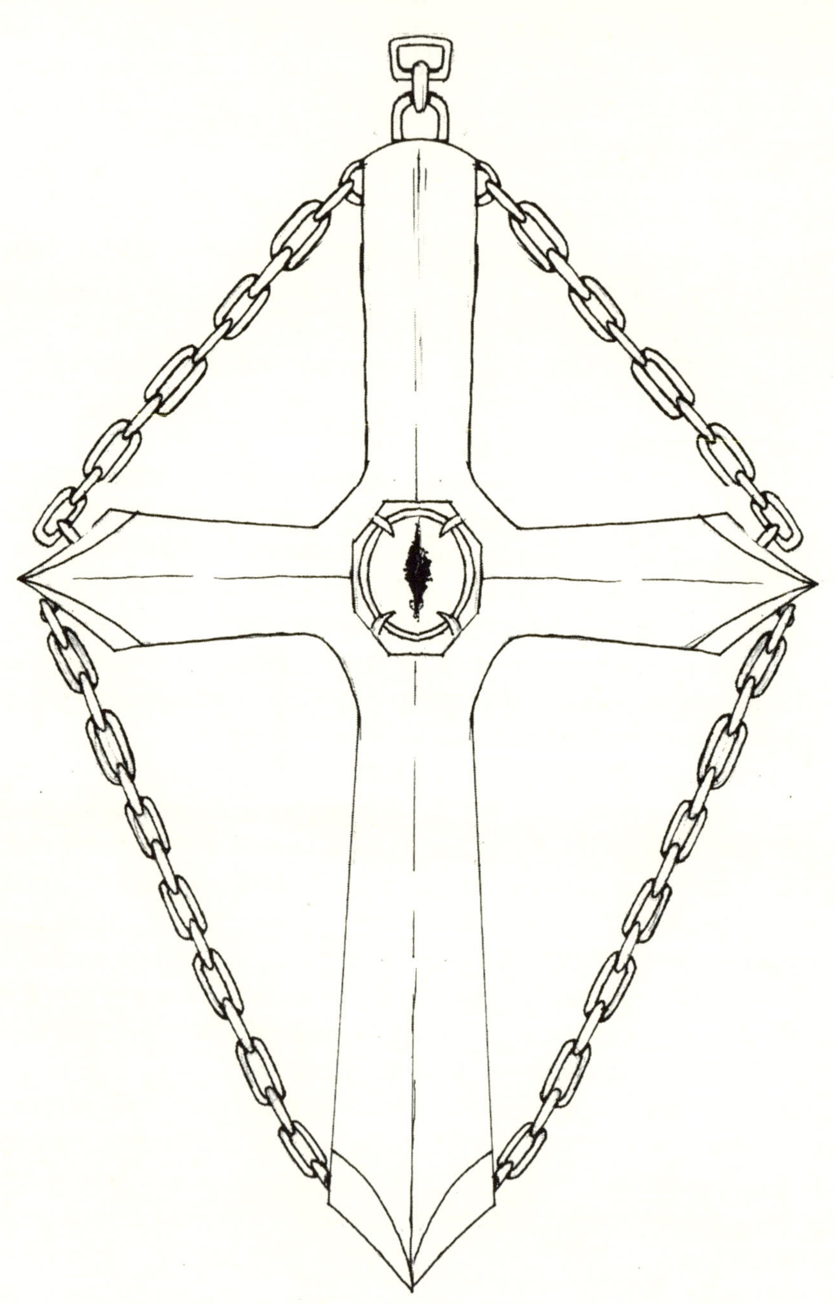

CHAPTER THIRTEEN

COMMITTEE OF ELEMENTS

When Mathew found himself on the other side of the monster portal, he realized they were inside a large cave . . . a very large cave. After his eyes adjusted, it was as though he had walked into another world. The cave itself was so immense that there were clouds above him.

Mathew gazed around in amazement. Everything he saw was so beautiful and pristine it was as if every good thing in nature had been carefully placed inside this cave. There were lush forests, grassy plains and, on the horizon, a large waterfall that created rivers that flowed into a large lake so big that it looked like an ocean.

Mathew assumed that the inhabitants of this world were segregated into their own unique areas. It was evident at his first glance where each Elemental race lived. The mountain on the farthest corner of the horizon was a large and worrisome volcano that was ominously producing black smoke. Mathew assumed the Fire Elementals lived there. Across from the volcano and closest to where the group stood was a glacial mountain and a vast tundra of ice. The ice field was populated with tiny houses scattered throughout it and, since they came out of the Ice Fortress portal at this location, Mathew guessed that they were in Ice Elemental territory. The Earth Elementals had the largest mountain with a huge forest growing on it. There was a large, ethereal looking castle on the edge of the ocean-like lake that Mathew assumed belonged to the Water Elementals. There were probably others who lived beneath the surface of the lake itself. He wondered briefly about Atlantis. Perhaps the legend was truth and could be found here.

The area that really caught his attention, though, was the Air Elementals'. They had the most surreal living area of all. They lived in a series of airborne mountains that were either flying or somehow suspended in the upper part of the cave. This reminded Mathew of a movie he had seen as a Human and made him wonder if Humans could access this area as well. He thought it unlikely that a Human could imagine a place like this so accurately. A giant castle rested on the largest flying mountain. There were separate buildings connected to the castle by rope bridges and small stone walkways that, even from where Mathew was standing, could be seen shifting as the mountains bobbed up and down.

In the assumed center of the cavern was a large structure that had multiple towers with walls. The walls were connected and formed some type of fractal shape Mathew could not identify from the angle he was at.

Mathew stood with his mouth open as he attempted to absorb every little detail. The 'sun' shining on them wasn't the actual sun at all. It seemed to be a replica of a sun or something with the same purpose. It covered a large expanse of the caverns' ceiling. Looking up at the 'sun' was how Mathew realized that the cave itself was a cylindrical shape that wrapped around the sun-like orb.

Mathew turned to get a different vantage point and noticed that the roads extending from the center of the cave were outstretched and appeared to curve upward with the cave. He didn't exactly understand the purpose for it so, like any tourist, he jogged to a nearby overlook and found the large, swivel binoculars that were common at Human scenic overlooks. Mathew peered through the binoculars and followed the nearest road up the mountain until he saw a town sitting sideways on the cave wall. To make sure it was actually sideways, he hopped over to a different binocular stand to check. Sure enough, the road was still sideways on the wall. A few clicks down the road, Mathew zoomed in and saw giant trees growing out of the cave walls, waterfalls with their water falling up towards the sky and small dots on the road that was actually a train running downwards. Mathew followed the train for what seemed like hours to understand where he was. The train defied gravity by following tracks that curved around the terrain until it looked like it was right side up again.

It was then that Mathew realized that he was in the very center of the earth. The reason the towns were on the walls was because the cylindrical shape of the cave caused the center of gravity to shift along with the individual's perspective. Depending where a person was, their location would seem normal and everywhere else was on the wall or ceiling.

"So what do you think of 'God's Step', Mathew?" Steven asked identifying the name of the new and truly amazing world.

"Mind blowing . . . This place is amazing! Do people actually live here?" Mathew asked dumbly for, even though his brain had solved the perspective issue, he was still not able to fully comprehend a town on the side of the wall.

"I'm sure you know the answer to that already," Steven said with a small chuckle. "We're going to be staying in a little town that's populated mostly by Water Elementals," he explained clearly enjoying Mathew's bewilderment.

A little confused, Mathew asked, "Why are we doing that?"

"I have three words for you; personal, hot and springs," Steven said getting excited as his eyes seemed to drift back into memory.

"So . . . is that the only reason?" Mathew asked with a lack of interest in the hot springs and wondered why any Ice Elemental would be excited about something related to boiling water.

"Trust me, Mathew. Yes, we are Ice Elementals and even we feel better after a long, hot soak . . . it feels a bit like melting," Steven said with another laugh.

Convinced, Mathew simply said, "Melting? All right, then. Lead the way," even though the idea of melting in a hot springs still did not interest him, however he had always wanted to visit one when he was Human.

Their only method of transportation was walking and Mathew was thankful that it didn't take long to get to their destination. When they arrived, they entered a little inn and the man behind the counter greeted Steven warmly. By the looks of it the two seemed to be old friends. Luckily, Steven was able to get the three best rooms available.

The rooms themselves weren't large but had more homey touches than Mathew had expected. He put his bag down to explore his room.

There was a bathroom, large closet and a small kitchen. Mathew opened a door and discovered the reason Steven was inclined to stay here; the bath was just like a picture-perfect hot spring from TV. It was steaming and incredibly inviting so Mathew did what he thought best; he ripped off his clothes and hopped in to the open-air bath. At that specific moment, the side of the cave he was on seemed to drift under a large object on the sky wall that blocked the sun. Mathew decided that there were small holes in the sky wall because specks of light shown through and gave it a starry, moonlit atmosphere that just seemed too perfect to be real. Mathew savored the heat that really did make him feel a bit breathless like he was going to melt but it was a warm and soothing feeling. He sat quietly with his eyes closed slightly, drifting off to sleep but, before sleep overtook him, a splash on the right hand side of the wall separating the baths spooked him awake.

"Oh! Hey, Bell . . . is that you?" Mathew asked.

"It is. Is that you, Mathew?" she replied.

"Yes, it is," he answered before letting out a loud yawn.

"Hey, guys! Don't forget about me," Julian's voice came from the opposite wall.

"You're enjoying the bath too, Julian?" Bell asked politely.

"Yes. It's my first time here and Steven has bragged about it every time he has come home from one of these large scale meetings," Julian explained just as more splashes came from her side. "Well, if you two would excuse me, I'm getting out. I'm not really supposed to be in here while pregnant, anyway," she said simply. Mathew could tell the heat wasn't exactly her thing.

"Hey, Bell. I'm going to get out too. I'll talk to you in a little bit," Mathew said before he hobbled out of the water.

After Mathew finished dressing, he decided to wander around the inn for a little sightseeing. There was not much of interest to see, a table here, a nice picture there so he decided to return to his room for a little rest. As soon as he saw a fresh swarm of people starting to mob the check-in desk, he cut short his small excursion and hurried back to his room. He didn't feel very social. There were some things that he had carried with him from his Human existence and not loving big crowds was one of them. Also, he was still adapting to this "no sleep" perk and felt like he needed a bit of rest. Just as he started to wobble into bed, he heard a few knocks at his door.

"Mathew!" Bell said barging into the room before Mathew had a chance to react. "My shoulders are killing me! Do me a favor and massage them out, please," she ordered desperately. It was quite obvious that her shoulders must have been really bugging her for quite a while for her to act like that.

"Okay, fine . . . would have been nice if you asked first," Mathew grumbled as he started the massage. "You're like . . . super tense, you know? It's ok to relax a bit every once in a blue moon or so," he suggested after a few moments of shoulder rubbing.

Mathew suddenly felt something through the shirt Bell was wearing. It started at her right shoulder blade and he traced it down with his fingers to the side of her hip.

"It's a scar, Mathew," Bell said calm and quietly and Mathew quickly went back to the massage.

"What happened?" he asked because he always heard the saying "every scar has a story".

Bell shrugged and said, "It was a fight with an Air Elemental; he managed to catch me off-guard," as she reached over her shoulder with her hand and felt where the scar started.

"Couldn't you just smooth out your skin . . . or something?" Mathew asked as politely as he could.

"I could, but it's a good reminder for me. Plus, some guys think it's sexy," she said with a small laugh.

"It's good to see you let your hair down, if only a bit," Mathew said still remembering the uptight Vanguard he first met who kept calling him "Commander".

"I took your advice about relaxing," she replied simply.

"Okay. You should be done; I don't feel the knot anymore," Mathew announced as he let go of her shoulders.

"Thanks, Mathew. I'll let you get some rest," Bell said standing up and started heading for the door. "I look forward to working with you," she said softly before she walked out.

After Bell left, Mathew became bored with his room and he couldn't get Bell's scar out of his mind, so he decided to head next door and see if he can bug Steven for information. He knocked a few times on Steven's hotel door until it opened.

"Oh hey, Mathew. What's up?" Julian greeted him when she answered the door.

"Hey, Julian. Is Steven around?" Mathew asked simply

"Sorry, Mathew. He left for a meeting but come in and I'll get you something to drink," Julian said stepping aside to allow Mathew to enter the room. "So . . . is there something I can do for you in his place?" she asked while she was in the little kitchen area.

"Yes, there is something that I would like to ask but . . . I'm not sure if I should," Mathew replied taking a seat in a nearby chair.

"Why? Is it something personal?" Julian asked bringing out a cup full of something-or-other.

"Well, I'm just curious about something," Mathew answered trying not to give anything away about his question.

"Here, drink this and I promise not to let anything you say leave these four walls," Julian said giving Mathew her almighty smile as she handed him a drink.

"Okay well . . . I know it's none of my business but . . ." Mathew began trying to figure out how to word his question correctly so it sounded like he wasn't prying into Bell's past. "Well . . . Bell has this scar on her back and I was just curious if you or Steven know anything about it?" Mathew asked before he took a sip of the liquid and instantly felt a fuzzy sensation course threw his body when the liquid hit his stomach.

"The drink is called Nether Brew. The Nine Tail Fox Demon makes it. The drink itself is for Elementals, not demons. It's like a liqueur that helps use our Art," Julian explained.

"Well, um, thanks for the drink . . . but you're avoiding my question," Mathew stated, fully aware that Julian was trying to distract him.

"Yes, I am. I do know why but, before I answer, what's your interest in this, Mathew? Excuse me for asking but it doesn't seem like you and I don't think it's your place to ask such an intimate question about another person. Seems like something you would ask Bell directly," she said calmly with her eyes closed but her tone, even though it was relaxed, was incredibly harsh.

"I suppose you're right, Julian. Sorry for asking," Mathew replied crumbling under Julian's small yet strong lecture.

"Mathew, just listen to me," Julian said taking hold of his shoulders and making him look her in the eyes. "Bell has had a hard enough life. She's my friend and I'm a bit over-protective of her. She may be a little older than a lot of Elementals here but her body and mind are still that of a young woman," Julian said simply with a look in her eyes that Mathew had never seen before.

"Okay . . . forgive me but . . . where is this going?" Mathew asked completely lost.

"It's not my place to tell you, Mathew, and I'm sure Bell will tell you on her own if and when she wants to. And, for the record, just because I know doesn't mean others do," Julian said and dismissed Mathew from the room because she was tired.

Disappointed and a bit embarrassed, Mathew went back to his own room. Julian's answer only served to pique his curiosity and made him want to know even more what had happened to his friend. He thought of hundreds of possibilities but made a point to forget all of them because he figured it would be best just to make sure that this wouldn't influence the way he acted around her.

Mathew put thoughts of Bell and her mysterious wound out of his mind and spent another night practicing magic. He was trying to make a continuous Ice Chain that would keep materializing like Spiderman's web as he flew it through the air. After several failed attempts, he decided the web chain was going to take too much time to perfect so he moved onto other things. He had fun making an elaborate chunk of ice and attempted to make it float in the air. Mathew practiced until he was finally able to make it hover a few inches off the ground but, as it was only a few moments in the air, he decided that wouldn't be useful yet. After a few more hours playing around, another knock came at his door.

"Okay, Mathew, it's time," Steven said pulling Mathew out of the room. He was with a few Ice soldiers who were dressed in full Ice armor. They looked awesome in Mathew's eyes but his admiration was cut short as he was pulled into some type of carriage. He thought the carriage seemed out of place—a bit weird even—for Elementals but Bell, in full Vanguard armor, joined him shortly after. The soldiers gladly welcomed her into their unit.

"This is a sudden move, Steven. What exactly is going on?" Bell asked trying to get a quick update.

"This is going to be Mathew's first appearance as the only Blood Elemental and tension is a little too high around here at the moment. We need to prove to the other Elementals that he isn't some type of secret project we've cooked up. We've decided to parade him around a bit in a hopefully strategic yet non-threatening way. You know, make him seem like a 'regular guy'," Steven said after they moved away from the Inn in the carriage-like transport. Mathew chuckled nervously as he saw the soldiers sitting on the outside of the carriage like Cinderella's mice coachmen while Steven, Mathew and Bell sat inside.

"Ok. So . . . what's my part of the plan?" Mathew asked getting a little jumpy because of the unusual seriousness in Steven's voice.

"For one, Mathew, you can relax! We can't have you all jittery and nervous looking. Most important, if you're asked a question, you answer the best you can but be smart about it. For example, if you are asked, 'Are you an Ice Elemental super weapon?' don't be a smart ass and say 'well, I could be.' This is really important because, in addition to negotiating for your very existence, we are also trying to negotiate for other things as well," Steven said trying to cover everything that crossed his mind.

The carriage came to a stop and a coachman announced their arrival. The door opened and Mathew was led down a path flanked by armed soldiers into a large room. He looked around and tried quickly to figure out the situation. They were in an enormous conference room where Elders of every race were in balconies looking down at him. He discovered he wasn't that nervous because this was just like the council room back at the Ice Fortress. There were five people in large chairs at ground level with Mathew. Each had multiple guards with different armor and banners to represent each Elemental race. All in all, it was a very regal sight.

"Is he in a daze?" one of the five people in the ground floor seating asked in a not-so friendly voice.

"Maybe he's daft and we have gathered here for nothing," another said.

"Pardon me, please. I was just taking in the situation," Mathew said trying to be as polite as he could.

"That was apparent when your nose was to the sky," the same man stated.

"May I start by first getting your names?" Mathew asked as politely as he could.

"Why should we give you our names?" another man asked.

"It appears by your position in the room that you are all incredibly important and I wouldn't want to be calling you 'Lord High Pompous,'" Mathew said turning response into insult. The man sitting in a chair behind Mathew started laughing.

"At least he has a sense of humor to him. But, he brings up a good point. If I remember correctly, which I am sure I do, this report said he isn't even two Elemental years old yet so he would have little way of knowing who we are," the man commented to the first man. "I am Earth King Stanly of the Diamond Dust," the man finished and Mathew now knew that this was the Earth Elemental king he heard about earlier. Mathew took a moment to give King Stanly a good once over. King Stanly was the most majestic looking person in the room and his face reminded Mathew of his grandfather's even though there wasn't a wrinkle on him. The dark brown hair made his eyes seem more sinister than they actually were and, while he was well built, he wasn't overly muscular.

"I'm Water Queen Dellina of the Tsunami but, please, I insist you just call me Dellina . . . or 'Mom' if you prefer," said one of the two women with a smile. Mathew thought she seemed a little quirky as she stared at him with a kind but spooky intensity. Her hair was light teal and looked more like seaweed than any hair he had ever seen. Along with her seaweed-esque hair, Queen Dellina had bright, intense emerald green eyes that added to her unusual appearance.

Next to speak was the man who had made the rude "nose to the sky" comment, "I am Fire King Ryan of the Inferno," King Ryan declared in a self-important manner. Mathew didn't think Fire King Ryan was too bad but his jet-black hair and his dark complexion made him look like he had just come through the back-end of an incinerator. This impression was so strong that Mathew expected to smell cinders any moment. Ryan was also trim and well dressed. He wore a crimson red suit that Mathew kept looking for scorch marks on. After confirming that there was no noticeable burn marks or even a dash of soot on his person, Mathew looked up and saw King Ryan's eyes were a dim crimson similar to his suit. Looking closer, Mathew saw what looked like tiny flames burning where the pupils of King Ryan's eyes should have been.

"I am Ice King Pompous-Pious," the man Mathew insulted earlier said with a little smirk on his face and his comment sent a ripple of laughter throughout the room. "I, too, have a sense of humor. My name is Ice King Marcus of the Black Ice," he concluded with a small chuckle, obviously pleased with his joke. Mathew analyzed him carefully since he was the Ice Elemental King. King Marcus had light blue hair and a horrible jagged scar on his neck. Mathew couldn't tell what caused it and, after the debacle with Julian the night before, he wasn't going to bring it up. While his demeanor was casual, Mathew really did want to make a good impression.

The final introduction was from a very young-looking girl. Mathew judged that she was in her late teens but, as Mathew knew elementals didn't age, the one thing that did stand out was that she didn't seem very noble. She looked very stiff and uncomfortable, out of place and appeared to be forcing the expected 'proper look'. She seemed very inexperienced and the only thing that made her stand out even more was that she had a person, some kind of helper, standing next to her when the other kings and queens sat on their own.

"Excuse me, Princess, but it is your turn for introduction," the royal helper said calmly.

"Oh! My apologies. I . . . I am the Air Princess Kallen. I don't have a fancy title; I'm just stepping in for my father. Or sitting in, rather. Air King Bradley of the Twister," she muttered after several pauses. She was kind of cute with her light pink hair that seemed to stick out more than her sleepy brown eyes.

"Excellent introduction, Your Highness," the royal helper praised her and Mathew then understood that the royal helper was one of the king's advisors and his purpose was to guide the young princess through this conference.

"A pleasure to meet you all. I am Mathew the Half Light Demonologist or you can just call me the Blood Elemental if you want. I'm not big on titles myself," Mathew said trying to give his introduction as best he could.

"It's a pleasure, young Mathew. Thank you for taking the time to see us . . . and by the way, who is the lovely girl by the door?" Queen Dellina asked noticing Bell who was keeping a very protective watch on Mathew.

"Ice Vanguard Second Class Bell, ma'am. I am here to ensure the safety of my charge," Bell said giving her usual quick introduction along with a small bow at the end.

"It's also a pleasure to meet you, Miss Bell," Dellina said with a smile and a nod.

"Dellina, are you quite finished yet?" King Ryan asked a little agitated by the delay.

"Yes, I'm finished! I suggest you cool down before I decide to extinguish you with a tsunami," Queen Dellina threatened with a crazy look in her emerald eyes.

"Enough!" King Marcus yelled. "Bickering and threats will not solve this issue any faster," the room quickly became quiet.

"Mathew, you are under suspicion of being a secret weapon developed by the Ice Elementals. Is there any truth to this?" an Elder finally yelled from above Mathew's head.

"No. There is not a single shred of truth in that statement," Mathew replied.

"Can you prove it?" another Elder asked.

"Give me a moment," Mathew said to mull over his thoughts. "Yes. I have all the proof within my short time as an Ice Elemental. My history in a nutshell . . . I accidentally ended up caring for a Succubus named Dee who is the daughter of a Succubus Matron named Catharine. After that and a lot of intense study, I earned my Demonologist license of which I am very proud of. The first assignment I was given was to solve a murder case, which I succeeded in doing within two or three days," Mathew said then paused a few seconds to think over the investigation. "A Fire Demonologist named Charles the Impulsive Blaze and his assistant, Keira, can confirm my story. Especially since the local authorities were preparing to accuse a nearby Vampire sect of the murders based solely on puncture wounds on the necks of the victims," Mathew explained and was interrupted by a deafening rustle of what seemed like hundreds of papers from each Elder. To have that much noise from a little paper rustling, there must have been hundreds of Elders present.

"Give us a moment, Mathew. Someone get that damn report!" Dellina shouted at a few Elementals who were just standing around, thus forcing them to frantically scramble around like ants. They returned in record time with copies of the files that they passed out to everyone else.

"There is record in Charles' report about a group of Ice Elementals escorted by a Demonologist who seemed to 'not know what he was talking about' . . . but that statement is questionable considering Charles' past inconclusive reports that did not hold up under questioning and even a few investigations . . . so please continue," an Elder said once the rustling papers stopped and everyone calmed down.

"Thank you. Where was I? Oh, yes. During the course of my investigation, I rescued a Vampire named Victoria who turned out to be the daughter of the Royal Vampire Count Dracula. If I remember correctly, and I'm sure I do," Mathew said with a small smile directed to King Stanly, "I mentioned this in my debriefing when I returned along with my evidence that the murders were committed by a Human and at that point the case was out of my jurisdiction," Mathew said which sparked the deafening sound of rustling of papers again through the room forcing him to wait until it was quiet enough for him to continue.

"Thank you. Later Dracula drew up a contract with the Ice Elementals. I was never apprised of the actual details of the contract. His daughter, Victoria, and I were engaged to be married to secure the contract. I'm not sure of the details myself but, logically, it seemed too important at the time to risk on some new procedure to fuse together two separate DNA codes," Mathew explained.

"How can we be assured that all this information you just gave us is actually true and not just an elaborate plan to make your existence look accidental? The entire process of you gaining such a significant reputation in such a short time seems too improbable and the story fits together just a little too well," King Ryan said as he studied a piece of paper that Mathew guessed was a timeline.

"I will personally vouch for him," a familiar voice rang out as the doors flew open and The Count himself made a royal entrance. Mathew tried to conceal a happy smile at the Count's arrival.

"Who are you?" King Stanly asked in a less than pleased voice.

"I am Count Dracula of the Royal Vampire lineage here to support my friend's testimony," Dracula stated loudly sending a mummer of scandalized whispers throughout the room.

"What evidence do we have to support that you weren't collaborating with the Ice Elementals to create a super soldier?" an Elder asked.

"My time is valuable and I would appreciate answering only intelligent questions," Dracula replied causing the Elder to curse rather loudly. "I am one of the original Vampires. My blood is of great value and is the key factor in the transformation of a Royal Vampire over a lower class vampire. Would I just offer it to Elementals and their doctors for experimentation? That, by the way, is a rhetorical question," he continued to explain but his voice was so loud he might as well be yelling. "My presence here alone should satisfy the validity of this young man's testimony. Now, if you will excuse me. My time here has expired and I have a meeting with the other originals and I choose not to be late," Dracula said calmly before turning back and exiting the building as quickly as he entered.

"Well, based off of Royal Vampire negotiations of the past, I'm sure we are all inclined to believe him. It is quickly becoming apparent that this was no secret project so we can put that point to rest," King Marcus said.

"I agree, but now we have to deal with the product of this twist of fate," Queen Dellina said.

"If the 'product' you are referring to is Mathew, then naturally he will remain within Ice Elemental territory and hence, under watchful eyes," King Marcus said with a hint of determination.

"But those 'watchful eyes' of yours got an officer of the Elemental Police Force arrested the first time they tried to bring Mathew in for questioning," an Elder stated causing side discussions to erupt loudly.

"The officer in question was under orders to arrest Mathew and escort him to the Earth Elemental capital. We are not denying that we were merely safeguarding Mathew by ordering the officer to stay away from him because Mathew's health at that time was unstable. He had committed no crime nor act warranting arrest either. In addition, he was unable to get out of bed and couldn't walk long distances without assistance," Steven's voice rang out above the others.

"What was the cause of this 'unstable' health? Why was he in such critical condition? According to these medical records, Mathew was put back into a medical shell for emergency surgery which was performed by Count Dracula," King Ryan asked sparking up more arguments from the Elders.

"Quiet, please! The Princess wishes to speak," the Air advisor boomed quieting the rabble.

"Thank you very much. If the medical records are indeed correct then the emergency surgery meant that unless they performed the surgery Mathew would have died . . . so all the official records confirm is that Mathew was hurt and then he was put into recovery for an untold amount of time which, according to every Elemental law, is usually enough reason to hold off an investigation by the Elemental Police or, in this case, an arrest," Princess Kallen pointed out with a quiet voice, but she surprised Mathew with her calm confidence.

"That is indeed an excellent point, believe it or not . . . who authorized the arrest?" King Marcus questioned.

"Elemental law states that the Elemental police can be commanded by anyone from an individual of low rank, like a Squad Commander, up to the position of a King or Queen," an Elder stated being the first person to come up with the correct answer.

"Where is the official record of the order?" King Marcus asked.

"Unfortunately, I looked into that out of curiosity, but we were not able to find any trace of the original orders so it is possible that Rune, who was the Demonologist sent to arrest Mathew, was acting on his own personal orders," King Stanly explained.

"Good enough for now I suppose. The situation about Rune is settled then . . . but allow me to backtrack a little bit. What exactly happened to Mathew that made him require the emergency surgery?" Queen Dellina asked.

"We can't say for sure what caused the initial blow to Mathew's health but The Count himself performed the surgery that fused both Elemental and Vampire blood. We have little to no way of knowing of how or in what way The Count managed to complete the transformation," King Marcus stated.

"Pardon me. Princess Kallen has a question for Mathew!" the Advisor declared quieting the rabble once again.

"Mathew . . . although we don't need to eat . . . Would you like to . . . have dinner with me tomorrow night?" Princess Kallen asked sending disapproving murmurs through the room.

"Kallen! What the hell does this have to do with the situation at hand?" King Ryan asked obviously irritated again it seemed as though he was quick to anger.

"My father and mother always said 'don't judge what you don't know.' I don't know Mathew at all . . . . so I can't possibly make any decision without knowing him," she said simply.

"I think that is a brilliant idea. We should not jump to conclusions in situations that are as serious as this and with something that could actually become a major asset to each Elemental race," Queen Dellina said with a more lively voice. "What about the rest of you? Are you willing to join us?" she continued to ask.

"My apologies but I have other engagements that I must attend to," King Ryan said simply with no actual regret in his voice.

"Marcus, what do you think? Should we reschedule our plans to next week instead of tomorrow?" King Stanly asked.

"I have no problem with that. It might actually be a pleasure to chat casually for once," King Marcus replied.

"Well . . . If you're all coming . . . it might as well be a banquet," Princess Kallen said and Mathew realized that the only official invitation from her was his.

"As for the meeting, I move we continue this at a later date," King Stanly said deciding there was nothing else to talk about until he had a better understanding of what he was dealing with.

"I second that motion and wish to end the meeting as well," King Marcus said and Mathew was shown out of the room by a guard.

Mathew again entered the fateful carriage, along with Bell who seemed to be a little tired, but the ride was quick and relaxing. He watched the scenery go by from the window which he often did while in cars as a Human. When Mathew got out of the carriage, he thanked the soldiers who escorted them and went to his room for a nap. He was feeling worn down and stressed from the pressure of the whole event.

Mathew woke up refreshed and it was dark out so he decided to take a bath in the hot springs. He hoped to remove any residual stress. After his bath, he went inside to practice magic. He was yearning to control blood again but he figured he should wait until he was safely in Dracula's mansion. In the meantime, he would practice rip-offs of Jujitsu he had seen in a show. Time passed quickly and, before Mathew knew it, a few hours had gone by. A knock at the door startled him back to reality.

"Hello . . . May I come in?" Bell asked when Mathew opened the door.

"Of course . . . You know you don't need to knock," Mathew said even though she barged in the last time she entered his room.

"I wouldn't want to walk in on you if you were with a girl," Bell replied softly.

"When has that ever happened? Anyway, where would I find a girl when I'm locked down in this place?" Mathew asked just for a joke.

"I don't know . . . but can I talk to you?" Bell asked as she took a seat on the couch.

"Sure. What's on your mind, Bell? Mathew asked.

"Listen . . . I don't know how to say this but . . . do you think I am pretty?" she asked making Mathew a little confused.

"What are you talking about?" Mathew said trying to understand where she was coming from. He had a growing sense of foreboding about this conversation.

"I know this doesn't make sense right now but just go along with it," Bell said seeing Mathew's confusion.

"Well . . . you are a very attractive woman," Mathew admitted but he was just trying to make her feel better.

"Okay . . . but what is it specifically?" she asked her voice getting a little shrill.

"What's the problem, Bell? Tell me first what is causing you to ask me these questions?" Mathew asked softly when he picked up on her tone.

"Well . . . it's . . . it's . . . it's just . . ." instead of finishing she just became silent with her head down and her hair blocking his view. Mathew was shocked when he saw something shine as it fell from her face.

It was that moment when Mathew realized what was going on. Bell was crying. Mathew did the only thing he could think of; he sat down next to her and put his arms around her. Bell clung to him and Mathew felt something hard against his chest.

"Bell? What are you wearing?" Mathew asked because it was making it uncomfortable for him to help her; whatever it was had rough edges that dug into his skin.

"It's . . . a plate of ice," she said in between her small sobs.

"Let's get that off of you," Mathew said looking for the opening but realized that the ice plate covered her entire chest and wrapped around her back like a suit of armor. He slowly removed the vest she had on over her regular clothes. The armor dropped to the ground with a loud twang. The plate itself was an inch and a half thick and looked really heavy. Now, with the plate gone, she reattached herself to him still crying.

"There. That's better. Tell me why you were wearing this?" Mathew asked trying to stop or delay the tears that froze on contact to his shirt.

"I just was . . . it's so I'm never caught off guard again," Bell said quieting her crying. "I'm sorry to be like this in front of you," she said after the crying stopped but she still clung to Mathew.

"It's okay . . . I am wondering, though, from whom you are protecting yourself? Bell, why are you so concerned about getting caught off guard?" Mathew asked risking the question.

"Because the last person to do that . . . was my husband," she said but it was more like a whisper. Nonetheless it was still a shock to Mathew.

"Your husband gave you that scar?" Mathew said with a knot in his stomach as he risked another question.

"Unfortunately . . . yes," Bell answered and Mathew didn't ask any more questions about that topic.

"To answer your question, a lot of things make you attractive; your looks for one and you're super flexible from all your training . . . you could probably stab and kick me in the head at the same time," Mathew said with slight sarcasm.

"Oh, yes . . . I know that's attractive," Bell said louder than Mathew expected as she laughed a little bit.

"Feeling better?" Mathew asked.

"Yes, I am . . . Thanks for telling me that . . . even though I don't think you have any clue what you're talking about," she said sitting up then she wiped away a few extra frozen tears.

"Thanks. I probably don't but whatever . . . I'll be right back," Mathew said leaving the room. He was back in a few minutes with a full bottle of Nether Brew that Julian donated after hearing the situation.

"What's this?" Bell asked when she was handed a cup of the liquid.

"It's something that makes you relax so don't complain and just drink it," Mathew said so she downed the glass faster than she was supposed to.

"Ah . . . the sweet nectar Nether Brew. It's been a while since I had a glass," she said before poring herself another glass.

"So what was the crying about?" Mathew asked because that was still concerning him.

"It's just that it's frustrating now and then because . . . despite everything, I am still a female. Ever since that night with us, you know, the trance and all, I have been dealing poorly with emotions I haven't felt for years," she explained her voice pitching up and down and Mathew was afraid she was going to cry again.

"Mathew . . . I may be attractive but, at heart, I'm just a killing machine by every definition of the phrase. Now that I'm retired I can't relax. I don't know who I am anymore. I suppose I am having an identity crisis. Years and years of training made me a certain way and I was planning on living my entire life doing what I do best; killing other races, men, women, children, Demon, Human . . . it didn't matter because orders were orders. But then I get this mission . . . to help out a green Demonologist with a murder case. I meet you . . . this strange person who ordered me to relax . . . and then in one moment in that strange room . . . bam! I don't know. One glimpse of that imaginary world caused my emotions to be brought out from the cage that they were put in. The next thing I know, I'm not able to function the way I used to. I can't explain it but the entire situation is incredibly stressful," Bell admitted as she slammed another glass of Nether Brew and became silent.

"Bell . . . I'm not going to pretend I know what you are going through but I understand what you're talking about. I felt the same way when I was ripped out of a depression that came on me when a good friend died. I couldn't understand things anymore but, the next thing I know, I had more friends than I knew what to do with. Do you want to guess what happened next?" Mathew asked just for fun.

"I have no idea" Bell replied sounding a little better.

"I got killed by a rabid Yeti and now I'm drinking Nether Brew with an emotionally disturbed ex-Vanguard," Mathew answered with a chuckle.

"I am not emotionally disturbed!" Bell snapped.

"That's the spirit! Now, how would you like another glass?" Mathew asked now that Bell was feeling better.

The next thing Mathew realized was waking up in his bed next to Bell, who was also waking up, and half the room was covered in ice. The other half had a thick layer of frost on it. Mathew tried to get out of bed but tripped on the ice plate and hit the ground hard.

"Damn it, you scared me!" Bell yelled as she was jerked awake from the noise and had a fully formed ice dagger in her hand.

"Sorry, sorry. Just fell off the bed. Which is covered in ice," Mathew explained as he stood up and quickly checked his body for a bruise of some kind.

"What the hell happened last night and why is half the room frozen?" Bell asked as she rubbed her eyes.

"I don't know. The last thing I remember was me saying 'cheers' or 'bottoms up' or 'skol' . . . something like that," Mathew said taking a new pair of pants out of his bag.

"I suppose we are going to have to deal with this thing," Bell said looking at the huge glacier-like form on the frozen side of the room.

Then both Mathew and Bell decided to put their efforts together so they could move the huge ice block into the hot springs where it quickly melted and made the water level go up a several inches.

"What are you going to be wearing tonight to the banquet? Mathew asked as he cleared up the remaining ice chunks.

"I have no idea. I'm sure I will find something," Bell replied calmly.

"I would appreciate you not wearing one of those ice plates today," Mathew ordered.

"And why would I not do that?" Bell asked.

"Because you need to look your best for the dinner tonight, that's why," Mathew said cheerfully even though his main source of motivation was to get her to start to believe in those around her and to learn to trust them with watching her back in case something were to happen. The first step to emotional healing was to get rid of that ice plate.

"I wasn't officially invited so I might just stay here," Bell said with a tone that Mathew couldn't identify.

"You are going with me. You can't possibly expect me to feel safe in a place like that when my personal guard is here taking a nap and eating bon-bons," Mathew said already determined to have her at the banquet. He figured it would be good for her anyway.

"Alright then. I had better go find more suitable clothing. Bonbons? What are those?" Bell asked with a funny yet happy tone in her voice as she left the room.

Mathew also needed to get ready so he scampered around the room looking for the fanciest clothes he could find. He found the retro Vampire suit that Victoria had given him and a more formal suit in his sack of clothing. He chose the more formal suit not wanting to offend anyone at the banquet by showing up as an Ice Elemental in Vampire clothing. Mathew threw on the suit and liked the way it fit so he decided that's what he was going to wear.

Time flew by quickly as Mathew worked to improve his look. He chained his demonology badge on, combed his hair (which he never did) and adjusted his attire slightly. Just as he was finishing up, the door flew open. It was Steven dressed just as fancy as Mathew. He yanked Mathew out and into the carriage once again where Julian and Bell were waiting.

"Steven, you're coming, too?" Mathew asked when he got comfortable.

"Of course, this banquet is a big deal and a lot of Elders are going to be there. A veritable Elemental 'Who's Who'," Steven said as he took a seat.

"I can't believe I chose to wear this silly thing. It's restricting my movements and I'll be completely unprepared if something happens," Bell complained as she fidgeted around in her seemingly new dress uniform.

"You look beautiful, Bell. And you know how it is for us women, pain and discomfort equals beauty," Julian said with a smile and a chuckle.

"Thank you very much, Julian. I like your dress," Bell politely replied.

"When we get back let's go shopping. My belly is popping out and I'm running out of suitable clothing that fits," Julian suggested.

"I could use a new wardrobe. I'm going to try other things than military attire for once now that I have an endless amount of free time," Bell said and the girls went into their girly talk.

"So Mathew, when we get back let's go to a gentleman's club," Steven said and, even though he was joking, both girls gave him a sour look.

Everything seemed to be progressing way too fast but Mathew figured he was just nervous. He was glad that King Ryan wasn't going to be at the banquet because of the way he came off to Mathew. Most of the other Elders seemed to be curious about him but Ryan had a barely concealed his hostility. Mathew found this puzzling especially since that had been their first actual meeting. Mathew pushed all those thoughts aside as this evening was a very important milestone and he realized he was going to have to think three steps ahead of himself to not do or say something stupid.

When they arrived, Mathew's nervousness increased. Right before his eyes was the largest castle he had ever seen. After a brief moment of shock, he remembered that this was a royal banquet and realized that a royal banquet probably would not have been held at the local VFW. Before Mathew could take it all in, his thoughts wandered off to the type of food that would be there.

A dozen royal guards directed their carriage to the entrance and assisted them as they got out. Mathew was caught in between the darkness of the carriage and the blinding light of the hall. When his eyes adjusted, he realized what he was dealing with. The lights weren't lights at all. They were glowing patches of mist and, if Mathew remembered correctly from his demonology class, they were called wisps. While walking to the entrance, Mathew, Steven, Julian & Bell were approached by a man who asked them their names, rank and type of employment. So, in the spirit of cooperation, they gave their best answers.

"Wait! Are you Mathew the Blood Elemental?" the man asked after hearing his name.

"Who wants to know?" Mathew asked back never seeming to tire of that response.

"I just want to ask you a question . . . off the record, of course," the man replied.

"Then yes, I suppose I am," Mathew said.

"Great! Please wait here for one moment," the man said leading the others inside.

"Now presenting Elder Steven, his wife Lady Julian and Ice Vanguard Bell," Mathew heard the man yell from inside the building.

"Okay, sorry about that but it's been busy. First of all, my name is Dagon," the man began. "So the question has to do with Demonology.

I'm seeing a Succubus. It's been about three years and I don't think she will be leaving me. So what do I do now? Do I marry her or do I just remain status quo?" Dagon asked and Mathew understood the dilemma.

"Well, if it's been three years and she hasn't left you . . . ask her to marry you if you can. I don't know how the Air Elementals view cross race marriages and, if you can't inter-marry ask her if she would like to have a child with you. If she is true to you she will undoubtedly say yes to either question. Beyond that, I can't help you," Mathew said answering the question the best he knew how.

"Okay thanks, man! I appreciate it. Well, let's get you announced," Dagon said heading inside first.

"Now presenting Demonologist Mathew the Blood Elemental," he shouted and the noise in the room diminished quickly. The announcement was the perfect situation to make Mathew nice and paranoid about every step he took coming down the stairs. He silently begged God to make sure he didn't trip or do something foolish. He had a flash of himself falling down the staircase like the Sesame Street baker with his 10 banana cream pies.

"What the hell took so long?" Steven yelled adding noise to the hall before it got too quiet and drawing Mathew out of his banana cream pie nightmare.

"Quiet, Steven! I was helping the man with something," Mathew replied as his body started to calm down a little.

"That was a lovely thing for you to do," Julian said patting Mathew on the head like a dog when she managed to get close enough.

"Good. I am so happy all of you could make it," a soft voice came from behind them.

"Oh, hello, Princess Kallen. It's good to see you again. Thank you for the invitation," Mathew said after he recognized who it was.

"No need for formalities . . . with things like titles," Kallen said simply.

"Okay. Just Kallen then," Mathew said trying to make a lasting impression on the young princess.

"Mathew . . . my mother asked to meet you so, if you don't mind and the rest of you would pardon us, I would like to introduce you," Kallen asked and it was obvious that she was not very assertive.

"No problem, lead the way," Mathew said.

He was led across the banquet room to a wind fountain. The wind fountain fascinated Mathew because, while being similar to a water fountain, wind fountains were used to provide power to mechanical sculptures by rotating fans to turn gears. This particular wind fountain provided power to a large, dancing puppet.

"Oh, Mother, there you are. I'm glad you made it," Kallen said running toward a very kind looking older woman. When Mathew caught up, he was surprised at how strongly Kallen resembled her mother. Their facial features were close to identical and they each had long, pinkish hair (that reminded Mathew of cotton candy.) The Queen's hair, though, was a slightly darker shade. Mathew couldn't tell the Queen's body structure because she was wearing a large, frilly dress but, age aside, they were obviously mother and daughter.

"Mother, it is my pleasure to introduce Mathew the Blood Elemental. Mathew, this is my mother, Lucy Queen of the Sky," Kallen said introducing both of them.

"It's a pleasure to meet you, Mathew," Lucy said doing a queenly curtsy.

"Oh, please. The pleasure is all mine," Mathew replied with his best rendition of a courtly bow.

"As I suspected, you are not at all as mean as you have been made out to be," Lucy commented with a smile that made Mathew feel all warm and fuzzy inside.

"Wait! People think I'm mean?" Mathew asked. Not even in Human form had anyone ever been able to call him "mean".

"Obviously rumors with no foundation," Lucy replied generously in a sweet voice.

"Well, well, well! What do we have going on over here?" a loud, booming voice questioned which, if it had been any closer, would have made Mathew jump out of his shoes.

"Good evening, Stanly. What brings you to this side of the room?" Lucy asked.

"I'm here to form some kind of opinion about this young man," King Stanly said and gave Mathew a good slap on the back.

"From what I can tell so far, he is a very polite young man," Queen Lucy said and Mathew got the impression she was supportive of his cause.

"A jolly good sense of humor he has as well. Did you hear what he called Marcus?" King Steven asked with a big smirk already creeping across his face.

"Unfortunately, I haven't. As you know, dear, I wasn't there," Queen Lucy replied calmly.

"Great tale. Marcus asked Mathew why he should introduce himself as he was clearly under the impression that Mathew should have already known of him. You know how Marcus can get with those sorts of silly things. The kid goes on to respond, 'So I don't call you Lord High Pompous'," King Stanly said then both he and Queen Lucy burst into laughter. Mathew honestly didn't find it that funny but realized it was similar to meeting the infamous Dracula. Legends were usually treated like kings and queens and, eventually they start to get detached from the real world. When that happened, even a small misunderstanding could be misconstrued as an insult and take on a whole different level of meaning.

"Hello, friends and Mathew, what are you laughing at?" King Marcus asked as he walked up to the group.

"Why hello . . . Lord High Pompous," Queen Lucy said merrily causing the group including Mathew to go into a laughing fit. It took them several moments more to regain their composures.

"Which one of you told her?" Marcus asked casting a glance between Mathew and King Stanly.

"Do you even need to ask? It was Stanly, dear. You know how he is about jokes and other nonsense," Lucy answered as if something like this had happened before.

"You are right, Lucy, I should have known. Mathew, would you excuse us? We have a few things to discuss," Marcus asked kindly.

"Of course. Have a nice time," Mathew said trying very hard to leave a good impression and, at the same time, to be a little discreet about it.

As Mathew explored the room, he was at his social best as he mingled with a few Elders. Steven had reminded him earlier how important it was to establish a positive persona and he was committed to seeing that through. He ate a few morsels of food but nothing was very satisfying at that moment. He began to noticing a funny feeling in his body and assumed that the source was the strange seaweed appetizer he nibbled on earlier.

As he walked aimlessly about the room, he managed to accidentally bump into a woman and knock her to the ground. Without paying attention, he scrambled to help her up and realized it was Queen Dellina.

"Oh! Pardon me, Queen Dellina! I wasn't paying attention as I'm feeling a little strangely," Mathew explained as he tried to help her up. He didn't have much success because a guard quickly pushed him away before he was able to help the Queen to her feet.

"It was a damn accident! Let the young man be!" Queen Dellina grouched at the poor guard who was only doing his job.

"It's quite all right, Mathew. Even I have been known to daydream now and then and, between you and me, it's much more interesting daydreaming then listening to all of this political drivel," she said with a harsh tone not directed at Mathew. Mathew did notice a few elders behind her casually walk away from them in the opposite direction.

"Agreed. I can't find the fun in that either but are you enjoying the party?" Mathew asked trying to make small talk.

"Honestly, dear boy, it's a serious bore. I would rather be playing a game or doing . . . just about anything else. I get so weary of these 'stand and talk' parties because I seem to hostess one every other day," she confessed.

"Well . . . there is a game I used to play with my friends but we would need a large, open space," Mathew said as a memory of a game he played when he was little popped into his head.

"They do have a large courtyard here at the palace. You have piqued my interest. Come, let's go," Queen Dellina said as she started pushing Mathew in front of her which caused quite a stir in the room. When they reached the courtyard, Queen Dellina ordered, "Okay, now tell me of this game!" Mathew sensed how desperate she was for a little bit of fun but found it a little odd that she was acting this way.

"I used to play this as a Human. It's called 'Kill the King'. The rules are relatively simple. There are two teams and it doesn't matter how many people are on a team as long as the sides are even. Both sides have a mascot . . . a snowman or whatever that can be knocked down," Mathew began stumbling his way through the explanation as he remembered how the game was set up and played. "Hang on, give me a moment please," he said as he closed his eyes and placed his hand to the ground.

He envisioned the old game and how it was played. He opened his eyes when he remembered exactly what he needed and used his ice magic to create the lines going across the field and human-sized snowmen at either end. The game setting made it look like a soccer field; except the goals were replaced by snowmen.

"Okay, now. This is my side and that's your side," Mathew said distinguishing both sides of the field.

"What exactly are the rules?" Dellina asked getting fidgety and impatient. Mathew decided that she must have an extremely short attention span.

"The objective of the game is to destroy the other team's snowman. The difficulty comes in because you can only throw things and you can't cross the centerline. This may be a bad time to ask but, Queen Dellina, can you make a water ball or something that won't break when it hits something?" Mathew asked forgetting about the fact that Dellina was a Water Elemental and water is, well . . . a liquid.

"Don't insult me, Mathew," she said and created an orb of water, which looked like a giant mercury ball, and quickly threw it at Mathew who managed to catch it. Holding it was a weird experience because the water ball defied natural physics. It felt like it was alive as it ran over his fingers and kind of tickled but, all in all, it stayed together and didn't even drip.

"Good . . . now let's say you threw this at my snowman and I caught it. Since I caught it, I can use it and throw it back at your snowman. If it knocks over your snowman, that's fair game. Okay?" Mathew asked just to make sure she understood.

"No crossing the line, you can catch and throw back. The overall objective is to destroy opponent's snowman. Got it. Let's play!" she exclaimed as she practically sprinted to her side.

"Oh and mental note, nothing that could hurt each other," Mathew stated and the game began.

Dellina threw the first ball. Mathew caught, returned it and threw one of his own. He was rusty and his first throw was really short. It didn't even go half the distance it needed to go. Mathew again caught Dellina's throw and whipped it back. It managed to curve, to around Dellina, and smash into the head of her snowman.

"Not bad, Mathew! Time for the next round!" Dellina yelled and replaced her demolished snowman with a waterman. Mathew thought that was super cool.

Dellina then did something that Mathew wasn't expecting; she threw her water ball high in the air and guided it into Mathew's snowman.

"Is that allowed, Mathew?" she asked after she already did it.

"I'll allow it. I'm technically rewriting the rules to this game to better suit Elemental abilities as we're playing it," Mathew said smiling as he realized that the rules needed to be tweaked in order for Elementals to play. "All right, let's do this thing!" he said after he rebuilt his decimated snowman.

Mathew threw his snowball high in the air, and with a snap of his fingers separated the snowball so it was more like a hailstorm. Dellina was clever, though; she got in front of her waterman and quickly created a water shield to assimilate the snow into her water ball. This created a giant water ball that she sent back at him. Mathew needed to think quickly. He knew instinctively that he couldn't catch something that big so he went for style points. He jumped up in the air and kicked it back with all the force he had. Dellina dove out of the way and the giant ball smashed into her waterman. Cheers and whistles came from the side of the courtyard.

Mathew didn't even notice that other party members had gather around in a large group to watch the game being played. Even members of the Elemental Royalty were enjoying the new sport.

"Excuse me, Mathew, but would you allow me to join you?" Queen Lucy asked with a smile.

"Of course but can we first see a wind ball?" Mathew asked. Her answer was to create something that looked like a mini hurricane in her hand.

"Well then, we need to even the sides," Mathew explained.

"Anyone willing to help out Dellina?" Mathew asked the crowd.

"I'll do it! I need to get you and Lucy back for calling me 'Lord High Pompous'," King Marcus said stepping forward as he took off his coat.

"Great! Now we have a game!" Mathew exclaimed as Queen Lucy threw the first punch.

Mathew seemed to be mostly on the defense with catching and returning the ice and water balls. The first point went to Mathew and Lucy and slowly more people came in to play. King Stanly went to Dellina's team and Bell decided to join Mathew. When King Stanly entered the game, Mathew re-established the game rules that there was nothing allowed that would hurt any team player so King Stanly created a quick sand ball and Mathew decided it was all right. The game started again with the additional players adding interesting creativity which made it all a lot more fun. King Stanly sent a jumbo sized sand ball which Bell, in a warrior stance, cut it in half with her blade. This caused a roar of cheers and gave Mathew an idea; he called a time out and gathered his team to tell them the plan that he intended to put in motion when the time out expired.

Mathew entered the game with his "snowball hail" move. As predicted, Dellina absorbed it and sent it back. Up next was Bell and she cut the ball in half; Both Mathew and Lucy then kicked both halves back. King Stanly blocked one half but the other half smashed into the waterman and a roar of cheers came from the growing crowd.

"All right . . . that's enough for me . . . I'm going to get a drink," Mathew managed to say while he was catching his breath.

"There is some type of Human drink inside so please, help yourself," Lucy said as Mathew left the field.

"Do we have someone to take my place? A Fire Elemental perhaps?" Mathew asked and someone eagerly stepped forward.

"Can you make a fireball that won't burn people?" Mathew asked just to be safe, so the man created one and handed it to Mathew. He held it for a few moments; decided it was a bit warm but all in all safe and sent the Fire Elemental into the game.

Mathew found the drink Lucy mentioned, got a glass and, to his satisfaction, found that it was a refreshing type of soda. He was so thirsty that he drank glass after glass of the delicious liquid until he felt bloated. He sat down next to the wind fountain, closed his eyes and listened to the cheers and the heckling because of his game.

"Quite a game you made, Mathew," Kallen's voice came and kind of startled Mathew.

"Oh hey, Kallen. What's going on?" Mathew asked rubbing his eyes.

"You just looked sad and lonely . . . are you tired?" she asked sitting down next to him.

"Elementals don't need to sleep but yes, my body needs to recover. That game saps a lot of energy with all those fancy tricks. It takes a lot to create the snowballs and all that," Mathew said trying to keep his eyes open.

"Would . . . would you like to spend the night here?" she asked kindly.

"If you have an extra room then yes, please. But I need to make sure that my friends know," Mathew said getting up.

"Oh don't worry, Mathew. I'll tell them myself. You came with that Elder over there named Steven, right?" Kallen asked politely.

"Yah, that's him," Mathew answered then realized Steven was dancing about with something that looked identical to lampshade on his head.

"Okay. Come on then," Kallen said helping Mathew up from the chair and leading him to a room with a normal queen sized bed. He plopped down on the bed and was instantly asleep.

Mathew slept soundly except for the feeling of motion sickness he had. He dreamt of playing "Kill the King" until a sharp, stabbing pain in his chest forced him awake. Even though he was drowsy he knew he was hurt. He looked quickly at his chest and saw a small dagger pierced in the left side. It was intended for his heart but thankfully missed its mark due to the luck of his genetics. His heart was in a different location than most people and, as he instinctively ripped out the dagger, he looked up quickly enough to dodge the next attack that was directed at his head. Mathew clumsily rolled out of bed and quickly created his blade to face the unknown enemy. He looked at his attacker who was dressed in all black and noticed they were using a similar dagger that seemed to be made out of a type of crystal that came with a sheath. Since Earth Elementals can create and dissolve any Earth weapon, they didn't need a sheath. Mathew knew his only choices were to capture or kill the assailant, for this was an assassination attempt.

Mathew took the initiative and swung first but was blocked by the attacker. However the assailant didn't anticipate Mathew's vampire strength and was knocked back; he stumbled to the floor but kicked Mathew's feet out from under him and proceeded to try and cut his throat while he was on the ground. Mathew rolled out of the way and took the only opportunity he had. With the attacker's dagger sunk deep into the floor, Mathew slashed at the back of his enemy's neck ending the fight and counting the first life Mathew took with his own blade.

Mathew had to crawl out of the room and pound on the nearest door for help. He hoped he would find someone there because he didn't have time to go anywhere else. He had already lost too much blood during the fight and was still bleeding out. He didn't even have time to perform his blood magic to try and save himself before his body began to shut itself down.

With his vision blackened and his consciousness fading, Mathew's thought and sense of urgency to save his own life slowly faded away. As everything went black, Mathew didn't dream this time and, even as an Ice Elemental, he felt a cold presence around him. He struggled one last time to regain consciousness but, with all the screaming and yelling going on, he couldn't think or even muster the strength to open his eyes to see what was happening. He tried to focus and listen to the words but they started to blur together. Eventually the words became an incoherent jumble to him and all he could hear was indiscernible sounds. It all became intolerable noise, just like a crowded room where everyone was talking at once about different things. As he lost all consciousness, he forgot. He forgot his friends, family, past, present, everything. There was nothing but a vast emptiness that kept getting smaller and smaller with each passing moment.

The next realization Mathew had was a painful sensation of something coursing through his body. A few moments passed then the same feeling again but stronger. This time it surged though his body, sending a strange warmth and fuzziness. Something appeared from what seemed like years of waiting. There were the sounds of words, clear and understandable words.

"What are you? A man or a Demon?" the unknown voice asked.

Mathew thought about it for a while and gave his answer.

"I'm both," Mathew said. He couldn't open his eyes yet but could tell the owner of the voice was pleased.

At that moment, something profound happened. There was an intensity of sound and lots of it. Mathew felt a surge of power from a source he couldn't define and everything started coming back slowly. First his memories, then his senses and last the thing to come back to him was ability to control his body. He opened his eyes once again and re-entered the world of the living.

Mathew

CHAPTER FOURTEEN

SAFETY AND DEVOTION

His body hurt, he was thirsty and his mind seemed dull and clouded. It was his chest, though, that was the worst of it all. Mathew tried to sit up but the pain sapped his strength and he collapsed back into the bed. It took several moments of heavy breathing to recover. The room he was in didn't look like an Elemental room. It was too dark but he felt it was someplace safe. He was in a large bed and especially happy about it. The room seemed familiar but he couldn't place it yet.

"Hey, anyone out there?" Mathew shouted in the loudest voice he could muster but found it harder than he expected and proceeded to become winded.

Mathew heard something from the other side of the door and, as it flew open, someone ran towards him and hugged him, which made him cry out in pain.

"I'm sorry, Mathew! It's just . . . . I have never been so scared in all of my life," Victoria said as she quickly loosened her grip.

"Where am I and what happened? The last thing I remember is pounding on a door at a palace," Mathew creaked out in a hoarse voice as his mind started to clear.

"You were attacked by an assassin and suffered a stab wound. The wound itself was not fatal but the blade was coated in a deadly poison. You were incredibly lucky . . . but that's nothing new for you," Catharine said as she entered the room carrying a strange looking bottle. "And, for the moment, you're in the safest place possible and that's all you need to know. Now here, drink this. It will make you feel better," she said as she handed Mathew the bottle of liquid. He drank some and choked on the disgusting taste as it went down.

"No, no, my dear boy. Drink all of it," Catharine said tipping the bottle up against Mathew's lips making him drink it faster than he should have.

"What is that stuff?" Mathew asked as his stomach rebelled with a heave and an indescribable aftertaste started to kick in.

"Just an old Succubus remedy for healing," Catharine replied.

"So is Dee here somewhere?" Mathew said lying back down and just glad to have company.

"Yes, she will be. She ran off to do something and is expected back soon," Catharine stated.

"What exactly is going on?" Mathew asked still not clear on the situation.

"Let's see. Where to begin . . . after you survived the assassination attempt, which was literally a shot heard round the world, you were on the front page of every newspaper. And I mean everywhere. That is, in the Demon and Elemental world, anyway. Dracula heard about it within a few hours and decided that you weren't safe in that place and had you moved back to the Manor to keep an eye on you. You are well protected here. In addition to us, there are approximately thirty Death Stalkers around the Manor. The other Vampires have returned and more seem to be arriving daily," Catharine explained in her sweet, calm voice.

"What about Bell? How did she take it?" Mathew asked remember the main reason she went on the trip to begin with.

"Oh, poor girl. I heard she was a mess when Dracula came to get you," Catharine said.

"Do me a favor will you . . . would you mind writing her a letter for me?" Mathew asked wanting to let Bell know how he was.

"Of course, dear boy. What would you like me to write?" Catharine asked with a compassionate voice.

"Just tell her how I'm doing and that it's my fault to begin with . . . and ask her to come see me so I can tell her myself," Mathew explained.

"Okay. I'll do that right now," Catharine said giving Mathew a kiss on the head that sent another warm feeling through his body.

"I'm sorry, Victoria. I just wanted to know what was going on," Mathew apologized for basically ignoring her.

"It's okay, Mathew. I understand what you must be thinking," Victoria said also in a calm voice.

"Thanks then. By the way, where is your dad?" Mathew asked out of curiosity.

"He is dealing with the political aspect of this situation at God's Step. You are a Royal Vampire and you were attacked so the entire Vampire community gets dragged into the dispute. Not to mention you're actually one of Dad's friends so he took the attack personally. Very personally," Victoria explained as she reached out and moved Mathew's hair out of his eyes.

"I'm sorry about that," Mathew said not sure what else to say.

"Oh, don't apologize. Just as long as you're okay, we're okay," she said giving him a peck on the cheek, which surprised him.

"What was that for?" Mathew asked out of curiosity.

"I needed some contact with you and can't exactly drink your blood at the moment . . . you need that," she said jokingly.

"Oh, so that's your game," Mathew said going along with the joke but discovered it hurt to laugh.

"That bastard punctured my lung, didn't he?" Mathew asked.

"Yes he did, that's what that bottle was for," Victoria said

"At least that explains why I'm having a hard time breathing," Mathew said simply.

"Mathew! You're up!" Dee yelled excitedly as she entered the room.

"No! Wait Dee! Don't . . ." Victoria tried to warn her but it was too late. Dee already had her arms around Mathew who screamed because of the intense pain coming from his chest.

"Oh! I'm sorry, Mathew! I was just so happy to see you awake," she apologized and quickly took a spot on the bed next to Mathew.

"Dee, how long have you been awake?" Mathew asked noticing the large bags under her eyes.

"Well . . . it's been about five days," Dee said which was astonishing.

"Okay . . . come on. Get in," Mathew ordered pulling the blankets over to make a spot for her."

"Thank you, Mathew," Dee said contentedly as she snuggled into the bed and quickly fell asleep.

"What is wrong with her? I mean she's not like you and me, she actually needs sleep," Mathew commented on the strange Succubus.

"She was worried. We all were. I need sleep as well, just not as much . . . think of it as catnaps," Victoria admitted making Mathew think of a conversation they had a while ago.

"That's right . . . why didn't I remember that?" Mathew asked himself.

"You should sleep with me more . . . wait a second. Victoria didn't think that through," she said aloud to herself and Mathew just smiled so he wouldn't laugh.

"I figured you would catch that," Mathew said trying not to laugh.

"Excuse me, Mistress," a man said as he seemed to appear out of thin air.

"Who the hell are you?!" Mathew asked out of shock then began to cough.

"I'm Renal, Captain of the Death Stalkers. Mistress, there is a woman here named Lucy, accompanied by an armed escort, requesting permission to enter," he said in a monotone that rivaled Bell's.

"Wait! Queen Lucy of the Air Elementals?" Mathew asked simply.

"Yes, Sir, that's what she named herself," Renal replied simply.

"She can only come in if she agrees to leave her guards at the entrance . . . and would you be so kind as to guide her here and inform Catharine about her arrival," Mathew asked because he couldn't do anything except lay in the bed.

"Lady Catharine has already been informed and I will guide Lucy here personally if she is willing to cooperate with your demands," Renal said quickly.

"Thank you . . . that's all," Mathew said feeling a little unusual giving orders and Renal vanished as quickly as he appeared. "Sneaky, sneaky. He is rather interesting," Mathew said aloud.

"Renal has been a loyal bodyguard of our family for years," Victoria said. "Who is this Lucy lady anyway?" she asked.

"She is a very kind woman. She is Queen of the Air Elementals. Please be nice," Mathew asked quickly because he sensed that Victoria might be a tad over protective of him in his current condition.

"Don't worry. If she's nice, I'm nice. If she's not, then it's her consequence," Victoria said. A few moments passed and Queen Lucy walked into the room.

"Mathew! So happy to see you again even after this unfortunate turn of events," Queen Lucy said as she turned to Victoria. "I don't believe we have met. I'm Queen Lucy,"

"It's a pleasure, Queen Lucy. I'm Victoria Dracula," Victoria replied reminding Mathew that Dracula was actually a last name.

"Oh, I see. A Dracula . . . Then the pleasure truly is all mine. Anyway, the main reason I'm here is because I wanted to apologize for what happened . . . I was horrified to hear you were attacked in my own home," Lucy said with a humble and apologetic tone.

"Did you send the assassin after me?" Mathew asked.

"Of course not! Why would I do such a thing and to someone I just met?" Lucy asked shocked by the question.

"Then I forgive you. By the way, do we know who the assassin was?" Mathew asked.

"You managed to kill him before the poison kicked in your system so that truth has been eluding us for a while. So, unfortunately no," Lucy said walking over to him. "Well, now. Who is that cuddled up by you?" she asked spotting Dee who was sound asleep.

"That's my daughter, Dee. She's exhausted from a long couple of days. I'm Lady Catharine," Catharine said when she walked into the room.

"It's a pleasure to meet you, Lady Catherine. So Mathew, is there anything I can do to help, anything you need or want?" Lucy asked trying to make up for the incident.

"Yes. You could do me a huge favor and watch after my friend, Bell. I heard she was having a hard time with this whole thing and I want to make sure she is okay," Mathew asked getting a little bit depressed when he thought of Bell crying her eyes out because in her mind she had failed.

"I can do that . . . anything else?" she asked with a smile.

"Hang onto that thought," Catharine said as she put another bottle of that liquid up against Mathew's lips and tipped it up again, forcing him to drink.

"Catharine! You know I'm a grown man, right?" Mathew asked as he spit up a little amount of the liquid . . . just like an infant.

"Yes, dear boy. I know . . . I just like to do that. I should have had droves of children," she admitted with a motherly smile and wiped his chin with a delicate lace handkerchief.

Lucy smiled and said, "I did the same thing with my daughter, Kallen. What is the purpose of the liquid?"

"It is an old Succubi remedy. We're trying to heal his left lung that was punctured during the incident. Not to mention, Mathew, your back is still a mess because the blade went all the way through," Catharine explained making Mathew feel a little worse because he didn't know the blade went through him.

"May I see the elements you are using?" Lucy asked. "Being also a mother, I could suggest some remedies I used to use."

"Please, follow me," Catharine said leading the way.

"I have a bad feeling about this," Mathew said to no one in particular.

"You know what mothers are like," Victoria stated. "But excuse me, Mathew, I need to check on something," she said pulling back the covers exposing Mathew's bare chest. Mathew, to his dismay and fascination, got a good first look at his new wound. It was a lot larger than he had expected and was neatly stitched up crisscross but the veins around the area were black . . . a clear sign of poison that was meant to break down and destroy blood cells. "This may sting a bit," Victoria said as she dabbed the wound with something that stung like fire and hurt worse than landing in a nest of hornets.

After she was done cleaning Mathew's wound, both front and back, they talked about this and that until he eventually dozed off. His body needed rest to repair itself. He drifted into dreams that were actually a lot more relaxing than the situation should have allowed and Mathew was thankful for that. What seemed like a moment later, when Mathew felt someone shaking him. He woke up to Dee draped over him; which wasn't all bad but he quickly changed his mind when he noticed both Lucy and Catharine watching him with funny smiles on their faces.

"What's going on?" Mathew asked a bit crossly after a few moments. He didn't think he would ever get used to someone watching him while he slept. It felt like an invasion of a private moment.

"We could ask you the same thing . . ." Lucy said with that same funny smile but Mathew understood what she meant.

"Listen. I can't even sit up straight without my chest feeling like it's ripping in half, so how do you expect me to mess around with a Succubus?" Mathew asked as he slowly started removing Dee's limbs off of his body. "Anyway, some things are supposed to be private, like sleeping."

"You would be surprised what the body is capable of, Mathew. Anyway, please sit up, dear boy," Catharine said.

"Here. Drink this," Lucy said handing him a glass.

"What is it?" Mathew asked.

"It's good for you so just drink it," Catharine ordered.

"Well, alright then," Mathew decided just to drink it quickly hoping the taste would go by just as quickly. Fortunately, though, the taste of this potion wasn't as bad as he anticipated. It had a sweeter aftertaste and was easier on his stomach, which he found refreshing compared to his first couple of batches

"Now that that's done, I really must be going," Lucy said after Mathew finished the drink.

"Thank you for coming, Lucy. Please remember to contact my friend, Bell, for me," Mathew said as she left.

"So Catharine . . . what does this drink do . . . because it's actually rather tasty," Mathew asked as he made his opinion about the drink.

"Just think of it as me trying to breed you into a good husband," Catharine replied not giving Mathew an answer.

"So what am I, your pet project?" Mathew asked with a slight chuckle with immediate regret it when the pain kicked in.

"In a way, yes. But that's as far as it goes," she admitted.

"I guess it's good that you're honest," Mathew said.

"Mathew?" Catharine asked.

"Yes?" Mathew replied but didn't see that Catharine had him locked within her gaze.

"Now sleep, Mathew," she said and Mathew fell fast asleep.

Once again his body was forced into a timeless sleep. This time, though, it wasn't as quick as before and his mind was still conscious enough to produce calm dreams.

Catharine put Mathew into a sleep of healing and Mathew felt the difference in his body's ability to recuperate. He sensed that his body was slowly recovering when he was awake but when asleep, the time it took to heal was drastically reduced. When he finally woke up, the pain at least was gone but he still needed to rest.

Feeling better, Mathew decided he should try walking. He slowly got up and started hobbling around the room, but not very well so he made his way back to the bed.

"Welcome back, Master. How are you feeling?" he heard a woman's voice say as he sat back down on the bed.

Master? Mathew thought to himself as he spotted the figure in the corner.

"Who are you?" Mathew asked the woman.

"I'm your personal attendant. I'm here to help you with anything you may need," the girl said quietly, her voice was soft and she was very cute. She had short, brown bobbed hair and darker skin but looked nervous and unsure of herself. Mathew noticed that she was dressed in a maid's outfit that, in itself, significantly added to her attractiveness.

"Hey, come over here for a moment," Mathew wheezed out in a funny sounding voice because his lung wasn't healed yet and he was short of breath.

"Yes Sir . . . I understand," she said as she began to unbutton her shirt.

"Um . . . what are you doing?" Mathew asked a little embarrassed.

"Didn't . . . you know . . . ?" she asked as a crimson blush spread across her face.

"No! Why would you think that?" Mathew replied.

"Well . . . your voice changed when you told me to go over there . . . I thought you . . . . you know," she said quickly buttoning her shirt back up.

"Oh, no. I only have one lung at the moment so my voice is weak," Mathew explained as he lay back down on the bed and took a moment to catch his breath.

"I understand. What could I do for you?" the girl asked, Mathew noticed her change of body language was rather quick.

"First of all, what's your name?" Mathew asked with a smile.

"My apologies, Master. People just call me Kyoko," she answered.

"It's a pleasure to meet you, Kyoko. If you don't already know, I'm Mathew. Now would you be so kind as to help me up," Mathew asked.

"Of course," Kyoko said helping Mathew stand up.

"So Mathew, you're up," Victoria said after Mathew was on his feet again.

"Ah . . . lovely Victoria. What brings you here?" Mathew asked feeling unstable as he worked on getting his balance.

"I'm here to check on you and you can go now, Kyoko. I can take it from here," she said with a tight, harsh tone in her voice.

"Yes, Mistress. Goodbye, Mathew," Kyoko said as she left the room.

"So Mathew, what do you want to do now that you're up?" Victoria asked giving Mathew a strange look.

"I know this will sound stupid but, would you mind helping just get out of this bedroom for a quick walk around? I could use the exercise," Mathew asked with a smile.

"Sure, no problem," Victoria replied letting Mathew take the lead.

The quick walk was the first time Mathew had been out of the room in a few weeks. Most of the servants had returned to the Manor, changing the atmosphere and making it lively and rather exciting. Mathew got a lot of smiles with a couple of weird looks thrown in but it seemed like a good, friendly place. Exhausted and in a small amount of pain, Mathew decided he needed to take a bath because he was just feeling nasty so Victoria showed him the way. When they arrived, Mathew looked around at the enormous bath the size of most people's bedroom. It reminded him of the hot springs at the inn in God's Step.

Mathew stepped in as quickly as he could and instantly felt a sense of satisfaction as the heat calmed the muscles around his wound, and the overall sensation of being clean was direly needed.

When he was finished soaking, Mathew felt a lot better and started back to his room for another bit of rest. Once there, he sat in front of the fireplace he had lit earlier for a little enjoyment. After watching the flames dance eagerly in random directions he heard someone close the door.

"Hello, Victoria," Mathew said after he saw who it was.

"Mathew . . . so what do you think of me?" she asked out of the blue.

"Where is this coming from?" Mathew asked a little concerned about the talk he was getting into. It already sounded far too close for his peace of mind to the talk he had with Bell.

"I don't want this to sound weird but . . . I want to know if we ever have a shot at a regular relationship . . . after our wedding was called off," Victoria explained making it clear this had been bothering her.

"Alright, I'll talk but I'm not going to hide anything," Mathew warned.

"That's good. I'm not one for lies," Victoria said sitting on the bed.

"When our wedding was called off, I was actually a little disappointed. I had gotten comfortable with the idea of you being my wife . . . but now I don't know how I feel. A lot has happened since then," Mathew began. "But, that doesn't mean that I don't want to have a relationship . . . just not at the moment . . . you know, with me basically on trial and everything," he explained.

"I feel the same way. But, until we get everything figured out . . . don't stop me from sucking," Victoria said.

And before Mathew could say, "Excuse me?" he quickly figured out what she meant when her teeth sank into his neck. Even though it hurt, it was a strange comforting pain. This feeding lasted longer than usual and Mathew didn't mind but, the longer she fed, the more Mathew pondered the fact that he didn't drink blood.

"Thanks for the meal," Victoria said when she finished.

"Victoria . . . do you think that I could drink your blood?" Mathew asked feeling a little embarrassed.

"I don't see why not . . . you want to even though it has a strange taste?" she replied with as a blush spread across her face.

"I want to at least try it once . . . and I don't know if I don't like the taste," Mathew admitted.

"Okay then. Let's make sure no one interrupts your first time," Victoria said as she got up, locked the door then returned to sit back down next to him.

"Okay, I'm ready," she said clearing a spot on her neck for him.

Mathew was a little nervous at first but his teeth sunk in like a knife through butter. It took him a few moments to figure out how to control the blood flow and the taste wasn't like anything he had expected or had tasted before. It was difficult to describe; it was like the taste of black raspberries with a hint of strawberries that were just a little too tangy to be fully ripe. But something happened to Mathew while he was feeding so he stopped for a moment.

"What is it, Mathew?" Victoria asked because it was obviously too soon for him to be satisfied.

"What the heck is that?" Mathew asked himself pulling off his shirt and saw his cross going haywire. The gem in the middle seemed to be vibrating with an unusual energy and the colors were all scrambling together. The cross itself was shaking, causing the chain on his neck to rattle.

"Victoria, I have a very bad feeling about this," Mathew said as he watched the cross and then Mathew saw his own ribs move. The intensity of the pain paralyzed him for a moment but Mathew wasn't afraid. He wasn't exactly sure what was going on but remembered going through something like this before when he drank the liquid that first allowed him to turn into a bat. This time it was different, though, and Mathew knew instinctively the source of this transformation was Victoria's blood.

While this reconstruction of his body lasted only for a few minutes, it seemed to Mathew to last for several hours. Extended pain never is a promotion for the quick passing the time. However, it wasn't as painful as his first experience but still it hurt. When it finished, Mathew was physically exhausted. After a short rest, he was able to get up and move around. There was no need for extended bed rest this time.

"What was that all about?" Mathew asked. He took quick stock of all his body parts and nothing seemed to change except his bone structure. He did, though, instantly notice that his lung and the wound were healed.

"Well that was . . . odd." Victoria said after the ordeal was finished. "Do you feel any different after all that?" she asked.

"Not much different. Thankfully my wound is healed. That's cool. Thank God that's over, though! That was just painfully annoying. Weird, though. The wound itself is no reason to go through a change like that," Mathew replied looking at his new scar.

"Can you still control ice?" Victoria asked looking at Mathew's cross.

Mathew quickly created a few random objects just to check and said, "Yeah, that hasn't changed. I don't know what that was about . . . I guess I'm going to have to sleep on it," Mathew said after thinking of one other thing he could try.

"Okay, then. I'll leave you be. Let me know if you figure out what it was about. I just wish Daddy was here," Victoria said leaving the room.

As soon as Victoria was out of sight, Mathew closed the door behind her and locked it. He searched the room for the bag of blood Dracula gave him but it must have been left at the Inn. Mathew thought for a moment and quickly thought of a plan. He rushed to the window and threw it open.

"Hey, umm . . . Any Death Stalkers out here willing to do a quick favor for me?" Mathew spoke out the window and luckily one of them responded quickly.

"What can I do for you, Royal Master?" the Death Stalker asked.

"Okay cool, I need you to do something top secret for me . . . no one else should know what I'm about to tell you," Mathew said getting a little excited.

"Of course, nothing I perform will come to light," the man replied.

"Okay good . . . so I've got this thing for one of the servants and I would like you to fetch her for me," Mathew said trying to be discrete.

"Understood. What is the servant's name?" the man replied with a slight smile.

"Her name is Kyoko. Tell her to wear something sexy and ask her to bring a vial of Elemental Blood, if we have any. Can you do that for me?" Mathew asked trying to give the impression that this was just a secret lovers' meeting.

"Sounds very romantic. Is there a time you wish her to be here?" the man asked making it clear that Death stalkers needed a lot of information to operate normally.

"Umm, good question . . . let's plan around midnight," Mathew said just throwing out a time.

"Sounds like a perfect evening, Sir. Is there anything else you would like from me?" the man asked.

"No, and for your good work, after you complete this task take the rest of the night off," Mathew said thinking that he might as well reward him for doing something like this.

"Thank you, Sir. It will be done momentarily," the man said before vanishing as quickly as a wisp of smoke.

And now we wait, Mathew thought to himself.

Time ticked by slowly because Mathew had nothing to do. He needed to see if his control over blood had been affected by this most recent transformation. Mathew noticed that his mind was sharper than usual and every problem, complex and not, he managed to think of in his boredom he quickly resolved. He was feeling incredibly good for some reason and deduced the source was the rearrangement he suffered earlier. He felt that he still needed more proof before he could be certain and, at the stroke of midnight, the knock he had been waiting for came at the door. Mathew flung the door open and quickly pulled Kyoko in the room.

"Hello . . . I came as you requested," she said with her eyes to the ground and Mathew knew that she was feeling nervous, uncomfortable and embarrassed all at the same time.

"Hello again, Kyoko. First, let me explain," Mathew said wanting to clarify the situation as he pulled her into the room.

"I understand and there is nothing to explain. You called me here to satisfy your urges . . . and I'm ready to serve you, Master," she said removing her work uniform exposing the most amazing lingerie Mathew had seen in a while. No, probably ever. He forced his mind back to the task at hand as he reminded himself that he had called her here for a specific purpose and it wasn't about sex.

"Umm . . . My sincere apologies for the misunderstanding but my true intention for asking you here was just to get the Elemental blood," Mathew said feeling guilty he had put her though this embarrassing display.

"Wait . . . you mean you don't want to have sex with me?" she asked obviously confused.

"I know seems strange but you will understand soon enough . . . by the way, do you want a drink of this before I use it?" Mathew asked holding out the bottle of blood.

"Yes please . . . I'm still trying to understand why you called me here though," Kyoko said taking a mouthful of blood. Mathew noticed that her ability to adapt to different situations was rather remarkable.

"Okay listen; I need you to keep your mouth shut about this. Can you do that?" Mathew asked making sure that his blood magic would be kept a secret.

"Yes, I understand, Master," Kyoko replied.

"Okay. Bottoms up," Mathew said before dumping the bottle of blood on the floor.

Mathew didn't need to concentrate because the blood quickly and easily obeyed his thoughts. As Kyoko watched Mathew enjoying himself making shapes and even a long rope-like strand which Kyoko took a bite out of just for fun, she understood why she was called so covertly to Mathew's room. What was taking place in the room was something revolutionary and potentially dangerous for Mathew. Several hours and a lot of fun later, Mathew's curiosity was satisfied that his ability to control blood was intact and he even managed to improve his skills significantly. Mathew coaxed the blood back into its original bottle and proceeded to hide it on a nearby shelf.

"Master, I understand now why you went through all the trouble to get that bottle. I am curious, though, about what you think of my lingerie?" she asked standing up and doing a little spin.

"It's super sexy. Why didn't you put your other clothes on?" Mathew asked realizing it had been a few hours since she had arrived and she might have been cold and uncomfortable during that time.

"Well . . . where else am I going to hang out while wearing this and actually have someone enjoy it?" she asked back.

"Fair enough. By the way, what's with the 'master' thing?" Mathew asked just out of curiosity.

"Lord Dracula assigned me to be your personal attendant and I am bound to you for life or until you dismiss me from service to you," Kyoko answered.

"Do you wish to leave my service?" Mathew asked wanting to understand her viewpoint on this.

"Oh no, half of the servants here are servants because we get treated well here. Much better that most places, that is," she said with a quirky look on her face and Mathew figured it wasn't his place to ask.

"Well then, you're dismissed for the night. I may need to call for you again in the same manner. Just a heads up," Mathew explained before she left the room.

Alone again, Mathew went through every aspect of his abilities to see whether or not the rearrangement did anything besides improve his control over blood. The only difference he noticed was when he bit his cheek and assumed his canine teeth grew a little bit larger again. After a while, Mathew decided he was going to go to bed. He still was not used to being awake for 24 hours a day and used sleep more of a way to pass the time.

When Mathew awoke, the high he had yesterday was gone. For better and for worse, he seemed to be back to his usual self. Mathew decided to take a walk around the Manor to explore. In all the time he had spent there he had never explored the entire property. As he started out on his exploration, he unexpectedly bumped into Dracula who was looking for him, then continued to pull him downstairs to a portal. This one was very similar to the one back at the Ice fortress and an additional thought crossed his mind as he wondered how long it had been here. But before Mathew could ask any questions about it, Dracula proceeded to push him through the center of the portal.

Stepping through to the other side of the portal, Mathew realized he was back in God's Step. He was quickly led into another carriage where he proceeded to confront Dracula about being brought back to God's Step without his permission.

"Mathew, we have decided it's time to announce your blood magic to the world," Dracula stated.

"Why now? Has something changed? We've been going through a lot of trouble to keep it secret," Mathew said trying to understand the situation. He was feeling a need for more control over his own life.

"Nothing has changed and, even with the days and hours spent on this investigation, we were unable to find out who hired the assassin. The plot was very well planned. We're now planning on luring out another one and you, dear boy, are the bait," Dracula explained.

"I need my blood bag then," Mathew said thinking ahead of himself.

"I have it right here. I'll give it to you when we get inside but I need to do something with it first," Dracula explained. "Okay, we're here. Get ready to do your best," he said as the carriage came to a stop.

Once again, Mathew walked down the line of soldiers and entered the room where the most powerful people in the Elemental world were. Most powerful or not, they were about to see something no one had ever seen before.

Dracula

CHAPTER FIFTEEN

THE POWER OF BLOOD

Just as before, Mathew stood in the center of the room except the only guards around him this time were the Elite Death Stalkers. Mathew actually preferred the fewer numbers of the Elite team and was reassured by their presence.

"What is the meaning of this, Count Dracula?" King Stanly asked when all the elders stopped barking at each other over the sudden interruption to their meeting.

"We are here to present an ability just uncovered in Mathew, the Blood Elemental. This new ability appears to have been awakened by the assassination attempt on his life," Dracula began presenting carefully selected details. "In a moment, you will all witness this but first, each of you please take a small portion of liquid from this water bag," he continued, passing around the blood bag to prove its authenticity.

"Alright, Mathew. Please proceed," Dracula said handing him the blood bag.

Mathew dumped the contents of the blood bag on the floor and a silence came over the room. To add a bit of drama to the already tense situation, he held out his hands and closed his eyes even though he knew he could easily control the blood without the theatrics. A bit nervous, he felt the need to concentrate just to make sure all went as well as possible.

In his imagination, he pictured a small stairs with a balcony on top. He heard gasps of astonishment so he opened his eyes to see the blood, still in its liquid form, but in the shape he had visualized. He quickly froze the form, causing another round of gasps from his vast audience. Just for effect, Mathew proceeded to walk up the frozen blood stairs and stand on the balcony.

"That will be all for now, Mathew. We need to leave immediately. I believe there is someone waiting to see you," Dracula said.

Mathew hopped down from his little creation and, just for the fun of it, stopped and snapped his fingers. Immediately the iced blood turned into beautiful red snow that fell softly to the floor. That little trick left the crowd speechless. Mathew felt like a magician.

"That was nice touch at the end, Mathew. Luckily you were able to pull something like that off," Dracula said when they were inside the carriage.

"So where is Bell?" Mathew asked.

"She has been staying at the Air Castle. Apparently Queen Lucy was enlisted to look after her," Dracula replied which was good news to Mathew.

"Hey, I've a question for you . . . What's the deal when your body rearranges but nothing happens?" Mathew asked wanting an accurate understanding of what exactly happened to him at the Manor.

"I thought you looked a little different. You entered an adolescent stage for Vampirism. Congratulations are in order, I believe," Dracula answered.

"So I'm a teenager, in Vampire terms anyway?" Mathew asked.

"Basically your body may rearrange one or two more times in your life," Dracula said calmly. "How's the love life?" he continued to ask for no apparent reason.

"What do you mean?" Mathew asked back not sure how to answer that question.

"Have you decided on your dream girl yet? There are many interesting choices available to you. There is my daughter or perhaps Dee . . . but then again, you seem to get along famously with any girl you meet," Dracula said giving him a light smack on the arm.

"I don't want to talk about it. I have enough problems to deal with at the moment," Mathew said as the carriage came to a halt.

Mathew walked inside the large hall and spotted Queen Lucy surrounded by a group of girls. He searched the room for Bell and, not seeing her, decided to ask where she was. To his astonishment, she was already there. Mathew had overlooked her at first because she was wearing a frilly dress and more make-up than he had ever seen on her.

"Mathew!" Bell yelled as her arms wrapped around his neck and her hug could have broken the back of a full-grown grizzly bear. "I'm so sorry you got hurt!" she wailed continuing to tighten the grip on her death hug.

"It's okay, Bell. I'm fine so don't cry. Please," Mathew said trying to calm her down so that she might loosen her grip.

"The dear girl is rather attached to you—especially for a Vanguard," Queen Lucy said with her sweet sounding voice.

"Mathew has treated me well in the short time I have known him. He has never said a cross word to me and he even tries to make me feel better when I'm down. He has seen me at my worst and has still been good to me," Bell replied which Mathew thought was a little extravagant. It seemed strange how a person could get attached to someone so quickly just because of actions he thought were normal, everyday things. Even so, they had only been through those events once or twice.

"What are you wearing?" Mathew asked not used to her wearing such girly attire.

"If you're wondering, this is your fault, Mathew. You told Lucy to watch over me so she figured she might as well change up my entire wardrobe or, at least, everything I brought for the trip," Bell complained.

"Why did you do that?" Mathew asked Lucy who seemed to be off in her own world.

"She is a striking young woman and I felt her beauty would be better suited to more feminine attire," Lucy replied. Mathew understood that, while her intentions were good, the way she went about it was not.

"Excuse me, Lucy. May I speak to you in private for a moment?" Dracula asked.

"Of course, my dear Count. By the way, I met your lovely daughter the other day. She seemed like such a nice girl," Lucy said as Dracula led the way to the other side of the room.

"What's the deal, Mathew? Why do you look so different?" Bell asked always noticing even the slightest change in Mathew's appearance.

"Oh . . . technically I went through Vampire puberty in record time and efficiency," Mathew said feeling stupid the moment he finished.

"I don't get it . . . but I'll buy it," Bell said with a smile, somewhat understanding the explanation.

"Mathew, would you like to join us in another banquet?" Lucy asked as she returned with Dracula.

"Seriously?" Mathew asked. "Honestly, I don't think that's a good idea . . . considering my current track record with parties. What do you think, Dracula? Would that even be appropriate after what I just did in front of everybody?"

"Oh, I think you will be fine, dear boy," Lucy said with a secretive smile.

"Don't be too quick to decide. Do you even know what I did?" Mathew asked well knowing that she wasn't at the meeting.

"Yes, I do. I'm Queen after all, and I learn things faster than even the King does," she said with another smile.

"So, you know about my blood magic?" Mathew whispered just to make sure.

"Of course, it's very interesting that you have abilities that even our greatest Kings don't have," Lucy said with an incredibly sweet and encouraging smile that made Mathew feel better about the situation. He wondered how such a small smile could make such a big impact.

"What is King Bradley doing, anyway, that he couldn't be here?" Mathew asked after mulling it over for a few moments.

"He is out on business negotiating with the local Demons about an occurrence in the nearby town," Lucy said simply.

"Well, that's a shame. I was kind of hoping I would get a chance to meet him," Mathew said to be polite even though he actually didn't want another king thrown into the mix.

"Mathew, if I were you, I would go back to the Inn to rest and properly prepare for the party tonight," Lucy said which was a clear indicator to leave.

"Oh wait, Mathew! I'm going with you," Bell said sticking closer to Mathew than usual. Mathew figured she just didn't want to wear the dress anymore, or get left behind and be forced to play dress up again.

"Very well. I'll see you later tonight, Lucy," Mathew said heading out of the room with Dracula and Bell.

As the carriage pulled away from the Castle, Dracula pulled both Mathew and Bell close so they could hear each other's whispers.

"We need to go over the plan. We need to draw out another assassin tonight. We just revealed that you could control blood, Mathew. Blood is the most basic form of life and your ability has undeniably shaken up the entire Elemental world," Dracula whispered to the both of them.

"Mathew, your only task tonight is to appear to exhaust yourself like you did last time. To avoid suspicion, we need to steer clear of duplicating the previous situation. We need you to wear yourself down in a different way. When we arrive at the Inn, you will practice making blood statues in the likeness of people. Your task will be making those statues of a few kings and queens at the banquet and, when you appear to be sufficiently worn down, Lucy will lead you to a room where you will go to sleep. Don't worry, my young friend, I will already be in the room, in bat form, silently watching over you. We hope to make the circumstances appear ideal for another assassination attempt on you without being blatantly obvious. I'll catch the assassin and will proceed to tear him apart, limb by limb, until we know who sent him," Dracula said as he finished laying out the plan. Neither Bell nor Mathew had a problem with the plan as the logic was there but Mathew was nervous just the same. There was something unsettling about being bait for a killer.

When they returned to the Inn, Mathew quickly greeted Julian and Steven. They were both glad to see him back in good health and on his feet again.

He began to prepare for the evening; Mathew decided he would use Julian and Steven as his first models for the blood sculptures. He had them sit or stand in different positions, closed his eyes and coaxed the blood to form exactly as he saw. Once the likeness was achieved, he froze the blood to form a solid miniature stature. Mathew was very pleased with his first attempts. The ice was red and looked like a giant, hand cut ruby that was also as smooth as a river stone. Steven and Julian were happy to have souvenirs as mementos of their time in God's Step.

After multiple successes along with a good share of failures, Mathew was satisfied with the progress he made and decided to spend the rest of his time preparing for the party before it got too late. As he was moving around the room, Mathew spotted a small brown parcel on the bed. He ripped off the paper and found formal Vampire attire, probably left by Dracula when Mathew was practicing the blood sculptures. Mathew decided that it was the perfect outfit to control blood in.

When the time came, the entire group climbed into the carriage and Mathew realized how big the small looking carriage actually was. Definitely bigger on the inside than the outside.

"So, Dracula. How have you been? We haven't had a chance to talk with everything that's been going on," Steven asked trying to be friendly.

"Things could be better but, then again, things could be worse," Dracula replied calmly.

"Mathew, after the party I have a question for you," Dracula said not giving Mathew any indication of what the question was.

"Of course, but just remind me because I'll forget," Mathew admitted. "So Bell . . . didn't have any other outfits?" Mathew asked just to poke fun at her because she was forced to wear another frilly dress.

"Oh shut up, Mathew! It's not like I had a choice in the matter . . . how am I supposed to say 'no' to a queen?" Bell asked giving Mathew an evil look.

"I think you look beautiful, Bell," Julian said with a smile.

"Still . . . I'm not used to wearing something so screamingly feminine," Bell said before she tried adjusting herself to the unusual clothing.

The carriage came to a stop and the group stepped out one by one. Just like the first banquet, the announcer was Dagon. He asked them their names and asked Mathew to stay back once again.

"So, what's up?" Mathew asked when Dagon came back from his quick task.

"Hey, Mac. Can you cover for me for a few seconds?" Dagon asked someone nearby.

"Got it covered!" the man yelled back.

"Okay Mathew, first of all I want to thank you for your advice. Because of you, me and my beloved are now married," Dagon said extremely proud of himself.

"Oh, congratulations! Just curious but did you get to see the Gaze?" Mathew asked having read about it multiple times.

"Of course . . . I should have asked about that before I asked her. It was terrifying. I thought she was going to eat me or something," Dagon said laughing. "Would you like to meet her?" he asked with a smile.

"Why not? Lead the way," Mathew said following Dagon through the door and up a few flights of stairs.

Mathew entered the room and he saw the Succubus. As he expected, she was really cute and, after Dagon told her who Mathew was, she greeted him with a hug and a peck on the cheek. They told him how grateful they were and asked him questions on how to keep their relationship stable since they were from different races. Mathew gave the best advice he could and, after giving them his best wishes, went down to join the others at the party.

Some people seemed to be afraid of Mathew now that they knew what he could do. Others, though, seemed overly friendly and shouted things like, "Welcome Blood Elemental!", as he walked by. Queen Lucy poked him from behind and Mathew figured this is when the plan would start.

"Excuse me, Mathew. Would you be kind enough to make a statue of me out of blood?" she asked and Mathew noticed that half the people nearby looked over to see what would happen.

"Of course!" Mathew exclaimed feeling he was going a little over the top with his acting. "Would you like it life or pocket size?" he asked just for effect, also it gave him a chance to change his tone.

"Life size would be lovely," Lucy said practicing a few poses before finally deciding which one she liked most.

Mathew went to work. He uncapped his blood bag and dumped the contents into an empty bowl that he found. He copied the image in his mind and coaxed it once again into the blood. When the blood finished taking shape, he froze it creating a smooth, shiny surface that reflected the dancing lights of the palace party.

"Wow. That's amazing!" someone from the crowd exclaimed as others gathered around the statue to examine it.

"Thank you very much, Mathew. I will treasure this for a long time to come," Lucy said as she admired the life-sized statue of herself.

"Would anyone else like one? I can make miniatures," Mathew asked the crowd and instantly a line began to form.

One after another, Mathew made statues of different people. Several statues into the project, he actually had to take a quick break so the gland in the blood bag could make more blood. The event was a huge hit and almost everybody wanted a personalized statue, including most of the kings who struck their best pose, like holding a sword to the sky. Queen Dellina even asked Mathew if he would create one of her in private. Mathew told her that, after everyone else got one, he would be glad to. The line slowly diminished and, when Dellina saw that Mathew was on his last customer, she quickly pulled him into a room away from the main hall.

"So what do you want me to make?" Mathew asked politely even though he was actually quite tired.

"Are you willing to do a nude of me?" she asked nicely but it seemed a little weird.

"If you're okay with it, I have no problem with it," Mathew said feeling a little uncomfortable with the suggested arrangement but tried hard not to show it.

"I don't mind," she said as she started to remove her clothes.

"Now what size do you want it?" Mathew asked.

"I would like a miniature for the moment," she said lying down on the bed and picked her pose.

"Don't mind me staring. It's my first time doing one like this so I need to really capture the image," Mathew said taking in the image of her body. He actually had to concentrate on this one so, when the blood properly arranged itself, he froze it creating the best work he had done all night.

"It's lovely. Thank you very much, Mathew," Dellina said as she started to put her clothes back on.

"You're welcome. Would you mind answering a question I have?" Mathew asked hoping that she would feel inclined to answer.

"Of course. Go ahead and ask," she replied as she fixed her hair.

"I would like to know where I stand. What's going to happen to me?" Mathew asked.

"Don't worry, Mathew. You are safe from any harm. Since you are a Royal Vampire, the stakes are quite high and any court action would need to be extremely well supported. We were investigating the details of your attack but unfortunately we found out nothing . . . that was a shame. Personally, I don't mind you. I might even invite you to a private dinner sometime. Perhaps to do a life size encore," she answered standing up and leaving the room with her statue before Mathew could reply.

Mathew went back to the party and chugged a couple glasses of Human soda that was apparently the hottest drink next to Nether Brew. He noticed that a few Elders had started a game of "Kill the King" in the court yard just as before. It was eerily similar to the night of the assassination attempt except the person to offer him a bed for the night was Lucy.

Mathew was led to the pre-planned room. It was farther down the hall than the room he was almost killed in. Mathew hopped on the bed, looked around quickly and, before he fell asleep, he saw a large bat hanging in the shadowy corner of the room.

Mathew woke up to something crashing into the floor. Startled, he froze the first object he saw which turned out to be nothing more than a coat rack, Mathew looked and saw that Dracula had the would-be assassin tightly in his grasp. Mathew knew that there was no escape for the assassin and did not envy him at all.

"Mathew, check his pockets," Dracula ordered. Mathew did and pulled out a few items that weren't unusual. There was a pocket watch, a deck of cards and some lint. But one of the items did look suspicious. It was a small vial with liquid in it.

"Mathew, destroy that vial," Dracula ordered without even breaking a sweat while holding the assassin.

Mathew threw the vial on the floor and smashed it with a chunk of ice. Just to be safe, he froze the pieces of glass, then changed it to liquid and smashed them some more. At that time, Queen Lucy arrived with a group of soldiers and ordered the man to be arrested.

The soldiers formed a square and used something like an air shackle to control the man's limbs so he was helplessly hanging in the air then they more or less floated him out of the room.

"That went perfectly!" Dracula said happy as his plan actually worked.

"I can't believe I actually fell asleep! Now what do we do?" Mathew asked.

"We go home and let the politicians battle it out. Come on, our work is done," Dracula said dragging Mathew along with him.

"Should we bring Bell along?" Mathew asked because he didn't want to leave her quite yet.

"Of course. Victoria knows her and it will be a nice little reunion for them," Dracula said.

As they exited the castle, Mathew and Dracula went to hop into the carriage that was waiting for them. Mathew's curiosity was finally satisfied as he caught a quick peek at what was pulling the carriage. He originally thought regular horses pulled the carriages but, in reality, Dread Steeds pulled them. Mathew had only read a few paragraphs about them during his Demonology training because, to an Elemental, seeing a Dread Steed was as common as a Human spotting the occasional rabbit. Mathew quickly took in their features and, all in all, they looked a lot like regular horses except for having eight legs instead of the four. Mathew guessed that the extra four legs gave them greater speed and allowed them to cover more ground with less effort. As he climbed into the carriage, he discovered what the 'Dread' stood for. The horses let out a ghastly and eerie 'neigh' that sounded like a polyphonic death toll from a horror film that a monster would scream when its last battle came to an end. Mathew clamped his hands over his ears as his body shook from the vibration of the horrific sound. He was paralyzed for the first few seconds until his mind could process what had just happened.

When they arrived at the Inn, Mathew picked up the rest of his belongings that had been left there during his first visit and woke Bell up. As she got ready, he said goodbye to Steven and Julian who had decided to stay on longer to support Mathew's case if need be. Mathew, Bell and Dracula decided to walk to the portal and enjoy the dark surroundings rather than take the carriage again. The walk was mainly at Mathew's suggestion because he secretly did not ever want to be subjected to the ghastly neigh of the Dread Steeds again. Once was too much for him when it came to that experience. Fortunately, they were relatively close so the trip wouldn't take them long on foot. When they arrived at the portal, Mathew walked in first because if he didn't, he had a feeling that he would be pushed in. After surviving two assassination attempts, he again felt the need to take some control over his life. He arrived in the basement of the Manor and was relieved that he was in a friendly and safe place again. Even Bell seemed to relax.

"Come with me, Mathew. I would like to speak to you in private and am reminding you as you requested earlier," Dracula said leading Mathew up the stairs into a library-like room and closed the door behind them.

"So, what's going on?" Mathew asked confused as to why he was brought here and curious about the secrecy surrounding the question.

"I have given this a lot of thought and would like to ask you if you would be willing to take my surname as your own," he asked simply as he sat down in a luxurious brown chair.

"Wait . . . you're talking about me becoming Mathew Dracula?" Mathew replied rather shocked at the unusual offer.

"Yes, I believe I know you well enough now to offer you a place in my family. You have my blood running through your veins and, as a Royal Vampire already, you would have no problem adjusting," Dracula explained.

"How will this affect my relationship with Victoria or Dee?" Mathew asked not wanting to be tied down quite yet. The urging to make his own decisions swelled up within him again. He had spent his entire Human life trying his best to follow other people's rules and he was finished with that. He hadn't realized until this moment how suffocated he had felt.

"I can suggest and express my wishes but will never force you to date or marry my daughter . . . or anyone else. And before you ask, no you are not brother and sister. You would be taking your place in my clan. Truth be told, I have never been officially married and all of my children are adopted," Dracula admitted with a hint of pride in his voice.

"What would change if I were to accept the name?" Mathew asked as he walked over to the library shelves to pull out an ancient looking demonology book that had caught his eye. He started flipping through it to mentally put some distance between himself and the current situation.

"Nothing much. You would be able to permanently live with us and have a voice in all Vampire affairs. As a Dracula, you will be an important and respected member of the community and, as I mentioned, you will be a part of my clan. In essence, nothing much will change. Your position has already been established here so why not make it official?" Dracula explained. "So . . . may I have your answer, Mathew?" Dracula asked.

"When have I ever said no to you?" Mathew said and, with that one sentence, he accepted his place within the infamous and centuries old family.

"Wonderful! Well now, Mathew Dracula, let us go and make the announcement to everyone," Dracula said literally dragging Mathew by the wrist out into the hallway.

"Everybody! Wonderful news! Mathew has accepted our family name so please welcome him into the family," Dracula announced enthusiastically, obviously making a bigger deal out of this than Mathew thought needed to be.

Mathew was congratulated by everybody with a round of applause, random hugs from females and slaps on the back from the males.

"You're worse than Steven," Mathew said giving Dracula an evil look.

"Glad to have you in our clan, Mathew Dracula," Victoria said giving him a hug.

"Why, thank you, Victoria Dracula. Thank you for allowing me into your family . . . or clan," Mathew replied.

"Hey, just remember we are not related. You're more like . . . my plaything," Victoria stated.

"I'll keep that in mind," Mathew said already informed on this topic.

Mathew enjoyed the rest of the day with his new family and his new name. Bell sporadically joined in the festivities as well but it was obviously hard for her to mingle because of her introverted personality. Mathew spent most of his time with her so she wouldn't feel left out. He was disappointed to hear that Dee and Catharine had left the day before so he wasn't expecting them to show. He had wanted to talk with Dee in private. When the party was over, Mathew went to his room but he was too wound up to sleep so he just sat in the dark thinking and messing around with blood.

Around midnight, Mathew saw a curious red glow on his wall. A moment later, a burst of fire came through his window. The thing Mathew had noticed about Elemental fire on the few occasions he had encountered it was that the fire didn't need to even smolder before it would ignite whatever it landed on. Anything the fire touched would quickly burst into flames upon contact and quickly spread as if doused with an accelerant. It would appear to spontaneously combust. By instinct, Mathew dashed out of the room because he realized it would have been stupid to stay there and spectate.

The Manor was full of frantic people screaming and running about. Chaos was everywhere. Mathew took action and began to freeze as much as he could until Dracula pulled him outside. There he saw the extent of what was really going on.

Fire Elemental soldiers were attacking the Manor. The Death Stalkers were giving them a hell of a fight but Mathew didn't think they could hold out for long on their own.

"Come on, son! Let's get in there," Dracula said dashing into what looked like a war of red and black uniforms.

Mathew had no choice but to go. This was real—not like the movies where you would reason with your enemy for ten minutes before they would make the first move. He joined the fight and noticed the Fire Elementals didn't use swords. Their strategy was more of a hand-to-hand combat or ranged tactics. This made them easy targets for Mathew and the rest of the Death Stalkers who used swords and various other weapons.

With his senses heightened from his recent transformation, coupled with the adrenaline from the current battle, Mathew heard someone coming up behind him. Not in time, though, to bring up his sword. He caught a glimpse of a red-hot hand closing in but, before the hand could find its mark, a sword came to his rescue. It flew into the attacker's head causing the body to burst into flame and vanish leaving behind only a liquefied mass of glowing red blood. It reminded Mathew of lava.

"Mathew! You all right?" Bell shouted as she ran up to grab her blade out of the molten lava.

"Yeah, thanks . . . don't stop on my account," Mathew said.

"I didn't intend to," she shouted back to him with a smile as she dashed and chopped her way through more Fire Elementals as if they were helpless chunks of firewood.

It was then that Mathew saw the true essence of his Ice Vanguard friend. She was in her element and at her finest. She moved with the grace of a ballerina and the force of a hurricane. At times, she wielded more than five blades simultaneously—each in different directions. Adding to the perfection of her combat skills was her use of Ice Magic. Every step she took created large patches of ice that she would stand and fight on but were the demise of her enemies. As he watched in fascinated amazement, Mathew saw Fire Elementals slip and fall to their deaths on her ice patches that seemed to consume the unsuspecting and dazed Fire Elementals. Mathew then realized why Bell had such a hard time showing her emotions. Decades of training, honing her skills and overcoming personal frailties had disciplined her into the perfect fighting machine. Mathew thought it was ridiculous for the Elemental court to accuse him of being a deadly weapon when Bell and others like her had existed for hundreds of years.

Somehow off to the side of the action, Mathew shook himself out of his daydream as he heard someone coming up behind him again. He saw another red-hot hand coming towards him but, this time, Mathew thought quickly. Using the element of surprise to his advantage, he turned into a bat, dodged the fire-infested hand and proceeded to fly up and take a bite out of the man's ear. The man screamed and tried to swat Mathew off like a fly but Mathew was too quick for the shocked Fire Elemental. When Mathew was tired of being swatted at, he transformed again and cut the man down with his ice blade.

Eventually the Fire Elementals were all dead or fleeing into the woods. Now that it was quiet, the Manor inhabitants just stood around in shocked disbelief. Because of the quiet atmosphere, Mathew was able to hear muffled cries coming from inside the still flaming Manor. He rushed into the building. It was hotter than anything he had ever experienced before and Mathew compensated by repeatedly freezing his skin for protection from the blazes.

Mathew followed the sound of the cries until he came to a large wooden door. He saw a metal coat rack wedged between the handle and doorframe. He grabbed the coat rack and freed it with a strong pull that would have scorched his hands if he hadn't thought to freeze them first. He opened the door and caught Kyoko as she rushed out. Because of the suspicious way the door had been jammed shut from the outside, Mathew quickly took mental stock of the room and understood why Kyoko was trapped in there. The room appeared to be a wine storage with only one access point and no windows. It was completely sealed off from the outside world.

"Master! Oh, Master, thank you!" Kyoko cried.

"Thank me later, Kyoko," Mathew said picking her up, running through the Manor, jumping over fallen beams and freezing a path as he went. He dashed out the front door of the Manor to safety, put Kyoko down and fell into the cool embrace of the grass.

Mathew turned to watch the once elegant and imposing Manor collapse to the ground. It was one of the saddest moments he had yet to experience; The Manor had become home to him even though he had only stayed there a few times.

Just then, Dracula appeared. "Mathew, carry Kyoko. She has passed out," he said firmly and authoritatively. "Gather around, family! Let's head into town . . . there is nothing more we can do here," he said to the group.

Mathew carried Kyoko as they walked down the path to town. He was thankful and relieved when Victoria approached him and then Bell a little while later. A moment later, a group of Werewolves came running towards them. They halted in front of Dracula.

"We saw the fire! What happened, Sir?" one of them asked. Mathew recognized the voice of Inspector Jonathan.

"Fire Elementals attacked us and burned our home down. We are on our way to the Succubus Palace to seek refuge until we can sort things out," Dracula explained.

"Is there anything we can do to help?" John asked sniffing the air a few times.

"We significantly altered their numbers but some of the attackers escaped. They could be regrouping but I don't believe them to be a credible threat," Dracula explained. "For surety sake, are you willing to do a little scouting for us, my friend? I am not able to spare any more Death Stalkers at this moment," Dracula asked with a pained expression of loss on his face.

"Of course. Pack! Spread out and search!" Jonathan yelled and the Werewolves sped off into the woods with howls that echoed through the woods.

The rest of the walk wasn't as depressing as Mathew thought it would be. The Vampires were a strong race of survivors. Mathew thought about their history and realized they would have to be as they had been constantly hunted and murdered by Humans and rival demons for centuries.

When they entered town, most of the remaining Death Stalkers went to the nearby bar to let off some steam. The others engaged in idle conversation with the various Demon races that gasped and cursed the Fire Elementals for their actions. Mathew was told to go inside with Dracula and Victoria to discuss provisions with Catharine.

"What the hell happened to you guys?" a young Succubus asked when they walked in. Mathew didn't notice that he was covered from head to foot in blood until he was in the light. His clothes were drenched in blood and it was splattered across his face. He had wondered why there was a strange taste in his mouth during the walk.

"We had a problem with Fire Elementals. Would you go and fetch Catharine for us?" Dracula replied.

A few moments later, Catharine came running down the nearby stairs.

"Dracula! What happened?" she asked taking out her handkerchief to wipe some off some blood of both Dracula's and Mathew's face.

"The Manor was burnt down by Fire Elementals . . . we need a place to stay," Dracula asked as best he could. It was clear he wasn't use to asking for anything at all but, then again, how often would a man who had everything need to ask for a place to stay?

"How many are there?" she asked as politely as she could.

"Around thirty five. We lost almost half of our Death Stalkers," Dracula admitted and Mathew saw the pain on his face again as he said it.

"You are welcome here," Catharine said ordering the girl who was attending the front desk to coordinate preparations for their dazed guests.

Dracula went outside to tell the others what was going on. They slowly came in and went off to their individual rooms. Mathew was told to go to his room which was one of the best rooms in the palace. He slowly walked up the stairs and opened the door. Luckily each room had its own bathroom so Mathew washed himself up and found a pair of clothes in the drawer. When he put them on they were a little large but he couldn't complain. The only thing he really wanted to do at the moment was sleep but sleep evaded him and, every time he closed his eyes, he saw the fighting. His mind was trying to process the trauma of the day's events so he just lay there awake until he saw the first glimpse of daylight.

Even though he had spent the night lying awake in his bed, Mathew still felt dirty. When he finally managed to get up, he took another bath and, even though he thought he had washed thoroughly the night before, the water still turned an unsightly brownish color of lifeless blood. Warm water wasn't appealing to him and he wanted nothing to do with heat at the moment so he froze the bath water solid. Even though the bath water was solid ice, he could still move through it as if it were liquid. This was something he had never done before and was amazed at his list of never-seeming-to-end abilities, and if only for a moment allowed him to forget the previous night.

Bell

CHAPTER SIXTEEN

HOME AGAIN

When Mathew came out of the bathroom, Kyoko was in his room making the bed for him. This surprised Mathew at first but he was quickly getting used to the idea of having a servant, especially a cute one.

"Good morning, Master . . . did you sleep well?" Kyoko asked with a smile.

"No, not at all. My nerves didn't let me and my brain was in trauma mode . . . I kept seeing Fire Elementals coming at me every time I closed my eyes. So I stared at the ceiling all night hearing dying screams instead," Mathew explained.

"Is there anything I can do for you . . . you know, to help repay you for your kindness in saving me?" Kyoko asked.

"I know this will sound weird . . . but do you think you would mind giving me a massage? My right shoulder and mid back are causing me a lot of pain," Mathew explained as nicely as he could. He did have a knot in his right shoulder that had been bugging him and a sharp pain in his mid-back when he took a breath. It felt like someone had yanked out one of his ribs and was stabbing him repeatedly in the back with it. He thought it was probably from repeatedly swinging his sword in awkward ways the night before. Over all, he was not in the best physical condition to face the challenges of the day.

"Of course . . . but don't expect a happy ending," she laughed.

"Do you want the shirt on or off?" Mathew asked after he finished laughing at her light joke.

"Off please," Kyoko said simply and her fingers made a loud snapping sound as she cracked them.

"Kyoko, why are you so comfortable around me? I mean, we haven't known each other long and had only really talked a few times before I got you out of the fire. Before that, you wore that lingerie around me for two hours even though you knew I wasn't going to make a move on you," Mathew asked as Kyoko began the massage.

"Well . . . I have no idea . . . it's just . . . I get this sense of security whenever I'm around you. I belong to you and am not allowed to say no to any Royal Vampire. Especially one that is my master," she explained as a few bones in Mathew's back cracked and popped back into place.

"Mathew, settle an argument," Dee said throwing open the door suddenly and walking in with Victoria. They both stopped dead in their tracks when they saw Kyoko giving Mathew a shirtless massage.

"Excuse us . . . it seems like you're busy," Victoria said pulling Dee back out of the room.

"But I want to see!" Mathew heard Dee whine from the other side of the door.

"Great. I just had to ask for a massage," Mathew complained softly.

"Forgive me, Master, but . . . would you be willing to do something for us? By 'us' I mean the local Vampires," Kyoko asked.

"What are you talking about?" Mathew replied unsure what the task was going to be.

"A Human has somehow gotten his hands on an old Vampire Slayer's hand book. Needless to say he has taken up a new hobby . . . I assume I don't have to tell you what it is. Would you be willing to acquire that book for us? I have informed Dracula about it but he refused to take action until it had been proven or . . . whatever. He never actually explained why he wouldn't take care of the situation immediately," Kyoko explained and Mathew understood that this was indeed a problem for his new family and others like them who may be passing through.

"Is he nearby?" Mathew asked wanting more details.

"Only a few miles away . . . I know exactly where he lives so I can take you right there," she answered.

"Alright, let's do this. We will leave tonight. Please go and find two black cloaks," Mathew said actually rather anxious to get out and run around even though he wasn't sure why.

The time ticked by slowly with Mathew continually going over the plan in his head until it was time to leave.

Kyoko knocked at the door and they headed off on their late night mission. Dressed mostly in black, topped off with the black cloaks, they quietly walked out of the Palace without anyone asking questions as to where they were going. Once outside, Kyoko led the way. To keep up with her, Mathew needed to sprint for the first time since he became a Blood Elemental. It took a few failed attempts to adjust to his newfound speed and, a few trips and tumbles later, he realized that he needed to actually watch where he was going to avoid obstacles.

When they reached their destination, a heavy fog was hanging in the air. Buildings big and small were slightly visible and Mathew thought the town seemed familiar but he couldn't think why. He and Kyoko rushed from alley to alley, hopped fences and scooted through the small streets. Both Mathew and Kyoko's eyes glowed red in the dark so they kept the hoods up and their eyes down when they came across another person. Eventually they reached the house where Kyoko said the book was.

"Is this the place?" Mathew asked.

"Yes . . . I hate this place . . . it reeks of evil," Kyoko said with a hiss in her voice. This was the first time Mathew actually saw from a Vampire's perspective. 'Evil' was subjective and murder was evil, no matter what side you happened to be on.

"Alright, let's move," Mathew said as he moved up to a darkened window and tried to open it. Luckily it was unlocked and opened slowly with only a small scraping noise.

Mathew and Kyoko crept throughout the house looking in every place they could think in search of the Slayer book. They dug through the cabinets and looked under the couch. Suddenly, a light flicked on and they silently hid in a darkened area of the living room. A man slowly walked down the hard wood stairs that creaked with every other step. He had an object in his hand that looked like a sharpened stake. He was furtively looking around as he peered into the darkened room.

"Come on out, bloody Vampires! I know you're here," the man said a little nervously so Mathew boldly stepped out of the shadows.

"Well! So they finally start to move on the offensive," the man stated in a false bravado that made his statement seem rehearsed.

"I'm just here for the book. Hand it over and I will leave," Mathew said loudly and clearly.

"That would be a no. Why would I give you filthy creatures the one weapon I have to fight your kind?" the man asked still sounding rehearsed.

"Because you're tormenting my kind and you're posing a problem. Just consider yourself lucky that I am here and not a Death Stalker," Mathew said trying to reason with the man.

"Death Stalkers are no match for a Slayer like myself! You should have seen how I cracked one on the head and left her for dead," the man said aggressively and it was obvious that he was getting ready for a fight. Mathew stopped breathing for a moment as he registered the comment. All he could think of was how he had first found Victoria with a head wound . . . left for dead.

"Did she have silver hair?" Mathew asked.

"What?" the man replied shocked by the question.

"Did the girl have silver hair?" Mathew asked again in a clearer voice.

"As a matter of fact she did. I lured her into the woods a few miles away from here with the scent of blood. I dropped a rock on her but she ran away before I could finish the job. I expect that the crack on her head did her in," the man boasted obviously proud of himself.

"So, you're the one!" Mathew yelled very angry now. He had strong feelings for Victoria and he hated the thought of her being hurt by this wannabe warrior.

"Oh, what a shame . . . Did you know her? Such a tragedy that she's dead now," the man taunted trying to provoke Mathew into a fight.

"Hate to be a buzz kill but she's alive and well," Mathew said as his muscled tensed and adrenaline started to flow through his veins. He had every intention of beating the man to an inch of his life just to get rid of the surging anger.

"So sad then that you won't be returning to her!" the man yelled and made a lunge at Mathew's heart with the stake.

Mathew easily caught the stake before it even came near him. He realized the difference in his strength now when this full grown man, who appeared to be twice Mathew's age and size, was no match for him when it came to strength or agility. Mathew was holding the stake back with one hand and threw the man back into the wall without even breaking a sweat.

"I'm not big on killing if I can avoid it but you're not giving me much choice so I'll say this one last time, give me the book and I will leave," Mathew said still trying to avoid a violent outcome.

"Shut up and die you unholy demon!" the man said with a mixture of fear and rage in his eyes. The man pulled out a gun from a hidden spot on a shelf and took aim at Mathew's heart.

Mathew reacted on impulse. He waved his hand that sent shards of razor sharp ice into the man's body. The man was dead before he could even put his finger on the trigger.

Mathew wasn't shocked or surprised at the outcome of this encounter but he did feel sick and proceeded to throw up. He reasoned with himself that he didn't need to feel too badly about the man's death. He gave the man honorable options to avoid fighting but the man still made the choice to try and kill him.

"You okay, Master?" Kyoko asked coming out from her hiding place.

"Yeah, just my first time killing someone who wasn't burning down a Manor or trying to assassinate me . . . not to mention it was a Human," Mathew replied. He quickly started to look through the house again for the book to take his mind off of his twitching nerves and shaking body.

The book proved to be well hidden and not easily found. After close to destroying the house, they finally found a safe hidden behind a painting. Mathew chided himself that he had not thought of such an obvious hiding place sooner. He could have avoided loss of time and perhaps loss of life. He had seen safes behind paintings in hundreds of movies and that should have been the first place he looked. The safe, however, was locked and Mathew tried force along with random numbers to open it until he suddenly had an idea. He poured blood from his blood bag onto the safe so it would leak through the cracks. He then went to work. Mathew closed his eyes and willed the blood to the combination dial. He visualized the notches and turned the blood a certain way until he heard the three clicks from the lock. He turned hard on the old handle and the safe opened easily with a loud creak. Inside he found a couple folds of money, some useless papers and the man's birth certificate but unfortunately no book. Mathew took a quick glance at the birth certificate and saw that the man's name was Ronny Elvender. The name sounded slightly familiar but Mathew just ignored it and proceeded to quickly stuff the money into his pockets because the dead man had no use for it.

Continuing the search for the book, Mathew looked around the house for anything that could be of use. He took a few books off the shelf and, after pillaging around the house some more, he looked out of the window and noticed that dawn was arriving. His body froze as he stared in dazed amazement. He had seen this sight before many, many times. The local church's bell tower was the center of town and next to it was the old and peeling barbershop billboard. He now knew why everything had seemed so familiar. Mathew had returned to his hometown.

Mathew had a hard time wrapping his mind around a Demon town so close to where he had grown up. He had just gone about his bland, unsuspecting life as a school student without the excitement of knowing that demons could be roaming around the town at any given time. With a second thought . . . he might not have been that excited as a Human knowing a demon town was so close by.

Nonetheless, Mathew had other things to focus on besides being home. He ripped apart shelves, flipped over furniture and finally found what he was looking for. The book was hidden under a floorboard that smacked him in the face when he stepped on it while moving a chair. The book was old, tattered and had a musty old book smell. It looked like a diary written in ink that was faded from centuries of use and age. It wasn't even the complete book. Several pages were missing and others were ripped in half. Mathew spotted handwritten notes in various places that looked about the same age as the original ink. An entire title of a chapter was scratched out and a simple statement was placed above the title. "Nothing but lies" was burned into the page as if whoever did that was using a hot iron brand. He marveled at the history of this book and wondered how many hands it had changed over the centuries to get here. Mathew continued to scavenge around the house and found an elaborate police uniform that looked so authentic that he decided to take it with him. He put both the book and the uniform into a small backpack he found, zipped it up and slung it over his shoulder. Several hours after their arrival, they were ready to head out.

"Why are you bringing that costume, Mathew?" Kyoko asked as she returned from her own scavenger hunt of the house. She was carrying her own prizes mostly made up of antique flatware that she hoped to be pure silver.

"This is my hometown and I want to grab a few things from my old house. I'll need a distraction," Mathew replied.

"You lived here?" Kyoko replied a little surprised.

"Yep, so on our way home we're going to make a quick stop," Mathew stated. "You don't mind, do you?" he belatedly decided to ask.

"Of course not. It's fine. We have all the time in the world . . . I guess," Kyoko replied hesitantly as she glanced out the window.

"Well then, let's go before somebody shows up. I'd like to stop at the mall on our way back to buy new clothes. I suspect that in this town we might draw a lot of negative attention walking around dressed mostly in black. That along with our smashing out-of-date cloaks," Mathew explained as he started to think through the situation at hand.

As they headed out of the house, Mathew led the way down the road towards his boyhood home. While they were walking down a dirt road a police car pulled up next to them. Mathew told Kyoko to stay calm and let him do the talking.

"Hello, why aren't you two in school?" the officer asked not truly interested and obviously just trying to do his job.

"It's kinda early yet and we're not from around here. Hey, do you know were 5930 Sutra Street is?" Mathew asked as he made up a non-existent address.

"Sorry, I don't. I could look it up on the computer if you want?" the officer suggested.

"No. That's okay, thanks anyway. I asked a gas station attendant a while back and he said if I head down this road I would find it. I just wanted to double check," Mathew lied with a sharp twinge of his conscience at how easily the lies were slipping off his tongue.

"Well, I'll leave you to it then," the officer said as his squad radio started chirping. He responded, turned on his siren and sped off in the direction that Mathew and Kyoko had come from.

They continued along their way and a school bus passed by. Mathew thought he saw Sophie's face so he quickly filled Kyoko in about his alias, James Arclight.

As they approached Mathew's old home, he asked Kyoko to change into the police costume. She agreed and changed in the nearby woods. She actually didn't look too bad in the uniform, fake badge and props.

"Okay, here is the deal. When you approach the house, ring the doorbell. If my father answers the door tell him that Ronny Elvender was killed last night. This is true but then tell him that there were documents stolen from a safe and you would appreciate his help in figuring out what might have been stolen. My dad owns a safe and knowing him, he won't argue with the police . . . but keep him talking. When he opens the safe for you, be smart about it. Ask him to show you papers in the safe but, like I said be smart. Don't pick out obvious documents like bank statements or car titles. If it is printed in big letters, don't ask what it is. Keep him engaged in conversation and I'll sneak in, head downstairs and grab the stuff I want. I will make my exit out the downstairs window and ring the doorbell when I have everything," Mathew explained the situation and quickly quizzed Kyoko on what she was going to do.

Before they reached the front door, Mathew turned into a bat and hid above the door where he couldn't be seen from inside of the house. Kyoko rang the doorbell and, moments later, the door opened.

"Hello, officer, how can I help you?" Mathew's father asked and Mathew noticed that his voice was a lot less chipper than it used to be. He also looked older and a lot more tired than Mathew remembered.

"Hello, Sir. Last night Ronny Elvender, a local who lived a few blocks away, was murdered and a safe stolen containing rather important documents and a large amount of cash. We believe that the culprit lives nearby so officers are going from house to house in search of any freshly acquired items, if you know what I mean. So would you mind if I come inside?" Kyoko asked sounding like a pro.

"Of course not, please come in," he replied.

"Sir, may I ask your name?" she continued.

"I'm Lucid Clarunde," he answered.

"And are you in possession of a safe, Mr. Clarunde?" Kyoko asked trying to lead Mathew's father away from the door.

"Yes, I am," Mathew's father replied.

"May I see it? We just want to make sure it's not containing any of the stolen items," she continued to ask which was just what Mathew wanted.

"Of course, please follow me," he said going up the stairs. Mathew made his move and swooped through the closing door down to the basement.

Mathew transformed back and stood motionless as he looked at his old wooden door with the dusty gold colored knob. How many times had he opened and closed that door throughout his early years? One last time, he opened the door and his own Human scent wafted to his nostrils. It was obvious the door hasn't been opened in quite some time. Mathew looked around at all of his old items, treasures and not, that were now covered in a thick, forbidding layer of dust. Mathew realized he had to be careful to not touch too many things to avoid leaving evidence of his return.

"What's this then?" Mathew thought to himself when he spotted an envelope on his bed that just had the words 'To Mathew' written on the top.

Mathew examined his bed and didn't remember making it the way it currently was made. It stumped him for a moment until he caught a very weak hint of perfume coming from the envelope. He eventually remembered that last person to actually use his bed was Sophie because she was stranded there the day before they left for the fateful ski trip. Mathew proceeded to rip open the letter and began to read it.

Hey, Mathew.

Yeah, it's me, Sophie. I'm leaving this message because this is the only way I can ask this. I understand that you might think this is a little silly but . . . you know how I am. I have wanted to ask you for a while but I wouldn't want things to become weird between us when we are trying to have a good time . . . But when we come back from skiing, do you think we could go on a real date?

P.S—Please actually think about it before you answer. I know how you usually are.

Love,
Your friend Sophie.

The words on the page tore at Mathew's emotions in an unusual way. The letter itself didn't torment him as much as the fact that he had died during the trip and Sophie never got an answer. As the enormity of his situation hit him, he dropped to the ground and tears started to fill his eyes. He read and reread the letter over and over until every word was burned into his memory. Mathew was close to a complete breaking point when he saw a small wooden box the size of a shoebox tucked under his bed. It reminded him of his mission. He got up slowly to retrieve an old skeleton key from its hiding place in a vent near the top of a shelf. Before he did anything else with the box, Mathew put the confession letter back on his bed were he found it and looked at it once again as if to make sure that it was actually there and not a figment of his imagination.

Mathew pulled out the old wooden box; he took the skeleton key and unlocked the small chest. His heart pounded so hard that he was sure it could be heard outside the walls of his old room. His emotions swelled again as he looked at the little black box that hadn't been disturbed in over a year. His hands shook as he gently pulled small items out and wrapped them in a symbolic cloth from the chest. His trembling fingers sorted through relics that were precious to him then and now, even after all he had been through since his death. There was a small rock broken in two pieces that fit together perfectly like a puzzle. There was also a little necklace made out of a string of beads. After looking through the chest, Mathew knew that the contents were too precious to him to leave any behind so he closed the lid and attached the key to his cross with some twine that was lying around. He closed the door to his room knowing he would probably never be back.

Mathew opened the window with his little chest under his arm and ran across the street to a small thicket where he left it nestled under an old dead tree. He quickly ran back to the front of the house, rang the doorbell and turned into a bat again to wait undetected for

Kyoko. She finally came out of the door, thanked his father for his time and set off down the driveway. As she reached the end of the driveway, an unfamiliar car pulled up so Mathew decided to stay behind to find out who it was. An older woman stepped out and walked up to the front door to greet his dad with a quick kiss.

"What was that about, honey?" the lady asked Mathew's dad.

"I'll tell you about it inside. I have a weird feeling we're being watched out here," he replied as he put his arm around her shoulders and they went inside together.

Mathew realized that this woman must be important in his dad's life. A myriad of conflicting emotions rushed through him. Mathew thought that now he was gone, there was no longer any reason to hide anything since he wasn't around any longer to stand in the way of his dad's happiness. The next moment, Mathew realized how petty those thoughts were and scanned his mind for another explanation. He finally decided that it was more likely that his dad had become lonely with Mathew gone. There wasn't anyone to greet him anymore when he returned from his long trips on the road or even share a few laughs with. After pondering this a few more moments, Mathew left his roost and flew off towards Kyoko.

"Welcome back, Mathew!" she exclaimed with a laugh as Mathew flew onto her arm like a hawk returning home just for fun. "So, how did it go?" she continued to ask as Mathew transformed back.

"Well. I got what I came for and now . . . I thought I would never say this in my entire life but . . . let's go shopping. I desperately want some new clothes and the mall across town was always the best place to shop," Mathew stated which instantly took Kyoko's mind off of their reason for being there. Mathew retrieved his chest from its hiding place and tucked it into the backpack. He made sure that he had zipped the backpack all the way shut so it wouldn't fall out.

When they arrived at the mall, Mathew gave Kyoko a few hundred dollars to buy new clothes and went into a store that carried his favorite jeans. They were the best jeans he had ever worn and he was suddenly homesick for them. He eventually found his new size, picked out a T-shirt and made his purchase. He changed in the store's changing room and ditched the black clothes he had been wearing.

After a while of walking around in his new clothes, feeling more out of his element with each step, Mathew decided that he preferred

Elemental clothing because of the fit. His Elemental clothes were loose and easy to move in unlike the clothes he had just bought that seemed a little too tight in several places and chafed him in places that should never be chafed.

A half hour later, Mathew decided he needed to find out what was taking Kyoko so long. He wandered around in the store looking like a thief with the backpack, which naturally made him get suspicious looks from security. Eventually Mathew spotted her going into a changing room so he took a seat in a chair that was placed in front of the changing rooms, obviously intended for weary husbands or other males that needed to wait for their female counterparts. After Kyoko noticed that Mathew was actually waiting, she asked his opinion and, to Mathew's frustration, went to pick out another new outfit. Mathew warned her that whatever she bought she needed to carry because he wasn't a pack mule.

"Mathew . . . is that you?" Mathew heard and turned around to see Kim all dressed up.

"Kim! What are you doing here?" Mathew asked not at all surprised but a little nervous.

"Me, Sophie and Angel are out for a girls' day. I snuck away when I thought I saw you in the other clothing store. If it was really you, I thought you would appreciate an advanced warning that we're also here," she explained.

"Thanks. I appreciate it. Is there anyone else here that I should know about?" Mathew asked hoping to avoid potential disaster by thinking several steps ahead.

"Tim will be here. We are meeting him for lunch. It sucks now that you're gone because we only have Tim's opinion and he's a pervert. His entire fashion sense for women is 'less is more'," Kim complained.

"Is that James you're talking to, Kim?" Angel said walking up to the two.

"Actually yes, it is," Kim replied happily.

"So what are you doing here, James? And what's in the backpack?" Sophie asked giving him a friendly slap on the shoulder.

"I'm waiting for a friend of mine. She's in the changing room, taking too long, of course. I would rather not talk about it," Mathew said and the topic of the backpack was dropped.

"This may be a little sudden but would you like to join us in the food court?" Angel politely asked.

"It's not just up to me," Mathew explained.

"Are Ilium and Sara here?" Sophie asked and Mathew guessed that there was something she wanted to discuss because of her serious tone of voice.

"No, it's my other friend, Kyoko. You haven't met her yet," Mathew explained.

They sat around and talked until Kyoko finished changing and purchasing her new clothes. Even though he hated doing so, Mathew gave the introductions and they went to the food court. Mathew encouraged Kyoko to order a soda because he had a hunch that the only actual drink she had in 24 hours was either water or blood. As they finished eating, Tim showed up and was shocked to see that Mathew was there.

"Hey, James . . . what are you doing here?" Tim asked curiously.

"The girls are out lingerie shopping today and needed an expert opinion so they called me in," Mathew said pulling out his best poker face just to screw with him.

"Why didn't you girls call me . . . especially since I haven't met your new friend?" Tim said with an eye on Kyoko.

"Because we wanted an actual, intelligent opinion, Tim. By the way, Kyoko, I was surprised to see that you regularly wear something that erotic," Angel said joining in on Mathew's joke Mathew remembered the similar statements the girls had made at the ski lodge. This made him think that they may have been joking then as well.

"Well, you know. It's just . . . something you get as a joke gift from a boyfriend and you try it on because you're curious and you find out that it's actually quite comfortable . . . except some of the hooks that connect the top to the bottom scrape my skin now and then," Kyoko said with all credibility. Mathew suddenly remembered the sexy outfit she wore for him the night he needed Elemental blood. The thought crossed his mind that that could actually be what she regularly wore.

"Okay fine, jokers. Be that way. So what are we doing after this?" Tim asked.

"We could go to the park," Angel suggested.

"Fun! We haven't done that as a group since . . . . Never mind," Sophie said quickly as a pained expression crossed her face.

"I have no problem going to the park," Kim stated her opinion.

"Well then, it's settled. We're going to the park. It's about time we went there again anyway," Angel said.

Finishing up at the mall, the friends went to the park where they had been regulars before Mathew's death. Sophie led the way to their "usual" spot under a large oak tree.

Everybody sat down at the bench and talked about something and nothing at the same time. Mathew had the urge to sit in the same branch of the tree that he used to sit on. As he was the only one out of the group who could actually climb up there, he resisted the urge because he didn't want to blatantly jeopardize his secret. Kim was the only one of the group who knew and he wanted to keep it that way.

"So what have you been up to, James? We thought you didn't live in the area," Tim asked after most of the groups' small talk had finished.

"I don't. I'm just visiting some family. We had a slight fire at our place so we are seeing if there are any places to rent until we've sorted things out," Mathew said adding in the fire so he wouldn't be completely lying.

"Seriously? A fire! Is your family okay?" Sophie quickly asked in her compassionate way.

"Yes, we are all fine," Mathew said with a hollow smirk. He knew that even though the fire itself didn't harm anyone, the fighting outside sure took its toll.

"That's good to hear. Was it on the news? My dad usually has it on all the time and I figured I would have heard your name if it was mentioned," Angel asked.

"I don't think it was but I might have missed it," Mathew answered rather blandly as he cracked open the can of soda he had grabbed from the vending machine next to the bathrooms.

"By the way, what are you all doing out of school so early? It's only like . . . 1pm," Mathew asked realizing that this was rather unusual.

"Huge drama, dude. Some guy got murdered last night and the school decided it's safer to send us home or something along those lines," Tim answered unusually quickly for himself.

"Really? Why did you go to the mall then? I would have gone straight home," Kyoko commented as Mathew noticed a bird fly into the tree behind him from the corner of his eye.

"We did think about it but, in the end, we decided it's too nice a day to hide inside. Besides, the murder happened at night and now it's day," Angel said logically as she rested her head down on the wooden bench. She sighed contentedly because it was nice and cool from the shade of the tree.

"I suppose we could also chock it up to strength in numbers, couldn't we?" Sophie commented after thinking about it.

"But then wouldn't it be best if we stayed in school? Call me loco but the school could possibly have the safest place to be. It's about the same amount of people as the mall during the school days," Tim argued and Mathew spotted another bird disappear into the tree behind him.

"That's possible. I know the gym by itself has a legal capacity of about 500 people," Kim said breaking her conversation silence as another bird flew to the tree.

"How do you know that, anyway?" Mathew asked.

"Duh . . . there's a sign on the outside of both the gym's entrances that says that," she explained as another bird flew into the tree.

"Well how much does a regular . . ." Mathew said but didn't get to finish his question before Angel began screaming and ran away from the bench.

"What's wrong?" Tim yelled at Angel as she was swatting and waving her arms around like a spastic mad woman.

"The tree! The tree! Look in the tree!" Angel yelled back as she continued to squeal, squirm and swat at invisible flies.

They all looked up into the tree. A branch, dangling a few feet over their heads, was weighted down with four large bats staring intently at them or, more in particular, at Mathew.

Mathew judged by their size and the slight color variations that they were not normal bats. Each one had a dash of red or green on their fur making Mathew believe that they were probably Death Stalkers sent to find him. He then realized that he and Kyoko had neglected to tell anyone where they were going.

"I'm SO retarded," Mathew said aloud with a groan. He and Kyoko were the only two left sitting on the bench. The others had joined Angel and were squealing and squirming around with the exception of Kim who didn't seem to mind the bats too much. Tim was squealing the loudest while wildly rolling around on the grass to get the imaginary bat off of him.

"James, Kyoko! Get away from there! They might swoop down and get caught in your hair or bite you and give you rabies or something!" Angel cried after calming down a bit. She was still squirming slightly but no longer doing the hilarious fly swat dance she was doing a moment before.

Mathew indulged her request not to appease her, but as he knew he should be getting back to the Palace. He was just about to open his mouth to talk when the girls started screaming in horror and ran away to the nearby bathroom to safety. Tim followed closely behind them still squealing louder than the girls. Mathew turned around and saw the four bats flying toward him only to stop and hover midair.

"Real subtle, guys," Mathew said sarcastically to the four bats. "Don't you think you could have, like, watched me from that other tree?" he continued to ask.

"Our orders are to find and escort you and Kyoko home, Sir. Lord Dracula was quite worried about you since as you left without saying a word," the bat in the middle whispered so no one would notice.

"Yes, I realize now that I should have left word. I just got caught up in the moment with Kyoko. We will say our goodbyes and head out. Just don't scare the girls . . . especially Tim, anymore," Mathew said and the four bats flew away to perch on a nearby swing set. This made both mothers and fathers snatch their children from the swings and scurry away out of fear.

"Do they seriously have no idea what they are doing?" Mathew continued to mutter to Kyoko out of frustration.

"They think it's funny. Death stalkers have a strange sense of humor," Kyoko responded not realizing that Mathew was just rhetorically complaining.

Mathew rounded up his friends that were now scattered around the park in fear of the bats. He explained to them that he had to go meet up with his parents at his relative's house to start settling in. The friends said goodbye and started walking their separate ways. Mathew looked back and saw Kim looking at him with a sad smile on her face.

Mathew gave her a goodbye nod and she gave a little wave back in acknowledgement and put her hand over her heart to let him know that she was still the only one who knew Mathew's identity secret. Mathew decided to step up the pace when he entered the woods as animal control arrived at the park and set out with what looked like butterfly nets. Good luck to you, Mathew thought with a chuckle.

Mathew and Kyoko brought their speed up to a brisk run when the death stalkers caught up with them and turned back into their humanoid form. They finally arrived back home later in the evening, they walked quickly back to the Succubus Palace in order to calm Dracula's nerves.

Mathew felt happy with the day's achievements and went to his temporary room with the two additions to his belongings. He hid the Slayer book in his room so that no one would find it. Then he took his black chest out of the backpack and gently hid it in the corner of a desk where no one would accidentally mess with it. He wanted to do his best to make sure the chest remained safe with no chance of something falling on it, smashing it or even come close to touching his box.

When he was finished straightening up his room, Dracula walked in. "Mathew! You scared the hell out of me! I was worried you had been kidnapped or worse by the Fire Elementals. Now that you are home safely, though, all is well. I also heard you acquired the troublesome Vampire Slayer's book. Well done, my son," Dracula said pleased with Mathew's accomplishments.

"Thank you very much, Sir. I do apologize, too. I was focused on the mission and didn't mean to make you worry," Mathew explained feeling rather proud at the compliment. "I have a question, though . . . why didn't you go after it? Kyoko knew the exact location and, once we were there, the acquisition was fairly straightforward. And I remember you mentioning it in one of our talks a while ago," Mathew asked.

"It didn't merit my direct intervention with the Humans at the time," Dracula replied. "Did you kill him?" he asked after a few moments.

"Yes, I did . . . unintentionally. He tried to pull a gun on me but my ice shards were faster," Mathew explained as the queasy feeling returned.

"Very good. If you hadn't, I was going to send Renal," Dracula said. Renal was the captain of the elite Death Stalker squad and was more than likely only called upon for significant matters.

"Why were you going to kill him?" Mathew asked because, even though he had killed the wannabe slayer in self-defense, he still didn't support random acts of murder.

"He was a Vampire Slayer. Even though he was a bad one, he was still a potential threat to the wellbeing of our family," Dracula explained.

"Maybe he wasn't so bad at it, after all. I should probably tell you he was the reason Victoria was about to go into a Vampiric coma when I found her," Mathew explained.

"Now I am truly pleased that he is dead," Dracula said with a grim smile. "Excuse me, Mathew, I need to go deal with other matters," he said as he started toward the door. "Oh and Mathew . . . I think you might want this back," Dracula said pulling out Vampire's Crucifixion from his pocket and gently handed it to him.

"Thank you very much," Mathew said as he tightened his grip on the cross.

Mathew stood a few moments in silence as emotions washed over him. It had been a big day and the cross was another reminder of his strong ties to humanity. He ran his fingers over the familiar patterns of his original cross and noticed the big blue gem was no longer there. He slowly put the cross on and felt the extra weight hang from his neck. Mathew knew with the chain digging into his neck that two crosses were too heavy for him to regularly wear. Together they were potentially dangerous, as the additional weight would throw off his balance too much.

This realization tore at Mathew's heart as he walked around his room trying to come up with a plan to keep Vampire's Crucifixion safe. He didn't want to leave the cross alone and risk it being stolen but he knew his options were limited. Mathew went to his wardrobe and pulled out one of his snow-white shirts, ripped it into one long strip and gently wrapped the cross. He placed it in his wooden box.

Mathew untied the chest's key from around his neck then made sure the chest was locked, before he left his room to hunt around the Succubus palace looking for a small combination lock. After a few minutes of looking, he bumped into Catherine who happened to have an extra stashed away in her desk. Mathew took the small lock and reset the combination to Merida's birthday, knowing that was something he would never forget. He then locked the key to the chain of his cross so he would never lose the key. Feeling like he had a foolproof plan for the cross' safety, Mathew went back to his room and eyeballed the hot tub that he had so far neglected to use. As he gave into temptation and stripped down to his boxers, he cranked on the hot tub jets and hopped in. He let out a long sigh as he enjoyed the pressure that waved over his back. The heat, which Mathew didn't overly care for, was relaxing and needed after all the physical activity he had done in the past day.

"You know, Mathew, I didn't think you would be the type to wear black under all that white," Victoria said as she slid in next to him.

"Hey, Victoria. I like your suit . . . and how did you know I was in the hot tub?" Mathew asked a little curious since she seemed to appear out of nowhere time and again.

"Thank you even though I'm borrowing it from Dee. I was talking with Dee and she heard the sound of the jets starting up . . . she should be showing up sooner or later," Victoria said leaning back against the water jets.

"You seem a little stiff, is everything okay?" Mathew asked after watching her.

"Well, you are one of the main problems . . . you disappear after the Manor gets burned down and Dad had to track you down . . . so the least you can do is give me a massage," she said with a smile that showed off her pearly fangs.

"Fine . . . turn to the side," Mathew said and he started pressing and rubbing her back. After a moment of rubbing, Mathew must have hit a nerve; because there was a slight popping noise that lead to her releasing a quick gasp and her back arched suddenly.

"You've done this before, haven't you?" she asked softly.

"I used to do this for a couple of my female friends so, yes, I have had some practice," Mathew answered as he continued to rub her shoulders.

"Hey! Don't start the party without me!" Dee said splashing water everywhere as she jumped into the small hot tub. "It's been a while since I have been in one of these," she said shaking her head to get the water off.

"Good of you to join us, girlfriend. I was starting to think you wouldn't show up," Victoria said splashing her back and then Dee splashed her, which led to a splash fight between the girls.

"You know I had a dream like this once . . . except you two weren't wearing anything," Mathew said completely joking.

"I'm sure that can be arranged. Dee, turn around so I can undo your top," Victoria said quickly.

"No, stop! I was kidding," Mathew yelled.

"Serves you right . . . pervert," Victoria said with a laugh.

"I may be many things but pervert I'm definitely not," Mathew argued but he knew it was all in good fun.

"I wouldn't mind if you were a pervert, Mathew. It keeps the relationships interesting," Dee said floating over to sit on his lap.

"Dee . . . I really do not need you on my lap at the moment . . . and put your tail away," Mathew said as calmly as he could.

"Why? It's not like it's doing anything," Dee said leaning back on Mathew as if he was a chair.

"It's wrapping around my leg . . ." Mathew said.

"I know" Dee replied calmly.

"Okay, off. I'm not a barstool," Mathew said gently lifting Dee and placing her next to him. He crawled out of the hot tub and went to change. "You girls are so frustrating. I was all alone, having a few badly needed relaxing moments until you showed up," Mathew said after he changed when he saw them lying on his bed still in their bathing suits.

"But isn't this like one of those ultimate fantasies for a boy?" Victoria asked as she stretched out on the bed.

"I would think so. That's what my classes said, anyway. It was either this or the school girl fantasies," Dee said recalling her Succubus training.

"You girls planned this . . ." Mathew said now extremely frustrated with them.

"Oh, come and sit with us, Mathew . . . I don't bite," Victoria said smiling so she showed her fangs and Mathew knew she was lying.

"I shouldn't but I'm tired and going to anyway," Mathew said as he sat down on the bed.

"So Mathew . . . would you mind telling us some of your little fantasies?" Victoria said pulling him down.

"No, I don't mind because I won't. Some things are strictly off limits . . . you know, PRIVATE," Mathew replied trying to sit up and get Victoria off him at the same time.

"Too bad so sad. Get over it and tell us the juicy bits," Dee ordered with a slight grin.

"Or what?" Mathew asked forgetting a very important rule to never argue with a Succubus and, especially, never look her in the eyes as you did so. Too late, Mathew remembered as Dee caught his eye.

"Mathew, would you care to answer a few questions?" Dee asked sweetly as she put Mathew into a trance.

"Absolutely, Mistress. Did you have a specific question?" Mathew asked with complete obedience.

"Cool! You weren't kidding when you said you could do that!" Victoria commented.

"Doubt me not Victoria. Mathew, what is it like dealing with Victoria and me?" Dee asked with a smile.

"My mind is constantly reminding me about my restrictions and inexperience when dealing with certain topics," Mathew replied in a monotone voice.

"Cool again! This is awesome. May I ask a question?" Victoria asked.

"Go ahead but wait one moment. Mathew, you will answer all questions you are asked until I snap my fingers," Dee said looking deep into Mathew's eyes. "Okay, go ahead, Victoria. Ask away," Dee said as she shared her control over Mathew.

"Umm . . . okay! I've a good one! Mathew, why are you friends with so many girls?" Victoria asked turning the inquisition into a game where Mathew was the only loser.

"My childhood. I rarely saw my mother and I sought out the missing motherly attention from multiple females. I also enjoy the perks, or touching, females require once they trust you and you are friends with them," Mathew answered.

"This is going great! What are those perks, Mathew?" Dee asked getting excited.

"Hugging, kissing, advice on body. Safety, loyalty and trust," Mathew replied with a few examples.

"What else could we ask him, hmmmm?" Victoria asked Dee.

"Well anything, but more fun than questions, we could even give him some simple commands and he will automatically do them on the spot," Dee said and snapped her fingers for the effect, obviously forgetting that snapping was the release from hypnotism. Mathew fell back onto the bed instantly drifting into a deep sleep.

When he woke up, Mathew did not remember anything that he confessed or explained. He rolled over to get out of bed and bumped into something. Surprised, he sat up quickly and saw Victoria lying there.

"Good morning," she said sitting up.

"Why are you in my bed?" Mathew curiously asked, not that he minded or anything. The idea of sleeping with her, though, was just a little weird for him.

"I don't know. I just felt like it," she answered with a stretch.

"Did something happen or something? Why can't I remember anything?" Mathew asked confused as to why he fell asleep.

"No . . . Nothing at all, you just got tired and fell asleep," she lied with a casual yawn.

"Highly unlikely," Mathew said. He looked at Victoria as she yawned and had an unusual feeling course through him when she licked her dry lips.

"Oh wow, my neck hurts from all this blood pumping through it . . . if only there was a cute girl that was also a Vampire to lend me a hand . . . or a fang," Mathew decided to say laying the sarcasm on incredibly thick.

"What are you playing at?" Victoria asked now looking at him with hungry predator eyes.

"Nothing really. It has been a while, though, and I don't know if you have had anything to drink recently," Mathew said not exactly sure why he had this sudden urge for intimacy with Victoria and before he could say anything else, his neck was quickly bitten.

Mathew noticed that Victoria was a little more aggressive this time. She was biting down harder than usual and not controlling the flow of blood well. When she was finished, she laid her head on Mathew's chest and had a small river of blood running down her chin.

"I know this is off topic but would you happen to know where Dracula is? I need to ask him about something," Mathew asked. He wanted to talk about rebuilding the Manor and pitch a few ideas if Dracula was in the mood to humor him.

"He didn't tell you?" Victoria asked back.

"No, I saw him last night but he didn't tell me where he was going," Mathew replied.

"Obviously Dad isn't one to take someone burning down his home very calmly, so he is again dealing with the Elemental politics with the council," Victoria replied angrily

"Mathew! You've got a message from the Elder Council," Dee yelled as she entered the room and handed him a letter with an ice seal on it. "Why do I never get to cuddle like that?" Dee complained when she saw Victoria lying on his chest.

"I have never woken up with you in my bed," Mathew replied.

"Is that all it takes?" Dee asked.

"Yep," Mathew said as he opened the letter and read it over.

"What does it say?" Victoria asked.

"I have to return to the fortress right away. It looks like I will be there for a while . . . apparently I'm needed to teach a few classes with Julian as a special guest or something," Mathew said summarizing the letter.

"You're leaving?" Victoria asked again.

"Not permanently. You know I'll come back," Mathew explained with a smile.

"Just stay safe, Mathew. Relations are very tense right now and you have an odd way of being in the thick of things. I have a strong feeling that things are going to get bad so just stay safe. Please," Victoria pleaded before getting up and leaving the room.

Mathew quickly tracked down Bell whom he hadn't seen in a while. His special instructions in the letter were to bring her back with him. Together again, like some strange kind of other-worldly dynamic duo, they headed to the teleportal.

They appeared on the other side and continued to wonder if they had been sent to the right place. The fortress was completely unrecognizable. Large walls and smaller buildings now separated the portal room from the inside of the fortress.

The two checked in at the new registry that was put in place to stop any "undesirables" from entering the fortress. Mathew looked around and noticed that it was very busy; everywhere he looked there were soldiers. There were watchmen on the walls, sentries at all gates and doors and foot soldiers making rounds like they were guarding the Queen at Buckingham Palace. Mathew exchanged greetings with a few soldiers and even saw an Elder that he had met during the party at God's Step. Bell ended up getting pulled aside by someone who looked like one of her old military buddies so Mathew returned to his room. It was exactly the same way he left it which made him a little depressed. He had gotten used to Ilium or Sara messing with his stuff but now his room just seemed lifeless and dull.

"Are you alright, Mathew? I heard about what happened," Julian said rushing into the room, effectively jostling Mathew out of the funk he was heading towards. Mathew understood and didn't mind when she started looking for any injuries he might have taken during the fire.

"I'm fine, Julian. Don't worry so much," Mathew said seeing for the first time how pregnant she was.

"Well, thank God you're okay!" she said giving him a friendly hug.

"So what am I here to teach?" Mathew asked wanting the rundown.

"I'm not exactly sure but I have some great ideas. I thought it would be a good learning experience for the students to hear from an Ice Elemental who has experience with Demons. I'm a good teacher but have my limitations. My pregnancy is going well but it still leaves me very tired, making this an opportune time for some additional help in the classroom. That and I only know a few Demons and not well. You, on the other hand, practically live with them. So . . . who better than you?" Julian explained.

"Ok. When do these classes start?" Mathew asked.

"Tomorrow morning and don't be late. It's the same room you were in when you were taking classes so you know how to get there," Julian said.

"I don't want to go to school again!" Mathew complained but he knew he was committed already.

"Mathew, you were top of my class but, then again, you should have been because you couldn't put that book down," Julian pointed out.

Satisfied with the fact that Mathew was in one piece and really there, Julian went back to her room to rest. Alone again, Mathew quickly became bored and playing with ice didn't pass the time like it did when he first started it. He had pretty much mastered most of the known Art and the challenge wasn't as strong as it had been. He still had fun using it but it was a common, everyday thing to him now so he just decided to head to bed and get up early in the morning.

Mathew woke up early the next morning with loneliness still hanging on him like a coat until he remembered that he actually had a purpose for the day. He quickly got dressed and was excited to get out of his room to go to the class thing. He had never been one to be to class early, or even on time, and this excitement was a new feeling that he liked.

When he arrived, Mathew found Julian in the so-called "Teachers' Lounge". Julian told him that Steven was still at God's Step working out the details of the assassination attempt along with Mathew's fate. They now knew that the would-be assassin had been working with the Fire Elementals and, after the attack on the Manor, the situation was looking extremely grim for the Fire Elementals, or King Ryan, if he was the one behind it.

"Alright class. Butts in seats," Julian said as she entered the room.

Mathew stood quietly behind Julian and caught some of the whispers going on around the room.

"Hey, who is that guy?" someone whispered.

"That's Mathew, the Blood Elemental," another person said.

"How could you not know that?" someone else replied.

"No way! Isn't Mathew supposed to be a terrifying Vampire that rivals Dracula himself?" another person whispered.

"Judging by the whispers already going on, most of you already know who our special guest is this morning," Julian began. "This is Mathew, the Blood Elemental. Now, before we begin class today, are there any questions for him so we won't have interference later?" Julian asked.

"Yes, I have one. Is it true that you survive off of the blood of your enemies?" a young girl asked.

"No. I don't suck the blood of my enemies . . . I have that ability but don't use it," Mathew replied.

"Excuse me, but is it true that you're actually the ghost of a legendary ninja who was born under the great banner of the Japanese Dragon clan during the Demon resolve of 1308 and you single handedly killed an entire Demon town and drank the blood of a Vampire lord and a year later was killed by a simple snowball then you were reborn into the Ice Elementals and that Vampire blood you drank caused you to turn into the Blood Elemental you are now?" a young boy intently asked with one incredibly long breath.

"No! What the hell? Where have you been getting your information from?" Mathew asked but heard a snicker from behind him and turned and saw Julian holding in her laughs as best she could.

"It was Steven, wasn't it?" Mathew asked.

"Yes, it was," Julian replied letting out her laugh.

"Okay. Class, if you don't already know, Elder Steven and I are friends. Friends to a point where he will make up stories about me just so I have to deal with the fallout later. Most of the stories about me are not true. Most . . . but not all," Mathew stated with a secretive smile trying to resolve the giant misconception Steven managed to set up.

"I heard you were getting married but now you're not . . . so does that mean you're single?" a girl asked.

"Well . . . my engagement was called off . . . so yes, I guess so," Mathew answered and noticed how half of the female side of the class perked up their heads and started paying closer attention to the interaction in the room.

"Julian, is there anything they should be doing before we end up with something similar to Dee's first day of class?" Mathew asked remembering their past argument.

"Actually yes, there is. Good point, Mathew, and a great opportunity to begin our instruction today. Class, please open your Demonology books to the chapter about the Succubi," Julian ordered.

Mathew spent the rest of the time answering questions from fifteen aroused girls who seemed to enjoy the chapter a little too much. The boys, however, were very inattentive which Mathew considered rather unusual. Even though Mathew was in the hot seat, class seemed to drag by slowly. By the time class was over, Mathew was so relieved to see the students walk out of the room that he could hardly contain his sigh of relief. The questions were tolerable but the student's eyes were like daggers making him even more uncomfortable.

"Julian, I forgot to ask you yesterday but has Steven sent you any detailed updates about the situation in God's Step? Not that I agree with this but I personally expected us to be in a war by now," Mathew stated.

"Not much. The Council is trying to keep things under wrap as much as possible and Steven has only been able to communicate with me sporadically. The last I heard from him, the Council was still in debate about the Fire Elemental attempted assassin. The biggest excitement of late was Dracula showing up and raising more hell than King Ryan could take. There's a saying that 'there's nothing more dangerous than a good man going to war' and this seems to be the case with the Count. For the meantime, though, they are still deciding the fate of his decision to go after you. There is a weird acceptance of a lone assassin but it's an entirely different matter when a large strike force is sent to assassinate one man, burn down homes and kill innocent civilians. You know as well as any that assassination attempt was enough to piss off Dracula but, now with the attack on his home, he is a force to be reckoned with. He has made it his current mission to make sure there are severe consequences for what has happened. Other than that, yes, there will probably be a war if King Ryan doesn't cooperate," Julian explained as best she could as she offered Mathew purple muffins on a pretty plate that, though attractive in hue, looked like death on a doily to him.

Steven

CHAPTER SEVENTEEN

WHAT ELSE BUT WAR

Time was passing slowly at the Ice Fortress even though a lot of activity was taking place. It had been barely a few weeks since Mathew started his duties as special unpaid voluntary teacher and the Ice Fortress was rapidly transforming into a medieval citadel. Mathew heard from Bell that the teleportals were all at maximum power and each day the Fortress saw the addition of troops from around the world. As they took their positions according to rank, region and special skill sets, it was awe inspiring to see how many their numbers were. A strong sense of unity and purpose settled over the Fortress and Mathew was even greeted a couple of times by unfamiliar and unique looking Ice Elementals who turned out to be from a different continent. Apparently he was fast becoming known around the world.

Whenever Mathew had spare time, he would go out and watch military drills that seemed to go on 24/7. The sound of the unified movements resounded throughout the Fortress making it difficult for everyone to relax so there was little downtime. Mathew saw Bell more than once barking orders at new recruits. She was officially retired but Mathew knew in her heart she would always be Vanguard and nothing short of an Elemental Council order would prevent her from participating.

He also spent his time thinking about the curiosities of Demon and Elemental culture. He was not able to sort out how a race of people to whom eating and sleeping were optional and could create whatever they needed would even consider war an option. A heavy sorrow started to settle on his heart as he searched for a viable, alternate solution. The Demon involvement with war was not a surprise to him because he reasoned that they still needed the essential things for survival, or extending their life, but the Elemental aspect really troubled him. In all of the Demonology classes he had taken, he couldn't remember the last time Demons and Elementals actually fought each other over such base necessities.

After a long and brutal thought process, Mathew came to understand that the overwhelming Human threat had forced Demons to unite for the survival of their various races. That common enemy unity eventually erased racism and formed a seemingly unbreakable bond between them. While there were still caste systems in place, such as Vampire and Royal Vampire, all other aspects of life seemed to sort out into companionable ebb and flow between each race that did not seem possible in the Human culture.

While Mathew was in thought that afternoon, an extraordinary event started taking place. Because of the rapid and large increase in numbers, more housing was needed. The Ice Council decided to create an entirely new area to house all the immigrating military personnel, their families and civilians seeking refuge from the threat of war. The immigrants were refugees in the Human sense as the Elementals evacuated God's Step during the threat of a potential war to eliminate civilian casualties. A natural cause of the effect was over-crowding for the smaller Elemental communities. To solve the over-crowding issue, a group of fifty Ice Elementals, classified as Shapers, unified their unique abilities to create an avalanche. The plan was to expose bare rock. Once the rock was exposed, buildings were formed, along with retaining walls, to create an entirely new district . . . the Wartime Barracks. Mathew was grateful for both the experience and the additional real estate that was created because the hallways had been getting extremely crowded. He wondered what would happen to the Wartime Barracks when the war was resolved and everyone went back to their original homes.

As Mathew walked around, he enjoyed the freed-up hallway space. The atmosphere felt electric with activity and there was never a quiet moment. The additional life energies and activities that took place merged together to create a buzz in the air that Mathew both heard and felt with every fiber of his being.

It was that moment when Mathew knew in his heart there was going to be a war. Though no official declaration had been given, there was no other reason he could think of to gather Elementals from all around the world into the limited space of the Ice Fortress. He had heard from Bell, his only access at this time to military information, that there was going to be a single vote to determine what would happen between the Ice and Fire Elementals. Mathew later discovered that, because of the acts of war committed in their respective territories, Air Elementals and Vampires had been dragged into the mix. Air Elementals were involved because the two assassination attempts on Mathew's life were in the Royal Air Elemental Palace. Vampires were involved because of the direct attack on Dracula's Manor. To this very moment, every time Mathew thought about the Manor being burned down, his blood still boiled. He had never in his Human life had such a desire for revenge. Mathew realized that he had never been passionately committed enough to anything to care about changing the outcome of any matter. Only in his death had he learned how to really engage in life.

Eventually news rushed in that the verdict of the single vote would be heard by the end of the day. Masses of people gathered together to wait outside the council's meeting room hoping to be among the first to hear the verdict on the two matters. The votes were being cast regarding the Fire Elementals' punishment.

Mathew waited with Julian and because of her pregnancy people stepped aside in respect allowing them to find front row spots. Pregnancies in the Elemental culture apparently weren't the most common way for adding to the ranks and were considered a special honor. The wait seemed like hours and the suspense kept building with each moment that ticked by. Some people were worried, some excited and others just tired of waiting. Bell showed up later in her full Vanguard uniform just in time for the verdict.

Finally there was movement on the Council Chamber terrace as a herald stepped out to announce the verdict.

"By judgment of the Councils of the esteemed Elemental races, Ice and Air, and by the decision of Royal Vampire Count Dracula, Fire Elemental King Ryan of the Inferno is hereby ordered to step down from his position as king. Due to his unforgivable and atrocious acts of war upon the brethren, Ryan of the Inferno is sentenced to imprisonment in a jointly controlled Elemental Prison for the next 400 years," the herald declared. Mathew looked around and no one seemed to be happy about the decision.

"Isn't this good news?" Mathew asked aloud to no one in particular.

"Mathew . . . all this means is that we are going to war," Bell said calmly.

"But . . . why? When Ryan steps down, there will be no one to war against," Mathew replied.

"Mathew, in the several hundred years that I have been an Ice Elemental, I have been to war thirteen times. Ten of those wars have been because a King or Queen was told to step down and they were unwilling to do so. I do not understand what or why this is happening. This doesn't make sense. Ryan's motive is not apparent . . . or even clear. He has always been purposeful and in control of his kingdom. He is not a stupid man and nothing adds up with all these sudden attacks. It just doesn't make sense . . ." Bell trailed off trying to sort out the mystery herself.

A few hours later, the same herald appeared on the terrace to announce that King Ryan refused to acknowledge the Council's verdict. Through his refusal to obey the reigning Council's verdict, King Ryan had declared that there was nothing else left but war. As if an unspoken command had been given, the Elemental troops immediately marched to their squads and proceeded to the largest teleportal in the land. This teleportal had been created solely to handle transport of vast numbers of people and goods at a time.

Then someone he never expected to see again approached Mathew. It was Marsh the Ice Tracker who helped Mathew solve his first murder case. Marsh pulled Mathew aside to talk in private.

"Listen, I know we don't know each other very well but it doesn't matter at the moment," Marsh began. "I'm just here to tell you that you're going to be joining me and a small envoy of Ice Trackers on a special operation mission into the Fire Elemental Royal Palace. Here is the Royal Order from King Marcus himself," he explained handing Mathew a letter with the royal seal along with signatures of a variety of high-ranking Elders who Mathew was familiar with.

"When are we leaving?" Bell asked as she walked out from around the corner.

"Seriously? How do you always do that?" Mathew asked realizing she always seemed to miraculously show up just before he was about to go somewhere he could be hurt or killed.

"Instinct wrapped up in experience," she replied simply.

"Well, who said you were coming, anyway?" Marsh asked rather annoyed at her implications that she could just tag along. Little did Marsh know that Bell never did anything close to just 'tagging' along.

"I said. As Vanguard 2nd Class, I outrank a simple Ice Tracker," Bell said with a cocky smile across her face.

"Damn it . . . you're right. Okay fine, we're leaving tonight. This is a cloak n' dagger mission so no one else can know about this besides us. Meet us in the new Wartime Barracks. We're going to be in a back alley across from a new bar 'The Slick Sailor'. Just be there before midnight," Marsh said before he walked away and vanished into the moving crowd.

"We'd better get ready . . . make sure to bring that creepy blood thing so we don't run into any easily preventable trouble," Bell said before she also vanished.

Mathew spent the afternoon sorting through and looking over his things to determine what he could pack. Deciding what would help him on a mission he knew very little about was difficult and time consuming. Details were sparse and were usually necessary when preparing for an offensive. Since he knew so little, he prepared as best he could and was especially diligent to not forget the "creepy blood thing". When it was time to leave, he grabbed his bag, walked out of his room and attempted to find the bar. Finding it was made more difficult because he couldn't remember the exact name of the bar . . . what was that again? Mathew thought to himself. Slippery Sam? Slick Willie? Pesky Parrot? He walked around for a long time before finally giving up. As much as he hated asking for directions, he was going to be late if he didn't. Mathew also needed to find out how to actually get into the new district.

Mathew found the bar easily once he remembered the name and after he asked for directions. He wandered into the alley and was greeted by a few people who seemed to be expecting him. He had a curious thought that this mission was rather unusual but then

Bell popped out of the shadows and scared him half to death so the thought vanished. At what Mathew assumed was about 11:00 pm, the whole group was assembled making 8 total.

"Okay now, here's the deal. Recently a Fire Elemental scientist came forward with a large collection of notes related to the creation of what are technically classified as Life Elementals," Marsh began making it obvious that he was the person in charge of this operation. "Mathew, you're mentioned multiple times within the first few pages but no specific notes as to why. The primary reason we are doing this is because the first notation in the collection dates back to when Mathew became a Blood Elemental. This is only a few weeks ago so we have been ordered to go and make sure there is no laboratory dedicated to the sacrilege of the creation of Life Elementals. Mathew, that's why you're coming. If there is actually a living Life Elemental, we will need someone to counter it. Otherwise we are ordered to destroy any laboratory and capture or eliminate any living experiment," Marsh finished explaining the mission so everyone was on the same page. Mathew, though, had to repeat it a few times in his head to fully comprehend what they were doing.

"How are we going to get there? It's not like we can just waltz into a heavily guarded Palace. They've probably beefed up security because of the verdict, as well," Bell asked as she pointed out the obvious.

"The scientist that came forward with the notes reportedly set up a single use portal for us," Marsh explained.

"Permission to speak, Sir. That sounds a little too convenient. What if we are walking into a trap? I mean, this sounds all too well prepared to come from a scientist. It just reeks of military tactics," an Ice Tracker commented.

"Now that it is out in the open, it seems that our mission is based on a lot of supposition. Why did the scientist give up the notes and why to the Ice Elementals specifically?" questioned another Ice Tracker.

"The Water Elementals originally received the information from the scientist and they passed it on to us. I have personally read a few of the notes and, if any of this is true, it would be fairly obvious why a scientist would defect from the project," Marsh explained as a grim look flashed across his face.

"Where is our teleportal, then?" Mathew asked simply.

"We're standing on it," Marsh stated, Mathew looked down and saw the carvings engraved into the ice.

"Let's do this," Bell said as the engravings under their feet started to hum, vibrate and glow.

CHAPTER EIGHTEEN

BLOOD, FLAME, ICE & FANG

The teleportal was hastily made and the shock from the rudimentary teleportation was too much for Mathew's system. As soon as they arrived at their destination, Mathew threw up and needed to take a moment for the stars to stop spinning and the drums banging in his head to silence. As soon as he felt better, Mathew looked around at the room they landed in. It was obviously set up as a greenhouse. Everywhere he looked, he saw creepy looking plants growing and it smelled of earth, mold and mildew.

"What area of the Palace have we teleported into?" asked an Ice Tracker.

"It doesn't really matter as it appears the scientist was courteous enough to leave us a map," Bell said as she looked over a paper that was stuck to the door.

Pointing out their route on the map with his finger, Marsh explained, "Apparently we are close to the area where the lab is supposed to be. We need to get down this hallway and in through this area here. Our target destination is way too big for a simple experiment and I have a bad feeling about it."

The group set off immediately and moved silently down the hallway. Mathew was flanked on either side, which seemed to him like he was being babied. He felt the others were being exceedingly over-protective of him. He guessed they had been given orders to keep him alive.

They stopped quickly as a patrol of about ten Fire Elementals walked by. Mathew initially thought they would wait the Fire Elementals out but quickly realized that wasn't the case. The Ice Trackers snuck up behind the Fire Elementals and made quick work of killing the group using a device that was thrown around each target like a lasso and tightened, quickly squeezing the life out of them. It reminded Mathew of death by boa constrictor. Mathew watched and realized that he wasn't as horrified as he figured he would or should be. Sure, it was horrible to watch people getting killed but Mathew figured his lack of emotional response was because he had killed Fire Elementals before in battle and he still carried a grudge.

Mathew took enough time to quickly collect some of the red glowing blood in a few vials he brought in his pack but, by the time he had finished, the others had moved along and he was alone in the long hallway.

"So much for being over-protected," Mathew commented under his breath. He then berated himself for being stupid enough to not tell anyone what he was doing or at least ask them to wait.

Mathew quickly moved down the hallway in search of his group. He was trying to remember the details of the map they were looking at earlier but took a left when he should have gone right. A short way down that corridor he bumped into several Fire Elemental guards. Both he and the Fire Elementals were taken by surprise and silently stared at each other for several awkward moments until the guards came to their senses. They surrounded Mathew before attacking in full force. He was thinking that it would have been a bit more honorable for the Fire Elementals to take him on one at a time but things just didn't seem to be going his way today.

Mathew quickly summoned his blade to defend himself. The fight was fast and furious and Mathew was thankful for the Manor conflict and the long, grueling hours of training he had put himself through in the past few weeks. There were three guards in total. Their main offensive was grabbing at him with burning hands but Mathew's blade was fast, true and sharp. He slashed at the guards' burning hands and took several fingers off. The guards screamed and Mathew saw his victory come together like checkmate on a chessboard. He remembered watching Bell and the poetry of her movements while in battle and felt a new sense of resolve and power surge through him.

Though he moved with great speed, Mathew felt like he was moving in slow motion because of the clarity of vision and purpose he had. He split his blade in half. With a blade in each hand, he lunged forward at one guard with the blade in his left hand and stabbed the other guard with a quick 180 spin. Each blade pierced into the heart of its intended target. A lucky grab by the remaining guard singed through Mathew' shirt material on his left arm. The pain was excruciating as the fire burned into his skin causing Mathew to cry out. Instead of cutting off mere fingers this time, Mathew aimed purely out of anger and he used his right hand to pierce through the attacker's chest. The attacker's body went rigid in shock and the hand that he had intended to scorch Mathew's face stood frozen in place only a few inches away from his nose. Mathew felt something unusual happening inside his head. He had a sense of something that reminded him of a trigger on a gun so he decided to mentally pull it. He watched in dazed satisfaction as the man literally exploded, disintegrating into pieces and covering Mathew in glowing red blood. Immediately an oddly peaceful silence settled over the hallway that looked like a violent murder scene. At that moment, Bell and the others quickly rounded the corner and stopped dead in their tracks when they saw the area.

"Mathew! What happened? We noticed you were missing and we only found where you were when we heard you shout," Bell said as she caught sight of Mathew.

"What the hell did you do!?" Marsh yelled in disgusted shock at the sight of the gore splattered everywhere.

"I have no idea," Mathew replied and clutched his arm in pain when he tried to move it.

Bell was on him instantly to inspect the wound. His arm had a black handprint with detailed fingerprints of the attacker scorched into his skin. If he were a murder victim, investigators would have had a quickly closed case. The fingerprint areas were much deeper than the palm of the handprint as the attacker had squeezed Mathew's arm to intensify the burn. It was starting to crack and spew out a puss-like substance. Mathew watched with gratitude as Bell gave him his first example of Ice First Aid that wasn't self-administered. She created a thin sheet of ice that was so fine and delicate it looked like cheesecloth. She secured it tightly around his arm causing a feeling of heavenly relief at the affected area. An Ice Tracker offered him a few painkillers, which he gratefully swallowed, and was thankful when they worked almost immediately.

As soon as Mathew was ready to go, the Ice group took off down the same hallway they had come from to find Mathew. They rounded a few corners without any more incidents and reached a wooden door that opened into a large room. Mathew noticed that Marsh seemed afraid of the room but when he asked him about it, Marsh refused to comment.

Silently they all crept into the room on the lookout for opposition. The room was dark, immense and had cavern-like features. In the far corner, they saw a large opening that looked like the mouth of a cave with an eerie light shining in. The room had an unusual odor and gave Mathew a chill up his spine as soon as the smell reached his nostrils. The feeling of being watched was so strong that he kept furtively looking up and behind to make sure nothing would get the jump on him. Mathew sensed the presence of a force far more powerful than him and quickly decided that he did not like anything about this room. Walking was difficult as the ground was spongy with slick patches here and there. Everywhere he looked there were oval shaped rocks that were smooth as glass to the touch. The group quickly moved through the tangle of rocks and out into an opening that was less populated with the smooth boulders.

"Hey, check out this funky rock!" an Ice Tracker said pointing at a large red, oval shaped rock with grey spots on it. Mathew instantly recognized what it was and tackled the Ice Tracker who was about to kick it.

"Stay away from the dragon eggs!" Mathew shouted and several people stopped what they had been doing to move away from direct contact with the eggs. One Tracker had been leaning up against an egg trying to clean the mucus off his shoe from their trip through what they now knew to be a hatchery. At that moment, a loud roar resounded through the room and the presence that Mathew had felt watching him landed directly in front of him. The gigantic mother dragon assessed him with coldly intelligent eyes to determine if he was friend or foe. Mathew's next move could be their very last. He watched intently as fire dripping from the dragon's mouth landed on a rock nearby melting it into the smooth stones they had climbed over earlier.

"Pardon us, Ma'am. We were just passing through and apologize for disturbing you. Thankfully, as you can see, all of your eggs are intact," Mathew said to the dragon as he swept his right hand around the room in confirmation of his statement. She tilted her head as if trying to understand what he was saying, gave him a funny look and moved closer to thoroughly sniff him. He must have had an unpleasant odor to her because she snorted, shook her head quickly and moved a few steps back.

"Oh, yeah. My apologies for the odor. It's Fire Elemental blood. I haven't had time to clean up from an earlier skirmish that got a bit out of hand," Mathew explained. His fight or flight instinct was urging him to run but he held firm and focused on his tone of voice as anything he said could potentially anger the monstrous reptile.

"Why is he talking to that big lizard?" a female Ice Tracker asked to Mathew's dismay. The mother dragon quickly turned toward her and immediately coughed up a sticky, black tar-like substance on the poor girl. The girl fell to the ground gagging and gasping for air as another Ice Tracker cautiously moved to help her.

"Seriously? How are you even an Ice Tracker? It's basic Dragon 1O1! They are highly intelligent beings and extremely protective of their young," Mathew yelled at the girl and turned back to address the mother dragon. "Pardon me, Ma'am. I hope you don't mind but I would be very honored for the opportunity to take a look at your young. Do you have any baby dragons running around? I have studied your kind in great detail and would really appreciate a firsthand experience with them," Mathew asked referring to the "Big Book of Creatures" which he had read through to pass time between classes. To answer him, the mother dragon lowered her head and gave him a sad look.

"Let me guess . . . Fire Elementals took them, right?" Mathew asked. The mother dragon gave him a nod. "That is not acceptable and I'm sorry to hear that. I have a thought . . . it might not be an ideal setting for your type but, if you are willing, I can make arrangements for you to relocate yourself and your eggs to the mountain where I make my home," Mathew sympathized and the dragon gave him an intrigued look. "It's a beautiful place on the American continent. I'm not quite sure where we are at this moment but the Ice Fortress where I live is called Illumination and it's filled with good and kind people who would let you live in peace alongside them. It's a bit cold there but the people are warm and welcoming and I'm sure we can find a warmer spot somewhere inside that will be more comfortable for you and your family. I wouldn't go there until for, like, another week or so, though. I will need to make it back to let them know that you and your family will be arriving," Mathew laughed and the dragon gave him another nod.

"Great. That's settled then. I'm looking forward to seeing you there but, in the meantime, is there another room around here? We came here on a mission and need to see that it is accomplished," Mathew asked remembering why they were there. For a response, the dragon pointed the way with her tail and a nod of her head in the general direction.

"Thank you very much," Mathew said with a smile.

"Wonders never cease when you are around. I can't believe you actually know how to reason with a dragon. We could all have had our gooses cooked, or flame broiled more likely," Marsh said and Mathew realized the whole group was in shock . . . including Bell.

"It's all about observation. You can get along with just about anyone if you know what they need or want and have a way of helping them get it . . . same with dragons," Mathew explained as he began to shake reactively as the adrenalin wore off.

"You know, that's the second time I have seen that dragon . . . Oh, my god. I thought we were going to die," Bell said shakily, her pupils dilated with shock. It appeared that her fearlessness did not extend to large, cold-blooded beings.

"When did you see it the first time?" Mathew asked to make conversation as they made their way to the other room that had more funny looking rocks in it.

"During my first war. It killed half my squad of 42," Bell said and Mathew didn't comment out of respect.

When they reached their destination, they found a secured door obviously designed to keep people out. The door, dancing with flame, had at least twelve high-grade locks preventing unauthorized access. After a moment of frustration, they came up with a plan to get the door opened. The team sent Mathew back to enlist the help of the dragon who kindly melted through the door with a short blast of her white fire breath. The combination of the dragon's breath meeting the flames of the door produced a reaction of heat so intense that the hairs on their arms were singed from over one hundred feet away. The flame on the door was extinguished by fighting fire with fire. Mathew thanked the dragon and the team walked through what was left of the smoking door.

They stepped into a room that was filled with medical extraction devices. The devices were so bizarre that they made the room look more like a torture chamber than a scientific lab. What the devices were supposed to be extracting, Mathew couldn't tell but whatever the intent, there was a lot of blood, fresh and dried. The scene reminded him of movies he had seen about the Nazi experiments during WWII. There was also an acrid, putrid smell that was overwhelming. Several Ice Trackers began gagging and rushed out of the room in search of fresh air.

Overcoming the horror of the moment, Mathew quickly started riffling through the lab in search of anything of significance. He found several handwritten notes and vials of what he assumed to be Demon blood. He shoved them all into a bag.

"So . . . what now?" Mathew asked taking as much information as he could fit into the large pockets of his pants and the bags he had brought with him.

"Now . . . we destroy everything. Per orders," Marsh said and the sound of shattering glass and the clanging of metal filled the room as they smashed the devices and vials of blood. They ripped apart the extracting machines, burned documents and coated just about everything else they could find in several thick layers of ice just to ensure maximum damage results. Mathew, though, acted on impulse and took every note that looked significant. He wasn't sure why but it seemed important at that moment to do so.

"Hey, Marsh! We got a seriously heavy duty door over here!" an Ice Tracker shouted from the other side of the demolished room.

"Well, open it up!" Marsh yelled back and, before Mathew could issue a warning about the purposefulness of heavy-duty doors, a loud crash and a scream broke through the room. Out of the corner of his eye, Mathew saw the Ice Tracker fall to the ground and a stranger standing over him. Mathew instantly unplugged his blood bag and sprang into motion. He sprinted over the wreckage in the room intending to use the blood to impale the attacker but the attacker was far quicker than Mathew expected. Mathew missed and quickly summoned his blade. The stranger easily blocked Mathew's ice blade with a mass of glowing red blood in his claw like hand. Taken by surprise, Mathew paused briefly to assess the situation more fully. He noticed that the stranger's stance seemed very casual and he had a superior smirk on his face. It was at that moment that Mathew realized he was fighting another Blood Elemental.

Mathew's senses went into high alert as he realized he was up against a worthy opponent. He quickly took in the other person, noticing his ragged body with telltale signs of experiments, torture or heavy drug use. There were injection bruises up his arm and his body was covered in scars of various shapes and sizes. Other than that, though, he seemed relatively strong and healthy. He was standing straight and his black hair looked clean and shiny meaning his captors were probably still allowing him basic privileges like bathing.

"So . . . you must be Mathew. Hello, brother," the stranger said with an arrogant, menacing smile.

"What? You have part of that right. I am Mathew . . . but certainly not your brother," Mathew asked.

"In case you've been a little slow on the uptake, I'm a Blood Elemental. You're a Blood Elemental . . . that would make us 'blood brothers'," the stranger chuckled.

"Whatever. What's your plan then, 'brother'? Anyone else you'd like to practice random acts of violence on?" Mathew asked still ready to take on the opponent.

"Sorry about the Ice Tracker—who should be fine, by the way . . . I think. I actually thought he was the scientist coming in to experiment on me again. A small case of mistaken identity," he explained as the Ice Tracker he attacked twitched a little. Mathew wasn't sure if it was a paralyzed twitch or possible revival but didn't have time at the moment to check it out.

"You seem awfully calm for someone who was 'experimented' on," Mathew said not ready to let his guard down yet.

"Torture does strange things to the soul. Can't really judge anyone till you've suffered in his or her shoes, eh? You might be a bit on the happy side, too, if strangers unexpectedly came into your personal torture chamber and destroyed the means and methods of that torture," the man said.

"Good point . . . anyway, enough of the annoying banter. Tell me your name so we can get out of here," Mathew instructed as he accepted the man into the group.

"Carter. Just call me Carter," Carter said as he joined the group and moved out.

They walked out of the room, back through the dragon's nest and down the hallway. Mathew noticed that they weren't taking the same way back to the teleportal. When questioned about their route, Marsh reminded them that the teleportal had been a single use only so they had to find their own way out. During their search, they engaged some guards and Carter was quick and ferocious with his attack. Mathew noticed it seemed as if Carter was trying to prove himself. It turned out that he was a Fire Elemental and Mathew was given his first opportunity to fight alongside a 'blood brother' who was also his direct opposite. Mathew was fascinated with how Carter controlled blood and picked up some ideas as he watched. Carter was not able to transform the liquid into a solid and back again, but instead could ignite the blood inside others to turn them into something along the lines of living bombs. He could also turn his hand into a demonic claw that he used to cut up those he was fighting. While the flames he had at his disposal couldn't harm other Fire Elementals, their color was beautiful; brilliant magenta flames fueled by blood he smeared over his hands.

Running down the hallway, the group turned a corner right into approximately 25 Fire Elemental troops. They were surrounded with no way out. Thankfully the troops seemed just to be holding their own ground and didn't look like they intended on attacking the small group of nine. As Mathew started to relax a little, something struck him in his right shoulder blade. He looked in time to see a glowing red claw pull away with drops of his silvery blood attached to it.

"Just as I thought . . . you're too trusting, 'brother'," Carter said controlling his blood that was flowing from the cuts on his wrists. Carter was trying to introduce Mathew's silvery blood into the cuts on his own wrists.

"Seriously? This was your plan from the start?" Mathew asked as he froze his shoulder. The pain was so intense it would have been crippling had his body not been pumping adrenalin. The frozen shoulder and adrenalin made it so he was still able to move about regularly.

"No, I improvised as opportunity presented itself. Clever, aren't I? I had no way of knowing that you and I would ever cross paths—especially not in that torture lab. Now I figure they will ease up on the experiments when they don't feel rushed to keep up with you. You, brother, set the bar rather high," Carter said simply and a creepy smile appeared on his face as he attacked Mathew. When Bell and the other Trackers moved to defend Mathew, the Fire Elemental troops attacked making it 26 against 8.

Mathew didn't want to fight against another Blood Elemental. It was tearing against his moral code and he didn't want to kill the only other member of his kind. Mathew also didn't know how to fight another Blood Elemental; every move was trial and error. He was now exceptionally thankful for the earlier opportunity to fight alongside Carter as this exposure gave him a small advantage. Carter, on the other hand, had been too busy trying to prove himself to notice much about Mathew's style and method.

"How are you able to manage the pain?" Carter asked offhandedly and Mathew noticed it seemed difficult for Carter to keep pace with him.

"What pain?" Mathew replied in awkward conversation before he threw a couple of strikes nicking Carter's cheek with the tip of his blade. Mathew noticed Carter's blood wasn't a uniform color. It was mixing and rejecting similar to when Mathew cut open his wrist. Mathew remembered how he watched his own blood flow from the cut and mix but not well enough for Mathew to function for long periods of time. This problem would eventually have led to his own death. "What were you fused with?" Mathew asked once he realized what was going on inside of Carter.

"Some weird blood drinker from Mexico," Carter replied after blocking another strike.

"That thing that eats all the goats? No wonder you're in pain! You were fused with a Monster and not a Demon. That's why your blood doesn't mix. Your genetics don't match up and now it appears as if you've tried to stabilize yourself with my blood," Mathew stated before making a lunge and caught Carter in the chest. Carter parried with a wave of fire. Mathew managed to block the fire with a wall of ice and quickly created a platform beneath his feet that launched him up in the air. Mathew's plan was to bring the blade down on Carter's shoulder from above but another wave of fire made him freeze his body before he was hit.

Dropping to his feet, the ice shield he had created in midair broke off and shattered against the ground. Mathew sprinted with everything he had toward Carter and swung his sword reverse. The blunt side struck Carter's forehead, throwing him off balance and making him do a flip. Carter landed on his back, unconscious, with a long swollen mark across his forehead.

"Well! That was easier than I expected," Mathew said to no one in particular before he turned his attention towards the other soldiers.

Fire Elemental numbers were quickly diminishing. Shortly after the skirmish began, the remaining soldiers started to flee. Mathew's group assessed damages and the only person they lost in the fight was the Ice Tracker who Carter jumped by mistake, or on purpose. Mathew hadn't been able to tell if Carter was telling the truth or not so, unless proven guilty, a bit of grace was necessary. When the room was clear of opposition, Mathew ran over to check on Carter who seemed barely alive. The others joined him and they froze his cuts and the stab wound as best they could but their first aid efforts weren't going very well. Carter was a Fire Elemental and they are not known for their love of ice. Marsh reminded them that "orders were orders" and they were to deliver Carter dead or alive. It seemed better to take him alive so Mathew threw Carter over his shoulder, which was extremely painful because of his wound, and exited the Palace. They had to take the long way around to avoid the war that had started just before they began their mission.

As they slowly made their way back to friendly territory, an intense burst of light followed by a strong gust of wind suddenly blinded them. Mathew turned to see what was going on. When he finally managed to get the dust out of his eyes, he saw one of the most unusual sights he had seen in a long time. A huge cloud began to mushroom against a large black wall. The haze from the explosion was shimmering with particles from the wall that looked like a curtain of thousands of falling stars.

"What caused that?" Mathew asked taking in the strange beauty of the sight as he dropped Carter onto an ice wagon Bell quickly created so Mathew didn't have to carry him on his wounded shoulder.

"By the looks of it, Ryan and Marcus are fighting," Marsh replied simply and they continued on their way.

They were stopped by friendlies and escorted to a safe zone behind the fighting. Air Vanguards took Carter to a secure facility and Mathew was glad to rest up. His shoulder got stitched up and frozen by the on-site medic so there would be no scar. As the war was against the Fire Elementals, the majority of the injuries and casualties were from burns on various body parts.

"You okay, Bell?" Mathew asked noticing her clothes were scorched from the fight.

"Yeah, I'm fine thanks to my faithful, multi-purpose ice plate," she replied with a glowing smile as she gave her chest a strong smack making the ice plate ring like a glass bell.

"Why is it every time I do something other than just sit around I end up wounded or passed out for a number of weeks? It's like my life is scripted or something," Mathew commented as he briefly pondered his life since his death.

"Mathew, just accept that's how things work for you here. I knew a guy back in my military group who had a scar from every single battle he was in. Great news is that he is still around today, even after all of those scars. It's just some people have that luck. You may be hurt but you build up a lot of stamina to keep your body in check. That makes you a lot more valuable than an average soldier who would just end up dying from a sword to the chest," Bell explained.

"I don't think Carter is going to live much longer," Mathew said more to himself than anyone else after he had thought about Bell's comment.

"Why do you think that?" Bell asked hearing the question.

"He was fused with Monster blood instead of Demon blood. And now it appears that he has tried to introduce my blood to his. Probably in an effort to stabilize the concoction he has running through his veins. From what I saw, it's not going to work out very well for him," Mathew stated his theory.

"Well, good then. I'm not one to trust backstabbers . . . no pun intended, Mathew," Bell replied in an unusually cruel tone.

"It's fine but what do we do next?" Mathew decided to ask.

"Protocol would be to take down Ryan but . . . I think Marcus will do that sooner rather than later. This war seems to be progressing faster than anyone expected," Bell openly admitted with a hint of sorrow in her voice.

"So we just sit, wait and hope things turn out for the best?" Mathew asked feeling a little dizzy for some reason.

"That's how it always works. Besides . . . we need to get back home to turn in all those notes you crammed into your pockets. Really, Mathew, did you even think of how much each pocket could hold? That careless decision could have impeded your movements and ended your life!" Bell ranted and Mathew noticed how bulged his pockets actually were.

"Well . . . I don't think we should leave just yet," Mathew said feeling like he needed to stay but wasn't clear why.

"I agree but, Mathew, you understand that this could be the end for us all if things turn out badly," Bell ominously said sending a shiver down Mathew's spine.

"I won't go rushing out anytime soon. I'm more concerned about these notes," Mathew replied pulling out all of the papers and set about the lengthy process of organizing them.

After sorting through to get a better understanding of the flow of information, Mathew realized that there were large gaps in the data making what he had unreliable. What he did find of value was data about the control and use of blood. Mathew pulled the notes dedicated to blood and spent the next few days reading through each note. Once Mathew was finished with a sheet, Bell took that sheet from him to study on her own. Some of the data was horrifying. The scientist's detailed experiments with the attempt to replicate a condition only referenced as "The Melding". He found a list of names of Vanguards and regular civilians who volunteered for the experiment. Mathew couldn't find Carter's name anywhere so Mathew assumed the list he was reading was experiment failures.

The most valuable information to Mathew was detail of several abilities Carter had managed to perform along with several that were theorized for different Elementals. The notes implied that Carter was not able to master the abilities because he hadn't been able to perform them for long enough to obtain an accurate evaluation. Mathew studied the details and practiced the abilities in what was seemingly was the center of town. Whenever he was in public, a crowd would gather to watch him practice. Being good at what he did was one thing; being gawked at another was and exceptionally annoying but practicing out in the open was not a choice for Mathew had made, it was a necessity born out of the need a space large enough to perform certain abilities. As he practiced that day, an Air Elemental captain brought his squad into the little camp to watch Mathew practice. His troops needed a morale boost and, by the end of Mathew's session, the Air Capitan was so impressed that he asked Mathew to create blood sculptures of his entire squad. Mathew gladly did but it took several attempts until he was satisfied. During the time that passed, word spread and half of the soldiers in the camp joined and wanted sculptures, too. By the end of the day, Mathew had created a sculpture of everyone there. He was exhausted and retreated to the small, private icehouse he was sharing with Bell. Happy with his work and thankful to be finished, Mathew admired his temporary home and surrounding structures. He was amazed at how Ice Elementals could create almost everything they needed, especially buildings. The entire camp was more like an Ice village than a military base.

"That was nice of you, Mathew," Bell said as Mathew entered the house.

"Working hard to keep morale up," Mathew replied happily even though he was completely exhausted from his day's activities.

"How about we give them a true show?" Bell said as her face lit up indicating she had an idea.

"What's on your mind now?" Mathew asked apprehensively.

"It looks like you are ready to have a few sparring matches to practice those new abilities," Bell suggested but her tone seemed to state 'you're going to fight me and it's not an option'. Mathew still found it strange to know a girl with such a love for physical combat . . . and a rather pretty one as well.

"If I must . . . and I know I must. Keep this in mind though, Bell. I have never hit a girl in either of my lives and I don't plan on starting now. Especially not you," Mathew replied.

"Think of this as sword play. It doesn't count because we're practicing, like theater," Bell said with a smile.

"Okay fine, but I need rest so we will duel tomorrow," Mathew replied as he hopped onto his soft bed. He quickly fell asleep thinking of potential strategies to win his duel against Bell.

Mathew woke up concerned about the duel. He didn't want to hurt Bell unintentionally but he was competitive enough to want to win. He knew Bell well and she would not hold back. Mathew knew that he would have to give it his all just to fend her off. Still planning, Mathew headed out to find a large crowd already gathered at a new, giant ice arena the soldiers had created just for the occasion. Mathew considered the giant ice arena a little over the top for a simple duel but, nonetheless, he walked into the arena and the crowd roared. Mathew felt like Maximus from the movie 'Gladiator'. He had a strong urge to throw his hands in the air and triumphantly parade around like he had already won the duel. Thankfully resisting the urge, the crowd roared again and Mathew turned to see Bell had joined him in the arena dressed in full Ice Armor. She was a remarkable and breathtaking sight.

"Mathew, don't you hold back. I want your best so give it all you've got," Bell said before they began.

As soon as Mathew signaled he was ready, the fight began. Bell was fast and lethal even in the bulky armor and put Mathew immediately on the defensive. This time, though, he was faring much better than he did during their first duel. The first duel they had was practice and worked well as preparation for this fight. It had given Mathew the opportunity to study Bell's methods of attack, making it easier to anticipate her next move so he wasn't being beaten to a pulp this time around. The ultimate goal of this duel was to put theory to practice and test different strategies about the viability of using blood as a weapon. Mathew quickly found out that some theories were successful and others left him unprotected. Bell's ice blades weren't able to cut through the blood while it was massed in its liquid form but, if the blood was frozen flat, it would shatter with even the smallest impact. Curiously, though, Mathew realized that if the blood was just the right thickness and shaped into a blade, it had the tensile strength of the finest metal.

Deciding to set the data from the notes he had read aside, Mathew took a deep breath and calmed his mind. To win this battle with Bell, he needed to use his creativity and hands-on experience from the countless hours he had practiced Ice skills and magic. His first idea caught Bell off guard. Taking a handful of blood, he extended his arm quickly throwing frozen blood spikes outward from his palm creating a shotgun-like splatter. Bell was caught by surprise and knocked back several feet upon impact. Mathew halted the duel to check on her and, when Bell assured him she was fine, they continued.

Mathew started to delve into his creativity more to develop new ideas. He was beginning to realize that his only limitation was himself. If he could visualize it and come up with the correct motion and pattern, it was possible. Not everything worked as he anticipated but the possibilities seemed to be endless. When Bell started using landscape obstacles in the arena as part of her tactics, he made the blood as thin as possible without it becoming too brittle and threw it like a Frisbee. The blood Frisbee cut through even the thickest fake ice trees and columns. Thankfully, none were of structural importance so Mathew, Bell and the spectators were not in any danger. He was beginning to tire but as soon as he realized that the only limitation he had was his own creative imagination, a fresh wave of energy washed through him.

After what seemed like hours on non-stop battle, Bell began to tire and made a mistake in her footwork causing her to trip. Mathew took his opportunity to end the duel. He tackled Bell and pointed a blood blade to her chest, ending the fight with a dramatic sweep of his blade. As the crowd cheered and shouted his name, Mathew checked on Bell to make sure she was uninjured. Despite this being a "friendly" duel, they had both taken some rather hard hits. As always, Bell professed to be fine. The warrior in her always put mind over matter and, unless it mattered in a life-threatening way, she overcame whatever ailment she had suffered. She did admit to having a few bruises and scrapes. The scrapes looked like a rug burn that was caused by the armor rubbing against her skin, but overall, she was none the worse for wear.

"That was an amazing fight, Mathew!" Bell exclaimed with a large grin on her face when she entered the house.

"I hope I didn't hurt you," Mathew replied putting a quick mist of ice throughout the house to cool himself down.

"I'm alright. This ice armor is tougher than it looks. I've been working on perfecting it and it appears, from the chafe marks under my arms, I still have work to do," Bell stated. She reached behind her back and pulled something that looked like a ripcord and the entire set of armor plates dropped off her body onto the floor, quickly turning into a pile of fine snow. “Enjoying what you see?” Bell asked as she struck a pose after she noticed Mathew staring at her.

“What? Where did that come from?” Mathew asked not use to her making sexual jokes.

“Just figured I should lighten up a bit. You know, live some life as long as I have the possibility of a never ending one,” Bell replied as a knock came at the door.

Mathew opened the door and was surprised to see King Marcus and Dracula. Not waiting to be invited in (something that caused Mathew to pause a moment and ponder the urban legend about Vampires and their legal entrance into a victim’s home), they entered the house without even saying hello.

“Um . . . Hello. What can I do you for?” Mathew asked as soon as they made themselves comfortable.

“We’re here on a very serious matter, Mathew. You are going to the frontlines with us. We’re going to use you as our trump card to take down Ryan,” Dracula calmly and decisively said.

“Do I have a choice?” Mathew asked.

“No, you do not. The war is not going as quickly or as well as we anticipated and you’re exactly what we need to get a clear shot at that bastard. Ryan seems to have been prepared for this battle long before we were,” Marcus grumbled.

“Mathew will not be going to the frontline,” Bell said after she had changed her clothes in the other room.

“Pardon? Who commands whom, little Vanguard?” Marcus said obviously insulted at her objection.

“I am not little and believe that I have been around here longer than you have. That alone should warrant some respect from even you, King Marcus. I will not allow Mathew to be put in any more danger than he needs to be,” Bell stated. “He is far too valuable to sacrifice on the altar of your arrogant vanity. He has saved more lives by just being true to himself than any war would solve using him as a pawn. I’d like to remind you of how he saved us by using only his brain when he reasoned the dragon into submission. Mathew is not a weapon. He is a valuable treasure and needs to be kept safe to do what he does best. Save people, that is. Which is what I believe your motive for this nonsensical war was,” Bell argued.

"This isn't a debate, Vanguard! Mathew is going to be on the frontline and he will help us take Ryan down," Marcus emphatically stated believing that he truly did have the final word on the matter. Obviously Marcus didn't know Bell very well.

"Enough! Stop the shouting! I hated fighting as a Human and even more now as an Elemental! It's my decision and I'll help but on one condition . . . it relates to Carter, the other Blood Elemental," Mathew stated.

"Wait . . . what other Blood Elemental?" Marcus asked distracted by Bell's opposition to his plan.

"The short version is the mission you sent us on to find the lab went exactly as planned. We found the lab, destroyed it and the research but discovered a poorly created Blood Elemental named Carter. Carter double-crossed us so I put a sword through his chest and smacked him on top of the head, knocking him out. After fighting about 50 Fire Elementals, we escaped and I carried unconscious Carter the whole way out of the Fire Palace on my jacked-up shoulder. When we arrived at camp, the guards met us and we handed him over to a group of Air Vanguards. I want to know how he is doing because I have a feeling he won't survive much longer. The DNA is not melding and his blood is not mixing," Mathew explained.

"Interesting . . . they actually managed to make one . . . well it's a good thing we destroyed that lab, then. Certainly don't want any one-off freak experiments running about. No offence, Mathew," Marcus said after realizing what he had just said. "Excuse me, I'll be right back," Marcus said quickly leaving the little icehouse.

"Bell, relax, okay?" Mathew said stopping her pacing to rub her shoulders. She was riled up and tense.

"I understand now," she replied simply but her response didn't make any sense to Mathew and, before he could question her about it, she stood up and walked into the other room.

"Mathew, as soon as Marcus is ready, we will be leaving. I suggest you pack a satchel and prepare for the journey ahead," Dracula explained clearly not in agreement with the plan.

"Again with the satchel? Alright, I'll go get ready," Mathew said with a sigh. He wasn't sure what he would be called on to do and, as he had never been "pro-war", he found cooperating with this plan exceptionally difficult.

Marcus returned after a few hours with King Bradley. Mathew hadn't met Bradley before and was impressed with his kingly appearance. Of all the Elemental kings, Bradley looked the most like a king and appeared to carry the burden of authority well. It also seemed as if he let less of his public life be ruled by character faults and quirks. Mathew mentally compared him to Zeus of the Olympians. King Bradley had an old grizzled face with deep lines that came from making hard decisions and understanding the consequence of each decision he made. There was a scar on his left cheek, a small one on his forehead and a large, puckered one from his right ear down to the top of the cloak he was wearing. His hair was long and the color reminded Mathew of the burnished Silver Eagle coin that his grandpa gave him when he turned 12. King Bradley looked like a wise sage. He definitely looked the part but, before Mathew was officially introduced, a man burst into the room and whispered into King Bradley's ear. King Bradley did not look pleased by the news.

"I see . . . you are dismissed. If it's not one thing, it's another," Bradley complained as he rubbed his tired looking eyes.

"What is it now?" Marcus asked obviously concerned. If King Bradley was troubled, it was a serious matter that probably affected him as well.

"The other Blood Elemental escaped and we don't have the man power to find him until this chaos with Ryan is resolved," Bradley explained.

"I will find him," Bell stated overhearing this new development.

"What source of help could you be?" King Bradley asked.

"I'm one of the few who has experience with Blood Elementals. I have met Carter and know what he looks like. I publicly sparred today with Mathew, whom we all know to be a Blood Elemental, and held my own. It should be simple considering Mathew's ability to control blood is far more effective than Carter's," Bell explained and Mathew agreed that she was the most qualified to find his 'brother'.

"We have limited options at this moment, King Bradley. I suggest that we allow the girl to find the Blood Elemental before he is long gone," Marcus stated and King Bradley agreed. "Bell, 2nd Class Vanguard, you are now reactivated for this specific manhunt mission and tasked to find and secure the fugitive Blood Elemental. You know what . . . screw the formalities. Get to it," Marcus said and Bell quickly created her Ice armor and was out the door.

After Bell was well on her way with her manhunt, Mathew, King Bradley, Dracula and Marcus got into a carriage pulled by the most impressive Dread Steeds Mathew had seen to date. Moments later, they arrived at the frontline of the war and the constant pit that had been in Mathew's stomach for weeks on end became a crater. He had yet to resolve his sorrow over this war and as far as his eyes could see was scorched and frozen earth. As he looked over the field to get a better understanding of the battle tactics, he noticed that the Fire Elementals kept well out of range of the Ice swordsmen because they were no match in hand-to-hand combat. They would be torn apart if the Ice swordsmen were to get close enough to draw their blades. Mathew had firsthand understanding of this from the Manor attack.

"You three go in and confront Ryan while I whip up a tornado as distraction. I'll keep the troops busy just trying to hang onto their pants," Bradley explained with an out of place chuckle. The mental image of that made Mathew laugh as well.

"Where exactly are we going?" Mathew asked wanting more details to the plan before going any further.

"The plan is to use Air Magic to launch you over to the main command post to the right," Bradley pointed at a small but stately looking red tent a few miles away.

"And my plan is to survive the launch," Mathew said wryly. That was not a detail of any plan he would have ever thought up and was extremely worried about his proposed method of transportation.

As they waited for confirmation on the launch time, Mathew worked hard to get answers about how he was supposed to land. He wondered why he was the only one who seemed to find the landing crucial to the success of the mission. Before he could get an answer, a guard ran up and talked to Marcus.

"Okay, it's time. Let's do this," Marcus said as two Air Elementals joined abilities to create a large vortex.

While Mathew apprehensively looked at the vortex (still trying to figure out how to land), he heard a large, roaring whoosh. Startled, he turned and saw King Bradley's tornado being formed. Even in his preoccupied state, Mathew found the tornado's formation interesting as it started small in Bradley's hand then slowly reached into the sky.

The larger it got, the more it threatened to pull away from Bradley's controlling hands.

The tornado increased in size and velocity by picking up dust and rotating it into the sky. As the tornado continued to grow, Mathew felt it tug at his clothes like a living being. It seemed as if it was trying to grab him and suck him in. As it spun and tugged repeatedly, Mathew moved farther away from the source and forced himself to concentrate on the task at hand.

"Mathew, my son! You are first," Dracula yelled over the noise of the tornado and, with a huge grin on his face, pushed Mathew into the vortex. Mathew was immediately launched high into the air in a slingshot like manner. He frantically tried to get his bearings as he was violently spun around. He couldn't tell if he was right side, sideways or upside down and knew it was crucial for him to get control of his body. He was going a lot faster than he ever imagined and didn't like the out-of-control feeling.

While fighting to gain some control over his body, Mathew came up with the landing plan. He decided that just before hitting the ground, he would transform into a bat. This, in theory, would enable him to glide to a graceful landing, safe and sound. What he didn't plan on was being distracted by the nightmare-like quality of dropping from the top of the vortex to the ground. It was exactly like the falling dreams he had as a Human that left him shaken and feeling out of control. Mathew had never considered himself a control freak but those dreams, better classified as nightmares, shook him to the core. As he thought about how much he hated those dreams, he was alarmed to see the ground approaching quickly. True to his initial plan, he transformed and was able to slowly glide down to a soft landing. He was still disoriented from the launch, madly spinning out of control and the falling but that was nothing compared to the shock when Dracula landed directly on his feet with Mathew in his small bat form only a few inches away.

"What's wrong, Mathew? I found that exhilarating!" Dracula exclaimed as he stood up and brushed dust off of his black vest and slacks in an attempt to return to his usual immaculate self.

"What's wrong?! Let's start with no one telling me that the thing was going to madly throw me into the fricken' air with no way of stopping! I was spinning out of control and still had to come up with a safe landing!" Mathew yelled back as several Fire Elemental guards rushed out to confront them.

Mathew was in no mood to deal with confrontation after his not-so-happy vortex experience so he fell on the guards like a rabid animal. He felt like an out of control madman as he ripped the guards apart without mercy or rational thought. Dracula took care of the others and together they left a bloody, nasty carnage all over the place.

"What did you two do?" Marcus asked in disgust when he landed.

"I don't know!" Mathew yelled, his body covered in blood. He was still on edge from the launch and mildly shocked at his inhumane response to confrontation. He then remembered that Dracula pushed him into the vortex so Mathew turned and gave Dracula an evil look.

"Come on, let's get this done with," Dracula said a little uneasy with Mathew glaring at him. Even he was surprised by the unbridled frenzy of Mathew's attack. Reminded of the importance of their mission, the small group cautiously entered Ryan's crimson tent.

"About time someone showed up. I was beginning to feel like no one cared," Ryan said standing over a map of the area with multiple colored pieces on it.

"Ryan, you have two options here. We can either take you to prison or we kill you. Either way, it's time to call it a day," Marcus said explaining the non-debatable options.

"Third option . . . How about we fight fair and see who wins," Ryan said throwing a few poorly aimed fireballs, which puzzled Mathew.

Mathew quietly stepped to the right hand side but Ryan kept his eyes on the location where Mathew had been standing. Mathew picked up a small rock and threw it on the other side of the tent. It crashed into a metal shield and made a loud noise causing Ryan to turn and harmlessly incinerate that general area.

"How long have your eyes been this bad?" Mathew asked.

"What are you talking about, Mathew?" Marcus asked.

"He's as blind as bat, how could the King of Fire miss with a fireball from such a short range?" Mathew asked pointing out the obvious.

"Very observant, Mathew. You're smarter than you look, I'll give you that. My eyesight has been diminishing because of the increased intensity of the more powerful Fire Art I perform. Smart or not, you are still a useless mutant needing to be purged from this earth," Ryan said throwing a few fireballs that didn't even come close to Mathew.

"I don't understand . . . you were attempting to create Life Elementals and yet you have the audacity to call me a "mutant"? What was the purpose of that, you hypocrite?" Mathew yelled irritated at Ryan's lack of rational reasoning.

"The friend of my enemy is also my friend. When you understand the essence of a matter, you can easily gain control of it," Ryan replied throwing larger fireballs like before, but still Mathew felt no sense of urgency to move out of the way.

"Why the assassins, then? What was the point of that?" Marcus asked completely relaxed and in control of the situation.

"Trial and error. First assassin was simply going to pierce Mathew's heart. The second was going to use a stronger dose of poison to stop that same heart. Both failed dismally, as we all know," Ryan said as he started to haphazardly throw fireballs in random directions. This made Mathew suspicious and uneasy because, out of all the Elemental Kings, the King of Fire was the last candidate that should be this bad at fighting. Also, it was obvious to everyone but Ryan that the tent was close to burning down.

"Poison? That was the vial that I smashed!" Mathew exclaimed remembering Dracula ordering him to destroy the vial he found on the second assassin.

"Exactly," Ryan said throwing a fireball directly a Mathew. Luckily Marcus was able to put up a wall of Black Ice before any harm came to him.

Ryan suddenly became a dead eye throwing waves of fire at all three of them with pinpoint accuracy. Mathew had to pull out his blood magic to create shields fast enough to provide protection for his group.

"That was a surprise," Dracula said still keeping his distance since the tent was now officially ablaze.

"I'm a Fire Elemental. I'm quite skilled at detecting heat sources, especially when I have enough heat around me. The heat filters out lesser degree temperatures so, the more fire, the more sensitive my perception is," Ryan said before creating yet another wave of fire. This explained the seemingly random fireballs.

The battle was officially on. Ryan had created an inferno all around them and the fire was consuming their oxygen. The heat was so intense that Mathew felt the hairs on his arms and brows singeing. Mathew knew they had to act fast or run for cover and there was too much at stake to run. Dracula moved first trying to flank Ryan but Ryan, due to the inferno around them, was much quicker and more effective with his battle tactics. A wall of fire easily stopped Dracula. Marcus attacked head on hoping to use Ryan's failing eyesight to his advantage. His weapons of choice were four short handled ice swords that were designed for stabbing. Marcus failed as well because the ice swords required an extremely close proximity to his target and the intense heat stopped him before he was able to do any damage to Ryan.

As Mathew watched, he learned. Realizing immediately that ice would instantly melt, he changed to blood tactics. Mathew formed a weapon out of blood based on a medieval lance. He was able to get close enough to rattle Ryan but, as Mathew had to constantly out-maneuver repeated fireballs akin to small nuclear explosions, he wasn't able to get close enough to make significant contact. Realizing that their efforts were valiant but not effective, the three quickly regrouped.

With only seconds to spare, Mathew, Marcus and Dracula came up with a plan to end the war. Instead of attacking separately, they decided to overwhelm Ryan with a collective effort. Individually, they were all fairly matched. Collectively, they would overpower Ryan. Dracula went in first again. He quickly dashed around the flames and caught Ryan unguarded. Dracula hit Ryan with a quick leg sweep (which looked to Mathew like an old 80's break dance move) and Ryan crashed to the ground. But, before he hit the ground, he was able to create a flame orb of protection around himself. Ryan was instantly on his feet again but unsuspecting of Mathew and Marcus' counter attack. Mathew and Marcus joined abilities and were immediately making progress freezing through Ryan's orb until Ryan caught Mathew off guard with a swift kick to his nose. Mathew doubled over in pain and backed off but Dracula attacked again and gave Ryan a vicious chop to the throat. Mathew took the moment to recover and reposition himself to a more strategic spot while Ryan himself recovered behind a wall of flame.

They had underestimated the King of Fire. Even with their consolidated efforts, Ryan stood his ground and the fighting continued like that for quite a while; just basic, dirty survival fighting that didn't take any intelligence or skill. Anything that could hurt your opponent seemed to be fair game and an onlooker might think he was at either an Ultimate Fight match or a theatrical comedy. It was difficult to tell being so closely involved but Mathew thought he was doing incredibly well fending off the onslaught of fire with blood or ice. He was not only defending himself but covering his allies as well. Mathew noticed that Ryan had a significant advantage over the Ice Elementals because fire was instantaneous and just needed to be released. Ice, on the other hand, was creative and needed to take form as a solid before assuming its official shape, which made it just a fraction of a second slower. Life and death were held between those fractions, though. Any hesitation or miscalculation during this fight could be rewarded with an entire body part being burnt to a cinder.

"Well it's been fun, but it's time for the dramatic finale," Ryan said jumping back amazingly far even for an Elemental. With a snap of his fingers, Ryan created a wide, intense flame that shot up in the air and continued to climb towards the upper atmosphere.

"Damn it, it's an inferno," Marcus calmly stated. "Well, boys, had a good run and it's been nice knowing you two," he continued which really angered Mathew. He thought the King of Ice would have more will to live than that.

"I'm not ready to die again! Get together!" Mathew ordered and knew their options were few and chances of survival even smaller.

"Marcus! Form an ice sphere around us now!" Mathew barked.

Marcus obeyed and the large dome encased them. Mathew quickly set to work and bit into both of his wrists to increase the volume and intensity of the blood flow he would have to work with. He also uncapped the blood bag and used everything he had on him. Mathew forced the blood to coat the inside of the orb then froze the outside layer making a thick sphere of three layers. The outside was black ice, the middle was liquid blood and the inner most layer was frozen blood.

Mere moments later, the entire sphere shook violently. Mathew was knocked off balance and fell to the ground as the shaking continued for what seemed like an eternity. He had never experienced an earthquake before and had a feeling that this shaking was way off the Richter scale. He smacked into Dracula and Marcus multiple times until everything calmed down and his body finally quit bouncing around. When Mathew realized that he stopped shaking, it was too dark to see what direction he was facing. All he knew was his body was banged up and he wasn't able to move just yet. He was too shocked from being shaken around like casino dice.

"Ouch. Am I dead?" Marcus' voice came through the darkness.

"Not quite yet," Dracula said and Mathew heard the dust and rocks hit the ground as he stood up and brushed himself off. "Mathew, my son, are you still with me?" Dracula asked shaking Mathew until he came to and his Vampiric vision kicked in so he could see clearly.

"Yeah. I'm still here. Ouch is right," Mathew muttered as he stood up. He looked around and realized something strange was going on. He was "seeing" sound waves as they radiated from everything. From his mouth to Dracula's footsteps, then back to his ears creating a decent sonographic image. It wasn't 3D but it created a vivid likeness of his surroundings. "Okay gentlemen, let's crack this egg shell," Mathew said as he ripped down the blood wall.

As it came down, the middle layer was revealed, pulsating red from the heat of Ryan's inferno. Mathew slowly moved it onto the ground and watched in fascination as it melted the surrounding rock. The Black Ice outer layer of the shell was so distressed it looked like Swiss cheese and Mathew was able to easily kick his way through it. They crawled out of their shelter of ice and blood and fell into a huge crater. They stood and looked around in disbelief. As far as they could see was a barren, smoking wasteland. Rock had melted under the extreme heat and pressure had turned into various textures of colored glass that Mathew had never seen before as a Human or as an Elemental. The colors were muted, not vibrant, giving the landscape an eerily beautiful glow as what little sun there was reflected off of shiny, smooth and razor sharp surfaces.

They hobbled their way up until Marcus grew impatient with the difficulty of the climb and created several flights of ice stairs out of the crater. The glass ground was too slippery to walk on where it had cooled and too hot and gooey where it hadn't. Mathew thought of all the adventures he had had as an Elemental and this experience was, by far, the lowest on enjoyment level to date. When they finally reached the top, they easily spotted their adversary.

Ryan hadn't moved very far from the general spot he had jumped to just before creating the inferno. He was safely out of the initial blast zone and, because of his poor eyesight and immense arrogance, prematurely assumed that the three were dead so they gathered their strength and seized the moment.

Dracula sped up behind Ryan and kicked him so hard that Mathew heard a sickening snap as Ryan's spinal column shattered. The force of the kick propelled Ryan's body high into the air where Marcus froze it solid. As Ryan's body started its descent in Mathew's direction, Mathew quickly wiped blood out of his eyes and, with all of his might, punched Ryan's frozen body, shattering it into a fine ice dust. A large red stone banged against Mathew's face and began to skip down into the crater. Thus ended the rule of the infamous Fire King.

"It's finished," Marcus said after several moments of silence.

"Well done, men," Dracula added as he helped Mathew up off of the ground where he had fallen, still shaken from the inferno.

"Are you okay, Mathew?" Marcus asked noticing Mathew shaking uncontrollably.

"I want to go home," Mathew managed to mutter.

"That makes two of us. Mathew, that inferno was too close for comfort and we owe our lives to you. Thanks only to your tenacity, creativity and unique abilities, we are alive to see the sun rise and set again," Marcus commended Mathew and they heard a small snap from behind them. Spooked, Mathew turned quickly and froze that general area.

"I think the poor kid is shell shocked," Marcus said shaking Mathew trying to calm him down.

"I'm . . . fine. I just need a warm bath. Or cake . . . yes, cake sounds good. Maybe chocolate. No, marble cake," Mathew replied incoherently.

"Let's get you home, son. This war has come to an end and now it's time to begin the healing," Dracula said helping Mathew up.

As they reached the top of the hill, they saw evidence of a war that had been. Ice and fire were mixed intermittently throughout the immediate landscape. Except for a few skirmishes here and there, the fighting was over. Fire Elementals were being gathered until the Council decided what to do with them. King Bradley, thankful and surprised to see them again, rushed over to hear the details of their mission. Everyone had felt the force of the inferno and had been waiting anxiously for news of the war. King Bradley was obviously overjoyed with the results and ordered a feast in honor of their victory but Mathew and Dracula departed quickly. Neither of them was up for celebration at that moment and both were exhausted from fighting and surviving an inferno. The severe shaking left Mathew with terrible vertigo that reminded him of the effect of a rollercoaster ride gone bad, really bad.

When they arrived at the camp, Bell was back from her unsuccessful manhunt. She had followed Carter's trail to a teleportal and there was no point in continuing the hunt when Carter's destination was undeterminable. Mathew encouraged everyone to get moving quickly because he was feeling sicker as time went on and he wanted to go home.

They went through the teleportal and came out to the friendly sight of the Ice fortress. Mathew walked into his room and found all of his friends in there.

"Oh, my God! Mathew! Aren't you supposed to be dead? Again?" Ilium exclaimed when she saw him, which explained why they all looked like they had seen a ghost.

"No, I'm quite alive. A little shell shocked, though," Mathew admitted still shaking from the trauma of it all.

"I told you girls but you wouldn't listen," Julian said in her usual calm, kind voice.

"All three of us survived with nothing more serious than a few scrapes," Dracula explained.

"Do we have any cake . . . ?" Mathew decided to ask because he still had these strange cravings.

"No, but we do have some soda if you want any," Sara said throwing him a can.

"How did you survive that blast? We were told that it decimated everything within a 5 mile radius," Dee asked as she latched onto Mathew, she buried her face into Mathew's dirty clothes just to make sure he was real.

"Layered blood ball," Mathew replied being quick and simple with his answers.

"Well, the important thing is that you're all okay. Now come and sit down," Victoria said pulling Mathew onto the couch next to her.

The group sat and talked for what seemed like hours until Mathew remembered something. He waited until most of his guests were gone and found the stack of notes related to the creation of Blood Elementals. He quickly made a Blood/Ice safe to store them in. He walked to the window and looked out on the peaceful, icy landscape where he had lived out most of his adventures since choosing the Path of Life.

As he stood there, Mathew reflected on his short life as an Elemental. He had made friends, learned how to control ice and blood and played a significant part in a senseless war where countless lives were lost. Lives that were meant to be timeless. Depression started to settle on him again as he realized that, if he hadn't chosen the Path of Life, those people would still be alive at this very moment. He wondered briefly if there was another life after this one. The weight of his decision sat heavily upon him, especially when he realized that he had supposedly been one of the main reasons the war started. All because some loser King guy in a red suit judged him and decided that Mathew didn't deserve to live. Mathew then remembered something Bell had said about the war "not making sense". He hadn't understood her seemingly off-hand comment at the time but now he agreed and was positive there had to be other factors involved in the war. It just "didn't make sense".

"Hey, Mathew, what do you think will happen next?" Victoria asked joining Mathew as they gazed out the window at the falling snow.

"I have no idea. I'm only Human after all . . . . wait . . . no, I'm not," Mathew replied letting out a small laugh before he decided to join the rest of his friends who were questioning the purple muffins Julian had left for them on a pretty doily.

CHAPTER NINETEEN

PILGRIMAGE

"There is something I need to take care of," Mathew said to the group and quickly left the room before anyone had a chance to ask him where he was going. It was rare he had the opportunity to slip out alone and needed privacy to finish what needed to be done.

Mathew went through the teleportal and came out in Dark Cove, the Demon town near his original hometown. He walked the distance to his former home and, when he arrived, he retraced his steps through several landmarks that were significant in his past. He found his way to a park that was blooming with bright yellow dandelions. He realized they were in bloom early this year and bent down to pick a handful to cheer himself up. At last he came to his destination, an old drain pipe at the end of the park's boundary.

He went down the worn path that he had walked down every day as a child. Hopping into the old ditch, Mathew landed in the same place he always did, right on top of two large rocks. Memories started to flood his mind as he looked hopefully for the hidden key that was kept under the only odd black rock in the area. The rock wasn't obvious to others but it had been the perfect hiding place for one familiar with the area. He easily found the key and was thankful it hadn't moved in all the years that he had been absent.

He dug out the key that was buried in a few layers of dirt, cleaned it off then walked up the pipe to the rusty lock. The key slipped in as if it were brand new. Mathew turned the key and heard a loud symphony of rusty parts that hadn't been used since his last visit. The gate's hinges were rusted together and, after a few attempts to open the gate, Mathew decided to ram into it to get it open. He backed up a few feet, ran and crashed into it causing the old gate to fling open. He hadn't adjusted for his new strength and Mathew fell hard onto the old, dusty cement floor.

"I never liked you, you stupid old gate!" Mathew childishly yelled at the inanimate gate.

It was dark inside and his eyes saw everything and nothing at the same time. He looked around seeing more memories than present reality. With a heavy sadness, he realized how old and neglected their secret place was as his hands reached for the ancient oil lamp that still stood on the small wooden table that he and Meridia had smuggled in when they were young. Naturally, the lamp's oil had vanished with the passage of time so Mathew reached for an old candle that seemed like it could still be lit. The matches he had left on the table were damp and the matchbox itself had decayed, leaving a thin layer of dust over the red tipped matches.

Mathew reached down for a rusty metal box, he opened it and grabbed the reserve matches that still were in good enough condition to use. He lit the old candle and placed the dandelions he had collected earlier into a small glass vase like he had done multiple times before, back when everything in the drain was new and still seemed friendly. There was nothing friendly about broken memories and heartache and their hideout seemed to reflect that.

Mathew broke free from the emotional downward spiral that always came when he thought about Meridia. He stood up and looked around with eyes that had more wisdom and experience than the last time he had been here. He felt that his heart had started healing but something was still missing to finish the process. He thought back to his Human death and Elemental rebirth. He thought about the adventures he had had and the friends he had made and decided that it was good. The One had been right when he had said that the path before him would bring many challenges but with those challenges would come great joy. He wasn't quite at the joy part yet but he was here, at this point and time, in the place, to settle the matter of his broken heart. There are things that can be changed in life and things that can't. Mathew had a flash of insight that freedom came when you could tell the difference between the two. He was ready for peace and ready for freedom. He was ready to accept those things that he couldn't change.

He turned from his thoughts and took action. He began examining the old silver wall of the drain that turned to concrete as it connected to the street. A lot of his Human history was on this wall and it contained records of every memory he and Meridia had shared together. Every day after school, they would make their way as happy and carefree children to their secret hideout. Meridia had better penmanship and would write the day's events in her favorite color, red. When she forced Mathew to participate in the ritual, he would always write in dark blue paint so it would show up better. They learned early on that thick paint was more visible and lasted longer on the silver surface than marker. Mathew was thankful for that insight now as the record of their friendship was still visible, even after all this time.

Mathew's mind drifted off into the past as he looked at the old wall. He touched every inscription as he read. The silver wall felt cool and impersonal to his touch. He thought it strange that something so impersonal could contain such vibrant detail from the most intimate relationship he had ever had. He remembered when they gave each other job titles for their club of two. They both agreed that Meridia would be the librarian because she was obsessed with recording on the wall and didn't like the word "secretary". One of the best memories on the wall was when Mathew's father, who had accidentally found out about their hideout, took a trip to the local junkyard to find free stuff to decorate the pipe so it was more homey. That was the best memory Mathew had of his dad and he felt a strong surge of love for his dad for supporting him and not disciplining him like he probably should have.

Mathew saw the slow transition that preceded his broken heart. He saw his handwriting show up more and more as Meridia's handwriting vanished altogether. Mathew paused for a moment and took a deep breath before approaching his personal turning point; the last entry. There, before his eyes, was the dark blue paint smeared across the wall with one big, solitary word, "disband", written on the wall. Mathew remembered that the only reason he wrote that was because he didn't know how to spell "separated".

Strangely, facing his deepest fear was not as terrifying as he thought it would be. Mathew realized that the fear was rooted in avoidance and that avoidance only increased the fear. It was a bad cycle that he was finally ready to break free from. To do so, Mathew knew he needed to put in his own final last entry. His dark blue paint was exactly where he had left it but the paint had dried, which was no surprise to him, so he bit his finger and used his own blood as the ink. He wrote down the date he became an Elemental along with the word "Rebirth". When he finished, Mathew froze the blood inscription before it had a chance to stream down the wall and disappear.

He stepped back to admire his work and heard someone calling his name. It was the same voice that had haunted his days and nights for the past several years. He instinctively reached for his gold cross for reassurance only to remember that it had been replaced by his new Blood Elemental cross. He heard his name again in that voice he had heard hundreds of times, in different tones, but always recognizable and always dear to him.

"Meridia?" Mathew's voice creaked out in a whisper. He frantically looked around but was only met with silence. He was still alone in this place where his past was meeting his future and his present was struggling to get free.

Mathew dropped to his knees like he had done years before when he made the last entry. Joy and pain, hope and despair were flooding through him at the same time and he didn't know which ones to cling to or which ones were real. His mind had tormented him hundreds of times with the memories of Meridia's voice or laugh. The worst were the dreams and Mathew hated them. They made him so happy he felt he could fly only to crash to the ground and burn when he woke up and realize that she wasn't there anymore.

His body felt frozen in time as his mind struggled to make sense of what was happening. Mathew knew he was here to settle his past but the memories threatened to overcome him. They tore at him as if they were razors and each one cut deeper than the last. Each memory seemed to mock his feeble attempt to bring his heart and his mind into agreement and finally move forward. They showed how close he and Meridia had been, as if they had been of one heart and one mind.

"Mathew . . ." He heard his name whispered again and then the final, dreaded memory of the last words he had heard from her lips that were the essence of every nightmare, "Mathew . . . my love . . . goodbye." Those terrible words shattered his struggling heart all over again. Mathew had finally come to the core of his torment; he had always felt it was his fault for not taking better care of her.

Someone was in the drain with him. Mathew saw a movement out of the corner of his eye and slowly turned to see what it was. Somewhere in the back of his mind he realized that he was the only one left on earth who knew of this hiding place. He wasn't afraid and didn't really care but his Elemental training had become such a part of who he was, making him unable to ignore it. His eyes were watery from his tears and, as he looked more out of discipline than care, the only thing he could see was the flame red of Fire Elemental robes.

"Excuse my appearance," Mathew muttered before he wiped his eyes, turned away and started crying again.

He felt more than saw as the robed figure drew close and sat down next to him. He didn't care when arms wrapped around him in a secure but comforting hug. They sat like that for what seemed like hours until Mathew felt like every tear had finally been drained from his heart.

"Thanks. I know you probably came here to kill me so go ahead. I don't care anymore. I'm done," Mathew said now that this final pilgrimage was finished. Though drained and emotionally exhausted, he had a new peace in his heart and knew that all was well with his soul.

"I didn't know you took it so hard," the robed figure said in a voice that shot through Mathew's mind. Mathew quickly cleared his eyes and looked at who had sat there comforting him as he walked through the darkest place in his soul. He saw a slender face with short red hair, familiar brown eyes and lightly tanned skin. This time, she was really here.

"Oh, my God! How? Why now? Why now of all times?" Mathew asked as he pulled her towards him to confirm she was not a figment of his imagination . . . again. He embraced this girl who was forever embedded in his heart and in his memories. The heat radiating from her body soaked into his clothes and into his body until he thought he would melt for joy.

"I couldn't find you until now. Trust me, I tried as soon as I found out you were one of us. Mathew, come with me. I need to show you something," Meridia said helping him up and they walked hand in hand down the street. They approached a corner with a large black gate that squeaked as they opened it and went down a stone path he had traveled many times in the past.

There were rows of gravestone that gave testimony to the lives that had passed out of this world but there was only one that Mathew actually cared about. That gravestone now had a partner.

"Even in death your body found its way back . . . it's a little romantic," Meridia said calmly with a light chuckle.

"Mathew L. Clarunde. November 1991-2009," Mathew read his own gravestone that would have been a more surreal experience if he hadn't spent the past year or so as an Elemental. What was weird was realizing that his body was supposed to be on the mountain. Mathew figured some poor hiker probably found it when the snow melted and told the authorities.

"Meridia T. Romare. June 1991-2005," Meridia said softly as she read her own.

"It's funny . . . every year I would come back on the anniversary of my death and you would always be here sleeping propped up against this stone. I was always so happy to see you but it was really painful. You were so close but unreachable. Then this year I was here alone. You never showed up and for a split second I hated you for forgetting about me so quickly after everything we had been through. However, after my fit I remembered how much confidence I had in us and knew you would never forget something that important. I knew in my heart something happened to you. I searched around town for a while and found no sign of you so I went to the library to search through the papers. I finally found mention of your disappearance in 2008 and just like you; I blamed myself for not being there for you when you needed me the most. About a month ago, the name Mathew kept popping up in different Elemental conversations and my curiosity was piqued," Meridia began explaining her own small adventure. "I returned again to this gravesite about a week ago to find your body being laid to rest next to mine. I joined the funeral even though I wasn't dressed for it and noticed this one girl out of a small group who wasn't wailing like the others. Her face had a peaceful look to it which gave me the impression that she knew something the others didn't," Meridia said with a smile as she causally hopped up on her own gravestone.

"Before she left I got her name and later showed up at her house threatening to melt her if she didn't tell me what she knew. She quickly got a newspaper dated a few months back and it had your picture in it . . . and even though it was black and white and you looked different, I knew it was you," Meridia said as she cast an irritated look at Mathew. "Even though you were fast becoming famous in the Elemental world, you don't make too many friends and you never stayed in one place for long. It took me forever to track you down. I followed you to our hideout and waited to see what you were up to. You were always an emotional boy but I never saw you so down before tonight. You looked so helpless and . . . I'm sorry for not telling you sooner," she finished then took a deep breath then stretching her legs out.

"It's okay . . . I know why you didn't tell me before but I'm better now and those memories can't torment me anymore. I had to go through what I had to go through to get free and move on from the past. It was all a process and I understand clearly now what The One was telling me. I just can't believe you are really here," Mathew said calmly before he grabbed her and pulled her in for a hug. Mathew stood there for a few moments so he could take in her sweet scent just to make sure he wasn't dreaming.

"So what do you want to do now?" she asked softly with that special smile that always made Mathew happy.

"Well, I did promise to push you on the swings when you got better," Mathew said recalling the very old conversation.

"Let's go, then. The park isn't too far from here," Meridia said with another smile. She took Mathew's hand and held it tightly as they walked slowly down the hill reunited after years of waiting.

A New Day . . .